Love, Legacy, and Little Green Aliens

An Over-40 Beach Town Romantic Comedy

Sadira Stone

To Duncan, my HEA
And to all the readers who take the time to review my books.
Your support keeps me writing!

Love, Legacy, and Little Green Aliens: An Over-40 Beach Town Romantic Comedy

Cover design by Wicked Smart Designs

Edited by Red Quill Editing, LLC

Learn more about Sadira Stone and her books at www.sadirastone.com. For up-to-date information about releases, giveaways, and more, please sign up for Sadira's monthly reader newsletter.

Quality Control: I strive to produce error-free books, but even with all the critique partners, beta readers, and editors, sometimes an error slips through. Pretty please, if you find a typo or formatting issue, let me know at sadirastoneauthor@gmail.com so I may correct it. Thank you!

Contents

Chapter One

The closer Xander got to his parents' home, the tighter he clenched the wheel.

Skipping Sunday dinner was out of the question, especially today, but he couldn't resist grumbling a string of curses as he searched for a parking space beneath the bare-limbed maples. He added a few more choice words when his dented Prius jolted over a monster pothole. Typical Seattle—even prosperous neighborhoods like his parents' had crappy, cratered streets.

The neighbors must hate it when the Anagnos clan assembled for a party. Luxury cars belonging to his siblings, aunts, uncles, and cousins filled every parking space in view, including several illegal spots. And no one in his extended family dared miss Aunt Zoe's seventieth birthday celebration—which meant all of his parents' generation were septuagenarians now, not that they looked it.

"Good Greek genes," his dad proudly proclaimed to anyone who'd listen. "Plus good Greek food and good Greek luck."

Unless you were a second son. Then you were screwed.

Xander checked his reflection in the rear-view mirror—no green in his teeth, no eye boogers, hair tamed for the occasion with enough product to subdue the unruliest curls, even in the February drizzle.

"Three hours, tops," he promised himself as he climbed out and fetched Zoe's gift from the back seat—a basket of gourmet goodies salvaged from his defunct shop, along with a few bottles from his recently closed wine bar.

He straightened his shoulders, pasted on a painfully fake smile, and strode up the flagstone walkway. Overhead, a crow squawked and dropped a splat of shit right in his path.

He glared at the feathered harbinger. "Yeah, yeah, I get it. I'm cursed. Now, fuck off."

On his way to the living room, he scanned the hallway photo gallery—a gilt-framed shots of Mama, Baba, and older brother Dimitrios in front of Niko's Taverna, the iconic Greek restaurant founded by his great-great-grandparents, along with elder sister Elena behind the counter of her artsy Capitol Hill coffee shop, and a glowing newspaper review of younger sisters Sofia and Irida's downtown lunch place.

But the photo of his wine bar's grand opening was gone, replaced by a picture of his nephew's soccer championship. The kid's team had been knocked out in the quarterfinals, but he still merited a place on the wall of honor.

And Xander did not. Not that he begrudged his siblings' success. The restaurant business had been his family's stock-in-trade for generations. Lacking a chef's training—he'd dropped out of culinary school after a series of unfortunate kitchen accidents—he'd taken a degree in business and tried his hand at food-adjacent pursuits. So what if his first few tries fell through? Failure is just a learning opportunity, as his favorite professor used to say.

He tapped his former spot on the wall. "I'll be back."

No one even glanced Xander's way as he strolled into the noisy, jam-packed living room, deposited his basket on the overflowing gift table, then wandered to the buffet and filled a plate with lemony stuffed grape leaves, flakey spanakopita, and tangy marinated olives.

Easier to evade questions when your mouth is full.

"Alexandros," a resonant alto voice called out from somewhere near the fireplace. "Come, give your auntie a kiss. And bring me some of those shrimp."

Juggling two plates and a glass of bone-dry Assyrtiko, he wove through the crowd until he found the birthday girl perched on a velvet armchair between a marble Hercules and a bronze Aphrodite. Zoe was in her glory today, dressed in a pink silk suit, her dark hair lacquered into a helmet, diamonds glittering in her ears and on her fingers.

"Here you go, Theía Z." He handed over her plate and pecked her cheek.

"My handsomest nephew. Let's look at you." Her eyes twinkled. "I don't care what they say, you're always a winner in my book, kiddo."

"Thanks." Ignoring the backhanded compliment—because why should today be any different?—he widened his phony smile. "And you're stunning, Theía. Sure you're not turning thirty?"

"Oh, you." Tittering like a schoolgirl, she swatted him with her napkin.

"There he is." His mother bustled across the room, elbowing her relatives aside. She planted her fists on her hips, narrowed her eyes, and inspected him from head to toe. "You look sickly, Alexandros. Aren't you eating up there in that drafty hovel?"

"It's not drafty, Mama." His studio apartment might be cramped and dark, but it was the best he could afford. And if his luck didn't change soon, he'd have to find lodgings outside the city to escape Seattle's insane prices.

"It's a bad neighborhood. My son deserves better." She patted his cheek. "Please, darling, come home. Baba will make a job for you at the restaurant."

Nope. Not happening. I'm nearly forty, and I'm not moving back into my childhood room. His fingers drifted toward the envelope in his pocket.

"I'll be fine, Mama. I've got a new opportunity."

She topped her scoff with an extra helping of stink-eye. "You and your opportunities. They never work out, and you know why?"

"Ma, for cripes' sake, lay off with that curse nonsense." Irida, his youngest sister, sidled up to join them. "Xander always lands on his feet, don't you, bro?"

"Absolutely." He grinned like a toothpaste model. "No need to worry about me."

"Enough squabbling," Zoe insisted, rising from her seat. "It's my birthday, and I say it's time to eat."

Mama clapped her hands. "Everyone, to the table."

Aunt Zoe plucked at Irida's sleeve. "And put on some music. Who's that handsome singer I like? The one with the bedroom eyes?"

"Panos Kíamos?"

"That's the one."

Greek pop music filled the air as the long dining table and three extra folding tables filled with hungry Anagnoses from seventy-eight to seven. Once everyone had wine or grape juice for the birthday toast, Konstantin, Xander's father and the oldest of his generation, tapped his glass with his spoon. At the kids' table, the littles echoed their grandpa's ting, ting, ting.

"Cut that out," Xander's eldest sister, Eleni, warned them. "You'll break something."

When Xander chuckled, she elbowed him, her glare the spitting image of their father's. "Just wait till you have kids."

Kids of his own? At almost forty, that didn't seem likely. Since his divorce fifteen years ago, his love life had consisted of nothing but brief liaisons, and that was fine with him. He had this ridiculously large, loud family. And he had friends—well, a few—plus his work, which left him with no time for relationships.

Baba stroked his thick mustache as he surveyed all their expectant faces. "It is good to see the whole family together." He furrowed his bushy brows. "Except for Gus. He should be here. Why is he not here?" His spotlight glare slid over the assembly, but no one made a peep.

"He should have driven up for his sister's party," Baba declared with a scowl as thunderous as Zeus's. "Family is more important than that stupid souvenir shop."

"That's enough, Konstantin," Zoe said with a sniff of wounded forbearance. "Augustus is doing his best, considering." Her gaze flicked to Xander, then away, a gesture repeated by several other family members.

Bruised by their pity and judgment, Xander remained stoic. How freakin' ludicrous that a bunch of twenty-first century Americans—well, Greek Americans, but still—clung to antiquated notions like family curses.

So what if Gus was less prosperous than the rest of his siblings? So what if he lived in a pokey little beach town instead of Seattle? So what if he'd broken free of the family restaurant business to go in a different direction? Gus was happy.

In fact, it was while helping Gus in Souvenir Planet, his sprawling beachside shop stuffed with everything from rare seashells to old-fashioned sideshow curiosities to alien-themed tchotchkes, that Xander had caught the entrepreneurship bug. His summer job there made him feel important and capable.

Unlike here, where everyone saw him as a bumbling loser, buffeted by bad luck beyond his control.

He strangled his napkin under the table. *Curse of the second son, my ass.*

As the family passed moussaka, roasted lamb, stuffed peppers, and Greek salad, Xander grazed his fingertips over the letter in his pocket—a talisman of hope.

"Come to Trappers Cove," Gus had written in his slanted, sloppy script. "I've got a business proposition for you, something out of this world."

Uncle Gus always had interesting ideas. True, they didn't always make sense, but between his vivid imagination and Xander's grounded practicality, they'd cook up something good.

And they'd better, because the wine bar's failure chewed through a big chunk of Xander's capital. He'd have to build up more funds before he could launch another business. And if that meant spending time in the funky little beach town he'd loved as a kid, there were worse fates—like overseeing supplies and laundry service from the stuffy back office of Niko's Taverna.

Family curse or no, Xander had bigger plans. It wasn't his fault his first few ventures failed, just a combination of bad timing and unforeseeable circumstances. He'd prove to his family, and to himself, that he was as capable, as creative, as responsible as any of them.

Dimitri reached across the table and snapped his fingers under Xander's nose. "Hey, space cadet, you gonna hold that salad all night, or you gonna pass it so the rest of us can have some?"

Sofia, his next older sister, tsk-tsked. "Quit picking on Xander. It's not his fault he was born under a bad star."

"Isn't that what you called your last place?" Dimitri teased. "Bad Star Wine Bar?"

"The Amphora," Xander grumbled and shoved the salad bowl into his brother's hands. He'd like to upend it over Dimitri's sneering face.

"That's a good name," Zoe reassured him. "You just had bad luck. Can't be helped."

With a grateful glance at his aunt, Xander pushed away his plate. His appetite had withered. Why did he subject himself to these gatherings? In his family's eyes, he couldn't win.

Mama speared him with her eagle-eye gaze. "What wrong, Xander? You don't like the food?"

Rule number one at a Greek family dinner: praise the food effusively. He'd fallen down on that job too.

He lifted a forkful of lamb. "Sorry, got caught up in my thoughts. Everything's delicious."

"That's better. Now, eat up."

According to Lydia Anagnos, the problem didn't exist that couldn't be solved with food.

After the dishes were cleared away, Baba poured Greek-style coffee, and Demitri handed out shots of ouzo and rose-flavored liqueur, while Mama and Eleni passed doily-lined platters of halva and loukoumades, balls of fried dough drizzled with honey. Xander helped himself, knowing it was futile to turn down dessert.

Besides, a shot or two of sweet booze would help him care less about the pitying glances and whispered comments. They were only trying to protect him in their warped, superstitious way. He wasn't unloved, just underestimated and pitied, and the only thing that would ever shake their belief in the family curse was a brilliant, showy success.

And how in the hell was he going to pull that off?

Aunt Zoe clapped her hands. "Come. I want my family to dance me into my new decade."

While Baba pulled out his collection of vinyl records, others cleared away furniture for dancing.

Lagging behind, Xander peeked at Gus's note again, trying to puzzle out his uncle's cryptic message. Something out of this world? What wacky scheme had Gus cooked up this time?

His mother plopped down next to him, her eyes sharp with curiosity.

He quickly refolded the letter and tucked it back into his pocket.

"What's that? A note from a new love?"

No, but hopefully a new start.

"Nothing that interesting."

She heaved a dramatic sigh and squeezed his knee. "My poor, unlucky boy. I worry about you."

He grabbed her hand. "Come on, Mama. It's not time for worrying; it's time for dancing."

The twangy opening notes of the Ikariotikos rang out, and Xander joined the line of laughing, swaying relatives, giving each stomp extra force.

Soon, they'd gather again to celebrate his success—whatever that turned out to be. In the meantime, putting some distance between himself and their smother-love would do him good. A man needs room to breathe, and Trappers Cove had room to spare, brisk sea air, and the only relative who had faith in him.

In fact, Trappers Cove was probably his best hope—and his last chance.

Chapter Two

What the hell was Mom doing?

Crouched awkwardly in the window of the Trappers Cove *Beacon*'s newsroom, Hannah's mother looked almost as green as the paper shamrocks she was taping to the glass.

Hannah hurried inside and dumped their takeout lunch on her desk. "Mom! Your back's never going to get better if you don't rest. Let me handle the decorations."

Mom pulled a wry face. "It's a slow news day. Might as well make myself useful." She ripped a length of Scotch tape with her teeth and pressed a grinning leprechaun into place.

As if they hadn't spent enough time in hospital waiting rooms lately. But stubbornly ignoring problems was a time-honored Leone family trait—one best confronted head on.

Hannah softened her tone and reached for the roll of tape her mother clutched with grim determination. "You don't fool me with this busy-bee crap. You're hurting, Mom. Is your ulcer acting up again? Another migraine?"

Wincing, Mom straightened and wiped her hands on her knit slacks. "I'm fine, just a little tired. Did Mo get my order right?"

"Plain chicken kebab, no spice." She handed over the sandwich, along with an iced mint tea, then sat at her desk and unwrapped her own lunch: a deluxe kebab with the works, the ultimate in greasy, garlicky goodness. She took a bite, closed her eyes, and moaned.

So did her mother, and not in an OMG-this-is-delicious way.

"Okay, enough of this stoic nonsense," Hannah snapped. "Either you go lie down or I'm calling Doc Rivas."

Mom waved away Hannah's concern with a flick of her paper napkin. "It's not my ulcer, and it's not a migraine." She pulled an envelope from her inbox. "It's bad news. This arrived while you were out."

Hannah extracted a sheet of foil-stamped letterhead paper and skimmed its contents. Each line knotted her stomach tighter. "They're cutting us off?"

Mom slumped in her worn desk chair. "Agnes Jankowski's heirs have withdrawn their support. This month's check is our last."

"But, but," Hannah spluttered, "how can they do that?" Without the patronage of their uber-wealthy benefactor, their small-town newspaper, one of the last in Washington State, would plummet into the red.

And then what? The *Beacon* was her whole world. Losing it was unthinkable.

Hannah's mental wheels whirred. "We'll cut costs. Take in more ad revenue."

"Pfft." Mom waved an arthritic hand. "The more we stuff our pages with ads, the more subscribers we lose." With a grunt, she pushed to her feet and hobbled over to perch on Hannah's desk.

A shiver crawled down Hannah's spine. Since when had Mom looked so pale and pained and...old? The lines bracketing her mouth seemed deeper today, and a slight tremor shook the hand she laid over Hannah's tight fist.

"The news industry is changing, love. Local papers are dying off like mayflies on a frosty night. Hell, even the big papers are struggling."

"But our digital edition—"

"Is also losing subscribers. We're down twenty-seven percent from last year."

Old Fred Knudsen shuffled by, pausing to snatch a fry from Mom's plate. "Afternoon, Hannah. Linda, I'll have that write-up on the water commission meeting by COB today."

Mom gave a tight grin. "Can't wait."

Once Fred was out of hearing range, she continued in a hushed voice. "There simply isn't enough news in TC to keep our doors open. It's time to put the paper to bed for good."

Heat rose in Hannah's throat. "And the minute we do, it'll all happen again." She shot to her feet and paced the timeworn black and white tiled floor, her hands karate-chopping the air. "It's our duty to expose that kind of back-room corruption. If the citizens of Trappers Cove can't see who's pulling the strings, those strings will strangle us."

Mom planted herself in Hannah's path. "Easy now. What happened to us was unfortunate, but—"

"Unfortunate? It was a tragedy! An outrage!" She smacked her desk, knocking papers to the floor. "And it's not gonna happen again, not on my watch."

Mom pulled her into a hug. "Honey, I get it. Journalism is in your blood, but it's a lost cause."

Hannah jerked free and resumed her frantic pacing. Give up? Lost cause? Not on her watch.

"All we need is one spectacular story that'll draw subscribers and save the *Beacon*. Otherwise, where will people get their news? Social media? An informed citizenry is the cornerstone of democracy, and..."

Mom chuckled. "Just like your grandfather, holding a beacon of light to the masses."

Hannah held only vague memories of her nonno sitting in the Editor-in-Chief's chair Mom now occupied. She remembered his striped suspenders, his walrus mustache, his ink-stained fingers. Always kind to his over-eager granddaughter, he printed her "stories" on the children's page. Nonno loved his work so much he never retired, heading the *Beacon* until his sudden heart attack at the age of seventy-five.

Fear snaked around Hannah's heart and squeezed. Would she come to work and find her mother slumped over in her desk chair, the way they found Nonno Leone?

As much as she loved the newspaper, she couldn't risk her mother's health and happiness to save it.

Mom grasped Hannah's shoulders and pressed a kiss to her cheek. "Change is inevitable, my love."

Grim determination tightened her jaw. "Not this time, Mom. There's too much at stake."

A loud rattle came from behind an office divider. Almah Reyes, another of their part-time reporters, poked her head out. "Printer's acting up again."

Hannah dragged a hand down her overheated face and muttered, "Why does she insist on printing out her stories?"

Almah harrumphed. "You young reporters and your digital newspapers. I proofread my work the old-fashioned way—with a red pencil."

Hannah and her mother exchanged a look of weary amusement, knowing whatever Almah turned in would contain several typos.

"What are you working on, Almah?" Mom called.

"Pet of the week from the animal shelter. Wait till you see this kitty. He's only got one eye, but he's so stinkin' cute."

"Be with you in a minute, dear." Mom rolled her eyes, then grasped Hannah's hands and lowered her voice. "My beautiful, hard-headed darling, I know how much the *Beacon* means to you, but I'm tired. My back is shot; my stomach is trying to eat itself, and my vision is going from staring at computer screens. It's time for me to retire." She patted Hannah's hand. "And without Agnes Jankowski's support, we'll run out of funds in a few months. So I'll give you until the end of April. If you can make the *Beacon* solvent by then, you can take over as Editor-In-Chief. If not, we're closing our doors."

"Ma," Hannah croaked and blinked back the sting of tears.

Mom cupped Hannah's cheek, her weary smile brimming with compassion. "I'm sorry, darling, but all good things reach an end. And Trappers Cove is too confining for someone with your drive and talent. You're wasting your potential here. Go stretch your wings, maybe even find someone to love. You've been single far too long."

Bristling, Hannah counted backward. It hadn't been that long since she and Nathan broke up. Just...

Her shoulders sagged. Wow, almost four years ago. His parting words still stung: "Your priorities are fucked up, Hannah. I'm offering you love, but you won't lift your nose out of that damned newspaper long enough to see it."

So what? She could get another man if she wanted to. She kept fit and took care of her appearance. Even at forty, plenty of guys still asked her out.

Besides, what were the chances of finding a partner who wasn't put off by her drive? A guy who didn't expect her to spend the rest of her life in the passenger seat?

Hannah closed her eyes and massaged her aching brow. "I'm not looking for a boyfriend, Mom. Journalism is my passion, and Trappers Cove is my family."

Mom's sigh spoke of weariness and defeat. "This newspaper has cost me too much already, baby. Don't let it cost you a happy future." She packed up her lunch and headed for the back staircase. "I'm going to lie down for a while."

She could use a lie-down herself, a little time to digest this wrenching news. But the clock was ticking, and she had a helluva lot of work to do if she was going to right this sinking ship in less than three months, so she collapsed into her seat and flipped through her appointment calendar.

City Council meeting, high school honors assembly, Mable Scarpetti turns one hundred...

"Come on, TC, I need a juicy story."

The oppressive silence of the newsroom left her flushed and claustrophobic. Weird—usually she felt as much at home here as in her tiny apartment upstairs.

She clapped a hand to her clammy forehead. *Oh no, is this what perimenopause feels like?*

She needed air. Grabbing her jacket, she bolted outside and lifted her face to the sky. Misty rain cooled her heated skin. Main Street was nearly deserted today—empty and frustratingly news-free. A brisk wind carried the scent of salt and sea from the beach, only two blocks away. If not for the cold, she'd head west and walk the shoreline, letting the surf's roar calm her buzzing thoughts.

"Dead, dead, dead," she muttered as she scanned Main Street. Between the holidays and spring break, raw weather and a paucity of fun events kept away the tourists who tripled the town's population in summer. Even locals mostly stayed indoors. No parties, no festivals...nada.

A seagull flapped down to perch on a fire hydrant and eye her intently, probably hoping for a snack.

"Why did things have to change?" she asked the bird, adding a childish foot stomp since no one was around to see.

The gull ruffled its feathers and squawked.

"You're right; it's my trauma talking." She gave a dry chuckle. "Ten years of therapy and I'm still chewing on that bone. But damn it, bird, how would you feel if you had to watch bulldozers demolish the nest where you grew up?"

The gull cocked its head and regarded her, a glint of accusation in its beady eye.

"Yeah, yeah, it was twenty-five years ago. I should be over it by now. But can a person really get over something like that?"

Dad's ultimate betrayal, worse than leaving her and Mom for a younger woman. He'd refused to let Mom have his share of equity in their cozy beachfront cottage, so the family court judge forced the sale of the property—to a greedy California land shark who didn't give two cold dog turds about Trappers Cove. To this day, she couldn't walk past the ugly block of apartments that took its place without stomach-churning flashbacks.

So who could blame her for pushing back against change? Change meant loss and heartache and bitterness.

The bird grumbled in its gull language, then fluttered down to her feet.

She dug in her pocket and found a crumpled paper napkin from her last visit to Garrett's bakery across the street. She shook it out, and a few crumbs fell to the pavement. The bird gobbled them quickly.

"All I need is one good story, buddy. Deep investigative journalism. Pathos, humor, irony…something people will be dying to read about. So if you've got any ideas, I'm wide open here."

The gull stretched its snowy throat, let out a yawp, then winged across the street toward Souvenir Planet, the sprawling, kitschy souvenir shop that shared a parking lot with the bakery. Odd, even during this slow time of year there'd normally be at least a half-dozen cars in the lot, but today it stood empty. And that was bad because tourist dollars were Trappers Cove's lifeblood.

Frowning, she gazed up at the chaotic façade where two silver-painted plywood UFOs and an assortment of stars and planets shared space with a pirate captain and a grinning dolphin. Beneath the porch roof, antique farm equipment and other mechanical oddities squatted beside benches and weedy planters.

So many happy childhood memories centered around this place. As far back as she could remember, Gus stocked her favorite saltwater taffy flavors: tangerine and peppermint. She'd loved impressing out-of-town cousins with his creepy taxidermized creatures, like the two-headed calf and the "mermaid," with a monkey's body and a salmon's tail. A good portion of her allowance went to seashell jewelry and other tchotchkes purchased at Gus's emporium of the weird and wacky. Back then, space alien-themed trinkets only made up a tiny portion of Gus's inventory. Lately, little green and silver ETs grinned from nearly every shelf in the store, and tourists gobbled it up. Seemed Gus found his market niche.

Come to think of it, she hadn't seen the mustachioed, grandfatherly Greek for a while now. She usually ran into him at the bakery or Cassie's Coastal Café. She made a mental note to check on him soon.

The wind was picking up, and the worst of Hannah's angst had eased into a dull sense of defeat, with a dash of impending doom. Might as well head back to the office and start making phone calls.

With Mom upstairs and Fred and Almah out covering stories, Hannah felt the weight of her solitude. Her footsteps echoed in the empty newsroom as she once again paced the aisle between the desks. "C'mon, Muse, hit me."

A shadow moved at the edge of her vision. She whipped her head around to stare at what had been her father's desk.

Nothing there but piles of mail and an empty chair. The caffeine must be making her jittery.

Ironic how bitter anger swirled with fond memories. Dad had such a nose for news. If he were here, he'd know what to do.

"But you're gone, aren't ya?" She glared at the vacant space. "Serves you right."

Immediately, guilt sliced her between the ribs. She had every right to hate him after he abandoned them for a shiny new job at the Portland *Oregonian* and the younger woman he'd knocked up while still married to Mom. But a heart attack had felled him before his little boy even reached kindergarten.

One destroyed home, two widows, four broken hearts.

Weird how, for long stretches of time, she wouldn't give that painful chapter of her life much thought, and then something would bring it all boiling up again like a foul-tasting, bitter burp. Why now? Must be the phase of the moon, or perhaps an extra-strong tide tugging at her psyche.

With a sigh, she sat and opened their database of digitized back issues. While the files loaded, she poked the space alien bobblehead atop her monitor to make him dance. Cute little bugger.

She clicked back in time—five years ago, six, seven... then smacked her desk and let out a whoop.

Shortly after her parents' divorce, Mom did a two-page spread on the twenty-fifth anniversary of Souvenir Planet. That story led to a feature on Seattle TV news and an influx of visitors. She checked the date—sure enough, that was in early March twenty-five years ago, which meant the shop's fiftieth anniversary was coming up.

Perfect! She could spin this into a big, juicy human-interest story—Gus's origins, his contribution to Trappers Cove, his antique arcade games, his fascination with aliens, which she suspected was mostly a marketing gimmick, but who cared? It was cute and endearing, and readers would eat it up with a spoon.

If she could pry enough information out of Gus, she'd have weeks' worth of material. And the old guy loved to talk. Ooh! How about a detailed digital exclusive to lure new subscribers?

Her whole body tingled with renewed energy as her fingers flew over the keyboard. Her prayers had been answered. She was going to by-God save the *Beacon*.

Chapter Three

Feeling more relaxed than he had in ages, Xander cruised through Trappers Cove on his way to Souvenir Planet. Despite the passage of over twenty years since his last childhood summer, Main Street had barely changed. So many happy memories: the arcade where he'd glee- fully bested Uncle Gus and Aunt Marty in Skee-ball; Gelateria Par- adiso, home of the world's best chocolate-hazelnut ice cream; Cassie's Coastal Café, where he ate blueberry pancakes with whipped cream smiles...

Idling at the main drag's only traffic light, he laughed out loud at the corny cartoon sign of Spee-Dee Go-karts. Would it be too weird for an almost middle-aged man to take a ride? Maybe Gus would race him again for old times' sake.

While his inner child rejoiced, his adult sensibilities cringed a little at the tackiness of it all. Mismatched buildings, a crooked streetlamp, faded paint, and kitschy shop names like Auntie Annabelle's An- tiques Attic, Ali Baba's Kebabs, Mermaid's Grotto Gifts, and Madame Zora's Psychic Emporium. He bet her patchouli incense still made visitors sneeze.

If he were in charge, he'd give the whole shopping area a facelift, starting with Gus's place—yikes! Of all the beachy-kitschy shops,

Souvenir Planet took the tacky cake. He pulled into the almost-empty lot and stared up at the gaudy façade, now even more crowded with grinning plywood aliens, shooting stars, a couple of lopsided planets, and a 3-D UFO made out of God knows what. Above the entrance, a new sign, hand lettered in neon green, shouted, *Visit the Cosmic Vortex.*

Was that some kind of kiddie ride? One of those optical illusion rooms with a tilted floor? Gotta hand it to Gus. The guy was creative, always throwing ideas at the wall to see what stuck.

Guilt poked Xander hard as he pulled on his rain jacket. He hadn't visited Gus's place since Aunt Marty passed, and that was...five years ago. To hear Gus tell it during his infrequent visits to Seattle, the shop was still humming along. Must be tough, running the business without his wife's help. They'd been so close, literally finishing each other's sentences and giggling over the goofy shit they stocked on their shelves.

If he could find a woman to laugh with the way Gus laughed with Marty, he'd be a happy man. But right now, he didn't have much to offer a partner, other than a night or two of fun. Better to forget about dating and focus on the task at hand—whatever that turned out to be. With Uncle Gus, you never knew.

He crossed the pitted parking lot, sidestepping around puddles. Weird, he couldn't recall ever seeing it this empty. Even in the dead season between school vacations, there was always someone poking through the shelves of seashells, snow globes, T-shirts, and other touristy crap.

A few cars sat outside Sweet Dreams Bakery, which shared the big parking lot. Was Miss Ella still around? His mouth watered at the memory of her giant peanut butter cookies—the perfect balance of sweet and salty, soft and crunchy.

As he walked past, a tall red-haired man stepped onto the bakery's covered porch, his arm crooked to steady an elderly woman as she descended the three stairs. Could that be the old baker herself? No, too short to be Ella. The man helped the old gal into her car, then glanced Xander's way and tilted his head as if trying to place him.

Holy shit. "Gary? Is that you?"

The guy laughed. "Nobody's called me Gary in years. Not since Granny Ella passed." He hooked a thumb over his shoulder. "This is my place now. Are you that skinny kid who worked at Gus's shop? His nephew, right?"

Xander strode forward, hand extended. "I'll be damned. I'm Xander Anagnos."

"Garrett Becker, at your service. If you're hungry, that is."

They clasped hands, and Garrett gave him that same wide grin he had as a gawky kid, all knees and elbows and big feet. Now tall and lean, he'd grown into those clumsy limbs. His friendly smile immediately put Xander at ease.

Garrett lifted his chin in the direction of the shore. "Remember when we tried to climb the rock wall to Ivan's Hollow?"

"Hell yeah." Xander rubbed his elbow. "We both fell—what?—ten feet? I've still got the scar."

"You in town to visit your uncle?"

"He asked me to come." He glanced over his shoulder. "Place is looking kind of sad."

Garrett nodded, his smile fading. "Afraid Gus hasn't been doing so well. The Pandemic hit us all hard, you know? Most businesses have bounced back, but Gus—" He spread his hands. "Anyway, I'm glad you're here." He backed toward the bakery. "Hey, I've got cookies in the oven, but stop by when you get a chance. Let's catch up."

"I'll do that."

Worry wormed into Xander's gut as he approached the shop. Its lights were off, except for a pale glow from Gus's office in the back. He tried the door. Locked. A handwritten sign in the window said '*Back at one.*'

Xander checked his phone. Four-fifteen.

"Uncle Gus?"

No answer. He called Gus's cell—probably still had his old flip phone. It went straight to a voice mail announcement that Gus's inbox was full.

Well, shit. He made his way to the "Employees Only" door behind the dumpsters. Maybe, if he was lucky…

Gus was notoriously bad about losing keys, so he used to hide a spare shop key…damn it, where? Scowling, Xander searched his memory.

"Gotcha!" Extracting the key hidden beneath a plaster alien in an overgrown, weedy planter, he let himself in.

The smell hit him first—the unmistakable whiff of mildew. He fumbled until he found a light switch.

"Sweet Jesus." How long since this place had a good cleaning? Cobwebs dangled from glass fishing floats and nets overhead, and dust coated mangey taxidermized creatures mounted high on the walls. The shelves were jumbled with no discernable order, which was out of character for Gus, who always kept his merchandise organized in his own oddball way.

Worry scrabbled in Xander's stomach. Something was majorly wrong if Gus let his beloved shop deteriorate to this state.

"Gus?" he called. "It's me, Xander."

No reply, not even the sound of Gus's ancient transistor radio, permanently set to a talk-radio station.

He made his way through the aisles, past an even bigger assortment than he remembered of space aliens, big and small, staring from mugs, ashtrays, wine glasses, and soap dishes. The once-impressive display of exotic seashells looked picked-over, and most of the penny arcade games bore *'out of order'* signs.

Even the "mermaid's" case was grimy with fingerprints. Actually a mummified monkey with false eyelashes attached to a fish tail, its aquarium home had a new label: *'Celestia, Space Siren from Planet Xormak, Crash Landed on Earth in 1942.'*

"Going all in on the alien angle, eh, Gus?"

He pushed through the swinging doors to the back storage area where Gus kept his office. A light burned behind the frosted glass office door.

"Uncle Gus?" He opened the door, then bolted backward and collided with rickety metal shelves, tumbling them and himself to the floor with a loud clang.

"No no no," he moaned, pushing painfully to his feet. "Please, God, let him be okay."

He wasn't okay. Gus lay face-down, his limbs sprawled at awkward angles, clutching a sheet of paper.

Stomach knotted, Xander stumbled to Gus's crumpled form and knelt beside him. He pressed two fingers to his uncle's throat. No pulse, just cold, waxy skin.

Gus was gone.

Xander's senses swam as he lurched to his feet and grasped Gus's desk to keep from toppling to the floor.

From somewhere in the shop, he heard a sharp knock. A woman called, "Hello? Gus?"

It took Xander three tries to find his voice.

"Call 911!"

"Call 911!"

A man backed through the swinging doors, swaying on his feet, one hand clutching his thick, dark hair. Was he drunk? A robber? No, he was too well-dressed for that, in stylish jeans, polished leather shoes, and a rain-damp jacket. He shook his head slowly, moving as if in a trance.

"Sir? Are you okay?"

He spun toward her, wan and wide-eyed, a grimace of sheer panic on his handsome face. "He's...he's... Oh, God." Stumbling forward, he collided with a display of snow globes that tumbled to the floor. Oblivious to the wet, glittery mess, he pointed a trembling finger toward the back of the shop.

She started for the swinging doors, but he yelped, grabbed her arm, and yanked her hard against his chest. Beneath her palm, his heart raced like a hummingbird's wings.

"Don't go back there," he rasped. "It's terrible."

Oh God, was Gus murdered?

Moving slowly so as not to further startle him, she pulled her phone from her pocket. "Okay, I'm calling now." While she waited for the call to connect, she inched him backward toward an old-fashioned park bench and eased him down beside a bedraggled life-size alien in a faded silver suit, a favorite photo spot for tourists. Afraid he might slide to the floor, she sat next to him, but their ET companion didn't leave much room, so she had to squish against the man's quaking body.

She hit Speaker on her phone.

"Pacific County Dispatch. What's your emergency?" a bored-sounding woman intoned.

The man yanked the phone from her grip. "He's dead. Gus is dead."

"Take a breath, sir," the dispatcher said. "What's the address?"

He speared Hannah with a pleading look.

She pried her phone from his hand. "Souvenir Planet, at the south end of Main Street in Trappers Cove. We're across the street from—"

"Got it, ma'am. Officers are on their way. Are you in danger?"

"Uh, I don't think so." She turned to the guy. "Did you see anyone back there?"

He shook his head, then crumpled forward, clutching his stomach.

"I think we're okay. The side door is open."

"Roger that." The dispatcher hung up.

Unsure of how to be helpful, Hannah rubbed his broad back, now shaking with silent sobs. When he leaned against her with a groan, she gathered him into her arms and held him, swaying slowly as he wept into the crook of her neck. His soft hair tickled her cheek.

Heart thundering, she battled between journalistic curiosity and compassion. This poor, traumatized man needed comfort more than she needed to gawk at a potential crime scene. Besides, earning his trust might unlock the juiciest story to hit Trappers Cove in ages.

Shocked at her mercenary impulse, she gave herself a mental slap. What the hell was wrong with her?

After a few minutes, he released her, swiped his forearm over his streaming, swollen eyes, and fumbled in his pocket.

"Here." She pulled a pack of Kleenex from her purse.

"Thanks." He sniffed hard and flashed a heartbreaking crooked smile. "Sorry, I'm a mess."

Something about his strong features reminded her of Gus—long nose with a slight curve, large, dark eyes, thick, straight brows. Even his sharp, scruff-dusted jaw and curly, dark-chocolate hair resembled the photos of a younger Gus she'd dug up in this afternoon's research. Thirty years ago, Gus was a hottie, and so was his...

"Are you, uh, related to Gus?"

He nodded. "He's—was—my uncle."

She clasped his hand in both of hers. In a weird way, it was an honor to help someone through that surreal moment when a loved one switched from present tense to past.

"I'm so very sorry. Gus was a wonderful man. Everyone in Trappers Cove loved him."

He chuffed a hoarse laugh. "Wish I could say the same about his family."

"But you're here."

"Yeah." He glanced toward the back of the shop. "He wrote to me. Actual snail mail. But that's Gus, right? Said he had a business deal to discuss."

"Any idea what he had in mind?"

He released her hand and speared long fingers through his hair, mussing it adorably.

She sucked in a breath, fighting for focus. She was here to help and to gather news, not to ogle a pretty man. A *very* pretty man.

"Honestly, I don't have a clue. Doesn't matter now, anyway." A tear rolled down his cheek, triggering a wave of sympathy so overwhelming she threw her arm around his shoulders.

"It'll be okay," she whispered and inhaled the enticing scent wafting from his warm, solid body—leather, she decided, and moss. Masculine and delicious. "We'll help you. Whatever you need, Trappers Cove takes good care of its own."

"I'm not from TC," he protested, his voice a sensual rumble.

"You're Gus's family. That makes you one of us." She patted his back, then released him when a siren whooped outside.

They rose to greet Police Chief Jess Hawthorne and Officer Ethan Jefferson, who made up slightly less than half of their town's tiny police force. Not much call for law enforcement outside of the tourist season, when the town's population tripled.

Jess removed her cap and smoothed her gray ponytail. "Hey there, Hannah. Scoping out a scoop?"

Gus's nephew scowled as he searched Hannah's face.

Heat painted her cheeks. "I'm with the Trapper City *Beacon*."

He narrowed his eyes. "Is that why you came? But how did you know?"

She raised her palms in a placating gesture. "I wanted to interview Gus for a story about Souvenir Planet. I had no idea he'd passed, I swear."

"Of course not. How could you? The place was locked up tight." Somehow, he didn't look entirely convinced, but his chest inflated in a deep breath. "Gus is back here, in his office."

"And who are you, sir?" Jess asked, her pen and notepad at the ready.

"Xander Anagnos. With an X, not a Z. I'm his nephew."

Xander. What a cool name. It suited him.

Jess jotted down Xander's contact information, then she and Officer Jefferson followed him back through the swinging doors. No one protested when Hannah trailed after them.

Before stepping into Gus's office, she braced herself. In twenty years of reporting for the *Beacon*, she'd seen several dead bodies, but all the breath left her body at the sight of the dear old man sprawled like a marionette with its strings cut.

"Oh, Gus." She clapped her hands to her mouth to stifle a sob. Such a sweet, funny guy. To have soldiered on through losing his wife, then the pandemic, only to die alone in this cramped, dingy office—it broke her heart.

The two cops stepped carefully around the corpse, snapping photos and taking notes.

"In my professional opinion, Gus expired from natural causes," Jess told them when they'd concluded their brief examination. "My condolences, Mr. Anagnos. Your uncle was a good man, one of the best." She leaned closer and lowered her voice—a useless gesture in the tiny space. "Between you and me, Gus seemed a little off lately, always muttering about alien visitors. Losing Martha kinda knocked him sideways, I think."

The two-way radio on the chief's belt crackled. She listened and nodded. "Ambulance is here. They'll take Gus to the funeral home. County Medical Examiner will confirm cause of death before releasing the body for burial. Any idea what Gus's wishes were?"

Xander shook his head, looking a little green.

"We'll figure it out," Hannah reassured them both. She hooked her arm through his. "Come on, Xander, let's get out of here. Where are you staying?"

"I, uh—don't know yet."

"Right. That's the second order of business. How about if we start with a coffee?"

He nodded and let her guide him through the shop and into the now-crowded lot. Seemed nearly half the town was there, drawn by the police car and ambulance.

"What's going on, Hannah?" Cassie, owner of the Coastal Café up the street, wrung her apron in nervous hands.

"I'm afraid it's Gus."

"Oh, Lord." Cassie whipped out her phone. Ten minutes from now, the whole town would have heard the sad news.

By the time she and Xander emerged from Garrett's bakery clutching large coffees and a paper sack of pastries, the onlookers had formed an impromptu honor guard, a family of the heart who stood solemnly in solidarity and respect as the ambulance crew rolled the gurney past.

Fred O'Malley, keeper of Gull's Point Lighthouse, doffed his fisherman's cap. "Safe journey, old friend."

A teen beside him added, "Gus is going home to Planet X."

Hannah shushed him. The last thing Xander needed right now was mockery of his dear, departed uncle. In fact, he looked entirely too shaken up to drive, so she bundled him into his car and drove him to the Mermaid Lodge—not exactly the finest accommodations, but they'd sort out something better once he'd had a chance to rest and absorb the bad news.

She helped him carry his bags into his "deluxe family suite," a wood-paneled room that hadn't been updated since the last century, and pried the cap off his still-warm coffee. "Here, have some. It'll help, I think."

He took a sip, then set it on the nightstand, shed his rain-damp jacket, and sat on the edge of the bed, his hands dangling between his knees.

"He asked me to come. Said he had a big opportunity for me." His voice wobbled. "He needed me, and I wasn't there for him."

The mattress creaked under their combined weight as she sat beside him. "Hey, you couldn't have known. I'll bet looking forward to your visit made him happy."

He released a shaky sigh.

"You really loved Gus, didn't you?"

He nodded slowly, his gaze focused somewhere past the olive-green curtains. "He was good to me. He and Aunt Martha took me in every summer. I mean, the whole family came to the beach for a week, but when they returned to Seattle, I got to stay behind with Gus and Marty to help in the shop." He huffed a bone-dry laugh. "Not sure how much help I was, but it made me feel special." His eyes brimmed with pain. "I needed that."

Unsure whether he'd welcome the gesture, she gave his back a tentative pat. When he leaned into her comforting touch, she rubbed slow circles across the broad expanse of muscle.

Xander's gaze dropped to his leather sneakers. "Then last week, he sent me that letter. Said he had some kind of opportunity for me, but he didn't go into any details. Whatever it was, I guess I'll never know." He slumped even farther. "The shop, his house—someone's gotta sort through all that, and I'm the only one in the family who'll care enough to do it right."

Hoo-boy, she should not be feeling this protective and fond of a near stranger, but the shock they'd endured together triggered big, warm, fuzzy feelings.

She squeezed him in a side hug. "Listen, you're not alone. I'll—we'll help you through this."

He leaned his head onto her shoulder, and her lady bits throbbed. *Totally inappropriate.*

As if he'd heard her thoughts, Xander straightened and heaved a huge sigh. "You've been wonderful, Hannah, and I'm grateful for your help, but right now, I need to be alone for a while." He gave her a heart-melting crooked smile. "You know, to soak it all in and figure out where I go from here."

"Of course." Shaking off her disappointment, she rose to her feet and pulled a business card from her jacket pocket. "Here's my contact info. As soon as you're ready, please give me a call."

"Thanks, I will." He stretched out on his side and clutched the pillow. A vision hit her of the adorable little curly-haired boy he'd once been, exhausted and tearful and in need of a good cuddle.

But he wasn't a little boy. He was a grown man about her age dealing with grief and all the complications that came with a loved one's passing.

She backed toward the door. "I hope I'll see you around."

The corner of his mouth not buried in a pillow lifted. "You will, I promise. Thanks, Hannah, for taking care of me."

"Anytime, Xander." Heart tapdancing with unseemly glee, she left him to recover.

Chapter Four

Xander stood beside vacation rental agent Cheryl Rossi in front of Trappers Cove's ugliest building. Puke-green paint peeled off the walls of a two-story shoebox pierced with small, salt-smudged windows. Judging by the beer swag, cannabis print curtains, and dead plant décor of the other three units, his neighbors were not upwardly mobile young professionals.

Then again, neither was he.

Cheryl, a fifty-something woman with a squirrel's chirpy energy, wrinkled her nose. "You sure about this, hon?"

No, he wasn't, but this was the cheapest option, and he had to conserve as much capital as possible. Besides, he'd be spending most of his time at the shop.

"I'm sure it'll be fine."

She let him into a dim, dingy upstairs apartment. At least he wouldn't have to deal with neighbors stomping on his ceiling, like he did in Seattle. The place had definitely seen better days—stained navy and white canvas sofa, mismatched chairs around a scratched dining table, a very small kitchen with cigarette burns on the Formica countertops. Ikea bookshelves held cheap, tacky nautical décor—a plastic seagull, a garden-gnome sea captain, desiccated starfish, and—

Xander picked up an ashtray shaped like a flying saucer. "Is this from Gus's shop?"

Cheryl grinned. "You'd be hard-pressed to find a rental in town that doesn't have something from your uncle's collection. It's a Trappers Cove tradition."

He forced a weak smile. "This'll do. Thank you, Cheryl, for finding me an apartment so quickly."

After showing her out, he surveyed his temporary lodgings and grumbled, "Definitely need to spruce the place up before having company."

An image flashed through his mind—sitting with Hannah at the wobbly dining table, watching candlelight dance in her dark, bewitching eyes. Their glasses raised in a toast, their fingers intertwined...

Where the hell had that come from?

With a weary sigh, he sat on the lumpy couch and pulled from his pocket another letter from Gus, the one he'd been clutching when Xander found him. The police chief had passed it on this morning, along with the coroner's pronouncement that Gus had died from a brain aneurysm.

If there'd been any doubt Gus was losing his marbles, that doubt was erased by his final message to Xander: *The visitors are coming for me, son. I can feel the star portal opening. My bones are vibrating to a new cosmic frequency. Don't feel sad for me. I'm going to a better place, and I'll be watching you. You're going to shine, agori mou, as bright as Sirius. Just rememb—*

Gus's shaky handwriting trailed off into gibberish.

Agori mou. "My boy." Warmth filled Xander's chest as he heard those words echoed in Gus's deep, raspy voice. Even through these mysterious, unbalanced ramblings, his uncle's love shone through.

As it did in his will. Seemed the news of Gus's death triggered a call from the police chief to Gus's lawyer, who left a voice mail while Xander ran on the beach. He'd needed that physical escape after fielding a thousand questions on the family text chain and a tearful call with his mother. Typical—Gus was Baba's brother, but Mama handled the emotional work.

"I'm so glad you're there, son. You've got the time to handle Gus's affairs. The rest of us are so busy. You understand, don't you?"

Yeah, he understood. In their eyes, his time was less important than the rest of the family's. No matter. In light of Gus's will, he'd be stuck in Trappers Cove for quite a while, because Gus had left him the shop: lock, stock, and leaky barrel.

"Don't you worry, son," the kindly lawyer had assured him. "Everything here was prepared four years ago, when Gus was definitely of sound mind. I'll testify to that fact if need be." She handed him a handwritten addendum Gus had penned before he spun off into outer space.

Xander, you were always my favorite. You've got a kind heart, a sharp mind, and a good head on your shoulders. I'm leaving you my business because I know you'll take Souvenir Planet to a new level of success and prove to those stubborn Greeks that this second son curse is bullshit. I did it, kiddo, and you can do it even better. All I ask is that you follow the three provisions, so when they come back, they'll know where to find me.

Unfortunately, Gus had sold his cute little beach cottage a few years back to cover his debts, and had been living out of the shop, a revelation that stabbed Xander with fresh guilt. How did the family not know Gus was doing so badly? Why hadn't he reached out?

Xander had no room to criticize Gus's secrecy, though, since he'd been hiding the full extent of his own financial disaster.

Was Gus's gift a lifesaver? Or an albatross around Xander's neck?

He flipped the thick packet of documents to page seventeen.

Xander Ioannis Anagnos will assume full ownership of Souvenir Planet, LLC, so long as the following conditions are met.

> 1. *The business will continue to operate as a souvenir shop.*
>
> 2. *The Cosmic Transmitter must be made available to visitors during business hours, and*
>
> 3. *The earthly remains of Augustus Xylon Anagnos are to be cremated and interred beneath the Cosmic Transmitter.*

What the hell was a cosmic transmitter?

If Xander failed to meet these conditions, the building would be sold and the proceeds donated to the North American Society to Document Extra-terrestrial Visitations.

With a grunt, he pushed to his feet and flung open the only decent-sized window in the place. He leaned out, sucking in a deep breath of salty air.

What an unappetizing choice—clean out Gus's cobweb-infested junk shop and make a go of the souvenir business, or return to the cramped back office of Niko's Taverna, working the books for his parents. Gus had him by the short and curlies.

No way around it. Souvenir Planet was his best shot at recouping his losses.

In the narrow residential street below, smiley neighbors greeted each other on their way to the beach or into town. Trappers Cove might be tacky and kitschy, but the town's soothing, friendly vibe was undeniable.

Gus's raspy voice rang in Xander's memory: "Are you up for a challenge, agori mou?"

The eager boy he'd been back then would've jumped right in with a whoop of delight. But that kid hadn't yet had childish optimism beaten out of him by sharp, cold reality.

With a sigh, he closed the window and trotted down the stairs to fetch his belongings from his Prius. On his windshield, he found a welcome message from Trappers Cove—a huge blot of seagull shit.

"Ugh." He pulled a paper napkin from the door pocket and scrubbed at the gross mess. "Is there even a carwash in this dumpy little town?"

He glared up at the muddy-gray sky. "What have you gotten me into, Gus?"

A peal of avian laughter rang out as two gulls—a snowy white and gray adult and a drabber juvenile—lifted off from a streetlamp and flapped seaward. On an impulse, Xander followed, hands stuffed into his pockets. Soft sea mist pattered his face. Well, that was one plus for this cruddy apartment—only two blocks from the shore, and the ocean's muffled roar grew louder with each step.

The cottage-lined street ended at a wooden railing. Stepping through a gap, he followed a path through the sea grass to the crest of a low dune.

"Wow." TC's eponymous cove stretched out before him, a long curve of pale, clean sand slicked mirror-smooth at the surf line. Comforting memories washed over him like a warm, buoying tide. So many happy, carefree summers he'd spent here, and that magic lingered, even amidst this perplexing crisis.

The tension rolled off his shoulders, leaving him peaceful and relaxed for the first time since he'd arrived in Trappers Cove. What a perfect place to sort out his next steps.

A smile curved his lips. "Okay, Gus, you're on. Thanks for this opportunity. I promise to give it my best shot."

Hannah scowled at her blank phone screen. Six days since she'd offered Xander whatever help he needed with his shop, and...nada. Okay, he'd dropped off an obituary while she was out covering a city council meeting, but otherwise, zip. After Sunday's front-page spread on Gus and his contribution to Trappers Cove, including quotes from over twenty friends, neighbors, and even the mayor, she'd expected at least a text of thanks. But nope, not a peep.

Well then, time to take matters into her own hands. Surely, there'd be a funeral or celebration of life, and her readers deserved the chance to bid farewell to one of the town's leading lights.

So what if she was itching for another peek at Souvenir Planet's oh-so-attractive new owner? That was beside the point—mostly.

"Mom, I'm going across the street for a bit."

Her mother looked up from the Saint Patrick's Day ad layout. "See if Garrett's got apple crullers today. I've got a hankering for one."

Caught. "Actually, I was going to stop at Gus's place first—er, Xander's place."

"I see." A knowing smile spread over Mom's face. "He certainly is handsome, isn't he?"

"You've met Xander?"

"Not yet, but Marquetta was in the bakery when he came in. Said he looked so sad and worn down she wanted to hug him." She waggled her eyebrows. "I'll bet he'd rather get a hug from you, though."

"Gah." Hannah flipped her scarf over her shoulder. "Enough with the matchmaking."

"All I'm saying is Gus's nephew is a hunk. What you do with that opportunity is entirely up to you."

Mom's not-so-subtle hint landed with a twinge of discomfort. In fact, Hannah did see poor Xander as an opportunity—not to date, as appealing as that idea sounded, but to lure more readers to the *Beacon*. Cute as he may be, she couldn't afford to let an inconvenient attraction distract her from that mission.

Last week's feature on Souvenir Planet had legs. She'd talked Mom into a larger than usual print run in honor of Gus's passing, and so far, sales were brisk. If Xander would grant an interview about his plans for the shop, she could put a teaser on the paper's social media and hide the rest behind a paywall—juicy bait for new digital subscribers.

Hannah slid into her lucky blazer, a scarlet classic with a nipped waist and lots of pockets. She loaded it up with her voice recorder, notepad, and extra pens before striding across the street, determined to charm a story out of Xander.

This situation called for the utmost tact. Poor guy had been through a terrible shock and might not be ready to talk about his relationship with Gus or his plans for the shop.

"Please be ready, Xander," she whispered, eyes on her alien-be-decked prize. "I need this story."

The interior lights were on, but Xander had pulled the shades, and the front door held a hand-lettered sign: *Closed due to death in the family*.

Before knocking, she snapped a photo of the impromptu memorial shrine beside the entrance: sympathy cards and handwritten messages tacked to the wall, along with Mylar balloons, supermarket bouquets in Mason jars, and heaps of alien-themed souvenirs, especially the metallic plush aliens Gus sold by the bushel.

Some smart-ass had spray-painted '*RIP Gus*' on the wall. On a poster board, someone more respectful had sketched a caricature of Gus with his trademark mustache and wide grin, dressed like an astronaut and pointing up to the stars.

Tears prickled her eyes. "Aww, Gus. You left us too soon. Don't you worry. I'm gonna help Xander keep your legacy alive—if he'll let me."

She knocked. No reply except the scrape and bang of someone moving around inside. Finding the side door open, she stepped through. "Hello? Xander?"

She followed the distant sound of masculine cursing. On the shop floor, she spied a very fine male behind in the air, the upper half of its owner bent over a cardboard box. Without looking up, he flung a plush spaceman her way, narrowly missing her head. Gu's nephew had a good arm.

So did she. She caught the next flying E.T. and hurled it back to bounce off Xander's butt.

He bolted upright, a plastic flying saucer clutched to his heart. "Jeeezus." He pulled off his headphones. "Sneaky, aren't you?"

"I called your name twice."

God, he was stunning. Mussed curls, a smudge on one cheek, and a soft navy Henley shirt with sleeves pushed to his elbows, exposing muscular forearms dusted with dark hair—her kryptonite.

She strode forward, hand extended. "Congratulations. I hear the shop is yours now."

He eyed her hand suspiciously. "Who told you that?"

"Oh, honey." She tutted and shook her head. "Have you forgotten how things work in a small town? Mavis from the county records office had breakfast at Cassie's café. By the time she finished her banana waffles, everyone knew."

"Super." He flashed a mirthless smile.

"Looks like you're dismantling the place."

"Just trying to find a starting point." He flapped a hand at the disarray surrounding them—half-emptied shelves, moving cartons and plastic storage bins, tarps and trash sacks.

Maybe the best way to get what she wanted was to pitch in. In her experience, men tended to open up better when engaged in physical activity.

"How can I help?"

He raked his fingers through his dark curls, accenting touches of silver at his temples. "Got any idea where to find the Cosmic Transmitter?"

"It's right over there." She pointed to Gus's most recent art project: an oversize hubcap etched with symbols and welded to a rebar pyramid wrapped in an iridescent metal screen. She supposed it was meant to be some kind of antenna.

"I think the switch is down here." She crouched and poked around until she found the button. LED lights wound through the supports flickered to life, pulsing in waves of blue, green, and purple.

"Pretty, isn't it?" She pushed to her feet.

He crossed his arms and glared at the thing as if it had personally offended him. "What's it for?"

"Coaxing money out of tourists." She leaned over the glass counter beside the register. "I think he kept it..." Her fingers closed around a cigar box covered in aluminum foil. "Here."

Xander's gaze jerked back up to her face.

Ogling my behind, eh? Interesting.

Biting back a grin, she lifted the lid to show him squares of metallic origami paper. "See? You write your message here, then put it in the cosmic transmitter, like so." She took a Sharpie from the tin can beside the register, scribbled *Help Xander*, then inserted her note into metal mailbox welded to the transmitter's frame.

"What happens then?"

She shrugged. "According to Gus, your message is transmitted to outer space. If you're lucky, yours will be the first one intercepted by intelligent interstellar travelers."

"And people pay money for this?"

"A dollar a pop, last I heard." She noted his sour expression. "If it gives people a giggle, what's the harm?"

Xander scrubbed a hand down his face and groaned. "How am I gonna bury him under this piece of crap?"

"Bury him? Pretty sure that's illegal in Washington State."

He pointed to an urn resting on the counter. "Tell that to Gus."

Hannah's throat tightened. With a trembling finger, she traced its surface, silver filigree and midnight blue ceramic painted with stars and nebulae. Truly, a beautiful piece of art. "He's in here?"

"Not yet. Found it in his office behind the coffee machine. I've got to deliver it to the funeral home." He flipped through a packet of documents and tapped a spot marked with a tiny Post-it. "His instructions were specific. Once cremated, his remains are to be interred beneath the cosmic transmitter."

"Hard to do without digging through the floor and the cement pad underneath." She tapped her pursed lips. "Wait. It doesn't say 'bury,' right?" She pulled out her phone and opened her favorite dictionary app. "Inter: to place a corpse or ashes in a grave or tomb, typically with funeral rites. Could you just—I dunno—build a metal box or something? Like a tiny mausoleum, just for Gus?"

Xander's full lips twitched upward. "Yeah, I guess that could work. Thanks, Hannah." His smile widened. "You're pretty sharp."

"Job requirement." She bit her lip hard to keep from grinning—a natural but totally inappropriate response to very gratifying praise. But now was not the time for flirtation. The poor guy was in mourning, and her goal was to unearth a story juicy enough to rescue the *Beacon*.

She struck a casual pose, elbow on the counter. "So, what'll happen to the rest of the shop?"

Xander sank onto the bench beside the giant cloth alien. "I'm waiting for inspiration to strike." He poked the figure's metallic, light-bulb-shaped head. "Bubba here is no help, are you, buddy?"

"I'm sure you'll do great."

He stretched out his long legs and crossed them at the ankle. "As it turns out, I was looking for a business opportunity. Et voilà. Shitty way to start, but I'm committed to polishing up Souvenir Planet, somehow."

Thrilled and relieved, she dropped down beside him and hugged him tight. "That's fabulous news! Welcome to Trappers Cove!"

He went stiff in her arms—and not in a fun way.

Awkward.

"Sorry." She released him and scooted as far away as the bench allowed. "I'm just so glad Souvenir Planet will live on. People love this place."

He cocked an ebony eyebrow. "People? Or just visitors from outer space?"

"Well, maybe them too. But look at it!" She circled a hand overhead. "Isn't it glorious? So quirky and weird and colorful. Tourists spend hours here."

"They do, huh? When does that start?"

"We get a small push around spring break, but the season really cranks up starting Memorial Day. Visitors come for the patriotic parade and street fair, and by the time school lets out, the town's population triples."

He rubbed his chin, looking thoughtful and so distractingly handsome she lost the thread for a moment, too caught up in his broody beauty to think straight.

Get the story, Ms. Horny-Pants.

And if doing so helped a hunky, troubled newcomer along the way, so much the better.

"Listen." She pulled out her notepad. "I'm doing a big feature on Gus. He's kind of a local legend, and I'd love to hear your memories about him."

Xander's mouth set in a hard line.

"When you're feeling up to it, of course. In the meantime, in TC, we take care of our own. That means you now. So if you need help—you know, hauling, reorganizing, painting—just give me a call. I'll put you in touch with someone."

"Pretty well connected, aren't you?"

"It takes a village, right?"

He scrunched his brow. "Wasn't that one about raising kids?"

"Yeah, well, for some of us, our business is our baby."

That was especially true for Hannah. Though she liked kids fine in the abstract, she'd funneled all her nurturing into the newspaper, and the threat of losing it brought out her mama bear instincts.

She reached across Xander's body to pat the big stuffed alien glued to the bench. "Gus loved this place like his own child. He poured so much love into it."

Might as well ask because she'd never get a better segue. "You have kids, Xander?"

He shook his head. "Never got around to it. Like my uncle, I guess." His gaze met hers and held it fast. "You?"

"I've never felt that maternal pull." She tapped her chest. "Hard-hearted career woman. That's what my father called Mom when she refused to give up the *Beacon* and be a stay-at-home wife. He'd say the same about me if he were still around." Which was a ridiculous double standard, since Dad had been just as driven as his wife and daughter.

She cracked a wry smile. "Family, right?"

Xander grunted. "Not my favorite topic at the moment."

"Well, you got lucky with Gus." She patted his firm shoulder. "He was a good one."

"That he was." A grimace twisted his features. "The guilt is eating me alive. If I'd visited sooner, I'd have noticed Gus was losing his marbles—holed up here, obsessing about UFOs, and neglecting his health." His deep voice cracked. "If I'd known, if I'd got him help, he'd still be here today."

"Hey now." She grabbed his hand and squeezed hard. "What happened to Gus was not your fault. We all should've noticed he was in distress. He was part of our family too."

Holding her gaze, he wove his fingers through hers, sending an electric zing right to her heart. For a long moment, she sat there breathless, vibrating with anticipation.

Then he averted his eyes, released her hand, and pushed to his feet.

Damn. Guess I'm the only one who felt that. Pity.

"Well, hard-hearted lady with connections, I need a way to unload all this dusty crap so I can see what I'm working with."

She tapped her lips with her pen. "How about a clearance sale? Saturday sound good? In honor of Gus's friendship, the *Beacon* will waive our usual advertising fee." Plus, a blow-out sale would provide yet another meaty story about Souvenir Planet and all the wacky merchandise on offer.

Xander scratched his head. "Um, I hadn't got that far, but yeah, that could work if I can get some temporary staff."

"Gotcha." She pulled out her phone and tapped out a message. "My friend Lisa sponsors the high school's honor society, and volunteering in the community is a requirement. We'll rope some reliable students into helping out. Anything else I can do today?"

"I'll need someone who can repair drywall. Check this out." He picked his way through the crowded, messy aisles to a ladder standing against the wall and climbed, thick thighs flexing. Reaching up, he tapped a lopsided painting of an alien on the ceiling.

"He's cute."

"He's rotten." Xander punched the creature's painted face. It crumbled like a B movie mummy.

He pointed. "There, and there, and there. Soft spots from a leaking roof Gus should've fixed years ago. And what did he do? Covered them up with effin' cartoons!" He slumped as if exhausted. "Leaky plumbing, peeling linoleum, slanted floors, cracks in the walls. This building needs a helluva lot more than a fresh coat of paint. I'm surprised it hasn't been condemned. I oughta just hire a wrecking crew to pull it down."

Hannah shot to her feet. "You can't do that!"

Xander poked a dusty taxidermized creature mounted up high—a badger? A beaver? "You're right. Gus's will says I have to keep the shop running. Otherwise, it'll be sold to benefit the... Damn, what's it called?" He pulled out his phone and tapped the screen. "NASDEV. The North American Society to Document Extra-terrestrial Visitations."

Hannah's heart rose in her throat. "Sold to whom?"

"Does it matter?" He clambered back to earth.

"Yes, it damn well does matter." Her voice rose to a shrill squeak. "Greedy developers, always sniffing around for their chance to erase Trappers Cove and remake our town into another Carroll Beach, all slick and bougie. You know the type—every shop has the same façade, selling expensive, pretentious crap. Before you know it, property values go up, and one by one, people who built lives here are forced to leave."

Remembered trauma heated her cheeks and tightened her chest—the unholy growl of the bulldozer pushing pushing pushing the walls of her childhood home until they splintered and crumpled. Even now, twenty-five years later, seeing the ugly, poorly maintained condos that took its place turned her stomach.

Xander clasped her shoulders, and that firm, grounding touch brought air racing back into her lungs. "Easy, avenging angel. I have no intention of letting this property go to a developer and a bunch of UFO nuts." He leaned in closer and peered into her face. "You okay?"

She sucked in another bracing breath. "Of course. I'm perfectly fine."

With a bemused smile, Xander shook his head. "Whatever you say."

Chapter Five

"Mama, no. That's not what Gus wanted. He spelled it out in his will."

Leave it to his mother's impeccable timing—her irate call landed during his coffee break in Sweet Dreams Bakery, currently packed with customers munching Garrett Becker's excellent pastries.

At the sound of Xander's raised voice, a trio of older women seated nearby swiveled and gawked.

Xander lowered his volume and hunched over his apple crumble cake. Should've known better than to pick up in a public place, but preparing for tomorrow's clearance sale left him so damn tired. The high-school kids Hannah had procured were a help, but at the drop of a google-eyed alien ball cap they'd break into giggles and start playing with the merchandise.

And now Mama was chewing him a new one over Gus's memorial service. "Your father is disgusted," she hissed into the phone. "All the Anagnoses are buried in Lake View Cemetery. We can't ignore four generations of family tradition because a wacko second son wants to be buried in his junk shop."

His jaw tightened. "It's a souvenir shop. And Gus loved the place."

"It's weird and dirty. What will people think?"

Blame a week of shoveling through plastic aliens, or perhaps it was space rays from the cosmic transmitter, but his filter was slipping. "Ma, Gus is dead. Let him rest in peace where he wants to."

She sniffed, no doubt offended down to her toenails. "Funerals are for the living."

"Listen," he snapped, "Gus was a good man, and people here loved him. I'm going to respect his wishes because it's the right thing to do. I hope you'll come, but that's your choice."

Really, he almost wished the Anagnos clan would stay home and hold whatever traditional service made them feel better about neglecting a relative. He and Trappers Cove would give Gus the send-off he wanted. If not exactly dignified, it would at least be heartfelt. Zora, the old hippie gal who ran the crystal shop, had pretty much taken charge, freeing Xander to handle his clearance sale without simultaneously planning a funeral. He probably owed Hannah a debt of thanks for that too.

At Zora's insistence, the service would be held inside Souvenir Planet, the place Gus loved most, even if it was drafty, damp, and badly in need of repairs. And why not?

Yeah, Trappers Cove was definitely getting to him.

Wiping his hands on his baker's apron, Garrett strolled over and dropped a copy of the *Trappers Cove Beacon* on the table. "Great article on Gus's shop."

Xander's stomach tightened as he skimmed Hannah's full-page story on the history of Souvenir Planet, from its early days fifty years ago, when a very young Gus and his pretty bride sold seashells and beach toys, to its present decrepit incarnation—though Hannah made it sound much nicer.

Garrett read aloud over his shoulder. "A fun, fascinating emporium-slash-museum offering everything from saltwater taffy to a mummified alien mermaid. And for lovers of all things extra-terrestrial, Souvenir Planet stocks out-of-this-world souvenirs from bobbleheads to star maps, plus the chance to send your very own intergalactic message into the void."

A series of photos showed a progressively older Gus in all kinds of weird space-man get-ups. Xander sent up a silent prayer of thanks that his uncle had elected to be cremated. If he'd opted for an open casket, God only knows what space suit he'd want for his final earthly appearance.

"Lots of nice quotes about Gus." Garrett tapped the article.

Wow, he wasn't kidding. A full sidebar column brimmed with praise for Gus's kooky sense of fun, wacky optimism, zany decorations—in other words, his affable craziness.

Xander's own name jumped out from the page. Crap on toast, here was a verbatim quote from what he'd assumed was a private, casual conversation with Hannah. Just a sweet reminiscence of his childhood summers with Gus and Martha, but still—the disarming, dark-haired beauty was first and foremost a journalist. Better watch what he said around her.

Xander skipped to the article's final paragraph: *Was Gus Anagnos a true believer in alien visitations or just a smart businessman? That's a secret he took to the grave. Rest well, Gus. May stars light your way.*

He folded the paper and muttered, "Well, shit."

Back at the counter, Garrett called, "Nice article, right?"

It was, but that wouldn't stop the family from shitting multiple bricks when they read this. *If* they read this. Who read newspapers anymore? Okay, Baba did, over his morning coffee, but what were the chances news from this Podunk town would travel all the way to Seattle? By next week's memorial service, the *Beacon* would have moved on to a more interesting topic anyway.

Returning with a coffee refill, Garrett squeezed Xander's shoulder. "I'll set aside a few copies for your family."

"No, thanks. This article makes Uncle Gus look like a nut."

Garrett shrugged. "Well, he kind of was, but a loveable one."

Xander smacked the paper. "And Hannah never warned me our conversation was on the record." In fact, he'd had the foolish idea she might actually like him. But no, it seemed she was just mining him for news copy.

Garret chuckled. "That's what you get for dating a journalist."

"Dating? Hannah and me?" Not that he wouldn't jump at the chance if he weren't weighed down with getting the shop ready to re-open by Easter.

The baker huffed a chuckle. "My mistake. I've seen her going into your shop three or four times this week, so..."

"She's just being helpful." Or so he'd thought.

Behind them, the electronic doorway chime beep-booped.

"Speak of the devil," Garrett whispered. "Hey there, Hannah. Your usual?"

"Yeah, plus a hot chocolate for Mom. Her ulcer's acting up again." She handed Garrett a pile of neon-colored fliers and dropped into the chair opposite Xander. "For Saturday's sale."

"I'll put one in the window." Garrett tilted his head. "You okay, Hannah?"

Xander noted the tightness at the corners of her plush lips. Dark shadows under her eyes too. Guess he wasn't the only one dealing with work stress.

She flashed an unconvincing smile. "I'm just grand."

While Garrett prepared her drink order, she peeled the elastic from her ponytail, shook out her glossy dark hair, then gathered it back into a knot at her nape, her long fingers sliding through the silky strands.

He crossed his arms, tucking away hands that itched to touch her. "Liar. You're not feeling grand."

Her chuckle rang dry and brittle. "Just came from another argument with my mom. She's trying to convince me to shutter the *TC Beacon* and move."

Her words landed like a sharp poke between his ribs. He'd just met her, and now she was leaving?

"Move where?"

"She says a smart girl like me should have no trouble picking up a job in Seattle or Portland." She snorted. "Girl? I'm forty. And in this economy? Mom's overestimating my chances by miles." She gave Garrett a warm smile, then sipped the coffee he'd brought. "Thanks, Gar. Parents, right? They always think we can move mountains."

Garrett made a wry face and moved back to his duties.

Huh. Maybe he and Hannah weren't the only ones facing family troubles.

Xander sipped his own drink, stalling his return to work. "At least your mom believes in you. Count yourself lucky." He reached across the table and grazed her knuckles with his fingertip. "Really nice story on Gus. It was kind and fair."

Her expression flattened. "I'm always fair."

And touchy, it seemed. This next bit called for the utmost delicacy. "Hannah, could I ask one more favor?"

She cocked an eyebrow. "Shoot."

He laid his hand over hers—partly to soften the request, but also because sitting this close and not touching her was an impossibility.

"If you do any more articles on Gus, could you tone down the alien angle? Our family is kinda... Let's say they're not exactly open-minded."

She took another sip but didn't pull her hand away. "Everyone here knows he believed in aliens. So what? He was a good man. He wasn't hurting anyone."

"Yeah, Uncle Gus was a special guy. I'm glad he landed here, where people are allowed to be...eccentric." He gave her fingers a gentle squeeze. "But it's hard to imagine him resting in peace while his family tears his memory to shreds."

Her dark eyes brimmed with sympathy. "Xander, he's beyond needing our protection."

She was right, but he couldn't shake this need to protect his uncle's reputation—a gesture of love from second son to second son.

"If you won't do it for Gus, do it for me—a hard-working entrepreneur who's trying to make a fresh start in your town."

Her expression shifted to a sly smile, her thumb teasing his palm in slow arcs, back and forth. And damn if his long-neglected dick didn't perk right up.

"I won't make any promises. You're not the only one fighting for his business. But I am on your side. I want the shop to succeed. I want *you* to succeed. See you at the sale tomorrow." She released her hold on him, and immediately, he missed her warmth.

When she left, he draped his napkin across his lap and thought hard about baseball and bugs and ugly little aliens—but his body remained unconvinced.

He wanted Hannah all the way to the marrow of his bones. But he didn't dare trust her.

"Will you look at that crowd." Mom stood at the window, staring across the street at Souvenir Planet's overflowing parking lot. "Guess I should go over there and get some photos."

Hannah's head snapped up from the letters to the editor she was screening. "I'll do it. The last thing you need is to wade through that mob."

Besides, she wanted to make sure Xander had enough helpers—and perhaps indulge in a tiny inner gloat over the success her publicity push delivered.

Maybe public relations could be her next line of work?

With a grimace, she quashed that irksome thought. She didn't need alternative career plans because she was going to spend the next two decades, maybe three, right here running the *Beacon*.

She snatched up her best digital camera, a freshly charged voice recorder, and her lucky purple pen, then trotted across the street to photograph the crowd streaming in and out of Souvenir Planet, its entrance embellished with a huge '*Prices Slashed. Everything Must Go*' banner.

Before Xander asked her to tone down the alien angle, she'd already called in favors to get her story about the close-out sale in newspapers as far away as Seattle and Portland. How could he object now, with all these people showing up?

Inside the shop, she was swept up in happy chaos: shouts of delight, jostling bodies, laughter over the oddball merchandise. At ten past noon, the shelves were already half empty. Arms loaded with plush little green aliens, a woman in a "Keep Portland Weird" T-shirt nearly stomped on Hannah's toes. "Sorry, hon. My grandkids will love these."

Deploying her elbows, she made her way toward the counter, past the bench with the cloth alien, now wearing a *Not For Sale* sign around its neck. Grinning, she gave its head a pat and muttered, "What do you know? Our Xander has a soft spot for aliens, after all."

She spotted another *Not For Sale* sign on the Cosmic Transmitter, but almost everything else appeared up for grabs, from tacky taxidermy to dusty mermaid-shaped bath bombs.

At the register, a frazzled Xander rang up purchases, his long fingers flying, his dark curls mussed, his sleeves rolled up.

Thank you, Jesus.

Hannah slipped behind the counter and grabbed a paper bag. "You're doing great! Where's the wrapping paper?"

He pointed, and she got to work wrapping up a dozen alien-themed mugs.

Xander wiped his glistening forehead and flashed a tight-jawed smile. "Didn't realize you were setting me up for a mob. Sir. Sir! That's not for sale."

"Aw, come on, man." A fuzzy-bearded guy yanked the handle of a penny arcade moving picture viewer. "It doesn't even work. I'll give ya fifty."

"Not. For. Sale." He rang up a heap of rubber snakes and reptiles.

"Give ya a hundred."

Ignoring him, Xander turned to Hannah. "Some museum historian read about the sale in the Portland *Press Herald*. Is that your doing?"

She nodded, watching carefully for his reaction.

He nudged her gently with his elbow. "Thanks, Hannah. He's sending an expert up tomorrow to appraise all the penny arcade games. Turns out some collectors will pay a fortune, even for the broken ones."

"Glad to hear it. Isn't that the one with the belly dancer? Bet you'll get a pretty penny for her."

"From your lips to God's ear. Emma, we need more bags."

"On it, Captain." A teen wearing a Souvenir Planet hoodie saluted and trotted toward the back. Hannah laughed. "Captain?"

"She's been calling me Captain Kirk all day. It's getting old."

"Why not take it as a compliment? Kirk was a total hottie."

With a grunt, he handed over a UFO soap dish for wrapping. "Don't you have something more newsworthy to cover?"

"In Trappers Cove? This is about as newsworthy as it gets—unless we have a repeat of the storm of eighty-seven."

"Hush your mouth, girl." Cassie, owner of the breakfast café, set her selections on the counter. "Don't rile up the weather gods." She hooked a thumb over her shoulder. "If you're aiming to buy anything, better get to it. These tourists are cleaning the place out like piranhas on a cow."

"Go on." Xander lifted his whiskered chin toward the melee. "Get while the getting's good."

"Sounds like something Gus would say." Laughing, she scooted around the counter and joined the fray, stopping here and there to snap photos, interview shoppers, and fill her shopping basket with souvenirs: a fridge magnet with an alien kissing a mermaid, a sexy merman mug for mom, a bag of pecan fudge, and a "Greetings from Planet Xormak" T-shirt, size XXL, to sleep in.

Bittersweet emotions swirled in her chest as she drank in her last look at Souvenir Planet. Mom was right: change is inevitable, but whatever Xander did with the place, she hoped he'd keep its wacky, eclectic vibe.

After ringing up her purchases, she fought her way through the crowd, now tripled in size, for a breath of fresh air. Outside his bakery, Garrett had set up a table where he offered coffee, hot cocoa, and cupcakes topped with green alien faces. She ordered a coffee, then surveyed the stuffed parking lot, noting license plates from Oregon, British Columbia, and even California.

A moment later, Xander staggered up, adorably disheveled with wild curls and his shirt half untucked. He grasped the table like a drowning man clinging to a buoy. "Coffee, I'm begging you."

Chuckling, Garrett poured him an extra-tall cup and proffered a cupcake. "You need this, brother."

Xander pulled a sour face. "Got anything without aliens?"

"Oh, hush." Hannah bumped him with her hip. "Isn't this great?"

Xander blew on his cup. "Those people are crazed. I caught one guy trying to chisel graffiti off the bathroom wall."

"Okay, that's a little extreme. But remember, when you re-open, they'll be back to see what you've done with the place. Gus left you more than a building—he left you passionate customers. Look." She pointed to a minivan rolling into the lot. "They drove out from Idaho!"

A multi-generation family tumbled out of the van, each clad in Souvenir Planet T-shirts. The littlest one aimed a plastic ray gun as he passed. "Pew pew! I'm a alien."

Xander huffed. "I'm trying to turn this freak show into a respectable business. How am I gonna do that with customers like these?"

Was he really that dense and hard-headed? She planted her fists on her hips. "Xander Anagnos, if you can't see the potential here, you're as shallow as a puddle. Gus must be rolling in his grave."

He glared back, just as stubborn. She'd met her match in this handsome Greek. "Listen, I loved Gus, but it's my shop now. I steer this ship."

"You're gonna run aground if you ignore Souvenir Planet's place in the TC..." She flapped a hand overhead— "galaxy."

Xander's voice rose to an outraged squawk. "It's a freakin' souvenir shop selling plastic crap and hokey T-shirts and—"

One of the teen helpers jogged over. "Mr. A, there's a big-ass line of people waiting to send messages to outer space."

Hannah fought a smug grin. "I'm not gonna say I told you so, but..."

With a sexy snarl, he knocked back his coffee and stomped off to deal with his customers.

After finishing her drink, Hannah flipped through the photos she'd taken, then started back across the lot for more.

An officious-looking older guy with a pot belly and military-style hat collided with her as he barreled toward the building.

"Sorry, ma'am. Got caught in traffic on the I-5. Hope I'm not too late." He eyed the camera around her neck. "You press?"

She stifled the urge to salute. "Yes, sir. Hannah Leone from the *Trappers Cove Beacon*."

He puffed out his chest. "James Malinowski, president of NAS-DEV, The North American Society to Document Extra-terrestrial Visitations." He smacked a star-embossed business card into her palm.

She bit back a grin. *Thanks, Gus. I couldn't ask for better material.*

A memory pinged. NASDEV was the group who'd inherit Souvenir Planet if Xander didn't make a go of it. Did this guy know of his potential good fortune? Better tread carefully.

She pulled out her voice recorder. "So tell me, Mr. Malinowski, did you know Gus Anagnos?"

The man straightened his spine. "Colonel Malinowski. Air Force, retired. And yes, Gus was an asset to our community. Just last month, he sent me a very intriguing report." He resumed his march toward the building.

Hannah trailed after him. "Anything you're willing to share, Colonel?"

"We're still processing the photos and data, but I can tell you this—there's undeniable evidence this very spot is an active site for extra-terrestrial communications."

Hannah's conscience twinged hard. Xander had asked her to tone down the alien angle, but this opportunity was too juicy to pass up. Besides, this kind of attention would benefit both Xander's business and the *Beacon*.

"That's absolutely fascinating, Colonel. Tell me more," she urged as they stepped through the door.

Shouts rang out from across the room.

The colonel made a beeline toward the ugly, mummified "mermaid," where a stout older woman in a bomber jacket with military-style patches waved a wad of cash under Xander's nose.

"Lois, you old sneak thief," the colonel hollered, "Get your hands off that alien."

A loud argument ensued, ineffectually refereed by a befuddled Xander.

"Sorry, sir, ma'am." He raised his hands in a placating gesture. "This item has already been promised to the Trappers Cove Historical Society."

The two foes grumbled and glared.

With a backward glance at Hannah, the colonel asked, "For the record, what are your plans to keep the cosmic vortex accessible to researchers like ourselves?"

His rival pulled a small electronic device from her jacket and waved it over the metal structure.

Peering over her shoulder, the colonel grunted his approval.

Lois tapped her gizmo. "All signs point toward an impending visitation. We'll monitor the data."

Xander rumpled his brow. "Data?"

She fished a business card from her breast pocket. "Lois Alterman. Washington State Chair of GUFON: Global UFO Network."

Xander eyed the card as if she'd handed him a live lobster.

"I'll take that, Ms. Alterman," Hannah chirped.

The colonel elbowed the older woman. "This girl's with the local press."

"It's *Doctor* Alterman." Lois asserted with a sniff. "I hold a PhD in astrophysics."

Xander rolled his eyes, but the two UFO experts didn't seem to notice or care.

"Quit bragging, Lois." The colonel threw a beefy arm around Xander's shoulders. "Let's brief this young man on the transmitter. Or has your uncle already trained you in its operation?"

Xander flushed and spluttered, "Oh for cripes' sake, enough with the UFO BS! There's no such thing as ETs." He smacked the cosmic transmitter, which wobbled on its metal base. "This hunk of junk doesn't transmit anything but suckers wishful thinking. And there's nothing beneath this building but a cement pad." His voice rose to a ragged shout. "There is no freakin' cosmic vortex."

Darting forward, Hannah yanked him out of the colonel's grip. The two experts gawked, as did dozens of customers drawn by the ruckus.

"You'll have to forgive Xander," Hannah cooed. "He's not thinking clearly after such a terrible loss. He's the one who found his uncle's body. I'm sure you can understand how traumatizing that must've been." She squeezed his arm hard, hoping he'd catch on.

They exchanged a loaded glance. His nostrils flared in a deep inhalation.

The colonel clapped Xander's shoulder. "Of course. Terrible loss. It's a grave responsibility you've inherited, son. When you're ready, you know where to find us."

Lois gave Xander a bear hug, her voice husky with emotion. "Gus was a good man. You've got some big shoes to fill."

When the colonel and the professor moved away, muttering over her tricorder thingy, Hannah smacked Xander's arm. "Way to drive away your best customers. Whatever you believe about UFOs, you need to zip your lip in front of these people."

Xander scoffed. "My customers will be tourists who come to Trappers Cove for fun and relaxation. I'll offer what they want, not this UFO crap."

Hannah crossed her arms and cocked a hip. "What can you offer that isn't already for sale on Main Street?"

His harsh glare softened as he tapped his pursed lips. What would those lips feel like against hers? Heavenly, she bet. And those strong arms around her? Mmmm, delicious.

"Good question," he said at last with a wry smile. "Help me figure that out?"

"Huh?" She blinked hard, struggling to recall what they were talking about.

"Show me Trappers Cove. My only hope of keeping this shop alive is to find out what needs and wants aren't already being met. Teach me what makes this town tick."

His words were all business, but playful energy sparkled in his mahogany eyes.

Well, why not? This might be her best shot. Once he saw the competition, he'd recognize the importance of maintaining his niche market.

She lifted her chin. "Okay, you're on."

"Excellent."

His smoldering smile ignited giddy tummy flutters.

Xander rested his palm on the "mermaid's" glass case. "Who knew people could get so passionate about this ugly old fish monkey?"

She giggled. "Correction: this ugly *alien* fish monkey. Mind if I take a photo?"

"Don't you have one on file?"

"Not with the handsome new owner."

He rolled his eyes. So much for her flirtation skills.

"C'mon," she wheedled, "it'll attract new customers. A smart business owner knows how to maximize his advantages."

He scoffed but flashed a panty-melting smile for the camera.

"So." He rubbed his hands together. "When can we get started with my Trappers Cove lessons?"

Her stomach rumbled, a reminder that she'd had nothing but a cupcake since breakfast.

Well, a woman's gotta eat. And there's no harm in mixing business and pleasure.

"Tell you what, how about if we talk over beers and dinner at the Salty Dog?"

He glanced around at the thinning crowd. "We'll close at four. I can meet you there at six."

"Excellent. I'll get us seats by the fire."

On her way out, she snapped a few more photos, then wiped away a surprise wash of tears. This was truly the end of an era.

Mom's words echoed in her memory: "Change is inevitable, kiddo."

"Yeah," she muttered, "but I don't have to like it."

A loud crash sounded behind her. She spun and spotted a coffee mug shattered on the floor a few yards away. No one stood anywhere near the mess.

Xander tsked and reached for a broom behind the counter. "That's been happening all week. Wobbly shelves."

A break in the clouds outside sent a beam of golden twilight through the plate-glass window and illuminated the cosmic transmitter, giving it an ethereal glow.

A shiver danced down Hannah's spine. "Sure," she muttered, "just wobbly shelves."

In the shifting light, she could swear the life-size alien on the bench grinned.

Chapter Six

By the time the last customer finally left, Xander's back and feet ached, his head buzzed from multitasking, and his ears rang from nine hours of noisy ruckus. But eager shoppers had bought out nearly all of Gus's inventory, and his till brimmed with enough cash to begin necessary repairs.

"Hannah worked a miracle, eh?" he asked the bench-sitting alien, now a little squashed from hundreds of hugs and not a few lap sits. "Hope she can do it again when I reopen."

As he pulled on his jacket, he took a deep breath of musty air. Something was definitely growing in these walls. On Monday, the building inspector would deliver the bad news, or worse news, or potentially disastrous news.

On the far side of the shop floor, a metal shelf toppled over with a clatter.

Xander's heart leapt like a startled rabbit.

Just a rusted-out shelf. Don't get your boxers in a bunch.

Expelling a gust of nervous laughter, he addressed the largest of the water-spot aliens. "Gimme a break, Gus. I promised to take good care of your shop, and I will. But now, I've got a date with a pretty lady."

A nosy, pushy lady, but still, he owed her big time for deflecting those UFO nuts.

Hannah's warm smile was a balm on his soul. Even though this was the worst possible moment to fall for someone, his thoughts returned again and again to her dark-honey voice, her plush mouth, her arms around him, her chestnut hair tickling his cheek. Not to mention her sharp mind. She was the perfect person to help him puzzle out Souvenir Planet's new direction.

Would he prefer to decide that all on his own? Absolutely. But Hannah knew this town inside-out, and if accepting her help came with a side of one-on-one time, so much the better.

The thought of diving into this project without a plan made him nauseated. Then again, he'd had a detailed plan for the failed wine bar, and the gourmet shop before that. Both times, developments he couldn't have foreseen punched holes in his immaculately researched plans.

Maybe it was time to try winging it.

After locking up, he scanned the shop's overcrowded façade. All this goofy shit would have to be cleared away—the plywood aliens, the fiberglass UFOs, the cement dinosaur, and the rusty antique farm equipment. What kind of aesthetic was Gus going for? Farming on the moon?

He switched off the exterior lights and headed toward the Salty Dog on foot. Hopefully, the brisk evening air would clear his muddled mind.

The sky had reached the indigo hour between twilight and total darkness. Halfway up Main Street, Xander slowed his steps to admire the inky heavens. Compared to the nighttime view through Seattle's city lights, out here the night sky glittered with millions of stars.

"Dazzling," he muttered, hands stuffed deep in his pockets. "No wonder you dreamed of going up there."

Should he be alarmed by his new habit of talking to his dead uncle? Well, they say everyone grieves in their own way.

So, this was home—for the next few months, anyway. His apartment in Seattle was another puzzle piece. Should he sublease? Though it was just a shabby little one-bedroom, he missed his familiar space, his neighborhood, his routine.

After a ten-minute amble, he reached Salty Dog Saloon and Brewery. The bar's front deck glowed with strings of Edison lights, propane heaters, and dancing flames from the big firepit table. At the hostess stand—a plank atop a wooden sea captain in a yellow slicker—a young woman in a fisherman's sweater greeted him with a broad smile. "Hi, Xander. Great job on the sale today."

He blinked in surprise. "Sorry, have we met?"

"I'm Kaitlyn. I snagged the last of your Christmas ornaments. My kids are gonna love those sparkly little green men." She lifted a pair of menus. "Can't wait to see what you do with the shop. Right this way."

She led him to the fire table, where Hannah sat chatting with two younger guys. One of them placed his hand on Hannah's knee. Xander's jaw twitched.

Look at me, going all caveman over a woman I've just met.

"Xander!" She stood and pulled him into a too-brief hug. Even through their winter jackets, the soft press of her body drew a potentially embarrassing reaction. She seemed oblivious, thank God.

"Guys, this is the man of the hour. Xander, meet Gary and Sean Rodriguez. They drove down from Bellingham for the sale."

"Really?" He shot her a quizzical glance. "That's a long way to buy cheap cra—I mean, souvenirs."

The handsy guy grinned. "We're making a weekend of it. I grew up down here. Graduated in Hannah's class." He squeezed her arm. "Go, Sharks!"

His partner piped up. "We cleaned out your sand candles and seashell soaps."

"And that driftwood thing." Handsy wrinkled his nose. "What's that supposed to be?"

"It's art, darling, and it's perfect for the Whidby Island cottage."

Hannah explained, "The guys have several rentals throughout the north Sound.""No aliens for you, huh?" Xander asked, shooting her a pointed look.

"Of course." Handsy showed him an enamel pin on his lapel: a grinning alien waving a rainbow flag. He drained his beer glass. "Come on, love. Don't want to be late for our twilight massage. Great to see you, Hannah. You take good care of our new alien herder, you hear?" He smooched her temple, then threw Xander a wink.

Hannah spared him an "I told you so," but she giggled as she examined her menu.

When their server came over, Xander ordered a red ale and smoked salmon chowder in a sourdough bread bowl. She ordered a clam strip po'boy, then unwound her woolly scarf. Reflected firelight gilded her skin and shimmered in her hair and eyes.

"What a triumph, eh?" She squeezed his hand. "You must feel great."

"I feel..." Searching for the right words, he watched the flames' hypnotic dance. "To be perfectly honest, I'm not sure." He tapped his chest. "It's kind of a stew, you know?"

She pressed her palm there, and—though it made no sense, considering all the layers of cloth between her skin and his—heat radiated from that point of contact, filling his body with tickly lightness.

"I understand. Your loss is still fresh. You must miss Gus terribly."
And now his eyes were growing misty. Swell.

He gave his head a shake. "This isn't like me. I'm usually more grounded. But something about Gus's shop makes me feel…off center, I guess."

"It's that cosmic vortex. It warps the energy field."

"Gah. Please tell me you don't believe in that bullsh—that nonsense."

Her laughter tinkled like bells. "You can swear in front of me, Xander. I'm not some delicate flower. As for the aliens, I keep an open mind." She tilted her head back to gaze up at the sky, baring her pale throat. "I mean, how arrogant to look at all those stars and think, 'Nope. We're the only intelligent beings.'"

He joined her in stargazing. "Honestly, I never really thought about it."

Just at that moment, a meteor streaked across the night sky. A good omen?

She nudged him with her shoulder. "You don't have a choice now, do you? Aliens are your bread and butter."

"Hmmph. We'll see." This was obviously going to be a sticking point between them.

She speared him with a stern glare. "You've got to keep the aliens, Xander. It's what Gus would want."

"I keep my promises." And technically, he'd never promised anything more than keeping the transmitter thingy in place. He could work around the ugly structure, maybe turn it into a planter.

"Uh huh." She arched an eyebrow, unconvinced. "Care to share your plans?"

"When I make a firm decision, I'll let you know." He nudged her back. "Considering how our conversations end up in your newspaper, you'll have to forgive me for playing close to the vest."

Rather than bristling, she regarded him like some intriguing puzzle she was determined to solve. "What are you afraid of, Xander?"

"Failure." The word slipped out before he had the chance to rope it back.

"Me too." Her eyes were so damn bright, reflected firelight dancing in her dark irises. "Want to hear a secret?" She beckoned him closer.

He complied—because how could he not?

"The newspaper's in trouble. We lost our sponsor. I have until April to pull the *Beacon* into the black. Otherwise..." She drew a finger across her throat.

"Sorry to hear that." His gaze drifted back to the fire. "There's something about a deadline, though. It's a powerful motivation, you know?"

Her hand settled over his, soft and gentle. "What motivates you, Xander Anagnos?"

He chuckled. "Are you interviewing me, Hannah Leone?"

"Nah. This is strictly off the record."

Just then, the server arrived with their dinner. Xander spooned up the velvety, rich chowder. "Wow. Better than I remembered."

"Don't change the subject." A dozen battered clam strips tumbled onto her plate when she lifted her po'boy. "You were going to tell me what makes you tick." She chomped into the sandwich and closed her eyes on a moan.

"I was?" A warning tickled down his spine. She was doing it again—teasing out details he didn't intend to share.

Then again, why not get an unbiased opinion?

He clasped her hand. "Promise me I'll never see these words in your newspaper?"

She crossed her heart, her expression solemn and attentive.

"I've never talked about this with anyone outside my family."

The corners of her mouth ticked up. "In that case, I'm honored."

Just do it, coward.

He sucked in a breath. "There's this family thing that goes way back to the old country. The curse of the second son."

"You're a second son, I take it?"

"Yeah. So was Gus."

"And what does this curse entail?"

He twirled his spoon in his soup. "Supposedly, second sons are doomed to failure. Business, divorce, you name it. Whatever we try, we fail."

She made a delicate snort. "Well, that's clearly not true. I mean, look at Gus. He was married to Martha for how many years?"

"But she died."

She shrugged. "Everyone dies."

"And they never had kids."

"Maybe they didn't want kids. I think the shop was his baby." She sipped her beer and wiped foam from her cheek. "He put a lot of love into that place. I felt it every time I walked through his doors. Souvenir Planet buzzed with upbeat energy. Every shelf, every wall, every corner was stuffed with something to make you smile."

He stifled a snarky laugh. "Spiderwebs make you smile?"

She grasped his forearm as if yanking him back to the topic at hand. "The point is, Gus was far from a failure. Everyone loved him." Her hand slid down to cover his, her touch satin-soft. "And you're not a failure either."

It would take a lot more than a pretty woman's kind words to make him believe that. "My last few business ventures tanked. But Gus's place is my chance to break the curse, to prove them wrong."

"Who, your family?"

"Yeah." Chuckling, he rubbed the bridge of his nose. "You'd think by my age I'd be over it, but their pity really gets under my skin. It's a shitty feeling, knowing they'll always see me through that lens."

She scooted closer on their shared bench and—God help him—squeezed his knee, her eyes brimming with sympathy. "I'm sorry you're going through that, Xander. You're a good man. You deserve better."

Face aflame, he ripped off a hunk of his bread bowl and dipped it into the soup. "How do you know?"

"I've got a sense for these things." Grinning, she tapped her nose. "A nose for news, my grandpa called it. And my intuition tells me you're going to make it this time. Trappers Cove is the right place for you. Now, tell me about your plans for Souvenir Planet."

"Nice try, newsie." He lifted his spoon. "Like I said, when I'm sure about my plans, I'll let you know."

"Can't blame a girl for trying." She took another giant bite of her sandwich. "A little advice. Take it or leave it."

"Shoot."

"Don't spoil a good thing just for the sake of change. Trappers Cove is a quirky town. We're..." she twirled a lock of hair around her finger. "Authentic. Not like more upscale beach towns where the whole main drag looks the same. Tourists love our funky vibe. That's why they come back year after year."

Upscale beach towns? He filed that thought away for further research. "Sounds like I need a better understanding of what makes

Trappers Cove tick." He bumped her knee with his. "Teach me quirky ways?"

One corner of her mouth ticked upward, then the other. Damn, what a gorgeous smile.

"Okay, when you can carve out a couple hours, I'll introduce you to the other Main Street business owners."

"I'd like that very much." Visions of strolling along Main Street hand in hand with Hannah warmed him down to his icy toes.

"After the celebration of life, of course."

That grim reminder popped his rosy bubble. He had one week to prepare for a horde of Anagnoses. And if Hannah wasn't overstating Gus's popularity, he'd better expect most of Trappers Cove as well.

"Don't worry, the Saint Sebastian's ladies' guild will handle the flowers. The Sons of Italy will bring tables and folding chairs, and everyone will bring food. We take good care of our own here. All you have to do is open your doors, say a few words, then sit back and listen to the speeches."

A smile stretched his lips. "You're kind of my guardian angel, aren't you, Hannah?"

"Oh, I'll get something out of it." A flicker of emotion passed across her face and was gone before he could get a read on it. Playful smile back in place, she held up the unbitten end of her sandwich. "Now, shut up and try these clams before they get soggy."

Interesting. He'd do well to remember that Hannah was in the news business and always angling for a story.

But right now, the sparkle of challenge in her eyes was irresistible, and so was that sandwich. He bit into fluffy brioche bun, tangy tartar sauce, and crunchy breading around tender clams so heavenly he let out a noisy groan.

The couple across the firepit table poked each other and giggled.

"Right?" Hannah took another big bite. "Are you starting to understand the TC vibe? Simple, but good."

Already, he was pretty sure that, whatever form the new and improved Souvenir Planet took, Hannah would not approve. But for now, why not avail himself of her institutional knowledge?

And her mischievous smile. And sparkling eyes. And soft touch, and...

He sucked in a deep breath. *Eyes on the prize, Anagnos.*

Chapter Seven

The following Saturday, dressed in a simple black shift dress and blazer, Hannah once again made her way through the packed parking lot and entered Souvenir Planet, transformed for the day into a makeshift chapel and reception hall. With the help of the handyman she'd recommended, Xander had removed the cute plywood aliens and fiberglass UFOs from the façade, but the cement T-Rex still stood vigil out front, and some smart-ass had attached a bunch of '*Rest in Peace*' balloons to its tiny forelegs.

Inside, the display shelves had been cleared away for rows of folding chairs. Hannah placed her peace lily among the jungle of floral tributes on the white-draped check-out counter, then scanned the crowd for her mother.

She found her chatting with her poker buddies. Seeing her in good spirits and walking without her cane lifted a load off Hannah's mind.

Really impressive, how the church ladies and the Sons of Italy Lodge had transformed the space into a dignified memorial chapel, even covering up the painted-on aliens with swaths of white bunting. A cloth-draped table next to the cosmic transmitter held Gus's star-spangled urn. The old guy certainly picked out the perfect vessel.

"Rest in peace, Gus," she murmured.

She followed the piano music to where her best friend Daphne tickled the electronic ivories beside a podium draped in purple satin painted with stars and a Latin inscription.

"Ad Astra per Aspera," Hannah read aloud.

"Through hardship to the stars." Daphne looked up from her electronic keyboard. "Perfect, right?"

"Your work?"

"Mostly Noah's. You know how he loves an art project." She flipped a page and played on, her long, slender fingers dancing over the keys. "I'm glad we could contribute something to a man who gave so much to Trappers Cove."

That was Daphne through and through, sentimental to the core. Noah too—like mother, like son.

"Quite the crowd. Even more than I expected." Hannah scanned the gathering. "Really makes you think, doesn't it?"

Daphne nodded in her wise, quiet way. "Testament to a life well-lived. I hope my funeral draws this many." She ended the hymn with a flourish. "On that heavy note..." Tapping a button on her keyboard, she switched to an eerie, spacy tone. "Talk to you after?"

"Absolutely. Is Noah here?" She scanned the gathering for a mop of sandy hair.

"Over with Ben's family. Poor kiddo. He loved Gus."

Hannah gave her friend's shoulder a squeeze, then found an aisle seat near the cosmic transmitter, decked out for the occasion with white ribbons and twining greenery. Most of the guests were still milling around, so she set down her purse to reserve her spot, then sidled toward a large cluster of immaculately dressed people with dark, curly hair like Xander's. One of them, a slouching teen, tapped his phone screen. The woman beside him snatched it away. "Show some respect, Niko."

"I hardly knew Uncle Gus," the kid grumbled. When Hannah gave him a sympathetic smile, he rolled deep-brown eyes that were the spitting image of his...uncle's, she guessed. Where was Xander, anyway?

She spied him in a corner conferring with Zora, their local psychic and crystal vendor, dressed for the occasion in a purple clerical robe and silver shawl. Poor Xander's shoulders slumped as if weighted. When Zora gave his arm a comforting pat, he glanced at the transmitter and wiped his eyes.

Hannah's heart squeezed hard, and it took every bit of decorum she had not to rush over and hug him tight.

Gaze downcast, Xander shuffled toward his family. A dark-haired, Chanel-suited matron intercepted him.

"It's a scandal!" she hissed loud enough for Hannah to hear clearly and speared him with a pointy gaze that raised the hairs on the back of Hannah's neck.

Xander's shoulders inched toward his ears.

Yikes on bikes. Was this his mother? She eased closer to catch the thread of their argument. Not that she needed much evidence to figure that out. From the perfectly coiffed grandmother to the school-age kids, the Anagnos clan gleamed with affluence and social polish. A family like that and an eccentric funeral like this? Oil and water.

Under the pretext of checking the AV system, Hannah moved as close to the kerfuffle as she dared.

A stocky, seventy-ish man with thick black eyebrows hooked his arm through the angry woman's. "Don't stress yourself, Lydia. Agustus was always an oddball. It's too late to change him now."

"But what will people think?"

Another older woman patted her glossy salt-and-pepper bouffant hair. "What do you expect from a second son?"

Xander flinched. His mouth opened, then snapped shut.

She couldn't stand it one more minute. Her new friend needed back-up, STAT.

"There you are, Xander," she cooed, lacing her tone with a thick layer of honey. She flashed her schmooziest smile and hooked her arm through his. "Sorry to interrupt, folks. I just need to borrow this handsome guy for a quick sec."

The mother raked Hannah with an appraising gaze.

Ignoring her and the rest of her hiss-whispering, judgy kin, Hannah towed him to the cosmic transmitter and turned their backs to his clan.

"You okay, Xander?"

Stupid question. Face pale, lips clamped tight, forehead dotted with sweat, he was clearly as far from okay as Trappers Cove was from Australia.

His nostrils flared in a deep inhalation. Who knew nostrils could be so sexy?

She rubbed his arm from elbow to shoulder and found his muscles so tense she might as well be stroking marble. "I thought you were exaggerating about that second son business, but it looks like you understated the problem."

He closed his eyes and shook his head. "I can't stand to listen to them shredding Gus. My uncle was a good man. An oddball, yes, but so what? He was generous and kind and funny and—"

"Hey." She grasped both his shoulders and turned him to face her. "You're doing the right thing. You are a loving, loyal nephew. And in a couple hours, all your bitchy relatives will leave, so you can get back to remodeling Souvenir Planet. I have faith in you, Xander. You're going to make this place shine brighter than ever."

His eyes widened. Okay, maybe she'd gone too far, but the only way through this debacle was forward.

"You've got this, my friend." She rose on her toes and pecked his cheek. At least, that was her intention, but a loud bang from across the room jerked his head around, and her chaste kiss landed on his lips. His soft, plush, slightly parted lips.

Xander gasped and blinked hard and fast, as if she'd blown dust into his eyes. "What the hell was that?"

A flush roasted her cheeks. "Sorry, I slipped." She took a step back—well, she tried to, but he gripped her elbows, holding her in place.

"That was totally inappropriate," she spluttered. "I apologize, Xander."

A flicker danced in his dark irises—amusement or something more interesting? A corner of his mouth ticked upward. "I meant the noise, not the kiss."

They both scanned the room. On the far side, near the door to Gus's office, a set of metal shelves had crashed to the floor.

Hannah tugged her neckline in a vain effort to diffuse the heat of her embarrassment. "I think Gus is telling us to get the show on the road."

Xander groaned and dropped his chin to his chest. His shoulders quaked.

Oh no! Desperate to undo the damage, she clutched his arms. "I'm so sorry. Me and my lame jokes."

Still quaking, he gripped her elbows and pulled her against his chest, burying his face in her hair. She wrapped her arms around him and rubbed soothing circles on his back—his broad, warm, muscular back...

What a perfectly awful moment for her libido to kick in. Tingles zapped up and down her spine as Xander's arms banded around her, snugging her tighter to his solid warmth. What a monster she was, getting all hot and bothered while he wept in her arms and...

Hold the phone.

She planted her palm on his chest and shoved. "Are you laughing?"

Grinning like a loon, he dragged a sleeve across his streaming eyes. "Thanks, I needed that."

"The kiss or the laugh?"

"Both." His gaze dropped to her mouth. "Especially the kiss. Can I have one more?"

Breathless, she bobbed her head.

He slid his broad, warm hand beneath her hair and cupped the back of her neck. Her body thrummed in anticipation as, with mesmerizing slowness, he moved closer until only a sliver of electrified air separated them. A quick brush of his soft lips over hers, a gust of breath, then he released her, leaving her with legs so wobbly she had to clutch the transmitter's metal frame to keep from falling.

"Okay." He grinned. "As you so eloquently put it, let's get this show on the road."

Moving with relaxed grace, he strode through the throng of Trappers Cove locals and dozens of strangers, many wearing T-shirts and hoodies with the Souvenir Planet logo, a caricature of a grinning Gus waving from an open-top flying saucer.

Rooted where she stood, Hannah stroked trembling fingertips over her tingling lips.

Holy shitakes, I just kissed him in front of the whole damn town—and his family!

To be precise, she'd kissed him, and then he'd kissed her, and then the whole room sort of wobbled, and...

Shaking off her horny buzz, she watched Xander advance on the Anagnos clan, his brisk stride radiating confidence. Judging by their open-mouthed stares and the teens' giggles, their kiss hadn't gone unnoticed.

Hannah trotted after him. Whatever smack-down he was about to lay on his family, she didn't want to miss a word.

"...and listen good." Arms crossed, stance wide, he glared at his red-faced parents. "Gus laid out his burial wishes, and we're going to honor them. He deserves that." He planted a stiff finger in his gawking father's chest. "All his life you put him down. But look at all these people who've come to celebrate his life. They knew Gus better than you ever did, and they loved him. If you can't respect that, if you can't appreciate what a wonderful soul he was, then it's better if you leave right now."

Xander's mother made choking sounds. His father's face darkened to an alarming shade of maroon. But a forty-something man stepped between the furious couple and Xander, his palms raised. "No one's gonna make a fuss today." He flicked a warning glance over his shoulder. "Right, Mama? Baba?"

Moving as stiffly as wooden soldiers, the older couple linked arms and stalked to their seats, trailed by the rest of their crew. As they departed, Hannah overheard one of the younger women mutter, "Check out Xander's shiny new spine."

The interceder flashed a smug grin and slugged Xander's shoulder hard enough to make him wince. "Introduce me to your lady, bro."

Xander stepped out of range and rubbed the sore spot. "Hannah Leone, meet my brother Dimitrios."

"Charmed." She pasted on a bland smile and extended her hand, which Dimitrios grasped in his clammy paw and lifted to his lips for a loud, smacking kiss.

"Cut the crap, Dimitri," Xander growled and draped his arm over her shoulders, deliciously heavy and warm. "My friend didn't come here to be pawed by you."

Dimitrios winked. "Just yanking your chain, bro." He hooked a thumb over his shoulder. "You know they'll make me pay for standing up for you."

Xander narrowed his eyes. "There's a first time for everything, I guess."

After a brief stare-down, Dimitrios cracked a wide smile and pulled Xander into a back-slapping hug. When they separated, both swiped at damp eyes. "Uncle Gus, huh?"

"Uncle Gus," Xander agreed.

Hannah's eyes prickled as she wrapped her hand around Xander's biceps and tugged him gently toward the front row of chairs. "Looks like Zora's ready to start."

As they took their seats, Hannah whispered in Xander's ear, "You were magnificent."

A blush painted his stubbled cheek. He gathered her hand into his and interlaced their fingers. "Thank you for shocking some sense into me." Leaning in close, he whispered, "Any time you want to lay another motivational kiss on me, be my guest."

There they went again, those damn butterflies dancing the Macarena in her belly.

Zora began the ceremony, her voice ringing out warm and rich over the borrowed PA system's static. "Friends, family, welcome visitors, thank you for coming. Today we gather to honor a truly unique soul."

Murmurs of assent swept through the room. Across the aisle, Xander's family sat stiff and silent.

"Death is not an end, my dear ones, it's a passage. Our stay on this beautiful earth may be long or short, comfortable or difficult, but when our time comes, we all must pass through that cosmic portal into the realms beyond." She patted the metal contraption beside her.

An Anagnos squeaked, then covered it with a phony cough.

Folding her hands over her broad bosom, Zora gazed heavenward. "Augustus Xylon Anagnos lived here among us, but he kept his eyes on the stars."

"Amen," rang out in a deep baritone.

Peering over her shoulder, Hannah recognized Colonel Malinowski, one of the UFO investigators from last week's sale. Arrayed beside him sat at least a dozen people in identical military-style jackets.

Zora continued her sermon, reminding the mourners to follow Gus's example and never lose sight of the great beyond...or something like that. Hannah lost the thread, too focused on Xander's hand wrapped around hers, his soft sighs and sniffles.

"And now, let's hear a few words from Xander Anagnos, Gus's nephew and the new proprietor of Souvenir Planet."

Xander squeezed Hannah's hand. "I could use another kiss," he whispered out of the side of his mouth.

Stifling an inappropriate giggle, she smooched his cheek.

He rose and strode to the cosmic transmitter, taking the microphone Zora pressed into his hand. Tears gleamed in his eyes as he scanned the faces before him. "Uncle Gus was, uh..." He cleared his throat. "He was a wonderful man. Warm. Accepting. No preconceived notions—" His sharp glance raked over his family, and Mrs. Anagnos developed a sudden fascination with the purse in her lap.

"Gus challenged me to think big, to stretch my mind and reach for the stars." Xander chuckled. "I didn't realize how literally he meant that."

Laughter echoed in the cavernous room.

He squared his shoulders and continued, his voice ringing out clear and strong now. "After all, who really knows what lies beyond this earthly plane? I sure don't. But I believe in Gus's vision—a connection between the known and the possible. Between people like us and beings that might be very different. Gus's life was about connection, and I hope to carry that lesson forward." His voice roughened. "I hope you'll join me."

Her eyes blurred by tears, Hannah dug in her pocket for a fresh tissue. As a journalist, she'd sat through too many funerals, wakes, and memorials to count, but never had a eulogy touched her like this one. Gus would be so proud.

"Thank you, Xander." Zora wrapped him in a motherly hug, the top of her head tucked beneath his chin.

When he made his way back to his seat, Hannah squeezed his hand tightly. "Beautiful eulogy. Absolutely perfect."

"I'm glad you think so. My dad looks like he swallowed a cactus."

Zora spoke into the mic. "Would anyone else like to offer a few words of farewell to our dear friend?"

Several chairs scraped back. Hannah craned her neck and spotted the stuffy UFO Colonel and his crew, along with Dr. Alterman, his alien-hunting rival and her own oddly uniformed followers, all marching military-style toward the podium. After some jostling and glaring, they arrayed themselves in two neat ranks, Malinowski's troops to the right of the transmitter, and Alterman's to the left. The leaders conferred. The colonel heaved an aggrieved sigh and stepped aside, yielding the microphone to Dr. Alterman, who pulled a velvet box from her satin bomber jacket and extracted a gleaming medal. "On behalf of the Global UFO Network, we honor our esteemed member Augustus Xylon Anagnos with the Asteroid of Honor."

She hung the medal's star-embossed ribbon on the transmitter, then snapped a salute. Her compadres did the same.

In a choked voice, Lois said, "Gus is returning to his home planet. Safe journey, old friend."

With a crisp nod, she handed the microphone to the teary-eyed colonel, who added own words of praise before attaching his organization's honors—a midnight blue flag embroidered with *NASDEV*, stars, and a silver spaceship—to the transmitter's framework.

Xander gave a little snort.

Hannah elbowed him. "Future customers."

With great solemnity, the colonel stepped to where Xander sat and snapped a salute.

"Um, okay." Xander stood and returned the gesture.

The colonel grasped his shoulder. "We're ready, son."

Xander's brow furrowed. "For the...?"

"Internment."

"Ah. Well, Gus wished to be—er—interred in the, uh—" He gestured toward the metal structure.

"And so he shall be." The colonel clicked his heels together, executed an about-face, and called his troops to attention. Marching in perfect synchronization, they closed ranks around the urn. Dr. Alterman's group joined them, and forty-something hands raised Gus's earthly remains high overhead like a sports team hoisting their trophy.

Xander squeezed Hannah's knee and made a squeaking noise.

"Quit giggling, you. Be respectful." She bit her lip hard to suppress a goofy grin.

Shuffling sideways, the UFO enthusiasts—as Hannah decided to call them in her feature on Gus's send-off—gently placed the urn inside a metal box at the transmitter's base.

"Kind of looks like it fits there, doesn't it?" Xander whispered.

"Yeah." She laid her hand over his. "In its own weird way, it's very beautiful."

The honor guard thumped their fists over their hearts like a bunch of movie space troopers.

"Oh, for God's sake," Xander squeaked.

The liquid notes of Daphne's keyboard filled the room. Hannah nearly lost it when she recognized the tune: Elton John's "Rocket Man." Voices blending, the mourners belted out the chorus.

Xander barked out a laugh. "Perfect. Gus would've loved this."

"That's Trappers Cove for ya. We honor our weirdness."

He swiveled in his seat and took her hands, his eyes large and luminous. "Hannah, I don't know how to thank you. There's no way I could've pulled this together."

"Zora deserves the credit. I just made a few phone calls to get the ball rolling."

"I'll be sure to thank her." He stood and extended his hand. "My family's going to ask about the woman they saw me making out with."

She giggled as he helped her to her feet. "If that's what you call making out, your love life needs resuscitation."

"Are you volunteering?" His mischievous smile twinkled.

What the hell is wrong with me? Flirting at a funeral?

Reluctantly, she stepped back. "Let's keep this professional for now. As soon as we're done here, I'm writing a story on Gus's send-off."

Still grinning, Xander nodded. "Right. For now." He inclined his head toward the Anagnos clan. "Since you'll be splashing my family's weirdness all over your newspaper, will you be my moral support for a few more minutes?"

Hannah returned his playful smile. "Sounds like a fair trade."

He took her hand, a gesture she enjoyed way too much, and led her through the milling crowd to his family, who held themselves aloof from the others—except for the slouchy teen boy from earlier, who hunched with Daphne's son over a portable gaming device.

Score one more for Team Trappers Cove.

Mama Anagnos puffed up at their approach. "Alexandros Ioannis Anagnos, that was—"

Her husband grabs her elbow. "Lydia, dearest, not now."

The older woman's nostrils flared, just like her son's, but she held her tongue.

The family resemblance was remarkable. The whole crew shared Xander's dark, curly hair, elegantly curved nose, strong jaw, and sturdy build. The men were broad-shouldered, the women buxom. From eight to eighty, they were strikingly good-looking people, and dressed to impress in expensive, tailored suits and sheath dresses.

Hannah tugged at her black blazer, a classic but well-worn find from Annie's vintage shop. She needn't have worried, though. Mama Anagnos's eyes were laser-focused on her face, not her outfit.

"Introduce us to your girlfriend, Xander."

"Just a friend," she blurted. Freeing herself from Xander's grasp, she proffered her hand. "Hannah Leone. Welcome to Trappers Cove, Mrs. Anagnos. I'm very sorry for your loss."

"Just a friend, eh?" The older woman smirked. "You always kiss your friends like that?"

"When they're hurting, sure. Why not?"

"So." Arms folded over his barrel chest, Xander's father executed a slow pivot. "This is my brother's legacy." His meaning was clear enough, judging from his pursed lips and wrinkled nose. And okay, there *was* a slight musty whiff beneath the cloying scent of funeral flowers, but Hannah associated that smell with good memories. Clearly, Papa Anagnos did not.

"Yes, Baba," Xander countered. "The shop is mine now. I'm looking forward to re-opening soon."

"Is that so?" The old guy's forehead pleated.

A loud whistle ended the father-son staring contest. As if by magic, the tables set up along the far wall had filled with food—Garrett's cookies and cupcakes, dozens of homemade pies and cakes, platters of finger sandwiches, fruit and veggie trays from Trappers Market, and enough paper plates and cups to serve the whole town.

Salvatore Verducci, head of the Sons of Italy Lodge, clapped his hands and shouted, "Food's on. Mangiamo!" He pointed a stubby finger at Xander. "Come on, son. You've got a big job ahead of you. Time to fuel up." Though the mustachioed old gent's words were bossy, his tone was kind.

"Coming, sir." Xander crooked his elbow. "Mama, let me introduce you to my new neighbors."

Hannah hid her grin beneath a tissue as she watched them go, trailed by the rest of the family. Only Xander's father stayed behind, glaring from beneath thick black eyebrows as he surveyed the remains of Gus's shop.

Finally, he turned to Hannah. "He's making a mistake, you know."

"Oh?" She forced a neutral expression. *More flies with honey...*

"Xander's wasting his time here. He oughta come back to Seattle and join the family business instead of draining his bank account to prop up this wreck."

Heat licked up her spine and tightened her jaw. "Let me tell you something, Mr. Anagnos. I've only known your son for a short time, but already I can tell he's got a sharp mind, a kind heart, and his uncle's determination. Xander is right where he's supposed to be."

The older man studied her for a moment, then cracked a faint smile. "Well, well, looks like Xander's got the family way with ladies. But you're wasting your time on this one. Second sons never amount to anything."

She crossed her arms and returned glare for glare. "We'll see, won't we?"

Chapter Eight

"Uh-oh."

Damn it, that was the third "Uh-oh" in ten minutes. Gripping the building inspector's ladder, Xander peered up at the grizzled harbinger of doom.

"What now?"

The inspector pointed. "See this here spaceman?"

"Yeah, I already found the soft spots. What's the verdict—water damage or dry rot?"

"The first one. Looks like Gus painted these little green men over water stains for years. I'm surprised chunks of ceiling haven't fallen on you."

Xander tensed, imagining his family's reaction if that had happened during the funeral service.

"I'm almost afraid to ask: are we talking leaky pipes or leaky roof?"

"I'll know more when I climb up there. Let's take a look at your electrical panel box first."

"Electrical panel. Right." Where in the hell was that? He scanned the vast, empty building.

"Probably in back, near the restrooms."

"Of course." Embarrassed, he swiped a hand across his sweaty brow. He'd been working on this wreck for over two weeks and still had no idea where the breaker box was. Or the electric meter or the water shut-off valve. Caught up in Gus's chaotic bookkeeping, not to mention moving his own belongings into his rented apartment, he'd barely paid attention to the building itself. He knew it had been some kind of auto-related business before Gus bought it—a showroom? A garage?

"What kind of mess have you saddled me with, Gus?" he grumbled, watching the inspector flip open the electrical panel and scribble notes on his clipboard.

The pipes running up the rear wall rumbled ominously.

The inspector rubbed his chin. "Does it rattle like that often?"

Xander gave a sheepish shrug. "Whenever someone flushes. The old building makes lots of noise. Gus would say it has personality."

"Cute," the older man deadpanned and jotted another note. "Don't suppose you've got some coffee around here?"

Xander's only attempt at making coffee with water from the bathroom sink resulted in a rusty, muddy brew. Never again. "I'll get you some from the bakery next door."

"Thanks, man. Cream and two sugars, please."

"You bet."

A cloud of sugar- and coffee-scented warmth greeted him as he entered Sweet Dreams Bakery. He'd come to think of this cheerful space as his second office. With white-painted brick walls, antique brass light fixtures, and old black and white photos of Trappers Cove's early days, he felt at ease here. Plus, the coffee was excellent, ditto the pastries, and getting through this renovation was going to take lots of caffeine and carbs.

On duty at the register, Garrett greeted him with a look of sympathy and two maple bars on the house. "Who's your inspector?"

"Frank something. Italian name."

"Giordano?" He wrapped the pastries in tissue paper and tucked them into a paper bag along with a handful of napkins. "He's good. Found termites in my front porch posts. I'd never even noticed the damage."

"Termites? Out on the coast?"

"It happens." He popped two large coffees into a cardboard carrier. "Don't worry. Gus never mentioned termites in his place."

"Bet he never mentioned soggy ceiling aliens either."

Garrett's eyebrows shot up. "Pardon?"

"I'll fill you in later. Thanks, neighbor."

He returned to find Hannah at the base of a tall ladder leaning against the roof, shielding her eyes as she peered up at Frank G... Damn, forgot his name again. Not since school had he had to learn so many names at once. Seemed like everyone knew everyone in this town.

The sight of Hannah lifted his spirits—and other parts inappropriate to the public setting. He hadn't seen her since the memorial service, but he'd damn well thought about her. That sweet, surprise kiss haunted his dreams. Was it really an accident, or a deliberate gesture to snap him out of his emotional overwhelm? Either way, he was grateful and eager for an encore.

"How's it looking up there?" she hollered, not yet noticing his arrival.

Frank peered over the roof's edge. "Hey there, Miss Hannah. I've seen worse." He chuckled. "Seen better too. She'll need a lotta work."

"Sea air is hard on buildings, right?" she called.

Warmth bloomed in Xander's chest as he drank in the sight of her, all sexy-businesslike in her fitted tweed blazer and dark jeans that cupped her shapely ass. The wind whipped her chestnut ponytail. Giving into a temptation, he gave it a soft tug.

She spun around, eyes fiery, then relaxed into a warm smile. "Hey, Xander. Saw Frank's truck, so I thought I'd drop by."

"Scoping out more details for your exposé? Let me guess—the Pulitzer Prize committee requested another story on my sad, crumbly building."

She socked his arm playfully. "It's a cool, funky building. And I'm about as likely to win a Pulitzer as aliens are to land on your roof."

Thank goodness Hannah didn't believe in that ET nonsense.

"I'd say your chances are better." He reached for her ponytail, fingers itching to feel those silky strands again, but she flipped it over her shoulder and out of reach.

Disappointed, he clasped his hands behind his back. The urge to touch her was damn hard to resist. "Your piece on Gus's memorial was—"

She raised her eyebrows and waited, lips twitching in a barely suppressed smile.

"Okay, I wish you'd left out the bit about Colonel Buzz, Professor Astro, and their space cadets, but it was mostly very nice. Your love for Gus shined through."

The prettiest pink washed her cheeks as she lowered her gaze. "I feel like a shitty friend for not realizing he was so ill."

"Hey, don't blame yourself. The pathologist's report says it was a brain aneurysm. No one could have helped him." That news had lightened his own guilt load a little.

A loud clatter from the roof yanked their attention upward.

"Well, shit," Frank grumbled.

Xander winced.

"Sounds like you could use some distraction," Hannah suggested.

As if her presence wasn't distracting enough already. "What did you have in mind?"

"It's a slow news day. Ready to start your tour of Trappers Cove?"

Oh, right. He'd asked her to show him what made this town tick—or some such flirtatious nonsense.

"How about if I text you as soon as we're done here?"

"Sounds perfect." She grinned and caught her lower lip between her teeth. Heat shimmied down his spine. How long since his body vibed like this with a beautiful woman? Too damn long, that's for sure.

The ladder clattered as Frank clambered down.

Xander tensed. "Well, what's the verdict?"

The old guy doffed his ball cap, raked grubby fingers through his gray hair, and shook his head. "I'll put it all in my write-up, but between you and me and this sweet gal, if it were my place, I'd tear it down and start fresh."

Hannah blanched and clutched Xander's forearm, her fingernails digging into his flesh. "You can't do that! Souvenir Planet is an icon. It's a cornerstone of our town's heritage. It's—"

"Don't worry," Xander assured her before asking Frank, "Can you give me a prioritized list? You know, what I absolutely must do before re-opening, things I need to do eventually, like that?"

Frank shook his head. "Whatever you say, son. But fair warning—the first part of that list will be mighty long." He retracted his ladder. "And you better call the exterminator right away. You got termites."

Thanks a million, Gus.

As the inspector loaded his gear into his truck, Hannah planted herself in front of Xander and leveled him with a piercing gaze. "Xander Anagnos, I want your solemn promise."

His stomach twisted. Under normal circumstances, he'd promise this beauty almost anything to win another of her sunshine smiles. But there was no talking sense to someone in love with a decrepit old building.

Upping the ante, she grasped his hand in both of hers—soft, warm, and surprisingly strong. "Promise me you won't tear down Souvenir Planet."

"Hannah, I can't afford to demolish the building and build a new one. I'll have to work with what I've got." And he wasn't just shining her on. After the failed wine bar and the ill-fated gourmet shop, he had no option but to make a go of Gus's business—somehow or other.

"And the aliens stay," she insisted with a stamp of her boot.

He gulped, his collar suddenly too tight. He hated misleading Hannah, but to turn Souvenir Planet into a business he could be proud of, he'd have to ditch the hokey green ETs.

"You heard the terms of Gus's will. I'm stuck with the—" he hooked his fingers into snarky air quotes— "'cosmic transmitter.' Though you and I both know that UFO business is utter bullshit."

She gave him a crooked grin. "For a guy with zero training in astrophysics, you seem awfully sure of yourself."

He inched closer. "I'm a practical man, Hannah." *One who'd like to pull you into the nearest dark corner and kiss you until you see stars and forget all about those stupid UFOs.* "Now, about that tour…?"

Her smile bloomed wide and dazzling. "Give me an hour."

She pivoted and strode toward the *Beacon*'s building down the street, her curvy hips swaying. Before disappearing from sight, she threw him a flirtatious glance over her shoulder and waggled her fingers.

"Hoo boy." Grinning like a fool, he sat on a weed-filled cement UFO planter. "That woman is dangerous."

A seagull swooped overhead, its mocking laughter cutting through the misty air.

"Enough of your commentary, Gus."

Chapter Nine

A little after four o'clock, Hannah's phone pinged.

Ready when you are, pretty newsie.

Embarrassing how her pulse revved like a Formula One car at the starting line.

"It's not a date," she muttered, checking her appearance in the restroom mirror. After all, she'd fix her lipstick before leaving for any errand. And she'd offer the same help to any new business owner in Trappers Cove. A rising tide lifts all ships.

For a moment, common sense wrestled with vanity, and then she removed the elastic band and fluffed her mane, now tightened into curls by the lowering rain clouds that threatened to cut their not-date short. She undid another button on her blouse, spritzed cologne in her cleavage, and checked her teeth for lipstick. "Ready as I'll ever be."

Back in the newsroom, Mom whistled. "Look at you, pretty girl. Has my nose-to-the grindstone daughter finally found a fella worthy of her interest?"

Irritation tightened her gut. Even at forty, she still bristled at her mother's playful button-pushing.

"I'm just helping Gus's nephew gather ideas for the new and improved Souvenir Planet."

"And using your charms to influence his choices?" Mom tapped her chin. "Let me guess—you want him to keep everything as it is, cobwebs and all."

Hannah indulged in an adolescent eye roll. "I just want him to respect Gus's legacy. What's Souvenir Planet without aliens?"

"Oh, my darling." Mom pulled her in for a comforting, squishy hug. "If you had your way, you'd dip this town in Lucite, so nothing ever changed. But change is life. It only stops when you're dead."

Hannah inhaled her mother's familiar floral perfume. "Not true. I get it. Change is inevitable." *I can understand that and still hate it.* "But Souvenir Planet occupies the biggest property on Main Street. If he gives it up, God knows what havoc a new developer would wreak." Her voice wobbled at the memory of bulldozers and destruction. "After what happened to us, I just can't..." She sniffed hard and dabbed her tear-blurred eyes with her fingertips. "I won't let it happen again."

Mom cupped Hannah's cheeks, her brow creased with concern. "Oh, honey, it breaks my heart how much you still miss that old house. I wish I could've saved it for you. But we're doing okay now, aren't we?"

Hannah gripped her mother's shoulders. "It wasn't your fault. It was Dad's. And that so-called developer. And the lust for profit at the expense of authenticity. And..."

"Simmer down, love." Though her eyes glistened, Mom managed a wry smile. "What's done is done. A wise man once said..." She scrunched her lips to the side. "Something about living in the present, which really is our only option." She patted Hannah's cheek. "And if anyone can turn that young man's head, it's you."

"Oh for—" Hannah threw up her hands. "I'm not going to seduce the guy just to get my way. That's manipulative. It's...it's...unethical. Besides, he's my most important source for this story. Romancing him would be a conflict of interest."

"Pfft." Mom waved away Hannah's scruples with a flick of her wrist.

"I'm serious. The regional editor of the *Olympian* asked for an in-depth follow-up piece. They love stories about UFOs." She knotted a sunset-hued silk scarf around her neck. "Our readership's growing steadily since that first story on Gus's shop. I can't endanger that."

"So we've got a few more subscribers. To pull the *Beacon* out of the red, you'll need thousands more."

"And I'll get them." *If* her deal with *PacNorthwest Magazine* went through: a full-color spread in with her byline, including a digital subscription discount code for the *Beacon* so readers could follow the developing story. And *if* her upcoming interview with that pompous Colonel Malinowski yielded juicy fruit. And *if* Professor Alterman delivered the documentation she promised on the cosmic vortex beneath Gus's building. And *if* her social media teasers were intriguing enough to sell subscriptions.

A lot of ifs.

Mom slurped her tea. "Aren't you a little old to be living on the plane of idealism? We're an itty-bitty regional paper, not the *New York Times*. And you've got your old sparkle back. I haven't seen that in a while, and I'm chalking that up to Gus's handsome nephew. So enjoy his company while you convince him to preserve Souvenir Planet. Two birds with one stone, eh?" She sank into her swivel chair, kicked off her worn loafers, and wiggled her toes. "Now, go have fun. It's good to see you excited about a new friend."

Her worldly wise mother would blush like a virgin if she knew exactly what Hannah yearned to do to that new friend.

She pulled her waterproof jacket over her blazer, zipped up against the chilly wind, and stepped out onto Main Street. A fat seagull fluttered down at her feet and stared up at her with greedy, beady eyes.

"You got any brilliant ideas for me, bird?"

The gull squawked and winged across the street, landing on Souvenir Planet's veranda to poke through the makeshift shrine, which had grown since the last time she saw it. Hannah trotted after the bird.

Surely, all Gus's Trappers Cove friends and relatives must've deposited their tributes by now. So who was leaving all these flowers, balloons, and alien knickknacks?

The seagull prodded the pile, then soared away with a tiny silver-suited spaceman dangling from its beak.

"That's gotta be symbolic," she muttered.

Right on cue, Xander emerged through the front door, wrapped in a weatherproof jacket. Fists on hips, he scowled at the heap of trinkets and poked a moldy-looking cloth alien with his toe. He gave her a weary smile. "Sure you're up for this? Looks like we're gonna get wet."

That's what she said.

She stifled a giggle. Damn it, this mission called for finesse, tact, professionalism. But every time he aimed those intense, mahogany eyes her way, her thoughts stalled out.

She gestured toward the pile. "Wow, this shrine keeps growing. Gus was well-loved."

"On my last coffee break, I spotted a car with California plates. They dropped off flowers, stood here a moment, then left."

"Like I told you, those aliens draw a lot of customers."

A smirk twisted his lips. "Lucky me. I get to fulfill my childhood dream of being a laughingstock."

"Why is such a smart, capable guy so hung up on what other people think?" A month or two in Trappers Cove would cure him of that affliction. *If* he didn't give up and flee back to Seattle, which would be tragic.

Fascinating, the way his jaw ticked as he digested her comment. He tilted his chin toward the mountain of love tokens. "Tomorrow, I'll clear this away."

"That's your decision, of course, but I'd keep it. Let people show their respects. Who knows? Maybe Gus's spirit is hanging around, enjoying the honors."

Could a man look any snarkier? "Right," he drawled. "It's Gus's ghost knocking over the shelves. The sagging foundation has nothing to do with it. And he's the one to blame for the flickering lights." He pinched the bridge of his nose. "Redoing the faulty wiring is going to cost me a fortune."

In an effort to tease him out of his dour mood, Hannah nudged him with her elbow. "You should call in one of those ghost-hunting crews. That'd bring publicity to your business." When he gawked, she added, "You know what they say—all publicity is good publicity."

"My family would absolutely flip out. Thanks to your story, all their friends know Gus was a UFO nut. Bring ghosts into the mix? I'd never hear the end of it." He stooped and picked up a bobblehead alien with huge, glittering eyes. "Poor Gus deserves to rest in peace. The family text chain has been buzzing ever since the memorial. Seems your profile on Gus got picked up by the *Seattle Times*."

She tamped down the urge to squee and pump a fist. "Yeah, I heard."

"Congratulations. I'm guessing that's helpful for your newspaper."

"It's a step in the right direction." She sidled closer and gave him her winningest smile. "Sure I can't talk you into an in-depth interview? You could drum up interest for your grand reopening."

Xander harrumphed. "Nice try. Like I said the other day, when I have firm plans, I'll let you know."

Crossing her arms, she glared in mock sternness. "You holding out on me, Anagnos?"

"On you? Never." He pulled his hood over his shiny curls. "I've been waiting for inspiration to strike, but my muse isn't speaking to me."

"Well, I've never been called a muse, but I've been told I'm amusing." She linked her arm through his and couldn't resist squeezing his biceps. "Come on, grumpy pants. Let's go before the rain starts."

And how did you get so muscly? Lifting boxes of junk must be a powerful workout.

"Should we drive?" He squinted up at the slate gray clouds scudding past.

She clucked her tongue. "The touristy part of town is all of five blocks. Afraid you'll melt before we reach the end?"

"Pshaw. I'm as Northwestern as you Trappers Covians. Lead on, pretty tour guide."

She guided him toward the shops lining Main Street, their springtime window displays glowing in the dim light of an overcast afternoon. "So, our goal is to soak in the town's vibe."

"And get to know the competition. Once I see what's selling well, I'll find holes in the market waiting to be filled."

She bit her lip hard. Was that a deliberate tease, or was he that oblivious to his effect on her?

"Mercenary, aren't you? How many of the Main Street shops have you visited?"

He flashed a sheepish grin. "Does Rossi Rentals count?"

"I suppose, but you're hardly competing with them. Did Cheryl find you a somewhere to live?"

He tilted his head toward the shore. "Yeah. Not exactly a palace, but it'll do for now. At least I can walk to work. Wouldn't want to brave this traffic every day."

A lone pickup rattled past, jostling over a pothole. The driver waved.

"Okay, Snarkmeister. Would you prefer Seattle traffic?"

He had the grace to laugh at her dig. "I'll take seagulls over traffic snarls any day." He hooked a thumb over his shoulder. "You know that guy?"

"That's Jesse del Toro. He has an organic herb farm east of town. Nice guy. Sells to local restaurants and at the farmers market."

"Does a good business?"

She laughed. "Are you seriously thinking of starting a farm?"

"No, no, I just—" He untangled his arm from hers and stuffed his hands into his pockets— "I like gourmet shops. Tried running one in Seattle."

"Tried?"

He shrugged, but his nonchalant expression didn't fool her one bit. "It did okay for a while. And then it didn't."

"Ah. Sorry. But don't most entrepreneurs try a bunch of ideas before finding the one that sticks?"

"I suppose." He raised an eyebrow. "How about journalists?"

"What about us?"

"Did you try lots of jobs before finding the right one?"

Turning away, she pretended to examine the window display at Sea Visions Art Gallery. "There are only so many news outlets: print, digital, TV, radio, podcasts. My whole career has been in print since I come from a long line of newspaper reporters." She stuffed her hands into her pockets. "I'd rather stay in print news, but if I can't resuscitate the *Beacon* by April, I'll have to go freelance."

As a deeply rooted homebody, she hated that idea right down to her marrow—traveling all over the Pacific Northwest, chasing down stories that someone, anyone, might actually pay for.

He stepped so close beside her, she felt his warmth through her thick jacket. "You're easy on the eyes, and you've got a great voice. You could go into TV news."

"At my age?" She snorted. "Stand aside, flawless twenty-something broadcast grads. Make way for grandma."

"Hey." Gripping her arm, he spun her to face him and held a warning finger an inch from her nose. "I won't tolerate anyone talking smack about my new friend."

His mock-stern expression was too cute not to play along. "Get that finger out of my face, or I'll bite it."

"That's the spirit." He patted her cheek, his touch light and warm and way too thrilling. "Now, shall we look at some art?"

And so, teasing and joshing, they made their way from shop to shop. Hannah introduced him to art gallerist Janice, who praised Gus's creativity; to antiques dealer Annie Scott, who gave Xander a vintage Souvenir Planet ball cap; and to Daphne Lee, her far-too-curious bookselling bestie who gifted him a slim volume of local history and asked pointed questions about his relationship status, all the while shooting Hannah knowing grins.

"Single as a Pringle at the moment." Xander waggled his eyebrows. "Why, are you looking?"

Daph fluttered a hand to her chest. "Not for myself. Just, you know, curious. In this tiny town, we single gals are fishing in a shallow pond." She shot Hannah a meaningful look.

Hannah bugged her eyes out at her interfering friend. "Xander's going to be busy rehabbing Gus's shop."

"Ah yes, too busy." Daphne fiddled with a rotating stand of romance paperbacks. "There's a lot of that going around."

Xander's rumbling laugh was much too sexy for Hannah's precarious composure, and so was the way he threw his head back, exposing his strong, oh so kissable throat. Not to mention the way his eyes crinkled with mirth, and that one dark curl that flopped over his forehead, only to be raked back into place again and again. Man, would she love to sink her fingers into his hair, and...

Her eyes widened when he pressed his palm to the small of her back. "It was delightful to meet you, Daphne, but Hannah and I have a lot of ground to cover before those rain clouds let loose. Thanks for the book." He wheeled toward the door, propelling her ahead of him.

She shouldn't like that lower-back touch as much as she did.

"Well, well." Once outside, Xander leaned against the brick wall. "Does your friend always bust your chops like that?"

"Nope. Seems you've inspired her." Flustered and a little ticked off, she smoothed sweaty palms down her thighs. "Ready for our next stop?"

"Could we grab a bite to eat?" He patted his flat belly. "I got caught up in Gus's cryptic bookkeeping and skipped lunch."

"Sure. Let's see—" She glanced up and down the street. "Cassie's café is only open for breakfast and lunch. This time of year, that leaves Chinese, pizza, or kebabs, unless you want to go back to Salty Dog."

"A kebab sounds perfect."

They crossed the street to Ali Baba Kebabs, where Mo and Nabila Abadi greeted them with huge smiles, open arms, and a brimming plate of garlic-feta fries on the house.

While Mo prepared their pita wraps, Hannah and Xander inhaled their fries.

She brushed feta crumbs from her chin. "So, seen anything inspiring yet?"

One corner of his wide mouth lifted as he held her gaze, eyes twinkling with flirtatious mischief. "You could say that."

Feigning obliviousness, she clasped her hands on the table. "Tell me."

"Well, Daphne's got the book market cornered, so no books."

"Good call. Though you might add a rack of books on UFOs."

His grin flattened. "No thank you."

Clearly, this was going to require more finesse. How to convince him the shop's reputation with UFO believers was an asset, not a liability?

Nabila bustled over with two foil-wrapped pitas stuffed with crispy meat, shredded cabbage, pickled onions, and oozing with garlicky yogurt sauce. She wiped her hands on her apron, then seized Xander in a tight hug. Hannah wasn't sure whether his goggle-eyed expression came from surprise or the strength of Nabila's squeeze.

"Oh, hon. Mo and I are so sorry about your uncle. Aren't we, Mo?" she bellowed over her shoulder.

Mo nodded solemnly from behind the counter. "Gus was a good man. A little touched in the head, but still—" He thumped his chest. "Heart of gold, that guy."

Nabila released Xander and scowled at her husband. "You hush. So what if he believed in little green visitors from outer space? We don't know what's out there. Or are you an expert in astronomy now?"

Mo shrugged and commenced wiping down the counter.

"Heck," Nabila confided, her eyes twinkling, "half the time, he doesn't even know where his keys are." She squeezed Hannah in a side hug. "You kids enjoy. Hope you got somewhere warm to snuggle tonight. It's gonna blow but good." She winked, flipped her dish towel over her shoulder, and sashayed back behind the counter.

Xander chuckled, a deep, enticing sound she yearned to feel rumbling against her cheek. Which was not a helpful thought at this moment.

He brought another fry to his lips. "Does she think we're spending the night together?"

She felt her cheeks heat. "Side effect of small-town living. The older generation are die-hard matchmakers. If you're not paired up by thirty, look out."

"Older generation?" He arched an eyebrow. "You and I aren't exactly spring chickens."

"You're younger than me, so bawk bawk." She lifted her napkin. "Here, you've got a smudge." He really did. It wasn't just an excuse to stroke the dark scruff on his dimpled chin.

He seized her hand. "You're forty, right?"

"Yeah. So?"

"I'll turn forty April fourth, so bawk bawk right back atcha."

"Interesting." She pulled out her phone and typed a quick note. "That makes you a..." She did a quick calculation. "An Aries, right?"

His brow furrowed. "Don't tell me you believe in that stuff too. Do you write the paper's astrology column?"

"No, that would be Zora's job." She lifted her shoulder. "But I'm not so arrogant as to think I know all about how the universe works."

Up flew both his glossy eyebrows. "Arrogant, am I?"

"Well, you're mighty quick to label UFOs as bullshit, even if selling alien toys and mugs and T-shirts kept your uncle afloat all these years and made his customers happy. Even if UFO believers are willing to travel into *our* little town to visit the shop. And you know damn well they always leave with *your* merchandise. But nooo." She dragged a fry through the garlic sauce on her plate. "Can't hang onto something that's working incredibly well. It's too embarrassing. What will the family think?"

Xander went stone quiet, his gaze focused on the napkin dispenser between them.

I've gone too far. Way to kick a man when he's down, smart-ass.

Regret flooded her, souring her stomach. She reached for his tightly clasped hands. "Xander."

He jerked them away.

She gentled her voice. "I'm sorry. I was completely out of line, especially when you're grieving. Please know that I loved Gus too. We all did. He was—"

"A legend, it seems. A dead broke, mentally ill legend."

"Mentally ill?" she squeaked, drawing stares from the other customers. Damn it, she had to get through to him, whether he liked it or not.

She seized his wrist. "Believing in something that hasn't been proved yet means you're crazy? How about people who believe in God? Are they certifiable too?"

Under the circumstances, she should not find Xander's frustrated growl so sexy.

He raked fingers into his dark hair, leaving a trail of crumbs. Without thinking, she reached out to brush them away. "Here, you've got cr—"

"Will you quit touching me!" he hissed, eyes blazing.

She jolted backward, mortified to her very bones.

"Sorry." He raised both hands and blew out a breath through flared nostrils. "It's hard to think when you touch me. Especially when you have a point, as much as I hate admitting it."

"Oh?"

"Listen, I..." Glaring at the table, he strangled his paper napkin. "Okay, it's true. I hate the alien crap. I hate the idea of people thinking I'm one of those tinfoil hat-wearing, conspiracy theory-believing nut jobs. But they do spend money."

At last, the man was seeing reason. "So you'll do the smart thing and stay the course?"

His brows snapped together. "You make it sound so black and white, Hannah. Why should I expect you to get it? You've got nothing to prove, no family curse weighing you down."

I am an insensitive asshole.

Appetite gone, she crumpled her napkin and tossed it onto her plate. "You told me about that. And I'm supposed to be good at remembering key details. It's kind of a job requirement, in fact. Guess I got distracted by—" Her shoulders slumped. "Never mind."

His brow smoothed, and he reached for her hand. "No, tell me." His broad, warm palm settled over her icy knuckles, massaging, soothing.

Ugh, this is so embarrassing.

She flapped her free hand. "You're a good-looking man, Xander, and I'm not immune to that. You're funny and smart, and I enjoy spending time with you. Plus, you're in a tough place. Anyone with a heart would want to help you." She sucked in a deep breath. "But it's not my job to tell you how to run your business. It *is*, however, my job to protect Trappers Cove from developers who'd gladly rip the heart out of our community."

"I see." His thumb traced hypnotic circles on her palm. Slow and sweet as honey, a seductive smile spread over his face. "For the record, you're a good-looking woman, Hannah. Stunning, in fact. You're sharp and insightful, and you know this town. I'd be a fool to ignore your advice. But,"—he squeezed her hand, then released it— "I've got to find a way to build Souvenir Planet into a business I can be proud of. And yeah, that damn curse is a factor. I've got something to prove, and not just to my family." He tapped his sternum.

"So, you could..." she twirled her wrist, waiting for inspiration to strike.

He beat her to it. "Keep the aliens, but add something new. Maybe divide the shop somehow. God knows the building is big enough—if it doesn't fall down around my ears."

"Like one of those antiques malls where different vendors have stalls?"

His grin widened. "Yeah, maybe." He scraped his stool back and stood. "But first, I've got a lot to learn about my temporary hometown. Shall we?"

Relieved to be back on track and, apparently, forgiven for her thoughtless accusation, she rose to her feet. "Yes, let's do it."

He arched an eyebrow, but thankfully let that unintentional double entendre lie. Lay. Whatever.

There was no denying it—Xander scrambled her brain and heated her blood. Keeping this relationship professional would take every shred of self-control she had.

Chapter Ten

An hour later, they'd scratched the west side of Main Street off their list and were crossing to the east side when the first drops hit—fat, icy plops that slid down Xander's collar. He pulled his hood up and glanced at his watch—a vintage Bulova Uncle Gus gave him for his college graduation.

"Wow, I didn't mean to take up so much of your day, Hannah."

Her smile shone so bright and inviting he'd willingly stand in the rain just to bask in its glow. But that wasn't fair to her, especially after she'd been so incredibly generous with her time and resources.

He crooked his elbow. "Shall I walk you back to your place?"

She chewed her bottom lip for a moment—slightly uneven white teeth digging into plump, pink flesh—and man, did he crave a taste.

"There's no need. I'm just up the street, above the *Beacon* offices."

"Huh. I guess Uncle Gus wasn't the only one living at the shop."

"We've got two apartments upstairs—one for Mom and one for me." She cocked her head and regarded him with those hawk-sharp chestnut eyes. "Did Cheryl find you somewhere nice to stay?"

He waggled his hand. "Meh. It's pretty dumpy, but it's got a view of the ocean." A tiny sliver of view, but still. "Want to see?"

She flashed a sheepish smile. "I didn't mean to intrude. I'm kind of hard-wired to be nosy."

"Comes in handy for a reporter." *Nothing ventured, nothing gained.* "You're cold and wet, thanks to me. Come up for a hot drink and satisfy your curiosity—though I've gotta warn you, my temporary digs don't reflect my usual style."

More lip nibbling.

"Just a coffee. Or tea, if you like. I picked up an herbal blend at Trappers Market—orange and spice." When she still hesitated, he bobbed a little bow. "My intentions are honorable."

For now.

She lifted a shoulder and let it drop. "Okay, a tea would be great."

The rain was gaining speed and strength, so they pulled their hoods low and jogged toward Narwhal Lane.

"Yikes, I'm getting soaked!" Her merry laugh rang out as they rounded the corner and nearly collided with a fire hydrant.

"It's just up ahead." He trotted to a stop in front of the ugly cement shoebox he now called home. Hopefully, she wouldn't be too put off by the peeling paint and utter lack of architectural charm.

She planted her heels and gawked at the building, her face a portrait of horror and disgust. "No," she choked out and stumbled backward, hands up as if expecting an attack.

He rushed to steady her before she toppled over the curb. "Hannah, what's wrong? Are you..."

Dazed and bone-white, she swayed on her feet as her eyes filled with tears.

He gripped her elbows. "Are you ill? Can I call someone?"

She yanked herself free and pierced him with an accusing glare. "In a town full of charming beach cottages, you picked this monstrosity?"

"Um...it was the cheapest choice."

"For good reason. It's an abomination." She whirled and stalked back the way they'd come.

"Hannah, wait." He caught up to her at the corner and pulled her beneath the awning of Gelateria Paradiso. "Okay, the building is ugly as sin, but is that a crime?"

She folded her arms tight across her chest, hunched under the weight of her emotions. For a long time, she stared at the sidewalk, her breath sawing in and out. Finally, she raised her watery gaze to his. "That was my childhood home."

"You grew up in one of those apartments?" Poor Hannah. No wonder she cared so much about preserving Trappers Cove's bohemian vibe.

"No." A tear rolled down her cheek. "I grew up in a cute little house that stood on the lot until my dad left us, and the judge split everything right down the middle." She stabbed a finger in the direction they'd come. "Absolutely everything. Mom couldn't afford to buy out Dad's share, so she had to sell the only home I'd ever known. I loved that place."

"And the buyer tore it down?"

"With bulldozers and jackhammers and..." Her voice cracked, and she swiped her streaming eyes with her sleeve. "I still have nightmares. Twenty-five years later, I can't walk past the site without wanting to puke."

"Oh, Hannah, that's terrible. I'm so sorry that happened to you." He gathered her into his arms, and she let him, thank God. What an utter oaf he was, spoiling their fun evening by stumbling into her childhood trauma.

"It's not your fault. People have to live somewhere."

He nuzzled his cheek against her damp hair. "You're absolutely right—the building is hideous and doesn't match anything on that street. Why was that even allowed?"

"Crooked politicians on the city council. As soon as we moved into the apartments above the *Beacon*, Mom wrote a feature exposing their back-alley dealings with a sleazy developer. It was too late to save our home, but she saved lots of others and got those scumbags voted out of office." She pierced him with a steely look. "And that's why a local newspaper is so important. If people don't know what's going on behind closed doors, they lose their power to shape their community."

Guilt weighted his chest. "I'll call Cheryl Rossi tomorrow and find another rental."

"No, you don't have to—"

He cupped her cheek. "Yeah, I do. I can't in good conscience stay in a place that causes you pain. And I may not be wild about aliens, but I like this town." *Because it's important to you. And to Gus.* "So if you need to do more stories on Souvenir Planet to help your newspaper, I'm in."

She gaped for a moment, then clutched his jacket and kissed him breathless.

She'd almost forgotten how soft Xander's lips were.

No, that was a lie. She'd thought about his mouth every frickin' day since that first barely there kiss at Gus's memorial service. No matter how hard she tried to ignore that persistent tickle of desire, Xander was always on her mind—and now he was in her arms, warm and solid. His lips parted on a gasp, and whatever was left of her good sense went AWOL because how could she possibly resist deepening this delicious kiss?

His tongue teased her lips apart and stroked into her as if savoring her taste. The tight, warm circle of his arms sealed out the wind and rain and horrible memories—

A seagull's scream overhead snapped her back to reality. And reality sucked to the utmost degree of suckage. Because no matter how much she ached for Xander, she needed to pump the brakes right now.

Gently, she planted her palms on his chest and pushed him away.

He searched her face, his rich brown eyes espresso-dark with desire. "Hannah, what is happening here? Do you want me, or am I just fooling myself?"

Despite the ache of disappointment, a giggle escaped her lips. "You are direct, aren't you?"

"Answer the question, please."

"Okay." She blew out a breath and prayed for clarity. "Here's what I know. That back there—" She pointed toward the fugly apartment block. "That knocked me off balance, and I don't make the best decisions in that state."

His nostrils flared. "I see." He released her, hands spread wide, as if demonstrating he was unarmed.

She grabbed his sleeve and towed him back in. "No, you don't." Giving into temptation, she ran her fingertips over the silky-rough stubble covering his jaw. "I'm very attracted to you, Xander. Distractingly so, but our timing is awful. I mean, you're probably not staying in Trappers Cove, and I'm trying hard not to leave, and we're both dealing with work crises, and—"

He halted her rambling with another kiss, gentler this time, less hurried, cradling her head and humming his pleasure into her open mouth. When he finally pulled back, his dark eyes glittered.

"You don't need to explain, Hannah." He chuckled and hugged her against his broad chest. His breath fanned her temple, soft against her leaping pulse. "I'm not usually a woo-woo kind of guy, but maybe this was supposed to happen. Holding you feels right." He pressed a kiss to her forehead, then feathered kisses down her cheek, over her jaw, behind her ear.

Her knees turned to water.

His voice rumbled, deep and velvety. "You said I should open my mind about aliens and such. Well, why not open our minds to what this could be? Because I've been so work-obsessed for so long, I can't remember ever wanting a woman as much as I want you right now."

She let her head loll back, inviting more hypnotic kisses. With each brush of his lips, her core throbbed.

"Xander." She gripped his arms—partially to enjoy his firm biceps, but also to halt this before she spontaneously combusted on Main Street.

"Yes, beauty?" His fingers teased open her scarf, and he trailed kisses along her collarbone.

"Hold on."

His laughter vibrated her bones. "I am."

"I mean stop." She gave him a gentle shove, and he immediately backed away, but his hungry gaze pinned her where she stood.

"Look." She dabbed her glowing face. "This is moving very fast."

His gaze drifted to her lips. "You want slow? I can do slow."

I'll bet you can. She imagined languid kisses trailing over her bare skin, between her breasts, down her trembling belly until he reached—

"Shit." She slapped a hand to her forehead and spun away, pacing beneath the leaky awning. There had to be a way around this obstacle, but right now, she just couldn't see it.

How could fate be so cruel?

He fell into step beside her, his feet splashing in puddles on the sidewalk. Why did he have to be so damn adorable?

She pivoted to face him. "Xander, I can't date you. It's unethical."

His eyebrows shot up. "I beg your pardon?"

"A romantic relationship with a source creates a conflict of interest, or at least the appearance of conflict." Her Ethics of Journalism professor had hammered that point home with cautionary tales of careers ruined and valuable reporting wasted. And Hannah was in no position to take risks, not with the *Beacon*'s fate hanging by a thread. Like it or not—and she damn sure did not like it—if she had the tiniest hope of using this story to rescue the *Beacon*, she had to maintain her journalistic impartiality.

He tilted his head and gave her a quizzical stare. "What's the big deal? You're not the Washington Post, and I'm not a politician. We're a small-town newspaper and a souvenir shop."

He just didn't get it. The men in her life never got it. Indignation simmered in her gut as she straightened to full height.

"I beg your pardon. The *Beacon* has been a respected news source since 1897. It's a big deal to this community, and my journalistic integrity is a big deal to me. Especially because I might be job hunting soon." She resumed pacing, because looking at his handsome, bemused face was too painful.

His footsteps dogged hers. "Okay, okay. Let's look at this logically."

She shot him a glare over her shoulder. "That's what I'm doing."

"Right. You're a paragon of logic and integrity. But what if—maybe we could—" he snapped his fingers. "What if we disclose our dating status? Like, on the record."

"We have a dating status now?"

He stepped into her path, halting her anxious steps. "I'd like to."

His hopeful expression was so cute, she couldn't quite restrain the upward twitch of her lips.

Encouraged by that tiny slip-up, he grinned and tapped his forefinger to the tip of her nose. "Or how about this? You could focus on the UFO angle. Report on the cosmic whatsis and the people who believe in it. You're not dating them, right?"

"That's a helluva turnaround. The other day, you asked me to tone down the UFO angle."

He shrugged. "Maybe I'm growing a spine. Took me long enough, but it's high time I told my family where to shove their judgy opinions."

Well, if nothing else, she could feel good about that. Cold comfort for her frustrated libido.

She shook her head. "I'm not sure that would fly, since the cosmic whatsis is on your property. Some might see that as inventing news to benefit my friend's business." She almost said 'boyfriend,' but caught herself in the nick of time. A few hot kisses didn't make him her boyfriend, for God's sake.

He crossed his arms and huffed. "Well, you're practically family with everyone in Trappers Cove, right? You said as much yourself."

"True."

"Yet you report on them all the time. And I live in TC now. Why should I be any different?"

She chewed her lip, noting how Xander's gaze followed the movement. "If it were just Trappers Cove, I wouldn't worry so much. But the story's already been picked up in Seattle and Olympia. If word gets out that I'm dating a source, I'll look like a joke."

He clapped his hand to his forehead. "It's a human-interest story, for God's sake! Just silly shit about flying saucers and wannabe space scouts."

Indignation sizzled along her nerves. "There you go again, belittling the people who could keep your business alive."

"That's not the freakin' point!" he roared.

She dropped her gaze to her soggy boots. "It kind of is, Xander. I want you to succeed."

"Gah!" He spun away, paced the length of the gelato parlor's storefront, then strode back. "Okay, you know what? We're not getting anywhere. You're upset. I'm upset. Let's just—" he flapped a hand— "go to our separate corners and think on this. We're both smart people. Surely, one of us can come up with a solution."

Frustration knotted her insides. How had their sweet afternoon crumbled into this debacle?

Because you kissed him, dummy.

Stepping in close, Xander grasped her hand and clasped it to his chest. "I'm warning you now, Hannah. I don't give up so easily. In fact—" He lifted her knuckles to his lips. And zowie! Even a hand kiss from him was enough to stiffen her nipples to diamond hard points. "I may be the most determined person you've ever met."

Chapter Eleven

Twenty-four hours later, and still clueless about how to overcome Hannah's scruples without coming across as a selfish, horny asshat, Xander fled the drywall crew's din for the sugar-scented peace of Sweet Dreams Bakery. Between Garrett's calm, the coffee's strength, and the sweet treats' carb rush, something would jolt him out of this pointless rumination.

Figuring this out would be easier if seductive sensory memories weren't derailing his rational brain. Because man—what a kiss! What a beautiful, brave woman, laying her heart's pain bare for a near-stranger. What a ridiculous barrier keeping them apart.

But Hannah's objections were important to her, and he'd have to respect that. So here he was, thoroughly stuck.

As he entered the sunny bakery, Garrett emerged from the back holding a tray of iced pastries.

"Mmm. Smells like just what I need." Xander peered over the counter. "What are these?"

"Grandma Ella's Danish. I've got rhubarb, apple, and lemon-ricotta."

Xander's stomach rumbled. "Tough choice. You pick. And a large coffee with extra cream, please."

"On it." Garrett plated a pastry and filled an oversize mug. "I'm curious. How does someone our age live on pastries and coffee and look as fit as you do?" He slid Xander's order across the counter and gave his arm a squeeze. "You got padding under your shirt?"

Xander snorted. "I'll have you know I ate a kale salad for lunch."

"Uh huh. Didn't I see you running on the beach the other day?"

"Exercise helps clear my mind." He slurped his coffee, then dosed it with two sugars. "If that doesn't work, bring on the caffeine and sugar."

Garrett shook his head. "Ain't gonna criticize. So many people these days won't touch sugar or flour, so I'm grateful for every customer I can get." He folded his arms atop the bakery case. "So, what's got you mainlining carbs today?"

"Ugh." He scrubbed a hand through his hair. "It's complicated."

"Life is complicated, my friend." Garrett looked past him to greet a pair of older women. "Afternoon, ladies. A pot of Earl Grey?"

The taller of the two eyed Xander curiously. "Let's try the green jasmine today."

While the baker saw to their order, Xander settled into his favorite armchair by the bay window and munched his pastry—so light and flakey his chambray shirt was soon littered with crumbs.

Once the waiting customers were seen to, Garrett joined him, stretching out his long legs with a sigh. "Feels good to get off my feet. Been up since o-dark-thirty."

"Sounds like you were military."

"Air Force. Cook of the year on three different air bases." He laced his fingers together behind his neck. "So, what's eating my new neighbor?"

"What isn't? The building's falling apart, the reno's costing way more than I budgeted, and now—" He lowered his voice. "I've got lady troubles."

Garrett let out a low whistle. "Already? Thought you and Hannah were getting along just fine."

"Jeezus. Does everyone know?"

"Small town, my friend. Being all up in each other's business is part of the deal."

"Is it worth it?"

Garrett pressed his lips together and gazed out the window for a moment before his easy smile returned. "Asked myself that question a lot when I first came here. From my point of view, yes, it's worth it. The restaurant business is hella competitive, and I burned out pretty hard. Here, I can take my time, experiment, and sink roots, you know?" He leaned his elbows onto the table. "So—you and Hannah?"

"Shh!" Xander glanced at the older gals seated two tables away. One of them quickly averted her gaze. "We were vibing hard, and then she suddenly announces she can't date me because it's a conflict of interest."

Garrett's spooky-pale blue eyes shone with amusement. "Quite the passionate reporter, our Hannah."

"She's trying to save her newspaper." *Shit. Should've asked her permission before mentioning that.*

"The *Beacon*'s in trouble?" Garrett glanced at the wire newspaper rack by his front door. "I'll have to push them harder." He half-rose from his seat. "Hey, Rosie, you get this week's copy of the *Beacon* yet?"

"Read it online. Loved that story about the UFOs."

Her companion chimed in, "That's the most interesting thing I've read in that old paper since the storm of eight-two, when St. Sebastian's steeple toppled over."

Garrett pulled his phone from his pocket and typed out a note. "Come to think of it, it's been a long time since I took out an ad in the *Beacon*." He returned his attention to Xander. "So, the lady needs your story to save her newspaper."

"Pretty much, yeah."

"And she won't date you as long as she can milk a story out of your business."

"Seems so."

"And your business is the biggest news in town." Garret scratched the back of his close-cropped head. "That's a puzzler. Have you talked to Zora?"

"Not since the memorial service. Why?"

"She's pretty good at untangling dilemmas like this. Helped me see my way through something even more complicated." Planting his broad hands on his knees, he pushed to his feet. "Might help you with your ghost situation too."

Shit on a stick. He hadn't mentioned those toppling shelves and flickering lights to anyone but Hannah. "What makes you think I've got a ghost?"

Garrett chuckled. "Where do you think your reno crews come for their coffee breaks? One of those drywall guys very nearly didn't go back to work after lunch today. I sent him to Zora's for a charm to keep the ghosties away." He rubbed his palms together. "So you're welcome. Now, I've got bread dough to knead. Hope you figure it out."

Xander sipped his rapidly cooling coffee and stared out the window at Souvenir Planet, soon to be renamed God knows what. "Give me a break, Gus," he muttered. "You're chasing off my workers and the woman I want. Can't you just rest in peace like a normal dead person?"

Three weeks ago, if anyone had told Xander he'd be turning to an old hippie mama for guidance, he'd have laughed in their face. But here he stood outside Zora's squat brick building at the north end of Main Street, inspecting her spring display: tarot-card butterflies dangling from fishing line above pots of crystal flowers. It'd be pretty if it weren't for the stone skulls grinning from beneath plastic foliage like freaky Easter eggs.

Was this complete insanity? His siblings would razz him mercilessly for consulting a psychic.

Hannah's voice echoed in his head. *Why is such a smart, capable guy so hung up on what other people think?* That still stung.

Perhaps there really was something to this woo-woo stuff. Maybe this weird little beach town held a lesson he needed to learn—a lesson Gus's ghost was trying to convey by pushing things off shelves and messing with light switches like a mischievous cat.

He shook his head. "I am well and truly losing it. There's no such thing as ghosts."

The door opened, and an attractive woman with light brown hair stood framed in the entrance, arms crossed over her hippie-dippy homespun sweater. "Hi, Xander. Zora's going on her coffee break soon. Are you looking for a reading?"

He stammered, unnerved at being recognized by a stranger.

"I'm Gemma, Zora's niece. I didn't get a chance to talk to you at Gus's service. So sorry for your loss." She inclined her head toward the shop. "No need to be embarrassed. Everyone in Trappers Cove ends up here, eventually. Your uncle was a regular customer."

No big surprise there. Why wouldn't a UFO nut put his faith in crystal balls and tarot cards? Still, the old soothsayer had been very kind during Gus's memorial service.

He shrugged and forced a grin. "Might as well."

"Excellent." Beaming, Gemma welcomed him into the shop with a sweep of her hand.

No need to consider stocking fancy rocks in his new store because Zora had that market sewn up tight. Rainbow-hued crystals from huge to tiny twinkled from shelves and display cases, sharing space with carvings of fairies, skulls, dragons, Buddhas, and Ganeshas, not to mention enough hippie-dippy ponchos, patchwork pants, and tie-dyed T-shirts to clothe the whole town.

Some kind of native flute tootled softly from hidden speakers, and ferns dangling from macramé holders added a homey note. Zora got points for solid branding, even if the heavy incense made his nose itch.

Gemma beckoned toward a carved wooden screen at the rear of the shop. "Zora will see you now."

Why did his heart thump like that? She was just a sweet old lady in weird clothes. Nothing to be nervous about.

Zora stood with her back to him, filling a mug from an antique-looking silver urn. Dressed in a riot of colors and sparkly sneakers, she hummed and swayed her wide hips to the music. Her dangly earrings added a tinkling counterpoint. Turning, she beamed and pressed a rustic ceramic mug into his hand. "Here you go, darling. This will warm you right up and soothe those nerves."

Suspicious, he peered into the brew.

Zora's laugh rang warm and merry. "Don't worry, dear, it's just tea. My own blend—chamomile, lavender, spearmint, and ashwagandha root." When he didn't immediately take a sip, she added, "Gemma drinks it all day, and she's perfectly fine."

Playing along, Gemma grunted and shuffled zombie-like back to the register, one foot dragging behind her.

"Gotcha." Zora cackled and lowered herself into an ornately carved armchair beside a table covered in purple velvet. "Have a seat, Alexandros."

He nearly spilled his tea. "How did you know my name?"

With a serene smile, she pulled a deck of tarot cards from beneath the table. "I have my ways."

She answered his gaping stare with a wink. "I Googled you, of course. What a shame about your wine bar. Such a lovely place."

"It was." He'd put so much time, work, and money into renovating that old diner, hunting down furnishings and decorations to create the perfect balance between sophisticated and cozy. The Amphora had reflected his personality and taste so well it felt more like home than his own apartment. Greek-inspired small plates complimented the wines—at least, as far as his uneducated palate could tell. He'd even snuck his cousin, a sommelier at the family's flagship restaurant, a hefty under-the-table payment to construct their wine list. And for six months, it ran as smooth as butter—until a new, bigger wine bar opened up the street. With live music. And a killer Instagram account.

Xander didn't stand a chance.

Zora patted his hand, a motherly gesture that pulled him from his ruminations and grounded him in the very weird present. "Running a business is hard, especially on your own."

"Oh, I had help." Every last one of his staff was a joy to work with. Letting them go crushed Xander's heart.

"And you have help here too, you know. Don't be afraid to call on your new community. We take good care of each other."

"Yes, I've seen that. Thank you again for everything you did to make Gus's memorial service so…memorable."

She chuckled. "It was that. Now, tell me." Her piercing gaze demanded his focus. "What guidance are you seeking today?"

"I, uh." It was the strangest sensation—his mind seemed to blank, yet words spilled from his lips. "I don't know how to make Souvenir Planet profitable."

She arched an eyebrow. "And?"

Yup, this old gal definitely had a sixth sense.

"How do I convince someone to look past her scruples and see… I don't even know how to say this." No matter how he phrased it, the sharp old bird would realize he was talking about Hannah, and that felt like a betrayal.

"Something is standing between you and the one you love?"

His throat tightened. "Love is a strong word, but we like each other, and, uh…"

"I see." She patted his hand again. "Is that all?"

"Yes, sure. That's all."

She pursed her lips and gave him a powerful mom stare, the kind that says *I know you're hiding something, and you'd better confess before I find out.*

Though beads of sweat prickled his forehead, he blurted the ugly truth.

"There's this curse."

"Oh?" A wide smile crossed her plump face. "Tell me about that, darling."

Stomach churning, he quickly summarized the burden he'd carried since birth.

"And so everyone in my family believes that I'm doomed to failure."

"As do you?"

"Ugh." He cradled his aching head in his hands. "I mean, after so much negativity, it's hard not to."

"Hmm. Let me think." She hummed for a moment, gazing into the distance. "You're carrying quite a heavy load, my dear. Not to mention the ghost issue."

Xander nearly toppled backward from his chair. Could this woman really see right through his skull?

She waved a be-ringed hand. "We can deal with that later. For now, let's start with the shop and the lady, then we'll tackle the curse."

This was turning into a major excavation. Maybe he should just forget the whole thing and return to Souvenir Planet. Hammers and ledgers and wiring—that he could wrap his brain around. But this psyche-delving stuff made him itch and squirm.

"Let's see what the cards say." She shuffled expertly. "You're an Aries, right?"

"Um, yeah." Had she found his birthday online too? Man, you couldn't hide anything these days. "Shouldn't we address my issues one at a time?"

"Ah, but they're connected, aren't they? Now, try to quiet your mind."

Vegas dealers had nothing on Zora. The cards slid through her fingers like water. She spread them in a perfect arc across the table. "Choose three cards that call to you."

Turning off his buzzing thoughts was not one of Xander's strengths, yet his fingers moved quickly, plucking three cards from the spread.

"Turn them over."

He scanned the mysterious designs. Well, the artwork was pretty, if nothing else. "What do they mean?"

Zora tapped the first card. "This one offers guidance for the change in your life. The High Priestess upright. She calls you to embrace your inner wisdom and trust your intuition. The answer lies within you."

Hard to imagine a less helpful suggestion. His inner wisdom urged him to chuck the aliens—or was that just his personal taste? Beyond that, he had no clue.

"The second card points to the best self-care during this time of change." A wide grin spread across her plump face. "Well, well, well. The Ace of Cups. This signifies a new relationship with the potential for a deep emotional bond. Does that call to mind anyone you've met recently?"

She knew damn well he was sweet on Hannah. By now, they'd been seen together all over town.

Nevertheless, he folded his hands on the table. "I'll think on that."

She tapped her temple. "Smart. Now, the third card reveals the best way to center yourself on this journey. The Six of Cups takes us back to happy memories from childhood. How apropos."

"Huh. I'm already in Trappers Cove. So I should just...?"

"Remember what you once loved about this place." She tapped the first card again. "Your inner wisdom already knows the right path."

It was all he could do not to stamp his feet like a petulant toddler because he had no freakin' idea what it all meant. That's why he'd come here, for God's sake.

Forcing a smile, he thanked Zora for her advice and asked how much he owed her.

"Not a cent, dear. First reading is on the house."

"Ah. Smart marketing."

She chuckled as she pushed to her feet. "Even a psychic needs to understand basic business principles." She enveloped his hand in both of hers. "Now, let's deal with that curse. Come."

She towed him to the front of the store, where, humming along with the mystical flute music, she filled a small wicker basket with packets of herbs and a six-inch rod of luminous white stone.

"Selenite," she told him. "For cleansing your energy field and breaking the curse's grip on you. Hold the wand above your head thusly and slowly sweep it down your body while you visualize the crystal clearing away negative vibes." She demonstrated with a dramatic flourish.

"Um, okay..."

Zora quirked a playful smile. "Worried about looking foolish?"

"Honestly, a bit, yeah."

She tapped his sternum with the wand. "That's the root of your problem, dear. Now, take a bath with Epsom salts and a palmful of these hex-breaking herbs. Let it steep like tea, then have a good, long soak."

"I, uh, don't have a bathtub at the moment."

She pressed the packet into his hands and folded his fingers around the cellophane. "Ask a friend."

Of course, his mind sped straight to Hannah, but how likely was she to lend her tub to the guy she was hellbent on avoiding?

"After your bath, infuse a bucket of hot water with the rest of the herbs, and clean your space with it—walls, windows, and doors—then toss the mop water out your back door."

"Um, are we talking about my shop or my living space?"

Zora raked him with an appraising gaze. "Both, I'd say. Here." She grabbed a few more packets from the display and added them to the basket. At the register, she packed them and the crystal into a purple mesh bag and tied it with a ribbon.

He pulled out his wallet.

"No charge, dear. Consider it a gift for Gus. If our old friend is truly resting uneasy, I'd like to do whatever I can to bring him peace." She squeezed his hand in both of hers, a motherly gesture that made his eyes prickle just a tiny bit. "Now, you take good care of yourself, and don't hesitate to reach out for help. This town's got a lot riding on your success."

"I will." His voice wobbled. "Thank you, Zora. And thanks for the tea."

Indeed, there must be something magical in that brew, because despite her frustrating, cryptic advice, he left Zora's place feeling lighter. The clouds had parted, and bright sunshine gilded the rain-wet pavement and raindrops clinging to the bare-limbed sycamore trees. He filled his lungs with clean, fresh air, then set off toward his shop.

"Now, inner wisdom, how do we convince Hannah to set aside her rule about dating a source?"

A young couple crossed his path, each holding the hand of a giggling toddler wearing a knit cap he recognized from Gus's shop—neon green with three googly eyes on top. "Again," the kid demanded, and his parents swung him high in the air.

"I flying," the little guy squealed. "Again!"

Smiling wistfully, Xander watched them pass. Lucky child to have parents who helped him fly.

A weird sensation sizzled down his spine.

"Family, huh? Is that the answer?" Instead of bitching about their oppressive negativity, why not focus on the one relative who believed he could fly?

And dear old Uncle Gus had provided him with just the juicy bait he needed to pique Hannah's interest. Over the past week, when not daydreaming about the stubborn reporter, he'd spent hours sorting through Gus's personal papers and found some truly far-out shit.

Maybe protecting a dead man's reputation was a futile waste of time—because Gus sure as hell didn't care who knew about his belief in interstellar visitors. From what Xander had read, his uncle had planned to shout it from the rooftops.

And if anyone thought he shared his uncle's wacko beliefs, well—his new store would set them straight. Okay, one or two shelves of alien souvenirs in Gus's honor, but the rest would be...

He'd figure it out soon. Like Zora said, his inner wisdom would show the way.

And right now, his inner wisdom wanted another chance with Hannah.

He pulled his phone from his pocket and tapped out a message.

> **Found something interesting in Gus's journals. Open for another interview?**

Chapter Twelve

Hannah hunched over her muffin-crumb-littered desk, crunching the numbers again. Nearly halfway through March, subscriptions and advertising were up, but not enough.

Last night, dogged by insomnia, she'd scribbled potential solutions in her bedside journal, but this morning, her sleepy chicken scratch was a complete puzzle.

Expand

Digonly

Savings

What the hell had she meant? She recalled it making sense right before she finally dropped off to sleep…and dreamt of Xander. Which was not helpful. How was she supposed to concentrate with his dark, lust-blown eyes haunting her dreams, her daydreams, her every waking moment?

"Arrgh." She cradled her aching head.

A soft hand fell onto her shoulder. "I'm worried about you, hon."

Crap on toast. The last thing she needed to do was burden her sick mother with this mess.

She flashed a tight grin. "I'm fine, Mom. Just didn't sleep well."

"Baloney." Mom crossed her arms. "You've been gloomy since yesterday, and I suspect it has less to do with the *Beacon* and more to do with a certain young man."

"Young?" Hannah snorted. "He's my age."

"All the more reason to snatch him up. Everyone in town can see he's gaga for you."

"Everyone?"

Mom shrugged. "Well, if you're going to make out on Main Street, you've gotta expect an audience. So, what's the holdup?"

Hannah's phone pinged with another message from Xander:

> **I could really use your help. 3 o'clock? 11A Schooner Lane**

Hannah quickly tucked her phone away, but not fast enough to escape her mother's eagle eye.

"Is that him?"

She nodded—because Mom would see through a lie in an instant.

"You know darn well why I can't date him."

"Uh-huh," Mom deadpanned. "Tell me, are you really hung up on your ethics, or are you just scared?"

"Me? Scared?" Courage and determination were her life's blood. Avoiding Xander had nothing to do with fear. It was just common sense.

Mom tutted. "You haven't let yourself fall for a guy since Nathan. Who was very nice, by the way."

"Moo-om." She cringed inwardly at her whiney, adolescent tone. "He didn't get me at all. He wanted me to quit working so hard, settle down, and make babies."

Guilt pinched her painfully. As an only child, her decision to forego motherhood meant that Mom would never be a grandmother—and she would've made an excellent grandma.

Mom pulled up a rolling chair, turned Hannah so they sat knee to knee, and grasped her hands. "Listen, this is not about grandbabies. Sure, I'd like one or two, but I have friends' grandchildren to spoil and your cousins' kids. What I care about most is your happiness."

Another pinch, this time closer to her heart. "Not everyone is meant to be paired up."

"True. Some people get everything they need from work and friends." She chuckled. "Since your dad left, I find I've lost interest in romance. But I had my great love. Even if it didn't last, I wouldn't trade those good years for anything."

Hannah stared agog. After the awful bitterness of their divorce, Mom still held love for her cheating, family-abandoning ex? Inconceivable.

"In my experience," Mom continued, "most people are happier with a mate. You certainly seemed happier when you were with Nathan. I hate to think you're putting your heart on hold to save the *Beacon*."

Like the good years before Dad left them, the good times with Nathan were something she hadn't let herself dwell on. She had to protect her heart.

Living with him had been nice. No, that was too wishy-washy a word for what they shared. Their three-year union was comfortable, cozy, safe. She'd liked having someone to come home to, someone to hold her after a hard day. But their balance was off. He wanted to be her main focus.

She'd never recapture that cozy feeling until she found a man as driven as she was, one who didn't see her passion for journalism as a rival. And maybe that could be Xander, if not for this stupid conflict of interest.

The cruel irony struck her like a slap. Xander probably would understand her in a way Nathan never could because his passionate determination to rebuild his business matched her drive to protect the *Beacon*. And though he was a thousand percent wrong about dumping the aliens, knowing his family history, she understood why he'd want to change the shop's focus.

If it weren't for their botched kiss the other night, she might've had a shot at changing his mind about that too.

Mom interrupted her useless mental wheel-spinning with a gentle arm-squeeze.

"It's your life, darling, and your decision. But let me lay a little old-woman wisdom on you." She cupped Hannah's cheek. "All this talk of ethics is a smokescreen. You like that man. He likes you. So get on with it already."

A phone rang in the back. Almah hollered, "Linda, it's the mayor."

Mom pushed to her feet with a faint groan. "Think on it, kiddo."

How could she not? Alone at her desk, Hannah stared at her phone.

He wants to show me Gus's journals?

The prospect of a juicy story sent a thrill of excitement through her, but sitting side by side with Xander, poring over Gus's notes? Bad idea. That kind of proximity would lead to touching and probably kissing and a flood of messy feelings she wasn't equipped to handle right now.

Hard enough to resist his magnetism from across the street. Since that blazing kiss two days ago, she fought the constant urge to dash outside every time she spotted him leaving Souvenir Planet.

"Morning, hon." Almah greeted her, arms laden with freshly printed papers. She lifted her load toward Hannah's face. "Hot off the presses. Don't you love that smell?"

Damn, she did love it. She loved the feel of newsprint between her fingers, the soft crackle as she turned the pages. She loved seeing her byline and Mom's and Fred's and Almah's and all their part-time and volunteer reporters who crafted stories about their community.

Faced with losing this and becoming just a digital edition—or worse, closing the paper permanently—spending an hour or two with the man she wanted but couldn't have wasn't such a huge sacrifice. After all, she was a professional. She had the strength to get through a short meeting with her sanity intact.

She typed,

> **Why not meet in your office?**

His answer came within seconds.

> **Workers making a racket. It's quieter here.**

Mom's words echoed—what was she afraid of? He wasn't likely to jump her bones over his uncle's journal.

Rationalization, thy name is Hannah.

> **Okay. See you at three.**

For the rest of the afternoon, she rushed to finish her story on Salty Dog's March specials, a German-style Märzenbier and an Irish Extra Stout, then upload photos of head brewer Lilo Eisinger checking her mash tun. Shots of the stunning beer goddess always sold extra papers.

"Sex sells, eh?" Lilo said with a laugh during their photo shoot. "Fine with me. Gotta use what you've got to get what you want."

Easy for Lilo to say. Hell, she was coupled up with Ryan, the brewery's owner. Clearly, "conflict of interest" wasn't a concern in their career field.

Later, as Hannah was packing up her interview gear, Zora Moore came sailing into the newsroom, her long scarf flying, a handful of papers clutched high overhead. "Finished the horoscope column," she sang out.

"Thanks, but why didn't you email it like you always do?"

"Oh, just wanted to stretch my legs. It's such a beautiful day out."

"It's raining, Zora."

"It stopped half an hour ago." Zora clasped her hands over her broad bosom. "Oh dear. Your aura is murky today. Very dark and drab. Let's do a quick one-card read."

Hannah slid one arm into her jacket. "Actually, I was on my way out—"

"Won't take a moment." She pulled a tarot deck from her copious fringed bag. "Sit."

With an aggrieved sigh, Hannah complied, enjoying the ffffrrrrt of the cards as Zora shuffled. She really ought to get back in the habit of a monthly reading, something she'd been neglecting since the paper started to flounder. Though she was skeptical of Zora's woo-woo philosophy, the old gal's readings always provided food for thought.

"All right, dear, concentrate on whatever's troubling you."

Xander, of course. No use denying it—ever since their date on Monday, her brain had been churning with frustration, ditto her sex-starved body that didn't give a damn about journalistic impartiality.

Zora spread the cards in a perfect arc on Hannah's desk. "The Eight of Swords. Interesting." She smiled serenely at the image of a person bound and blindfolded, standing on wet, boggy ground, surrounded by eight upright swords.

A shiver prickled Hannah's skin. "That can't be a good sign."

"This card points to the dangers of overthinking. When we indulge in rumination, we risk anxiety, overwhelm, even paralysis. See?" Zora tapped the card. "This person is trapped by worry and blinded to the options around her. The question to ask yourself is, what is my obsessive pondering costing me? An opportunity? A new ally?"

With a snort, Hannah crossed her arms and leaned back in her chair. "You've been talking to Xander."

With a cryptic smile, Zora packed up her deck. "My spiritual guidance is confidential. But suppose a handsome newcomer came to see me, all tied in knots, because the woman he cares for won't give him a chance? And suppose all signs point toward an advantageous match for both of them? Wouldn't it be my responsibility to encourage one of the smartest, stubbornest, most loyal people I've ever met to look at things from a different angle?"

"For frick's sake, Zora." She tempered her language out of respect. "You're such a matchmaker."

"Not at all. Who you let into your heart is your affair and no one else's. I just want my loved ones to be happy." She squeezed Hannah's hand. "Use that regal Leo creativity and determination to overcome whatever dilemma's been spinning your wheels. Leos can't flourish when they're confined."

"What does my star sign have to do with—"

Ignoring her question, Zora fluttered off with excuses about being late for an appointment.

"Just want you to be happy," Hannah grumbled as she wrapped up against the chilly wind. But Zora's words swirled with Mom's, itching under her skin as she set off for Schooner Lane.

Xander lit a pine-scented candle he'd picked up from the Sea Queen Spa's gift shop. Then blew it out. Then lit it again. If he looked, or smelled, like he was trying too hard, she might be put off. But after ruining their last date, he really wanted Hannah to like his new temporary home.

When Cheryl Rossi suggested this renovated RV as another cheap option, he'd nearly walked out of her office in frustrated disbelief. But a nagging voice urged him to take a look before turning it down. Good thing he had, because this cozy vintage camper was perfect—freshly repainted and refurnished with white walls and cabinets, wooden flooring, a snug dinette, comfy couch, queen-size bed, hanging plants, and a skylight that let in sunlight filtered through the surrounding pines. Less than a block from Shoreline Road, the RV court smelled of sea and green and resurrected happy memories of childhood visits to Uncle Gus.

Besides, since they were months away from Trappers Cove's high season, the two sisters who were rehabbing old RVs into tourist lodgings gave him an excellent deal. And God knows he needed every penny of capital if he hoped to reopen the shop by Memorial Day.

Because opening for spring break? Not gonna happen. Already, it was mid-March. Necessary repairs to the building were barely started, and he was still at sea regarding the shop's new branding and focus. Not just at sea, bobbing in the Bermuda Triangle.

He crunched another of Garrett's iced cookies and pushed the rest aside. At this rate, he'd gobble them all out of sheer nervousness before Hannah arrived.

Turning his attention to the papers strewn across the dinette table, he flipped open a cracked plastic binder labeled *For Xander*. It was a miracle he ever found it, since Gus had left it in a moldy cardboard box beneath brochures from a half-dozen UFO organizations.

"Thought you'd have more time, eh Gus?" He thumbed through painstakingly drawn diagrams overlaid with spirals representing... Cosmic energy? Gamma rays? Hannah could help him figure it out. He had a hunch she was the sort of person who couldn't resist a puzzle. Or a challenge.

"She sure as shit can resist me, though." With a sigh, he pushed the papers away and opened his laptop to his growing list of potential merchandise for Souvenir Planet 2.0. Thank the intergalactic gods, Gus's will didn't stipulate anything about keeping the name, just the cosmic transmitter.

"So, what to call you, sweetheart?" Something Greek would be nice, to reflect their family's heritage. The Agora? Would shoppers know that means "marketplace"? No, the name had to be catchier, more accessible. "Shoptopia? Marketplace of Mysteries? Bazaar of...ugh." He clicked another tab. No use trying to name the place when he still had no idea what he planned to sell.

A Steve Jobs quote from his college marketing classes stuck in his memory: "The only way to do great work is to love what you do. If you haven't found it yet, keep looking. Don't settle."

Xander tapped his stylus on the table. "That's my problem, Steve. I love lots of things, but I'm an expert in nothing. Not wine, not gourmet food, and definitely not beach souvenirs." He closed his eyes and massaged his temples. "Come on, inner wisdom, hit me with some inspiration."

No answer except for the sound of female voices outside—probably the Delaney sisters, his landladies, arguing about building materials again. At least they weren't running their table saw today. Another voice joined in, forming a three-part harmony between Diane's raspy laugh, Donna's high-pitched giggle, and the newcomer's mellower tone.

He grinned. "Harmony. I like that." He didn't have to settle on just one type of merchandise as long as he found a common thread, a theme to inspire his brand and his store's name.

"So, what connects you guys?" He ticked through his list of typical tourist fodder not yet peddled in Trappers Cove.

- *designer pet gear*

- *high-end leather goods*

- *smelly candles and luxury bath stuff*

- *trendy kitchen accessories*

- *those wooden plaques with cutesy sayings*

- *gourmet oil and vinegar*

- *upscale linen beach wear*

"I'll call it...A Touch of Class? A Cut Above?" He tossed the stylus onto the counter and closed his laptop with a snap. "Hannah's right. I do sound snooty."

A knock sounded on the door. He opened to find the object of his affection, the haunter of his dreams, the pricker of his conscience, wrapped to her chin in a woolly scarf, her dark hair lifted by the wind.

Flanking her stood the Delaney sisters, their weathered faces wreathed in knowing grins.

Well, fabulous. More grist for the Trappers Cove gossip mill.

"Hi, Xander." Hannah shoved her hands into her jacket pockets and gave him a wary smile. "Donna and Diane were just showing me around. Really impressive what they're doing with these campers."

"DIY queens, that's us!" Donna chirped and fished a bandana from her pocket to wipe her sweat-dotted forehead. "We installed a gas fire pit like yours in front of the '72 Airstream."

Eyes sparkling with interest, Hannah pivoted slowly on the wooden deck, taking in the dilapidated RVs waiting their turn for a makeover. "What model is this one?"

Donna patted its red and aqua aluminum wall. "1950 Vagabond travel trailer. Found it in a field south of town, covered in blackberry brambles. Can you believe it?"

Xander huffed, impatient for one-on-one time with Hannah.

She noticed—because her sharp eyes noticed everything—and turned to the sisters with a smile. "I've got an interview with Xander today. How about if I come back tomorrow, and you can tell me all about your plans for this place. We'll do a full-page spread for the Sunday edition."

"That'd be grand." Diana grabbed her sister's sleeve. "Now come on, spotlight hog. Let Hannah get back to work."

"But I was just—"

"Showin' off, like you always do." She threw a wink over her shoulder.

"Skillful deflection," Xander said once they'd departed.

"It'll make a good story." She gazed up at the tall trees. "This will be beautiful when they're done. Nice twist on the usual mini log cabins you find in beach towns."

"Well, that's Trappers Cove, right? Full of unusual twists." He held the door and made a sweeping gesture. "Care to see what they've done with the interior?"

She chewed her lip for a moment, then mounted the stairs and stepped inside. "Nii-ice. Love the colors." She lifted a moss green pillow from the cream-colored sofa.

He slid behind her, close enough to inhale the scent of her hair—some magical mixture of fruit, flowers, and spice. "Hannah, I still feel terrible about the other day. If I'd have known about your house..."

She turned quickly, which put her an inch from his nose, then jolted backward and bonked into the sofa.

"Tight quarters." She giggled nervously. "Listen, that wasn't your fault. There's no way you could've known. And I'm sorry for flipping out on you. Anyway, I like this place much better."

Thank God for that.

"Have a seat." He pulled the tea cozy from the ceramic pot and filled two mugs with sweet, spice-scented tea.

"You don't seem like the tea cozy sort."

"Came with the kitchen. They thought of everything, those two. Must've scoured every yard sale from here to British Columbia."

"I'm surprised you even know what it's for."

"Aunt Marty had one." Smiling at the memory, he sat facing her on the dinette bench. "She was a great old gal. Funny, snarky, and her baklava could bring you to tears. She kept Gus grounded. Losing her probably sent him spiraling into...you know." He twirled a finger at his temple.

"Yeah, she was a character." Hannah sipped her tea. Her eyebrows flicked up. "Really good."

"Zora's special blend." Garrett sold it in his bakery, a smart idea. When neighboring businesses promoted each other, everyone benefited from the increased exposure. He'd find a way to do the same once he figured out his non-alien angle.

"Speaking of Zora—" Hannah's eyes narrowed. "Did you sic her on me?"

"Sorry?"

"Never mind." She reached for the plate of cookies between them. "So, what's this interesting discovery you promised me?"

Here we go. Gotta hook her good.

"While sorting through Gus's papers, I found this." He slid the plastic binder toward her. "It's—well, I'd love to hear your thoughts."

For several minutes, Hannah pored over each page, pausing to scribble in her little notebook, silent but for soft grunts and the occasional breathy "Wow."

Finally, she looked up, her face solemn. "Gus really believed he was communicating with aliens."

"Yup. Did you see the bit about the probe?"

She shuddered. "Since Gus's memorial, I've been reading up on this phenomenon. Some scientists blame sleep paralysis. Like, if you already believe in UFOs and you semi-wake up but can't move, your mind automatically goes there, and poof! Another alien abduction." She wiggled in her seat. "That doesn't explain the butt stuff, though."

She held his gaze for a long moment, until the corners of her eyes crinkled, her lips twitched, and they both dissolved in laughter.

Finally, Xander straightened and wiped his streaming eyes. "God, I adore you, Hannah."

Still giggling, she blotted her cheeks with a paper napkin. "I think you're pretty cool too."

Throwing tact and caution to the wind, he clasped her hand, damp napkin and all. "What are we gonna do about this situation?"

She exhaled a long, cookie-scented breath. "Zora says I'm over-thinking."

"Huh. She says I should trust my inner wisdom and be open to a new relationship." He chuckled. "Think she invents predictions based on what she wants you to do?"

Her playful smile detonated a firework of giddy sparkles in his belly. "Hmm. Let me consult my Magic Eight Ball." She mimed shaking a sphere. "All signs point to yes."

She's giving you an opening. Don't botch it.

He cleared his throat. "Hannah, we've only known each other for a few weeks."

"Three," she added. "Twenty-one days today."

"Always a stickler for facts." He ran the pad of his thumb over her knuckles. "You're a hard-charger, but you balance that determination with kindness and generosity. It's a killer combination."

She bit her lip, and man, did his dick sit up and take notice of that sexy gesture. Ignoring his horny sidekick, he continued, "You've done so much to help me already. I hope that means you care at least a little."

She leaned onto her elbows and fixed him with a fierce look. "I like you, Xander, but know this—Trappers Cove is my heart, and I'll do whatever it takes to protect it. And Souvenir Planet is a big part of TC's charm. I won't let it go down without a fight."

His besotted smile remained stubbornly stuck in place. "Your eyes sparkle when you get riled up."

"Flatterer." But her grin glowed with pleasure. "Zora says we Leos are very protective of our friends and family."

"And am I one of those friends?"

Her eyebrows shot up. "Would I put in all this work for someone I didn't care about?"

"Hmmph. Sometimes I wonder if you care more about the shop than me. What if we'd met somewhere else?" Giving into temptation, he lifted a strand of hair clinging to her cheek and tucked it behind her ear, then traced the delicate shell with his fingertip. "Would I have caught your eye?"

Hannah's cognac-brown eyes darkened. "Definitely." The tip of her tongue slicked the full curve of her lower lip.

Xander's mouth went dry, and his dick went rock hard.

"I've been wrestling myself since that amazing kiss." Hannah said, fiddling with crumbs on her plate. "And I probably have been over-thinking it. You need to make Souvenir Planet a success. I need to increase readership, and you're handing me the perfect story on a platter."

"I'd like to hand you a lot more than that." *Oof!* He'd meant his heart, not his dick. Could he be clumsier?

She tipped her head back and laughed. "Quit trying to derail my train of thought with your dirty talk."

"Sorry. My brain short-circuits around you." He hid his flushed face—and his hopeful grin—in his hands.

Soft fingers threaded through his hair, and the pleasure of that simple touch ricocheted through him. If she lit him up like this with just her fingertips, what would happen when she pressed the length of her bare, supple body against his?

If, he corrected himself. Her consent was far from given. He'd have to proceed with caution.

"You have a good heart, Xander. You're trying to honor Gus and all the hard work he put into his business."

Thank God she saw it that way. And her assumption was true, sort of. He'd never surrender Gus's legacy to some developer who didn't give a monkey's ass about Trappers Cove. His goal was to remake the shop into something that would enrich the town as well as his bottom line, and Hannah would see that once he opened his doors.

He grasped her hand and pressed a kiss into her palm. "Yes, I do want to honor Gus's legacy, even if we don't agree on the best way to do that."

A beautiful pink flush tinted her throat and cheeks, and man, did he want to see what that color looked like on the rest of her skin.

Hannah plucked at the neckline of her blouse. "Whew. It's warm in here. What do you say to a walk on the beach? That always helps me think."

"Fantastic idea." Because what could be more romantic than strolling hand in hand over the sand? If he played his cards right, he'd get another kiss before they parted ways. Or maybe even more?

Don't push your luck, Anagnos.

Chapter Thirteen

As she followed Xander through the dune grass, Hannah's heart thrummed like she'd mainlined espresso. A sharp wind whipped her hair into her eyes, and when she paused to secure it with an elastic band, he immediately whirled to face her. "You okay?"

"I'm great. Just need a sec." *Jeez, he has the ears of a fox.*

Funny how that was the first animal that came to mind. Not a big cat or a wolf or bear or some other apex predator—no, Xander had a fox's sleek beauty, sharp senses, nimble movements, and determination, not to mention his large, liquid, foxy eyes. With her heart trembling inside a flimsy chicken coop, she watched him plot his approach.

What a weird metaphor. Good thing she was a journalist and not a poet.

"Not too cold, are you?" he asked, all sweet concern.

"Are you kidding?" She tossed her head in feigned nonchalance. "I grew up here, remember? I've seen winds that'll peel the flesh from your bones."

He chuffed a laugh. "Noted. You're an old salt, cleverly disguised as a beautiful lady."

"Go on with ye, flatterer," she said in her best movie pirate accent, hoping the heat in her cheeks wasn't visible. She had enough miles under her hood to know that men used sweet talk as a means to an end, yet Xander's compliments lit her up like Christmas.

When they topped the dune, they stopped to drink in the wide curve of beach stretched out before them. The sun was sinking low, and already the horizon blushed rose-gold. The angled light burnished the surf and glimmered on the wet sand.

Coming here with Xander was a turning point, a transition from mere flirtation to real connection. The beach was her healing place. When troubles overwhelmed her, the sea breeze held magical powers to blow them away, leaving her clean and clear. It was also here she came to connect with friends and family—really one and the same in Trappers Cove. Nights spent singing and laughing around a bonfire counted among her fondest memories.

So when Xander drew her arm through his, snugged her to his side, and started down the dune onto the beach, it felt like crossing a threshold.

A few pickups and SUVs sat to the south, halfway toward Ivan's Hollow, and the faint sound of salsa music carried on the wind.

Xander inclined his head. "Too bad the tide's in. I'd love to see the Hollow again. Which way shall we start?"

She turned toward the partiers because she didn't quite trust herself with Xander on the more deserted end of the beach. With the stiff breeze tousling his dark curls and the golden sunlight glinting in his eyes, it took all her strength to keep her hands to herself.

For a while, they walked in companionable silence, breathing in the tangy salt air and listening to the surf's whoosh and hiss. Gulls tap-danced on the surf-slicked sand and ruffled their feathers. Busy little plovers darted to and fro, pecking out their dinner. A galumphing

Golden Retriever ran to intercept them and dropped a soggy tennis ball at their feet.

"Max, get back here," someone hollered from the cluster of pickups.

Laughing, Xander dropped to one knee and gave the happy pup a thorough head-scratch before pitching the ball back where it came from. Tongue lolling, the dog tore off after it.

"Good arm," Hannah observed, and patted his biceps.

"Who's the flatterer now?" But his grin gleamed with pride.

"Just a simple statement of fact. You're very muscly. Weights?"

"Belonged to a neighborhood gym up in Seattle. Now it's just boring calisthenics and running. You?"

"Beach walks and yoga. Yoga Bliss on Main Street has a great juice bar."

He nodded, but his eyes seemed glazed over.

"Guess yoga's too boring for a guy like you."

"Not at all." He gave a sheepish grin. "Imagining you in downward dog pose kinda blew all other thoughts right out of my head."

"Shut up." She socked his arm, secretly tickled to her core. "Did you ever camp out there as a kid? In the Hollow, I mean."

"Only once. Gus and Marty packed enough food for an army, but it was just the three of us."

She pictured a skinny, mop-headed boy of seven or eight squirming with excitement as his aunt and uncle set up camp. "S'mores?"

"Of course. And hot dogs, corn on the cob, basically anything you could put on a stick and roast over a campfire. Martha played her ukulele." His steps slowed as he sank into the memory. "Good times."

"Right? Beach kids are the luckiest, I think." She bumped him with her hip. "I'm glad you got to be one, if only during the summer."

They started forward again, but he wheeled her around to face him. "Do you think we ever met?"

She searched her memory but couldn't retrieve a trace. And she'd have remembered a kid with a cool name like Xander, not to mention his playful smile—something she hadn't seen enough of before now. Seems the beach was doing him good.

The same held true for her. Out here, it was easy to forget all the complications separating them and just *be.* Two simpatico people exploring a new connection and enjoying the moment.

She shook her head. "Sorry, I don't think so. I mean, chances are we crossed paths, but there were so many summer kids, you know?"

"Did you make friends with any of them?"

"Only for the summer. After they left, well..." She smiled at the bittersweet memory. "Like most townie kids, I learned to focus on friendships that would last, because visitors always forget about you once they leave."

His expression shifted, suddenly solemn. With his bent forefinger, he traced the line of her jaw, igniting shivers that had nothing to do with the cold wind.

"Hannah, I could never forget you."

"But you'll leave, right? Once you've got Souvenir Planet up and running again?"

His face blanked. Answer enough.

Her stomach fell. Since Nathan's departure, she'd been more than content with brief liaisons, a little meaningless fun to take the edge off. But the thought of Xander leaving Trappers Cove? It hurt.

He stuffed his hands into his jacket pockets and stared out to sea. "Honestly, I'm not sure. Which is weird for me. I'm usually the man with a plan, you know? This is my first time flying without a map."

He nudged a smooth, flat stone free with the toe of his leather sneaker, pulled it from the sand, and tossed it into the churning surf.

"Hey." She rubbed gentle circles between his shoulder blades. "Forget I asked. You're going through enough. You don't need extra complications."

Still gazing at the rosy horizon, he smiled wistfully. "The more time I spend with what Gus left behind, the more I realize there's no getting around life's complications. Maybe that's why I've failed before now. I tried to keep everything too simple."

Her heart brimming with sympathy, she leaned into his shoulder. "Insert wise quotation about how failure is an opportunity to learn."

Laughter shook his ribs. In an excellent Yoda impression, he rasped, "The greatest teacher, failure is." He held her softly against his chest, his cheek nestled into her hair. "You're good for me, Hannah. I hope I get a chance to return the favor."

Emotion washed over her, as overwhelming as a rogue wave. She should break away now, before she fell too far, but she couldn't force herself to let go of his warmth. Inhaling deeply, she savored his scent—moss and leather and clean skin.

Later, when he'd gone, she'd remember every crystalline detail of this moment.

A rough finger tilted her face up. "Hannah, can I kiss you?"

Eyes still closed, she nodded.

Soft lips brushed hers and lingered, caressing, tasting, learning her mouth. She pressed her palms to his cheeks, relishing the scratchy-soft texture of his short scruff.

She whimpered in disappointment when his lips trailed away, but he wasn't finished with her. He feathered kisses over her cheekbones, her temples, her closed lids, then sealed his mouth to hers again in a deep, fiery kiss.

Lust roared through her, hot enough to fuse the sand beneath their feet into glass. Their kiss burned on and on—until icy surf drenched them both.

Gasping, they broke apart and dashed toward dry land, hooting with laughter.

When they reached the dunes, Xander toed off his sodden, sand-caked shoes, then held Hannah steady while she did the same.

She straightened and draped her arms loosely over his shoulders. "That was amazing. Where do we go from here?"

Heat and hope glinted in his eyes. "My place? If nothing else, we can shower this sand off our feet."

Anticipation sizzled over her skin. Showering with Xander, naked, hot, and slippery? Nothing had ever sounded more delicious. Well, one thing did, and she was running out of reasons to resist.

In fact, it was starting to feel inevitable.

Xander's first thought on seeing this RV had been *Hannah would like this.* While waiting for her to answer his text about Gus's journals, he'd speed-cleaned the interior, changed the sheets and towels, even lit one of those froufrou scented candles he'd picked up from the Sea Queen Spa during his market research, all in hopes of making the tiny space appealing to her.

And now, here they stood on the RV's little deck, potentially on the cusp of a life-changing encounter—if he didn't blow it by rushing her or saying the wrong thing.

He hadn't been this helplessly horny since he was a teen. And while he craved her body with every cell of his, in this moment, earning her trust felt more important. Because he wanted so much more than a quick hook-up with Hannah. All he could do now was go slow, pay careful attention to her reactions—and pray.

While her back was turned, he quickly adjusted his erection, then toed off his sandy shoes and banged them together. Sand showered down with each loud clap.

Following suit, Hannah giggled.

"What's funny?" he asked, unable to restrain his grin.

"Nothing." She bit her lip and snickered again.

He nudged her. "Come on, share with the class."

"It's so juvenile."

"I won't judge."

The prettiest shade of pink painted her cheekbones. "When Daphne asks about our meeting, I can tell her we went back to your place to bang." She dropped her shoes and hid her face behind her hands.

A smart, beautiful, hard-charging woman who could laugh at goofy jokes? *I'm in love.* He set her shoes alongside his on the top stair. "Don't worry. What happens in the RV stays in the RV. Here." He handed her one of the towels he'd left on the patio table, a habit from childhood summers, when Aunt Marty would scold him for tracking sand into the house.

She wiped the sand from her pretty, bare feet, but it clung around her scarlet-painted toenails and to her jeans, soaked halfway up her thighs.

She scrunched her face and plucked at the damp denim. "I can't go inside like this. I'll get sand everywhere."

"Hang on." He checked for passersby before reaching for his belt. "Turn around, please." The last thing he wanted her to see was his goofy patterned boxers. Or the stiffy still tenting them.

"Okaay." Grinning, she complied. But as he fiddled with the door lock, a musical giggle rang out. "What are you wearing?"

He glanced down. Dinosaurs.

Eyes twinkling with merriment, Hannah giggled into her hand.

"I said no peeking. And they're a gift from my nephews. Wait here." He dashed inside, pulled on joggers, and grabbed his bathrobe—another Christmas present, fluffy and two sizes too big.

"For me?" Hannah asked when he went back outside.

He couldn't resist. "Wrap up in this, then drop your pants."

She spluttered with laughter. "There you go again with the dirty talk."

He joined in, unable to hold back a laugh. "You're gonna have a lot to tell Daphne." He watched her gyrate and wiggle until her jeans dropped to her ankles. "Unfortunately, I don't have a dryer here, but I'll give you something to wear."

"Something with dinos?" Still giggling, she followed him inside.

He gestured toward the little bathroom. "The shower's all yours." Though the thought of showering with Hannah steamed up his brain, he calculated his chances were better served by being a gentleman.

Her gaze darted from his face to the door and back. "Oh, I don't need to—"

"Listen, beach babe." He took both hands. "We both know the only way to get rid of all that sand is to shower it off. Besides, you're shivering."

She pulled the bathrobe tighter. "You go first. I'll look over Gus's notes."

No point arguing with a woman who looked ready to bolt. "Right. Make yourself comfortable."

He quickly stripped down and washed his sandy feet and legs, along with everything else, for good measure. Who knew how tonight might end? That thought sent his half-chub pointing skyward again, but it felt creepy to take himself in hand with Hannah so near, so he ended his shower with a bone-jarring blast of cold water.

He ducked into the bedroom for clean clothes—not much to choose from until he made a trip to TC's only laundromat. Gray sweats and a worn blue Henley would have to do. For Hannah, he selected his best joggers and a pair of thick socks. He found her hunched over Gus's notebook of chicken-scratch and conspiracy theories.

He set the clothes on the table. "Find anything good?"

She jolted upright, eyes wide. Her cheeks flushed, and her gaze drifted down his body before jerking back up to his face.

"Sorry, I was, uh—this is very interesting." She tapped the page, then tittered as she examined the socks printed with Sasquatch chugging coffee. "How perfectly Washington State."

"Yeah, well, now you've seen half my Christmas haul: socks, underwear, bathrobe." He moved to the little propane stove. "How about more tea while we wait for the water to warm up? Or I've got some decent coffee."

"Coffee sounds great." She bent over the journal again.

When he returned a moment later with two mugs, he caught her holding the joggers to her nose. "Your, uh, laundry stuff smells nice." Forget pretty pink—her cheeks were flaming red now.

She's smelling me! That's gotta be a good sign.

Keep it together, Anagnos. "A little rum in your coffee?"

She bit her lip, *God have mercy on his soul*, then nodded, so he added a glug of Kraken to each mug.

She sipped her drink and shivered. "Delish."

He sat beside her. "Still cold?"

"Just my icy toes."

This wouldn't do. He fetched a fuzzy blanket from the couch and laid it across his lap. "Give 'em here." He hauled her feet onto his lap, wrapped her bare legs in the blanket, and massaged her feet through the thick fleece.

Hannah squirmed. "I'll get it all sandy."

"I'll wash it. Now quit arguing, woman."

She giggled again at his gruff tone. *God, he loved making her laugh.*

While kneading her calves, he glanced at the open book. Huh. She'd been reading the same page for five minutes. Did he fluster her as much as she flustered him?

Curiosity made him as squirmy as a first grader with a head full of questions. He wanted to learn everything about Hannah, from her favorite snack to her secret fantasies. He cleared his throat.

"At the risk of sounding cheesy, how is a beauty like you single?"

She crooked a snarky smile. "I happen to love cheese."

"Deflecting much? Don't tell me if you don't want to. But I'm feeling—" Searching for the right words, he dug his thumbs into the arch of her foot. Hannah closed her eyes and moaned. His dick hardened instantly.

Her chuckle turned low and throaty. "I can tell what you're feeling."

"Ignore him. Rude little bastard, always butting in when the conversation gets good." He shifted on the seat and kneaded her calves.

She lifted her gaze to his again, and wow! Those eyes, deep enough to drown in, gleaming with promise.

"I want to know you better, Hannah, and I want you to know me—if you're interested."

She scooted closer, laying her thighs over his. "That kiss on the beach wasn't clue enough? I'm interested, Xander." She held his gaze for a long, smoldering moment, then sighed and leaned back against the bench. "Okay—obligatory relationship history rundown. Never married, but I've had serious relationships. Three, if that matters. They all ran their course. I've been single for a few years now." Her sardonic laugh sounded desert-dry. "You know what they say about three strikes. Maybe I'm just no good at relationships."

He gave her leg a squeeze. "Or maybe those three guys weren't good at relationships."

She lifted a shoulder. "They're all good people. We just had different ideas about what makes a good life. The last one wanted to get married, but after Mom and Dad's split, I didn't have the stomach for it—standing up in front of all your friends and family, swearing to love each other till you die... Half the people who make those vows are lying."

A weight settled in his chest. She'd been honest with him about her history, an act of trust. He owed her the same. "I wasn't lying when I made them."

"Oof." She scooted backward, lifting her legs from his lap. "Let me pry this foot out of my mouth. I'm sorry, Xander. That was mega insensitive of me."

He shrugged. It took a few years of therapy to get to this point, but he was finally able to think about his brief marriage without regret or bitterness. "We were college sweethearts, both business majors. We got married a week after graduation."

She waited patiently, her eyes never leaving his face.

"We were too young, neither of us fully baked, you know? After a few years, we drifted apart. She went into green cosmetics, got all crunchy granola, moved to SoCal, met a guy who makes kombucha, had a bunch of free-range kids. We're still friends." In fact, he looked forward to Heather's Christmas cards adorned with photos of her family. This year, they'd dressed as chefs and posed in the middle of baking cookies, their faces dusted with flour and smeared with icing. They seemed happy.

Hannah stroked his arm with her fingertips. "Nobody since then?"

His cheeks heated. "I mean, I'm not a monk, but I haven't really prioritized relationships. Kind of hard to do that while building a business." Since his divorce, he'd nearly convinced himself he wasn't the coupled-up type. He had his family, a few friends—though not as many as he'd like. And he had no trouble finding willing women for casual hookups when the loneliness got to him.

He laid his arm across the seatback. A tendril of chestnut hair had escaped her wind-whipped ponytail. He wound it around his finger. "Meeting you has been a wake-up call, Hannah. I can't stop thinking about you, can't stop wanting you."

The corners of her lips lifted as she removed the elastic, freeing her hair to fall in shiny waves around her shoulders. "A little crush can be a powerful distraction."

If that wasn't an invitation, he wasn't Greek.

He plunged his fingers into warm silk, and she let her head loll back into his touch.

"A crush?" he murmured into her ear. "Is that what I am to you? Because what I feel for you is so far beyond that." He gently kneaded her nape.

She didn't answer his question, just stared out through the window at the gathering darkness outside.

Damn. He'd killed the mood with this heavy talk of feelings. He cleared his throat and shifted away. "Well, the water should be hot by now."

Hannah chewed her lip, a tell she displayed when debating with herself. Then, bless all the tiny angels, she lifted her legs onto his lap again and placed her palm over his thundering heart. "You know, I can't get Zora's words out of my head."

Xander froze, unsure of her intent. Moving gingerly, he rested his hand on her knee. She nestled into his side and nuzzled the crook of his neck with a sexy hum that electrified his nerves.

"Zora says my rumination is blinding me to possibilities." She traced his jawline with her fingertip. "And meeting you has opened my eyes to what I've been missing."

Desire roared through him, as powerful as the surf. He held his breath while she studied his face for a long moment, then pressed her lips to his.

It took every ounce of control he had not to plunder her hot, wet mouth, but he restrained his inner beast and let her take what she wanted.

Her breath fanned over his cheek. "Is this okay, Xander?"

"Okay? This is fuckin' magnificent." He pulled her to straddle him and filled his hands with the soft curves of her ass.

Kissing Hannah was a revelation of all that a kiss could be, a gliding dance of thrust and parry, an exploration, sharing breath and heat and taste. She suckled his lip, and each deep pull echoed in his groin until his whole body pulsed with need.

She shifted, pressed her heated softness against his erection, and *sweet Jesus,* she felt so good he nearly died. When he clasped her bare thighs, she moaned, low and sultry. But while he was fumbling with the belt of her robe, she gracefully slid off him and rose to her feet.

"You know," she said with a devilish grin, "It's always tricky figuring out the hot and cold water in a new shower. Come give me a hand?"

With a swift gesture, she dropped the robe and stood before him wearing only her clingy sweater and green satin panties. Crooking a finger, she beckoned, then turned and sashayed to the bathroom, her lush hips swaying.

"Yes, ma'am." He scrambled to follow her.

Heart hammering, core tingling, Hannah pumped feigned confidence into her sultry walk and prayed Xander would take the bait before she chickened out.

The way he ran his fingers through her hair ignited a flame. Hell, everything about the man was enticing—his voice, deep and rich as dark chocolate; his seductive, long-lashed eyes; his flirty banter, his slow touch, as if he wanted to memorize every inch of her body.

He followed hot on her heels, but the RV's little bathroom was barely big enough for one. So much for her idea of a sexy shower à deux.

She turned to find him inches away, his eyes glittering.

"It's, uh, tight in here." She gestured lamely toward the tiny shower stall.

His lips spread in a devilish grin. "There you go again with the dirty talk." He inched his hands inside her pullover. Callused fingertips scratched deliciously over her bare skin. "May I?"

Breathless, she nodded.

He slid the sweater up and over her head, drinking her in with his ravenous gaze. "Ooh, Hannah." He tossed the garment onto a towel rack, then skated his palms over her from ribs to hips, leaving a wake of goosebumps.

Glad she'd worn a matching bra and panty set for once instead of her usual mismatched undies, she sucked in her stomach and cocked a hip. She needn't have bothered posing, though, because Xander's rapturous expression made it clear how much he liked what he saw, not to mention the erection tenting his gray sweatpants.

"My turn." She reached for the hem of his Henley, but he beat her to it and whisked the soft, worn shirt over his head, revealing breathtaking, sculpted pecs dusted with dark hair that flowed into an arrow down his taut belly.

"You are stunning," she murmured. His back was a landscape of rolling muscly hills, his waist narrow, and the contrast between satin skin and crisp chest hair stoked her desire.

"Quit stealing my lines, woman." He bunched her hair in his fist and pressed a hot kiss to the sensitive skin behind her ear. And then, God help her, he gently tugged, and sparks of pleasure skittering down her spine to pool between her thighs.

This was beyond want. What she felt in Xander's arms was urgent need, the kind that couldn't be denied.

His hands slid down to her ass, snugging her tight to his body while he clutched and kneaded her glutes. His hot, heavy cock pulsed against her stomach.

"I've got to taste you, Hannah," he growled.

"Ah ah ah, not before washing off all this sand." Teasing, she wriggled from his embrace and flipped her hair forward. "Help me with this clasp?"

The noise he made landed somewhere between a groan and a laugh, but his nimble fingers quickly unhooked her bra and peeled off her panties.

Funny, she expected to feel tight with self-consciousness. She certainly had the first time she stood nude before past lovers. But Xander's worshipful gaze urged her to be bolder, wilder.

She reached for the shower faucet. "Hot is this way?"

"Hot is anywhere you are, beautiful." Reaching past her, he adjusted the water until it flowed perfectly warm. "Can I scrub your back?"

"Of course." She gave him her wickedest smile and stepped under the spray. With Xander watching her through the open shower door, the droplets felt like tiny kisses on her sensitized skin.

When he shoved his sweats down his strong legs, Hannah's mouth watered at the sight of his long, sturdy cock bobbing up to smack his belly.

She crooked her finger, then gathered her hair to one side and gave him her back. With no real room to maneuver, Xander pressed tight against her, his water-slicked skin sliding over hers as he filled his palm with shower gel and glided his hands over her from nape to ass.

When he reached around to mold her breasts with hot, soapy hands, she leaned back onto his body and moaned in bliss.

And when his thumbs circled her taut nipples, her knees buckled.

His hand glided down her belly and over her mound, and she saw stars.

With a light, teasing touch, he soaped her throbbing sex, then pulled the shower head from its bracket to part her folds with a gush of warm water.

Hannah jolted and yelped.

"Too much?" Chuckling, he continued down her body, hosing the sand from her legs and feet. She watched it swirl down the drain as she struggled to catch her breath.

When the water turned cold, Xander apologized for the tiny tank and stepped out. He enfolded her in a fluffy towel. "Your throne, my queen."

Laughing, she sat on the toilet lid. "You really are a cheese monger, aren't you?"

"Can't help it. The sight of you naked fries my brain." He crouched at her feet, his erection jutting as he blotted the water from her legs and feet. Grasping her knees, he eased them apart and stared at her pussy, his eyes glittering. "So pretty, all flushed and pink."

He kissed the inside of her knee, then feathered kisses up her thigh.

She clutched the counter to keep from falling. "Xander."

"Mmm?" He nibbled and licked the sensitive skin of her inner thigh. His hot breath fanned her clit.

"Xander!" Bolting upright, she planted her foot on his chest and pushed him away.

He blinked up at her, face flushed, lips wet and glistening.

"Don't you have a bed in this place?"

He gaped for a moment, then doubled over with laughter, his damp curls soft on her thigh. "Forgive me, beauty. Lost my mind there for a minute."

With a sexy grunt, he stood and let her blot most of the water from his body before encircling her waist and towing her to the bedroom.

He flung the accordion door open, seized her mouth in a searing kiss, and tumbled backward onto the mattress, carrying her with him.

Hannah straddled him, planted her hands on his heaving chest, and pushed up to drink in the sight of his strong body, the muscular curve of his shoulders, the rapid rise and fall of his belly, and the naked hunger simmering in his eyes. Something dangerously close to joy simmered in her veins and danced over her skin. Trailing her fingertips over his pecs, she rocked her pelvis against him, and he bucked his hips, bringing his marble-hard cock into perfect alignment with her clit.

The room around receded into soft focus until all she saw was Xander, all she felt was his skin, his firm body beneath her, his breath in sync with hers. He gripped her hips, strong fingers digging into her flesh, and arched up off the bed as his cock slid between her slick folds in slow thrusts that turned her blood to flame.

Her muscles jolted, and she felt the electric tingle of approaching climax. Though she yearned to prolong this delicious sensation, she was rapidly losing control.

Folding forward, she claimed a deep, hot kiss. "I need you now, Xander."

He smiled into their kiss. "Let me taste you first."

"No." She hadn't intended to sound so harsh, but her hunger was too strong. "I mean, later, and yes please, but right now I need to feel you moving inside me."

"You're bossy." He flashed a feral grin. "I like it." Banding her ribs with one arm, he scooted her up to suckle first one breast, then the other, each deep pull drawing sharp pleasure from her clit. With his free hand, he fumbled the nightstand drawer open and extracted a strip of foil packets.

She watched, panting, as he quickly rolled the sheath over his ruddy cock. She lifted onto her knees, notched him at her entrance, and sank down on a long, ragged moan. *Heavenly* was too weak a word for this sensation as he stretched and filled her, impossibly hard inside her softness. Together they undulated, swaying slowly at first until they found their rhythm. Xander's eyes fluttered closed on a gasp. Gripping her nape, he pulled her to his chest and breathed her name like a prayer.

She rode him, and he rocked against her, slow and deep, each thrust a delicious shock, tightening her nerves to the point of unbearable bliss. For a moment, they poised together at the top of the wave, eyes locked, mouths gasping—and then the surge crested, tumbling her down, down into a vortex of ecstasy. Xander followed, head thrown back, strong throat working as he growled her name one last time, his cock pulsing deep inside her.

Panting, slick with sweat, they clung together. When she finally moved to roll off him, he held her tighter. "Stay with me, Hannah."

"Can you breathe with me on top of you like this?"

He chuckled into the crook of her neck. "Breathing is overrated. I just want to feel you." His hands stroked lazy arcs and spirals over her skin. "Every inch of you is delicious."

She rose onto her elbows and smoothed his hair back from his damp forehead. "That was—" She giggled. "I don't even have words."

"Right?" He kissed the tip of her nose. "Indescribable." With a playful whoop, he rolled her underneath him. Propped on one forearm, he peppered her breasts and belly with comically loud smooches. "I want to spend the rest of my life naked with you."

Laughing, she squirmed beneath him. "How are we going to do our jobs from this bed?"

He nuzzled her ribs. "Work from home is a thing. Haven't you heard?"

She wriggled away. "Your beard tickles."

"I'll shave it off." He sprang to his knees.

Up till now, she'd had only glimpses of his playful side. She liked it. A lot.

"I happen to love your scruffy jaw." She looped her arms around his neck and pulled him down for a kiss, soft and sweet. "It's sexy. You're sexy."

When he came up for air, something had shifted behind Xander's eyes. His expression became solemn.

She braced herself as a thread of fear wound around her heart and squeezed.

"Hannah, I'm falling in love with you."

She opened her mouth, but all that emerged was a squawk.

"That's what I was afraid of." He rolled onto his side, snugged her against him, and stroked his fingers into her hair. "But hear me out, okay?"

She nodded, too tongue-tied to do otherwise. Because love? Holy flaming poop on a stick, how had they leapfrogged so far in just one hot encounter? And why was her heart dancing a frantic samba inside her ribs?

She couldn't be in love with Xander. It was too soon. She hardly knew him...and couldn't stop thinking about him, about ways to help with his shop, about how to keep him in Trappers Cove...

He rested his cheek on his biceps, a sight so entrancing she nearly swooned. What would it be like to wake up to that view every morning? To fall asleep in his arms?

She yanked hard on the reins of her runaway imagination and tried to focus on his words, and not the mesmerizing play of his fingers in her hair.

"I know how crazy this sounds. And I don't expect you to be there yet. But I've spent so many years telling myself I wasn't destined for love, that I could do without it."

Damn it, she did know, because she'd told herself the same lie.

"And maybe it's Zora's tarot cards, or some kind of beach magic, or even Gus's ghost pushing us together, but this,"—he took her hand and placed it over his heart. Its strong beat thrummed beneath her palm. "This is real, and I'd be a fool to deny it just because it arrived at an unexpected time."

"I, um…" She couldn't think straight while pinned by those pleading eyes, so she trained her gaze on his broad chest instead.

If I let myself love you and you leave me, I'll crumble to dust.

Her rational brain knew that wasn't true. She'd weathered breakups before, and she had the strength to do it again. But leaving Xander? That would be devastating. On the other hand, shutting down this amazing attraction because it scared her? That would be stupid and cowardly.

She stroked his flat pec. "I'm not ready to talk about love yet, but I like you a lot. And I want to explore this connection we've got." She gave a dry chuckle. "That's a bit terrifying to admit, considering my history."

"Hey." He cupped her cheek, his touch warm and reassuring. "Your past doesn't define you."

"And your curse doesn't define you."

"Huh." His gaze shifted away. "You know, it's funny. I've made that stupid imaginary curse the focus of my life for so long, I haven't stopped to consider what would happen if I just…let it go."

She traced a circle around his heart. "I'd love to see what happens when you do."

His smile bloomed slow and sweet and a tiny bit naughty. "Well then, I'll have to stick around." His fingertip circled her areola. "Would you like that, Hannah middle name Leone?"

She laughed, and God, did it feel good to laugh with this delicious man. "It's Elisabetta. And I'd like that very much, Xander shmrr-shmrr Anagnos."

His laughter shook the mattress. "It's Ioannis. That's Greek for John."

"Ioannis. I like it." She grasped his hand and flattened it over her breast.

"I'm so glad." His smile simmered with wicked mischief. "Now, about that taste you denied me." He waggled his eyebrows and slid down, down, down until he was crouching between her thighs. "Look at you, Hannah. You're glorious."

One swipe of his tongue, and her mind blanked. All she knew was Xander, wanting him, needing him, and God help her, loving him.

Chapter Fourteen

The third Saturday in March dawned blustery, clear, and bright, one of those days where Xander's ability to concentrate on boring plumbing repairs flagged whenever he glanced out the window.

The plumber doffed his stained ball cap. "For the record, I think you're making a mistake."

Not the first time he'd heard that line from a contractor, but desperate budgets called for desperate shortcuts, even if it meant holding the building together with duct tape and bubble gum.

For the time being, if he had any hope of re-opening by Memorial Day, he'd have to get by on a wing, a prayer, and the bare minimum patchwork repairs to bring the old hulk up to code. Next winter, once he built up his cash reserves, he'd tackle more in-depth upgrades to pipes, wiring, and roofing.

Time to put Hannah's big talk about 'Trappers Cove takes care of our own' to the test.

He conjured up his best sad-puppy expression. "Listen, Joe, I'm really backed into a corner here, and I need your help."

The old guy snorted. "Okay, son, don't get weepy on me." He lifted an enormous pipe wrench. "I'll patch 'er up again, just like Gus has been doing for the past five years. But I can't guarantee how long it'll last. Best you put up one of those signs about what not to flush."

"Right—paper towels, lady products, hopes and dreams." He'd make the biggest sign ever seen in a public restroom.

Feeling a buzz in his pocket, Xander pulled out his phone. A big, goofy smile stretched his lips as he read Hannah's invitation.

> **You work too hard, X. Take a break? We'll check out few more places in TC.**

> **I'll have you back by two. Space Scout's honor.**

What did she have planned? Maybe a quick nooner in her apartment over the *Beacon*? Though his hips and back were a little stiff from all their bedroom activity since that first delicious romp on Wednesday, the thought of more naked time with Hannah made his mouth water.

"Hey Joe, you okay without me for a while?"

The plumber gave a dismissive wave. "Go enjoy the day, kid. You're no use to me here."

Humming under his breath, Xander pulled on his jacket and trotted outside, happy and energized despite his heavy workload. Chalk it up to the power of mind-blowing sex.

Though they hadn't yet discussed their relationship status, Hannah had spent the last three nights in his bed. Already, it seemed natural and right to wake wrapped around her soft warmth in what he'd come to think of as their little love nest.

Of course, he couldn't live forever in an RV. He'd need bigger quarters in TC, especially if he ended up relocating here permanently—an appealing possibility with Hannah in the mix.

Who'da thunk it? Me, city boy to my bones, happy in a Podunk beach town?

His head filled with sunny daydreams, he trotted kitty-corner across the street to The *Beacon*'s office. Just like every other building on Main Street, his own excepted, Hannah's was decked out for Saint Patrick's Day with glittering green tinsel garlands crisscrossing the front windows and paper shamrocks taped to the glass.

Funny, he'd been crushing so hard on Hannah, but he'd yet to visit her workplace. It reminded him of a 1970s newsroom movie set, with its worn black and white tile floor, old-school metal desks, and olive-green partitions covered with photo calendars and sticky notes.

The attractive, sixty-something woman with Hannah's bright eyes and thick, wavy hair stood to greet him, wincing as she pushed to her feet. "About time, darling." The strong family resemblance extended to the warm smile she gave him. "I'm Linda Leone, Hannah's mom."

Not content with a handshake, she pulled Xander into a tight, squishy hug. "I'm so sorry about your loss. Your uncle was well loved. We're all glad to know you'll be continuing in his footsteps."

Guilt pinged behind Xander's forehead. Had Hannah led her mom to believe he'd be hawking alien schlock? Or did she just assume, like all her fellow Trappers Cove-ians? He would disabuse them of that notion soon enough. And despite their sweet, stubborn attachment to Gus's little green visitors, they'd come to appreciate his new, improved, classed-up shop when it brought even more shoppers to Main Street.

"Delighted to meet you, Ms. Leone."

"Oh bosh. It's Linda." She gave him a quick once-over. "You're the spitting image of your uncle when he was your age. I was married back then, but all us young women envied Marty her handsome husband." She chuckled. "Hell, that went for the older gals too."

Xander smiled on the outside but winced inwardly. If this was how Gus looked at almost forty, did that mean he'd end up a pot-bellied, flush-faced oldster like his uncle? Because if Hannah aged as attractively as her mother, he'd need to stay on top of his game.

"So, I hear you've got big plans for the new and improved Souvenir Planet." Linda smiled expectantly.

He chuckled. "Like mother, like daughter. As I told Hannah, I'll share my plans when I'm ready and not until then."

Still smiling, she shrugged. "Can't blame a reporter for trying."

"Xander, there you are." Hannah bustled out from behind one of the room dividers, hair rumpled, blouse askew, a smudge of black across her cheek. "Sorry, had to wrestle a paper jam."

Heat licked his skin at the sight of her, beautifully mussed, as if she'd just emerged from his bed—exactly where he wanted her right now.

He sucked in a deep breath and forced a casual smile. "You print the newspaper here?"

"No, we use a printer in Pacific Shores, but we still need the copy machine, and it seems to be possessed by demons at the moment."

Mrs. Leone gestured to her cheek. "Darling, you've got toner—"

"Ugh." Hannah snatched a tissue from a box on her mother's desk and scrubbed at the spot. "That's me, always professional." She stood patiently as her mother straightened her blouse, then pecked her mom's forehead, shrugged into her blazer, and grabbed her camera. "All set. Ready for a little adventure?"

Xander cocked his arm. "Where are we going?"

He admired her unconscious grace as she slid her arm through his, like they'd been moving in tandem all their lives. "Farmer's market first. It's opening day after the winter hiatus. Then I've got a surprise for you before lunch, if you have time."

"Sea Dragon?" Mrs. Leone called after them.

"Yup. Want your usual?"

"Please and thank you. Have fun, you two. Don't do anything I wouldn't do." Her laughter tinkled with merriment. "And there's not much I wouldn't do at your age."

Hannah tugged him out the door and away from her mother's teasing. "Sorry. Mom worries about me ending up alone like her. Makes her a little too eager to see me paired up."

"I don't mind. She's sweet. Also pretty and sharp as tacks, just like her daughter." He spun her around and smooched her lips. He liked kissing her in public, claiming her for everyone to see. And judging by her glowing smile, she didn't mind being claimed.

"So, farmer's market, huh?" He slung his arm over her shoulders as they walked.

"Yup. First of the season is always extra fun."

"You know what'd be even more fun?" He waggled his eyebrows.

Hannah bumped him with her hip. "This is my job, Xander." But her grin and flushed cheeks proved her thoughts were just as dirty as his.

Most of Trappers Cove streamed toward the sound of guitar music and the scent of kettle corn wafting from the town's little park. Flowerbeds surrounding the lawn had been refreshed with bright pansies, and vendor booths lined the gravel paths, their awnings snapping in the coastal breeze. In the quaint gazebo, town council members handed out fliers for community events. Squealing kids chased each other around a bronze statue of a fishing crew hauling in a net.

Hannah snapped shots of the merry ruckus. "This one's a memorial to fishermen lost at sea. And that one—" she pointed to a marble bust of scowling, jowly man— "is George Arthur Baron, founder of Trappers Cove." A fat seagull flapped down to roost on the founding father's head. Served him right, grumpy old fart.

"Is he the guy who built the castle up on the north bluff?"

"That's him." Hannah panned the crowd, snapping more photos. "Hey, did you hear? The castle's occupied now. Some tech investor guy bought it and is converting the old school building into a community center."

"Rich benefactor, eh?" Xander gave her waist a squeeze. "Why not tap into that?"

Hannah bristled. "I beg your pardon? Besides, he's dating Annie Scott from the antiques shop."

"No, no, I—" He doubled over, laughing at his own ridiculous blunder. "I mean, why not ask him to bail out the *Beacon*?"

She tilted her head back and regarded him through narrowed eyes, though the beginnings of a smile twitched her lips upward. "You sure about that?"

"Sweetheart." He grasped her hips and snugged her tight against him. "I have zero interest in sharing you with another man."

"Even if it means saving the *Beacon*?" She was teasing now, her eyes alight with mischief.

"I'd deliver every newspaper personally before I'd agree to that."

When she gave him a skeptical look, he added, "In my dinosaur boxers."

Giggling, she goosed his butt. "Don't tempt me. You know I'm desperate to save my newspaper."

"Then seriously, why not ask the rich guy?"

Her sigh fanned his cheek. "Honestly, I've thought about it. But I need the *Beacon* to succeed on its own merit. Old Mrs. Jankowski never tried to influence our reporting, but a new benefactor might. And relying on some rich guy's good graces makes us vulnerable, you know?"

Xander nuzzled her hair. "I get it. You've got something to prove—to your mom and to yourself." He, of all people, understood exactly how that felt.

"Something like that, yeah." She held him for a long, sweet moment, then stepped back and blinked hard. "Okay, let's go explore."

They stopped at every booth, chatting with vendors of everything from empanadas to gleaming fruits and veggies to goat-milk soap. They joined a gaggle of kids listening to a local author read from his picture book about pelicans. The musician warbling about spring days and bumblebees turned out to be Alysson Lee, sister of Hannah's bookseller friend Daphne and brewery owner Ryan. He shook her hand, grateful she didn't ask about aliens or UFOs.

Farther down the path, they passed a purple tent with flapping Tibetan prayer flags. Inside, Zora was giving a tarot card reading. The old hippie mama glanced at their joined hands and gave him a wink.

Their last stop was a plant vendor, his already picked-over shelves holding potted herbs with hand-lettered signs. "Good Vibes Garden," he read aloud.

A familiar face popped up behind the shelf. "What's up, Hannah? Hey, Xander." Gemma, Zora's niece from the crystal shop, grinned knowingly. "Did you take Aunt Zora's advice?"

A beefy, bearded dude in a flannel shirt and overalls draped his arm over Gemma's shoulders. "Always take the Moore women's advice."

"Hi, Jesse." Hannah introduced them. "Meet Xander Anagnos, Gus's nephew. This is Jesse del Toro, herb farmer extraordinaire."

Jesse gave him a solemn nod. "Sorry to hear about Gus. Good guy. So, you guys together now?"

Gemma poked his ribs. "Duh. They've been together for a while."

Jesse raised his bushy eyebrows. "Well, how would I know? I spend most of my time on the farm, minding my own business." He lifted his chin. "Congrats, man. She's a good one. Helped me out with a big story when last year's storm destroyed my greenhouses. That online fundraiser saved my bacon."

Hannah ducked her head and blushed cotton candy pink, a shade so pretty Xander wanted to taste her skin—again. "No need for thanks, Jesse. That's what family's for."

"You guys are related?" he asked Hannah.

Gemma laughed. "She means our TC family. You're part of it now."

Xander reined in an eye roll. They were laying it on thick with this town-as-family stuff. In his experience, family equaled pressure to do things the family way. He sure as shit didn't need more of that in his life.

Moving on, they picked up croissants and coffees from Garrett's stand, which earned them another knowing grin. Each loaded up complimentary cloth tote bags with fruit and veggies for their respective fridges. Xander reflected—he hadn't really cooked a proper meal since coming to Trappers Cove.

"I'll have to make you dinner sometime. Show off my amateur chef skills."

"When?" Hannah's smile sparkled with challenge.

"Uh, let me check my calendar."

She nudged him. "Right. I'll never see a crumb, will I?"

Oho, so it was like that. Never one to leave a dare unanswered, he snapped back, "Okay, you're on. Tomorrow night, my place, Greek dinner."

"Can't. Tomorrow's the St. Patrick's Day party at the Salty Dog Saloon. You're my date. And wear green. I may get violent if other women pinch you."

"Noted." Neither of them owned the other, of course, but hearing her claim him like that filled him with a rosy glow.

"Ready for our next stop?" Hannah asked.

"Does it involve privacy and the chance to pick up where we left off this morning?"

She pecked his lips. "No and no. I've got another story to cover, and it involves you."

He took her sack and looped his free arm around her waist. Side by side, they crossed Main Street and strolled up Dunes Avenue.

"Mini golf? Are you kidding me?"

"I never kid about the important stuff." Her tone was perfectly serious, but she didn't quite hide her grin as a gangly teen handed them clubs and colored golf balls—neon pink for her, acid green for him.

"Gram's running a little late," the kid said. "She'll come find you in a minute."

They teed up behind a family with three squealing preschoolers. The oldest rushed over to hug Hannah around the knees, clobbering her with his tiny golf club.

At the first hole, a six-foot lighthouse, Hannah wiggled her butt enticingly while lining up her shot.

Xander leaned on his club. "Really? We're doing this?"

She waved him off. "Relax and have some fun! You must've come to this place as a kid."

"Yeah, sure." He scanned the chipped, faded obstacles. "Looks like it hasn't been painted since then."

Hannah sent her ball gliding up the plastic turf path. "It's all part of the Trappers Cove vibe. Nova adds a new obstacle each year."

Smooth as butter, her hot-pink ball rolled through the lighthouse door, triggering a flash of light from the glass cupola. She hooted and pumped her fist. "Hole in one, baby! You're up."

Xander was a mediocre golfer at best, and he hadn't played in years, but he couldn't have Hannah thinking he was a no-fun stick in the mud. He made it to the lighthouse in three putts, the pelican's mouth in two, and by the time he sank a hole in one in the metal loop de loop, his forced grin gave way to genuine laughter. "Move over, Tigress Woods. I'm coming for ya."

Hannah smooched his cheek. "Oho. Our Xander has a competitive streak."

"It's my Aries nature." He hooked his fingers into curly horns. "We keep battering away until we reach our goal."

She ruffled his hair. "Didn't you say you weren't a woo-woo kind of guy?"

"Must be the TC vibe sinking into my bones." Capturing her waist with his free arm, he snugged her close and nuzzled her neck. She squealed with laughter, and if they weren't surrounded by families with kids, he'd explore what other ticklish spots she was hiding under that businesslike blazer.

"Careful," she protested, "Don't wanna scare the littles."

"They've gotta learn about the birds and bees somehow."

A raspy laugh broke them apart. A seventy-something woman stood behind them, hands on hips, her salt and pepper hair in a long braid, a merry grin creasing her weathered face. Just his luck, she wore a Souvenir Planet hoodie, the one with the surfing alien.

"Put that in your article, Hannah," she crowed. "Treasure Chest Mini Golf is the perfect spot for a romantic date."

Red-faced, Hannah introduced them. "Xander Anagnos, meet Nova Reyes, owner of this fine establishment."

Her face went solemn as she enveloped his hand in both of hers. "I'm so sorry about Gus, hon. He was a good man, and so are you for filling his big ol' shoes." She turned to Hannah. "Ready for the unveiling?"

She raised her camera. "Can't wait."

They followed Nova past a lumpy cement dragon, a neon orange crab, and a mangey pirate.

"Here he is, the pride of Trappers Cove." The old gal yanked away a tarp, revealing a four-foot, bug-eyed alien, painted a bilious green and waving from an open-top flying saucer. "Meet Gus, our newest obstacle."

"He's beautiful." Hannah elbowed Xander.

He choked, cleared his throat, and tried again. "Really, uh, special."

Nova thumped her fist over her heart. "I wanted to honor my old friend, and what better way than to memorialize him in sculpture?"

"Indeed." He pinched his lips together hard to keep from laughing in the kind old woman's face.

Not one tiny bit fooled, Hannah stepped between him and the sculptor. "He's touched, Nova. Truly, this is lovely. Right, Xander?"

He nodded, feeling his face heat.

The old gal fished a packet of tissues from her hoody pocket.

"Thank you, ma'am." He turned his back and pantomimed wiping his eyes. Good Lord, what was with these people and their attachment to Gus's little green men? Everyone he'd met—and with Hannah's help, he'd met everyone from the shoe repair guy to the librarian to the mayor—they all asked about his plans for the damn aliens.

What they didn't know, and what Xander wouldn't share out of respect for his well-loved uncle, was what Gus's UFO obsession had cost him. His bank records revealed a once-fat balance worn down to whisper-thin over the past five years. If Gus hadn't passed, he'd probably have been forced to sell the place. So Xander's distaste for the schlocky alien merchandise wasn't just a personal preference—he was pissed at the little green buggers for hijacking his uncle's nest egg *and* his sanity.

To rebuild Souvenir Planet, Xander had to find a new focus.

But what? After visiting every shop in town and taking copious notes, inspiration still eluded him. Next week, he'd expand his search to nearby beach towns.

Ideas would probably flow faster if Hannah wasn't so damned intent on preserving Souvenir Planet as a shrine to her beloved past. Would she still care for him once he changed things up? The more he learned about her history, the more he understood her desire to cling to the good old days, but nostalgia wouldn't pay the bills. She and all the other UFO fans would have to be content with an alien corner in the new shop. Or an alien middle, since he can't move the damn cosmic transmitter without disturbing the so-called cosmic vortex. Just thinking about it curdled his stomach.

Hannah kissed the old gal on both cheeks. "Thanks so much, Nova. We've got to scoot now. Xander needs to get back to work soon."

Nova gave them each a tight hug. "Good luck to you, son. I know you'll make us all proud."

I will, but you might not like it at first.

Hannah hooked her arm through his and started toward the beach. "Sorry, Nova's a talker. I hope you're hungry."

"I am, actually. Must be the sea air."

She led him to a low brick building with an ornate painted dragon arching over the doorway.

"Sea Dragon Chinese Cuisine." She tugged the door open, and a cloud of garlic and spices enfolded them. "Not fancy, but their lunch buffet is truly kick-ass."

A youngish guy showed them to a table by a trickling waterfall. His little daughter, who couldn't be more than four, trailed after and pointed to the goldfish swimming in the water feature's base. "That's Peppa and Zoe, and the black one is George."

"Very fine fishies," Xander assured the cute little squirt, who giggled and dashed behind her father's legs.

"Help yourselves to the buffet," her father said. "I'll bring your tea."

They filled their plates with fragrant noodles, savory and spicy stir-fried dishes, crispy fried wontons, and puffy battered prawns.

"Try the almond duck," Hannah urged him. "You won't be sorry."

"I'm gonna need a nap after all this." He added another scoop to his brimming plate, then waggled his eyebrows. "Care to join me for naptime?"

"Can't. I've got three interviews this afternoon. News is picking up, for once."

"I'm glad." He took his seat across from her and unwrapped his chopsticks. "So, things are looking up for the *Beacon*?"

She wrinkled her nose. "A little. Not enough."

"Anything I can do to help?" Crunchy batter shattered down his shirt as he bit into a succulent fried prawn.

She leaned an elbow onto the table and fluttered her eyelashes. "The bigger and sooner your grand re-opening, the better." She chomped into a spring roll and moaned, and his dick sprang to attention.

"I'll do my best, beauty." Which meant he'd better make up his mind about branding and merchandise damn quick. The dry wall guys were nearly done patching the ceiling, and the electrician would finish on Monday, putting an end to the flickering lights.

Unless Gus had other plans. One more big repair bill would blow his budget to smithereens.

As they pushed their empty plates away and patted their overstuffed bellies, the little girl appeared again, followed by an elegant grandmother in an embroidered scarlet jacket. With a shy smile, she set a plate on their table and nodded encouragingly at its contents—two green blobs with teardrop-shaped eyes.

"Ma Ma made a special dessert for you," the little one told them. "It's aliens!"

"Why, that's so sweet of you, Mrs. Wong," Hannah cooed.

The girl bounced on her toes. "They're delicious. I already ated mine."

Her grandmother looked on expectantly.

Hannah lifted one and nudged his foot under the table.

"Right, let's see what aliens taste like."

Turns out this variety of E.T. was a fluffy steamed bun filled with sweet red bean paste—tasty indeed. He wiped his lips. "Really tasty. Thank you so much, Mrs. Wong."

The old woman gave a little bow. "You take good care of the store, okay?"

The young man joined them. "Ma loves shopping for her grandkids at Souvenir Planet."

"Seventeen," Mrs. Wong added, pantomiming sizes from tiny to tall.

The little girl thrust out her arm to display a slap bracelet. "Ma ma bought me this. It glows in the dark! It's my favorite." She removed it from her tiny wrist and slapped it around Xander's. Taking his cue, he admired it, then replaced it around her arm.

Hannah made a funny squawk and dabbed her eyes with her napkin.

Never wanted kids, huh?

The thought of disappointing the little cutie pinched his conscience. It wouldn't hurt to expand his limited selection of alien schlock just a bit. He owed that much to Hannah and the town that seemed intent on adopting him.

After a brief squabble over the check, which he insisted on covering, he helped Hannah into her jacket—not that she needed his help, but he enjoyed the smile these little courtly gestures brought to her lips. As they strolled arm in arm back toward Main Street, he asked, "So, was today part of your campaign to keep Souvenir Planet locked in a time loop?"

"Listen to you, Mr. Sci-fi." She bumped him with her hip. "I just want you to meet everyone and see how much they support you."

A noisy sigh slipped out before he could stop it. And of course Hannah noticed—the woman noticed everything. She spun him around to face her. "What's wrong?"

"Bills, mostly. Looks like I'm going to have to take out a bigger loan than I'd anticipated."

"For repairs?"

He nodded. "And inventory. Gus was operating on a paper-thin margin."

She planted her fists on her hips. "Then let us help."

"Us?"

"Trappers Cove." She circled her hand overhead, taking in the whole town. "There are lots of people with building skills who'll give you a friends and family discount."

"I'll, uh, think about." What he needed was qualified professionals, not a bunch of local fix-it dudes with good intentions.

"Promise me," she urged, eyes bright. "I want you to succeed, Xander."

She was hedging about something. He could see it in her twitchy expression. He could feel it in her tense body.

"Beauty, why are you so invested in Souvenir Planet?"

Her gaze shifted away, and her chest rose in a deep inhalation. "Because I'm sentimental. Gus's shop holds a lot of happy memories from before my family life went to shit." Scooting closer, she tucked her hands into his jacket pockets. "But mostly, because I want you to stay."

So many sensations ricocheted through his body—a bloom of warmth in his chest, a rush of desire that fizzed in his veins, and a prickle of tears that blurred his vision. She hadn't exactly declared her love for him, but this was one important step closer, but maybe this was her way of telling him.

He cupped her face in his palms. "Hannah, I need you to hear me."

She nodded, her glistening eyes never leaving his.

"Whatever happens with the shop, I'm committed to what we're building together. You're special to me, and I'm not going to run off and leave you, okay?"

Her forehead rumpled. "Oh, Xander." She threw her arms around his neck and slanted her mouth across his.

Onlookers be damned. He kissed her back with everything he had.

Chapter Fifteen

Xander pushed through the door of the Salty Dog Saloon and into a raucous green mob. Hannah was running late, so he'd agreed to meet her here, but how was he ever going to find her in this sea of partiers bopping to the "Irish" band's merry drinking songs?

The bar's crew had gone all out with the decorations. Green balloons floated in clusters from the deck railing outside and crowded the ceiling inside, interspersed with dangling metallic shamrocks and Irish flags. The glowing octopus at the corner of the bar had a green bowler hat, as did the wooden pirate captain at the entrance. Bartenders wore sequined green suspenders and headbands with glittery shamrocks that bounced as they whirled from taps to counter, filling orders for whiskey drinks and green beer.

Every table, booth, and spot at the bar was jammed with customers dressed in green T-shirts, hoodies, shorts, and even tutus, plus Mardi-Gras style beads, oversize sparkly glasses, and goofy hats.

He glanced down at his own pitiful costume: a T-shirt with three cartoon aliens in the classic 'See no evil, hear no evil, speak no evil' pose. His only green shirt was still in his Seattle apartment, so he'd raided Gus's leftovers. Oh well, at least it was green.

He squeezed into a corner of the bar facing the entrance and ordered a Jameson neat—much-needed liquid cheer to pump up his mood after the latest estimate: twelve thousand dollars to level the floor and replace the worn-out linoleum with something a little less tacky.

A young woman in spangled cut-off overalls bopped up beside him and poked the slogan across his chest. "Cute shirt! What happens in Trappers Cove stays in Trappers Cove." She batted her green-tipped false lashes. "I'm only here for the weekend. Wanna stir up some shenanigans?"

"Sorry." He wasn't, but there was no need to slam her for a request he'd have welcomed a month ago. "I'm seeing someone."

She pouted prettily. "Lucky girl. Hey, barkeep, we need five more Irish coffees." She pointed to a booth filled with equally young and tipsy giggle bunnies.

"Here ya go, Xander." The buxom, bristle-haired dandy set his drink on the bar and rolled her eyes. "Tourists, am I right?"

"Sorry, have we met?"

She extended a sticky hand and gave him a firm shake. "Quinn Zacoski. Sorry to hear about Gus, man. He was good people." She chunked ice into a tall glass, then poured green liqueur into her cocktail shaker. "I'm thinkin' I should create a drink in his honor. Something green and sweet and a little kooky, right?"

Her tone held no malice, but he winced all the same. Poor Gus, immortalized as a nut job.

A stout older guy muscled his way to the bar and greeted Xander with a broad smile and a back-slapping handshake. "Hey, it's Gus's nephew, right? Heard you might need a hand with your reno." He fished a business card from his wallet. "Sam Sparks. When you're ready for framing, gimme a call."

He scowled at the card. "Did Hannah send you?"

Sam rubbed the back of his neck. "Well, ah, she might've mentioned in passing…"

Xander's jaw tightened. No doubt she meant well, but he was perfectly capable of finding and vetting his own contractors. This was *his* project, damn it, and the more help he accepted, the more say those helpers would expect in his business decisions.

A buff, dark-haired young guy at Xander's elbow chuckled. "Living in TC is kinda like landing in a spider's web."

The older man snorted. "Terrible metaphor, Matteo. You're gonna scare the poor guy to death." He smacked Xander's shoulder. "Don't worry, son. TC ain't got no more spiders than any other town. What this knucklehead means is we're all connected here. Makes it hard to keep secrets, but it's easy to find help when you need it, as long as you're willing to help in return."

He tucked the card into his pocket. "Thanks. I'll keep that in mind." The old guy moved off, and Xander scanned the crowd again. Still no sign of Hannah.

Matteo nudged him with his elbow. "Sorry about Gus, man. Good guy. He never let life squash the fun out of him, you know?" He offered his broad, callused hand. "Matteo Verducci. I refinish furniture, upscale old pieces, do a little creative carpentry. Hey, I've got some salvaged sheet metal we could use to rebuild that UFO out front. You could put in some seats, make it a selfie spot for tourists."

Again with the space crap. Was the whole damn town conspiring to keep him mired in little green aliens?

Or was this Hannah's doing? And why was she twenty minutes late?

Matteo grinned over the rim of his beer glass. "Or I could help with new shelving. I heard yours keep falling down."

Xander's brows snapped together. "Did Hannah—"

"Naw, man. I help out at my uncle's gelato shop up the street. Your dry wall guy has a sweet tooth. Jittery type. He was spooked by the falling shelves. Said you've got a ghost." Matteo scoffed. "It's obviously just uneven floors, right?"

"Heyyy, Matteo." Two of the giggle squad trotted over and grabbed him by the elbows.

"See ya," he called over his shoulder. "Can't wait to see what you do with the place. Hi, Han." He shook off his groupies long enough to enfold Hannah, who'd just rushed in looking beautifully disheveled, in a big, rocking hug.

The sight of his lover's hands clutching Matteo's muscular back did nothing good for Xander's mood.

She extricated herself and hurried to his side, where she kissed his cheek and huffed her green-glitter-dusted hair out of her eyes. "Sorry. Mom had an episode. I had to make sure she was okay."

His irritation melted away. "What's wrong?"

"She gets migraines. This one was wicked. It made her throw up, and that twinged her bad back. I had to help her to bed and call Doc Rivas."

He grabbed her hand. "You should've called me. I could've helped."

"How?"

"I don't know, driving? Fetching medicine?" He pressed her palm over his heart. "If you're in need, Hannah, I want to help."

The irony smacked him full in the face. Here he'd been for the last twenty minutes, grumbling to himself about her interference with Souvenir Planet—most of which turned out to have nothing to do with her. And now he was butting his stubborn ram horns right into her family business.

She cupped his cheek. "Okay, Sir Galahad. Next time we have a crisis, I'll give you a call. Anyway, Marquetta came over to sit with Mom until the doc gets there. She'll be fine."

"Uh huh. Then why does your face look like that?"

"Like what?" She massaged the furrow between her brows.

"Like you want to rush back home and take care of your mom." He upended his glass and shivered at the sweet burn of Irish whiskey. "Let's go."

Just then, Hannah's phone shrilled. She pressed it to her ear. "Yeah? Uh huh. Okay." Her worried frown smoothed out. "Wonderful. Thanks so much, Doctor."

"Good news?"

She pocketed her phone and gave him the sweet smile he'd craved since he left her after lunch. "Doc prescribed something strong. She's feeling better already. I'll check on her later."

That meant no cozy night in his RV, but her mom's health came first.

Hannah greeted Quinn and ordered the cocktail special, an emerald martini garnished with sugar-dipped mint leaves. She sipped, then closed her eyes, licked her lips, and hummed a sexy "Mmmm."

Of course, Xander's dick responded as if she'd issued an invitation. He quickly adjusted himself so as not to embarrass her in public.

She surveyed the rowdy scene. "Great party, huh? Did you recognize Allyson from the farmer's market?"

"Right, the owner's sister."

Speak of the devil, Ryan Lee appeared behind the bar, all gleaming teeth and cocky posturing. "Hannah, babe, how's my favorite reporter?" He grabbed her hand and lifted it to his lips for a loud smack.

"Hanging in there." She firmly extricated herself and leaned her cheek against Xander's shoulder.

That's right, beer bro. She's with me.

Xander grinned, pleased she'd trusted her bad news to him and not to this model-perfect schmoozer.

Seemingly oblivious to Xander's discomfort, blondie guy gave him a wide grin. "So, how's it going with Gus's place?"

"It's Xander's place now," Hannah corrected him.

Ryan raised his palms. "Of course, of course. My bad. Old habits die hard, you know? So, Lilo and I were talking. If you give us a heads-up for your re-opening date, we'll dedicate one of our seasonal specials to you—Intergalactic Ale? Starship IPA?" He shot finger guns across the bar— "Pew pew, right?"—then took off to greet other customers.

Xander scrubbed a hand down his flushed face. "Why does everyone assume I'm all gung ho for Gus's aliens?"

She tilted her head and looked at him as if he'd asked why it was necessary to breathe. "Because that's what people love about your shop. Haven't you seen enough evidence of that?"

He sucked in a deep breath and summoned all the tact he could muster. "If the new shop is going to be a success, it has to reflect my own interests. It takes passion to make a small business thrive." No need to mention how this was starting to feel like a personal battle between him and those little green bastards.

He clasped her hands and kissed her knuckles. "I can't fake being passionate about UFOs the way Gus was."

She gentled her tone. "But you have to give your customers what they want, Xander. You've got a ready-made market." She angled her head and batted her lashes. Here it came, another pitch for the same old, same old.

"So listen." She snuggled beneath his arm. "I got an interesting message today from Colonel Malinowski."

That blowhard was the very last person Xander wanted to discuss right now. Or ever.

"He wants to meet with you about creating a retreat center for UFO believers. Says they can study the cosmic vortex, host conventions—"

"No!" He slammed his fist on the bar. "Absolutely not. How could you even suggest something so—" He grimaced, fighting for control. Had she heard nothing he'd said over the past month? Was she faking interest in him just to get her way?

He squashed that ugly thought down hard. After the passion they'd shared, after she'd opened her heart to him, he was beyond wrong to doubt her. But damn, when it came to this UFO bullshit, she was like a dog with a bone—and not in a fun way.

"Hey." She squared her stance and jutted her chin. "Look at me, Xander."

He complied, jaw clenched tight to bite back words he'd regret.

Her eyes glittered under the green lights. "It's *your* business. You and I can disagree, but that doesn't mean I don't respect you or care about you, okay?" Her brows contracted. Her nostrils flared. "I won't mention the aliens again, if that's what it takes to be your friend."

All the air left his lungs in a whoosh.

For his sake, this smart, beautiful, hard-headed woman was releasing a cherished memory. After such a traumatic loss, her attachment to those little green buggers made sense if seen through the convoluted logic of the heart.

"Hannah," he cupped her face in his hands. "I want to be so much more than your friend. And I don't want you to censor yourself around me." He pressed a soft kiss to her rumpled forehead. "But can we put a moratorium on the aliens for a while?"

She nodded.

"I promise you, I'm conducting solid market research."

She bit her lip, a sexy gesture that heated his blood.

"So, I have a question for you, beauty. It's kinda out of left field."

A seductive smile spread her lips. "Fire away."

"Do you have a bathtub I could borrow?"

Chapter Sixteen

Hannah's heart danced a nervous bachata as they mounted the narrow back stairs from the *Beacon* newsroom up to her apartment. She'd cleaned the place top to bottom last week in anticipation of this possibility, for cripes' sake. She'd even changed the sheets this morning on a weird hunch. But it wasn't the exertion or fear of dust bunnies that made her so jittery, it was the symbolism.

She was inviting him into her private sanctum to indulge in some very dirty fun, and her mother was sleeping—hopefully!—right across the narrow landing.

This was a big honkin' deal.

And here they stood, Xander's hands tunneling under her top as she fumbled for her elusive keyring. The bewitching sensation of his lips nibbling her nape wasn't helping her manual dexterity.

After a few bungled attempts, she fitted the key into the lock and whispered, "Come in before Mom sees us." Hell, she probably had seen them already, drawn to her peephole by the creaky stairs.

She hung her coat on a hook beside the door, toed off her boots, then nibbled her lip while Xander did the same and gazed around at her itsy-bitsy living space. "Make yourself at home." She hooked a thumb over her shoulder. "I'll, uh, go check on Mom."

She found her mother's bedroom door closed, and a note from Marquetta, TC's head librarian and Mom's good friend, on the dining table. "Doc sent some strong meds. Linda will probably sleep through the night. I'll check on her in the morning."

Just to be sure, she cracked open the bedroom door. Mom lay on her side, cuddled around the body pillow Hannah had given her for Christmas, her breaths deep and even.

Relief washed through her, quickly replaced by tummy butterflies as she crossed the landing. Xander sprawled on her sofa, his arms stretched across the back, his stockinged feet up on her coffee table. He glanced up at her approach, mouth curved in a smile. "I like your apartment. It really reflects you."

"How so?" She sashayed over to join him, faking confidence she didn't feel. Seeing him so at ease in her private space made their relationship—because as much as she feared admitting it, that's what this was—made it all seem inescapably *real*. Visiting him in his temporary quarters was one thing, but the sight of Xander all cozy and adorable between her sofa pillows, his feet beside her pile of *Vanity Fairs*, *New Yorkers*, and *Rolling Stones*...just *wow*. Her favorite guy in her favorite place was a powerful combination—and a tiny bit terrifying.

Xander laced his fingers behind his head, nestled among those silky, dark curls. "It's cozy here, colorful, welcoming." He threw her a killer grin. "Like you, love."

Oof. There it was again, the big L word, the one she'd been studiously avoiding since his declaration four days ago, because saying it aloud meant so much more than flirtatious fun and earthquaking sex—it meant big changes, maybe even rethinking her life's direction.

Nope, nope, nope. Coping with work and Mom's ill health was all she could handle right now. Her giddy heart would have to wait.

Needing a moment to breathe through her anxiety, she went to the kitchenette and brewed a pot of blackberry tea. "This place is charged with good vibes because it was built with love. When we lost our house, lots of people pitched in to renovate the *Beacon*'s upstairs offices into two apartments—one for Mom, one for me."

"Why two? Why not just one bigger apartment?"

"I was fifteen. Mom was looking ahead—figured her best shot at keeping me close was to give me my own space. And thank God she did. I doubt we'd get along as well if we shared the same apartment." Chuckling, she tapped her temple. "Linda Leone's a smart cookie."

"Like mother, like daughter." Xander accepted a steaming mug and inhaled the fragrant steam. "You've always lived here?

His question stirred up memories of living with Nathan—their sunny kitchen, the covered porch, the little veggie garden out back. When she realized she'd miss the house more than she'd miss the man she shared it with, she knew it was time to go.

"I've lived other places in the area, but I always come back here. It's tiny, but it's home."

His gaze shifted to the window and the glowing streetlights beyond. "Since I graduated from college, I've lived in..." He counted on his fingers. "...seven different apartments. I kind of like the starting over phase."

She forced a laugh past the lump clogging her throat. "You're not the rooted type. Me, I get attached to a place—not just the building, but the people, the vibe, the natural surroundings. It all combines in a way that feels right. Deep in the marrow of my bones, I know this is my home."

Xander set down his mug and swiveled to face her, winding her ponytail around his fingers. "You think you could feel that way somewhere else?"

"You mean leave Trappers Cove?" She shuddered. "I hope I never have to find out."

An awkward silence thickened the air between them. What must she look like to him, stubbornly clinging to her dinky apartment and her tiny newspaper? He'd promised not to leave her, but when the initial infatuation wore off, he'd grow restless and move on. How could she expect someone as bright and ambitious as him, someone who'd grown up in a big, glittering city like Seattle, to mesh with her small-town life?

She gave herself a mental shake. Xander was here beside her, warm and solid, his dark gaze glowing with desire. Yes, their future together was uncertain, so why not enjoy this sweet, fleeting moment?

Leaning into the pleasure of his touch, she lowered her lids and purred, "So, about that bath."

He nuzzled the sensitive crook of her neck, his lips soft and insistent. "Yes, please. Naked with you is my favorite place to be."

"In that case, follow me." She pushed up from the squishy couch and strolled to the bathroom, putting an extra swing in her step.

Xander followed with a low whistle that unleashed a waterfall of goosebumps. He detoured to retrieve a cellophane packet from his jacket pocket. "I've been carrying this around since last week. No bathtub in my RV, so..." He flashed a devilish grin.

She recognized the silver and purple label. "Zora's?"

"She says it'll wash away my curse."

"Well then." She cranked the hot water faucet to full blast. "Let's get to washing."

"Mmm." Winding one arm around her waist from behind, he tugged the elastic from her ponytail. "Sounds delicious."

How could she be anything but delighted by this playful, loving, horny man? She reached back and goosed his firm, jeans-covered butt. "You've got a bathing kink, don't you? First the shower, now this."

His laughter shook her. "You're opening up new worlds to me, Hannah."

She wiggled her ass into the cradle of his hips. "Here's where I say something about getting wet with you, right?"

"Always a welcome development, beauty." He slid his fingertips beneath her green satin blouse.

"Ah ah ah." She slipped out of his grasp. "Take off your own clothes while I set the scene."

Thanking Past Hannah for her foresight, she lit candles scattered around the tiny, cornflower blue bathroom, then switched on soothing saxophone jazz and dimmed the lights.

A very naked Xander drew her tight against his heated skin. "You have excellent setting-the-scene skills." His lips teased the shell of her ear. "I should hire you to decorate my shop."

"Nope. I'm keeping my nose out of your business decisions, remember?" She wriggled out of his embrace and whisked her blouse over her head. "Now, let's get to work lifting this curse."

She shucked her jeans and, clad only in a mint-green bra and panties, emptied Zora's potion into the tub and bent to swirl twinkling salt crystals into the gushing water.

Xanders hands settled on her hips. He hummed his appreciation, a low rumble that triggered an echoing pulse between her thighs.

But experience had shown her bathtub sex was better in horny imaginations than in cold, porcelain reality.

"Bath first. Let's clean away all that dark energy." She pivoted to face him. And hoo-boy, was he a glorious sight—full lips parted, broad, naked chest rising and falling as his glimmering gaze drank her in. And that cock! Ruddy and straight, bobbing with his pulse, its plush crown tipped with a crystal tear. *Yum.*

"Besides, I like ogling you. You're a beautiful man, Xander." She ran her fingertips over his pecs and down his sides to trace the indentation on the side of each muscular ass cheek.

Xander's eyes drifted closed. "Hannah, your touch is so... I don't even have words to describe the feeling. It's like you open me up and pour in starlight."

She felt it too, this sense of slipping the bounds of gravity and floating, weightless, just the two of them—a fragile joy made all the more precious because it couldn't last. Nothing this good ever did.

"In you go." She guided him into the tub. "Let's clear your aura so we can get on with the bedroom part of our St. Patrick's party."

While he settled against the porcelain curve, she sat on the low stool that usually held her bathtime tea—or wine, depending on how rough the day had been. With a plastic pitcher shaped like a pelican—bought long ago from Gus's shop—she sluiced water over his skin, admiring the artistic swirls it made in the dark hair on his chest and abs.

"Mmm, Zora's herbs smell nice."

"Very relaxing," he agreed.

Unable to resist a bobbing target, she swirled a fingertip around his stiff cock. "Part of you isn't relaxed."

Wicked intent sizzled in his grin. "Well, you're near, so..." He clasped her arms. "Come in, beauty. Share this curse-banishing bath with me. There must be some bad vibes you want to wash away."

He had a point—and not just the one pointing skyward between his sturdy thighs.

Ever since Mom broke the news of her impending retirement, Hannah had lived under a cloud of anxiety about the paper's future, which dulled her enjoyment of this blossoming connection with Xander. Why not give Zora's potion a go?

Humming along with the sexy sax, she stood and unhooked her bra, then shimmied out of her panties and carefully stepped between Xander's spread legs. The warm water felt silky against her skin. As she folded herself into the narrow space, his heated gaze glided over every inch of her.

"Oooh, Hannah. You are breathtaking." He skated his slick hands over her arms, down her sides, and up again to cup and knead her breasts, his thumbs teasing her nipples to stiff peaks. She closed her eyes and let her head loll back, reveling in the delicious sensations—warm water, strong muscles dusted with soft hair, satin skin beneath her palms, strong hands that gripped her hips and urged her forward.

"Hold on now." She wiggled away. "Bath sex isn't really as fun as it seems. Besides, we're gonna need more room."

His lips quirked up in a mischievous grin. "Bath foreplay?"

"First, we have a job to do." She cupped water in her hands and poured it over his collar bones, watching it slick over his flat nipples.

"Right." He settled back against the tub. "Let's get on with the curse-lifting before we get all pruney."

Giggling, she filled the pitcher and poured water over her tingling breasts. "I call on these magic waters to clear my fears and all the bad vibes dragging me down. Show me the way to new success for the *Beacon*. Abracadabra, alakazam. Your turn." She dunked the pitcher into the water and dumped its contents over his head.

Spluttering with laughter, he wiped water from his long, thick lashes. "Hey, warn a guy."

"Anointing your head is part of the process." She poured a stream over his bobbing dick. "You too, handsome. Okay, state your intentions."

He pulled a sour face. "I feel like an idiot."

She leaned forward to address his cock. "Your friend is killing the vibe, little guy."

Xander threw back his head and laughed. "Oho, ganging up on me? All right, here goes." He adopted a deep, ponderous tone. "Sacred waters, release the curse's hold on me. Let me..." He flapped a hand, "fly free and...find my own destiny. And if anyone tries to squash me down, let them..."

Hannah raised an eyebrow and whispered, "Pretty sure you're not allowed to curse anyone else. Kinda spoils the cosmic harmony, don't you think?"

He huffed a dramatic sigh. "All right, Ms. Buzzkill. If anyone tries to block my growth, may the force of this magic release them from their foolishness. Amen and Hallelujah." He punctuated his declaration with a huge splash of water that flew right up her nose.

"Oh yeah?" She splashed him back, dousing three candles.

"Yeah." He snatched the pitcher away, filled it, and dumped it over her head.

"You...you...sea monster!"

Splashing, squealing, and hooting with laughter, they flailed until the tub was half empty and the floor was soaked.

"C'mere, you." Ignoring her protests, Xander scooped her onto his lap. With nowhere to put her legs, she crossed them behind his back and surrendered to a wet, slippery hug. His lips claimed hers in a deep, passionate kiss that went on and on.

Finally, he broke the kiss and pressed his forehead to hers. "I think it's working."

"How can you tell?"

"I'm feeling all tingly." His fingertips traced dizzying spirals over her back, then down her flanks to dip beneath her knees. He scooped more water over her head and stroked his fingers through the wet strands. "Where's that shampoo of yours that smells so good?"

She handed him the bottle. He poured shampoo into his cupped palm and sniffed. "Ah, here it is. I love this scent. May I?"

When she nodded, he smoothed the fluid over her hair and worked suds into her scalp, pressing firmly with the pads of his fingers, a seductive, sensual massage that soon had her moaning.

"You know," he confessed as he wove his magic, "that day when we first met, finding Gus felt like a tsunami knocking me ass over heels, dragging me under." He filled the pitcher and cupped her nape while he poured warm water through her strands. "But you held me so tight. I remember burying my face in your hair, breathing in this scent." He pressed his forehead to hers. "You kept me from drowning, Hannah." His lips feathered over her arched throat. "I'm so grateful to you, so grateful to Gus or the aliens or whatever brought me here so I could meet you, know you, love you."

A heady swirl of emotion coursed through her—desire, joy, and the sweet, aching burn of new love, as intoxicating as whiskey, as irresistible as sirens' song. It would be so easy to whisper 'I love you' into Xander's kiss. But hard-won experience taught her that waves like this always crashed against the rocks.

She speared her fingers into his dripping curls and sealed her mouth to his, hoping her kiss would say all the sweet words she couldn't yet force from her tight throat.

His body tightened, just a flicker of tension. He knew.

But the tightness quickly passed. He relaxed into her kiss and stroked his tongue deep. "It's okay," he whispered when they broke apart on a gasp. "Just because I fell fast doesn't mean you have to. I know I'm asking a lot of you. I'll take it as slow as you need, Hannah."

Grateful, she nodded and dove in again, greedy for his taste, his skin, his firm, hot body beneath her and over her and in and all around her. She grasped his wrists and pulled his hands to her breasts.

"Listen," she panted against his temple, "I want to be with you, Xander. I want to know you, to share...so much with you. And I hate that I'm scared. But I promise you, I'll keep pushing through the fear."

His tongue swirled behind her ear, then his sharp teeth bit into her lobe, a flash of exquisite pain. Her clit throbbed in response.

"Maybe Zora has a potion for your cold feet."

"You goof." Grateful for the comic relief, she grabbed a handful of his slippery ass and pinched hard.

"Whoa!" He thrashed, splashing them both. "Let's get out of here before we drown."

She pressed her forehead to his. "On one condition."

"What's that, angel?"

"Are you cured?"

He blinked for a moment, as if translating in his head.

"Of your curse."

A wide grin spread over his face. "Curse? What curse?" With a whoop, he scooped her under the arms and lifted her to her feet. "I'm healed! Whole! A new man! To bed, good woman," he roared. "Now."

Giggling, she pointed, and he hoisted her into his arms and, still dripping, half strode, half skated over the floorboards and into the bedroom, where he tossed her onto the bed with a bounce. "Wow, you should see your tits jiggle. Magnificent."

With a comical growl, he dove on top of her.

"Shh." She clawed at his shoulder. "Mom's sleeping next door."

"Oh, that's right. Sorry," he stage-whispered and sat back on his knees, his cock bobbing upward. "Do you have condoms?"

"In the drawer."

Hannah considered her next move carefully. Whether she did or didn't call this feeling love, she craved more of Xander—more of his goofy jokes, his adoring gaze, his satin skin, his electric touch. "About the condom issue—"

He froze, curiosity written all over his flushed face.

"I'm on birth control, and I got checked out at my last doctor's appointment. Would you mind getting tested too so we can—"

He beamed. "Beauty, I got tested after my last, uh, liaison, and that was months ago."

A smile stretched her lips. "Well then." Heedless of the dampness, she lay back on the pillows, gave him a seductive smile, and parted her thighs.

He prowled over her on hands and knees, then lowered himself until only millimeters of heated air separated them. "Beauty, I'm going to love you so hard, you won't ever want to leave me."

The fat, blunt edge of his cock nudged at her entrance, once, twice. He shifted and rubbed his shaft over her clit, sparking pleasure so bright her whole body jerked with it.

"Beautiful Hannah," he murmured, peppering kisses over her face, down her arms, all the while grinding his shaft through her sopping folds—exquisite torture that had her undulating with each slow stroke. His mouth closed over her nipple—soft lips, sharp teeth that held the sensitive nub in place while his velvet tongue swirled and stroked.

A cry escaped her. She turned her head into the pillow to smother it.

"Don't hide, beauty. Let me see your eyes the first time I love you with nothing between us."

Barely breathing, she held his gaze and waited. His first shallow thrust parted her folds. The next nudged her open. And then he filled her in one smooth rush.

"Oh God Oh God Oh God," she moaned as he rode her, each stroke driving her higher until she quaked on the edge, helpless to do anything but hang on and ride.

"We belong together, Hannah." His fierce thrusts shook the bed frame and rattled her bones. "Even if you won't say it, I know you feel it."

She did feel it, an undeniable, irresistible surge of pleasure and emotion. Her will to resist him faltered with each delicious plunge into her flesh.

"Xander, I, I..." A blinding climax stole her words and blanked her mind. She was pure sensation, clutching his body so tight as his hips churned, hard and fast. With a feral groan, he reached his peak, and his cock pulsed inside her, flooding her with heat.

Slowly, as light as falling snow, she drifted back down to her damp bed and her panting lover, heavy atop her, his fingers snarled in her hair, his breath hot on her cheek. When he finally opened his eyes, so full of love and hope, her thundering heart overflowed with sweet, golden joy.

"Yes, Xander." She caressed his soft curls and pressed her gasping mouth to his. "I feel it too."

Chapter Seventeen

When the electrical crew deserted him, spooked by tools that seemed to move of their own volition and lights that flickered despite having the whole damn building rewired, Xander threw in the towel. Literally—he shut off the washroom's new faucet and chucked his soggy hand towel at the rumbling, quaking pipes.

"Okay, Gus, you win this round. Time to fire up the big guns. I'm calling Zora."

He hesitated before texting Hannah as well. On the one hand, involving her in this weird ride might open the can of aliens again, and he'd been enjoying their truce on that subject. On the other hand, she'd probably find Zora's ghost-removal process fascinating. Come to think of it, Hannah made an excellent filter between his skepticism and Trappers Cove's...well, quirkiness was a polite word for it.

> **Zora's coming at one to deal with my ghost problem. Want to come?**

They arrived together. While the psychic set up her paraphernalia, Xander huddled with Hannah behind the cosmic transmitter, now covered with a paint-speckled tarp.

"Listen, Han, you're not going to write this up for the *Beacon*, are you?"

"Of course not," she answered with a huff. "This is a private family matter."

"Right, it's between me and Gus's ghost, who seems determined to drive away all my workers."

Her eyes twinkled with amusement. "So you believe in ghosts now?"

"The contractors damn sure do." He circled a hand overhead, indicating the abandoned ladders and paint trays, gaping holes in the drywall, and crumpled tarps. "And I don't know how else to explain this. As soon as we fix a problem, it breaks again—the plumbing, the wiring, the tippy shelves."

This morning, he'd set a folder down on Gus's old desk—he was absolutely certain of that—and found it across the building under a worker's toolbox. The guy swore he hadn't put it there, much less even seen it.

"It's like Gus is sabotaging me from beyond the grave." He sank onto an overturned storage crate and massaged his tense shoulders, a task Hannah quickly took over, much to his enjoyment.

He leaned into her touch. "Gus loved me. I was his favorite freakin' nephew. Why would he leave me the business and do his damnedest to thwart the renovations?"

Zora stepped up, holding three bunches of dried leaves. "Supernatural activity often peaks during construction in haunted buildings." At least a dozen silver bracelets jangled on her wrists as she gesticulated. "Spirits attach to a specific place because they have unfinished business there. And we all know how much Gus loved this shop. It must be very hard for him to watch you tear it apart, even if it's necessary."

Xander envisioned Gus floating above their heads, his beefy arms crossed, scowling beneath his walrus mustache.

I am well and truly losing my mind.

Hannah hugged herself and shivered. "I can feel his presence. It's like the air is thick in here, full of static electricity."

Zora patted Hannah's arm. "Our job is to reassure Gus, so he'll feel safe moving on. Now, let's begin by asking what he wants from you."

Xander fought an eye roll and lost the battle. "Sure, of course. Why not? Let's chat with my dead uncle."

Zora shot him a sharp look. "First rule of communicating with spirits—be polite."

He chuffed a sigh. "Sorry, Gus. No disrespect intended."

"That's better." She pulled a piece of jewelry from the pocket of her embroidered kaftan. "Sometimes, a ghost doesn't even know it's passed over. Gus died suddenly, yes?"

Xander nodded. "Aneurysm."

"So let's make sure he's aware of his ghostly state." She held the slender silver chain between her index finger and thumb. Dangling from it, a dark blue stone carved into a point hovered over her palm. "Sodalite is especially good for communicating with the spirit realm." She closed her eyes and breathed deeply until the stone hung motionless. "Right, here we go. A circle means yes, and a back-and-forth movement means no."

A tiny scoff escaped Xander's lips. Hannah elbowed him.

"You want proof?" With a low laugh, Zora intoned, "Is Xander Anagnos here?"

The crystal thingy shuddered and began to sway. Soon, its point was inscribing a clear circle in the air over her palm.

Xander wasn't impressed. With practice and subtle hand motions, anyone could make that stone rotate or sway or dance the macarena.

Zora raised one eyebrow. "Your skeptical vibes are not helping, son. Here—try it yourself."

She passed him the pendulum.

"Right." He held it as she had and concentrated, but no matter how still his hands were, the stubborn rock refused to cooperate. It jiggled and jumped, but no circle.

An odd little shiver slid down his back.

"There you go." Zora took the pendulum, stilled it by touching the point to her palm, then lifted it again until it hung perfectly still and asked, "Am I faking this?"

The pendulum slid into a clear back-and-forth movement.

Zora chuckled. "Now then, let's get started." She gazed intently at the blue stone. "Is the spirit of Gus Anagnos with us in this room?"

The pendulum trembled and slowly began to move.

Xander reached for Hannah's hand. She squeezed his fingers tight, just as nervous as he was.

The blue stone inscribed a circle over Zora's palm, round and round, causing the hairs on Xander's nape to rise.

"Do you have something you wish to share with us, Gus?" she crooned.

The stone gave a jump and wiggled at the end of its chain.

"Hmm. Unclear." Zora eyed Xander. "What would you like to say to Gus, dear?"

Feeling not a little foolish but definitely spooked, Xander gazed up at the ceiling. "I'm doing my best, Uncle. I'm trying to make you proud, and I've nearly run through my reno budget. What do you want from me?"

Again, the stone jumped.

Great. I'm debating with a ghost.

"Try a yes or no question," Hannah whispered.

"Okay." He closed his eyes and tried to picture Gus as he'd been years ago, a smiling, portly man, light on his feet despite his fireplug physique, his pockets stuffed with saltwater taffy and his head stuffed with silly jokes and riddles. He'd been happy back then, a shining example of how to enjoy life. Gus would halt a business transaction to pull Aunt Marty into a whirling dance behind the cash register. He could wiggle his ears and sing Greek folksongs in a booming baritone voice, and he entertained customers by juggling the tchotchkes he sold.

Uncle Gus was the pure embodiment of fun.

"Gus, I want to love this shop just like you did. In your letter, you said I could make it shine even brighter, right?"

The pendulum began to stir.

Encouraged, he continued. "But we both know the building needs lots of repairs, and you're scaring away my contractors. So what I need to know is, will you trust me? Will you let me update the building so I can reopen the shop and make you proud?"

The stone jumped and wriggled.

Damn it, the stubborn ghost wasn't convinced.

"I love you, Gus, and I'm so grateful for this gift. So please, let me do what I need to do."

The pendulum settled into a circular path.

Well, I'll be damned.

"Very good, old friend," Zora cooed. "Now, are you aware that you've passed on?"

The stone continued to rotate over her palm.

"Would you like our help to leave this place?"

The spiral tightened and grew faster.

"What does that mean?" Hannah whispered.

"Most likely, our old friend is conflicted." Zora gentled her voice to a near-whisper. "Gus, I'm sure Marty must miss you terribly."

A low moan sounded from somewhere in the bowels of the building, causing all three of them to jolt.

Xander hugged Hannah to his side. "It's just the pipes." He didn't believe that, but he felt compelled to comfort her all the same.

If someone had told him a month ago he'd be a willing participant in a séance, he'd have questioned their sanity. But the energy in the cavernous room had shifted to a palpable melancholy that pricked his eyes with tears. Gus was lonely. He wanted to go home.

"Right, let's get to it." Zora pocketed her pendulum and pulled out a silver lighter inscribed with flying saucers and stars. "Bought this from Gus years ago." She handed them each a bundle of twigs and leaves.

Hannah held hers under her nose. "Mmm. Smells like Thanksgiving. Did Jesse grow this sage?"

Zora nodded. "It's been blessed under a full moon. Powerful stuff."

The down-to-earth guy he'd met at the farmer's market didn't seem the woo-woo type, but he was dating Zora's niece, so...

Zora lit her own bundle of sage, then Hannah's, and finally his. After a moment, she blew out the flames and motioned for them to do the same.

With eyes as wide as saucers, Hannah watched fragrant smoke waft up to the ceiling.

Zora glanced around. "We need an object Gus cherished."

Xander yanked the tarp off the cosmic transmitter. "Will this do?"

"Perfect." Zora stepped slowly around the metal contraption, waving her smoking sage to and fro. Xander and Hannah fell into step behind her.

"Remind me, what's his full name, hon?" Zora prompted.

"Augustus Xylon Anagnos."

Maybe it was the force of his voice that set the smoke to swirling—or a draft from the leaky windows. He and Hannah exchanged goggle-eyed glances as the three plumes merged and danced upward in lazy spirals.

"Augustus," Zora spoke his name like a magical incantation, "it is time to go home. Your journey here on earth is done. Go forth to new adventures and reunite with your beloved wife."

A breeze ruffled his hair, just like Gus used to do when Xander was a kid. And though he shivered, a comforting warmth filled his chest.

He gazed down at the metal box containing Gus's urn. "I'll be okay without you, Gus. You can go home to Marty. I love you."

Silence enveloped them. No rattling pipes, no creaking beams, no drip, drip, drip. Just peace.

Xander's knees wobbled, and he grasped the transmitter's rebar to keep from falling to the floor. Hannah hurried to grab him around the waist, grounding him in her solid warmth.

"Huh." Grinning, Zora gazed up at the ceiling. "What do you know? It worked."

"Does it usually go like this?" Hannah asked.

The old gal shrugged. "Never helped a spirit cross over before. I looked it up on Google an hour ago. Figured it was worth a try."

Dumbfounded, Xander shook his swimmy head. "No way."

"Seems to me Gus was ready to go. He loved you fiercely, you know. Probably stuck around to make sure you could handle this mess." Zora clucked her tongue. "Sorry, I mean this challenge. And I'm sure you'll make him proud."

Xander walked Zora back to her car and returned to find Hannah running her fingertips over the transmitter's metal frame.

"Hey there." He spoke softly so as not to startle her, but she jumped all the same.

He drew her into his arms. "You okay?"

"I think so. You?" She nuzzled the crook of his neck, a gesture that would ordinarily fire up his libido. But this afternoon's eerie events left him oddly disconnected from his body, especially the lustful parts.

He stroked her whisper-soft hair. "That was the strangest experience I've ever had. I feel—shaky."

Understatement of the century. While he'd always assumed the energy that made up a soul had to go *somewhere* after death, he'd never spent much effort contemplating the great beyond. But now—

He rested his chin atop her bowed head. "Unless we've shared a group hallucination, I've got to admit, I'm convinced. Ghosts are real."

"Makes you look at everything differently, doesn't it?" She gave a little shudder. "It's a lot to take in."

"Want some company while you work through it?"

She raised tear-sheened eyes to his. "Xander, I'm so honored you asked me to share this experience, but I need some alone time to write about this."

His heart jolted. "You promised you wouldn't—"

"Not for the newspaper," she hurried to reassure him, "just in my journal. It's how I process difficult things."

"Oh. Okay." A bit disappointed, he pressed a kiss to her forehead. He'd much rather work through this strange experience while wrapped around Hannah's soft body, her satiny skin against his. But he'd asked a lot of her since his arrival in Trappers Cove—her connections, her time, her love. To convince her he truly was in this for the long haul, he'd have to learn when to back off and give her space.

She pecked his lips. "I'll text you later." Turning, she started toward the door, then spun back. "And Xander?"

"Yeah, love?"

"You did the right thing."

Chapter Eighteen

It was like static electricity, but stronger and with no ZAP when I touched metal. It was cold, but not scary, heavy, but not painful. It was like...

Hannah grunted and shut her journal with a snap. "And I call myself a journalist."

She'd been writing for hours, but was no closer to finding the perfect words to capture what she'd experienced. That's what she got for neglecting her journal, which she'd left untouched on her nightstand since last week's midnight scribbles. Usually, with enough time and ink, her thoughts and feelings solidified into something concrete, something she could deal with. But this?

There was no doubt in her mind that what they'd experienced was real. Which meant ghosts were real, and living people could communicate with them.

Mind blown to smithereens.

Though she talked a good game about journalistic objectivity, she hadn't really expected to see or feel anything during Zora's woo-woo ceremony, just some nice smells and soothing chants to quiet Xander's worries. Sure, she'd heard the rumors too. How could she not in a town this small? Plumbers, electricians, carpenters—seemingly everyone working on Souvenir Planet told of weird sights and sounds and sudden chills. But she hadn't given much credence to their complaints. After all, it's natural to be spooked where someone recently died.

She'd never forget seeing Gus's body on the floor of his office, limbs at odd angles, dark eyes flat and staring.

Poor Xander. Bad enough that his living family didn't believe he could revive Souvenir Planet—or succeed in any other business, for that matter. But even his dead uncle doubted him? How horribly disheartening.

And some kind of girlfriend she was, abandoning him to deal with the emotional aftermath.

For the fourth time, she promised herself she'd text him. Just a few more pages.

Shivering despite the toasty heat from the electric heater, she drew her TC High School Sharks stadium blanket tighter around her shoulders and turned her attention back to her journal. It fell open to last week's entry.

Expand

Digonly

Savings

Ah, right. Sleep had eluded her that night, worries about the newspaper's future itching like poison ivy. So she'd tried the old trick of writing down her intrusive thoughts. But what the hell had she meant?

Expand made the most sense. If she expanded the paper's scope—say, to the surrounding coastal towns or even the rest of Pacific County—she could attract more readers. She jotted a checkmark by that one.

Digonly? Had she been dreaming about kid wizards? Or…She rolled her eyes at her own stupidity. *Digital Only.* A possibility she'd resisted, hating to give up the traditional printed newspaper. But time marches on, as Mom was so fond of reminding her, and as much as she hated the idea, ditching the print edition would free up much-needed funds. She scribbled *Last Resort* in the margin.

Savings. Holy shit on a flaming stick. Had she really been contemplating that? Because cracking into her not-large nest egg to keep a sinking business afloat would be thirty-one flavors of stupid, right?

Then why did that sound so tempting?

A soft knock on the door jerked her head up. "Xander?" She bolted upright and nearly face-planted when the blanket tangled around her feet.

Smiling in that patient way of hers, Mom stood in the doorway, holding a tray. "Brought you some banana bread and tea."

"Maahh," Hannah protested, "you're supposed to be resting, not baking."

"Bah," she countered and bustled in, casting a disapproving glance at Hannah's messy apartment. "Baking is restful. Besides, the bananas were going black."

Hannah took the tray and pressed her mother into the only armchair not covered with papers and laundry. "Doc said three days, Mom."

"It's been almost three days, and I'm bored." She stretched out her legs, then winced. "Headache's gone, anyway. Sciatica's kicking up, though."

"And your ulcer?"

"Nothing I can't handle. So." She laced her hands behind her head and regarded Hannah with an X-ray gaze. "What's got you holed up here on a Tuesday afternoon? Shouldn't you be out covering the town council meeting?"

"Almah's got it." She plated two slices of banana bread. "I'm working on—something personal."

"Uh huh," Mom deadpanned. "Does it have something to do with that handsome guy you've been dating?"

"As a matter of fact, yes." She set a plate and napkin at her mother's elbow. "And before you ask, I promised to keep it between the two of us."

Mom's teasing smile grew wider. "I'm glad you two are getting closer. Now, let's talk brass tacks."

Hannah chuckled. "Brass tacks? Mom, you're sixty-eight, not ninety-eight."

"You'll discover, my dear, that one of the blessings of age is not giving a flying crap what the youngsters think. So, how's your salvage mission coming?"

She'd probably already checked the *Beacon*'s accounts, despite the doctor's warning to stay away from screens, a common migraine trigger.

Hannah's shoulders tensed, but she forced a nonchalant smile. "Subscriptions are up. We're on track." Not enough to be back in the black by April, but if this upward trend continued, they'd make it by May or June, at the latest. If she presented her mother with the data, plus her projections, surely she'd relent and keep their doors open a little longer. She had to.

"Uh-huh." Mom did not look convinced. In fact, she barely looked interested. Maybe those migraine meds were stronger than Hannah realized?

She cleared away the end of the couch closest to Mom and sat, fixing her with a no-bullshit stare of her own. "Mom, you have more connections than I do in Trappers Cove, yet as far as I know, none of them have come forward to help save the *Beacon*. Why is that?"

She lifted one shoulder. "You know where I stand. Community newspapers are a lost cause. It's time to pull the plug."

Hannah leaned closer. "Buy why?"

Mom squirmed in her seat, then winced and repositioned her legs.

"You don't think I can manage without you? Is that it?" After all these years of working side by side, that thought hurt like hell.

"Oh for cripes' sake." Mom dropped her head backward. "You always were persistent. Like a bulldog, kiddo." She gave Hannah a look brimming with sadness. "You are destined for greater things, daughter mine. I'd have closed the paper years ago, but I didn't want to disappoint you."

"Mom, I—"

"No, you listen to me." She shifted in her chair, planting her elbows on her knees, and for a moment, Hannah saw the old Mom again, the one who defeated a bribe-dealing developer and rooted out corruption in the city council.

"Hannah, you are too smart, too beautiful, too talented to end up like me—old, alone, discarded, stuck." Tears brimmed in Mom's brown eyes. "So if I have to jolt you out of your rut, that's what I'll do."

"Mom!" A flush washed over Hannah's face. "I am forty years old. You do not get to make that decision for me. You can't just—"

Mom grabbed the chair arms and half-rose, then froze, a grimace of pain twisting her features.

"What is it? What's wrong?"

"Back," she gritted through clenched teeth. "Can't move. Hurts." She raised pleading eyes to Hannah. "Call Doc."

Hannah gently grasped her mother's arms and tried to lower her into the chair, but she let out a gut-wrenching wail of pain.

"That's it. I'm calling an ambulance."

"Back spasms." Hannah pressed the phone to her ear and paced the hallway of Trappers Cove's little community hospital. "Doctor says it can feel like an electric shock." She chuckled. "Mom concurred, at the top of her lungs. She'll be on some strong muscle relaxants for the next few days. That means I'll have to stay close. Knowing her, if someone's not keeping an eye on her, she'll try to come downstairs and carry on as usual."

The thought of her mother crumpled at the bottom of the narrow staircase brought back the image of poor Gus, struck down in his office. A whole-body shiver quaked through her body. She wasn't ready to lose her mom.

Xander's voice grew sharp. "I'm on my way."

But as much as she craved the reassuring warmth of his arms around her, she'd reached her absolute limit. "No, please don't." She softened her tone. "I know you want to help, and I'm grateful, but it'll be easier if I handle this on my own." She cut off his protest with, "You're the best, Xander, and I'm so glad to have you in my life, but we've both got a lot on our plates right now. How about if we meet up again in a few days when the dust settles, okay?"

His sigh whooshed into the phone. "I'll miss you, Hannah. Promise me you'll call if there's anything I can do."

"I promise. I'll miss you too. And Xander?"

"Yeah, beauty?"

Her heart pinged at the sweet nickname. "This isn't me putting distance between us. I just need to focus on Mom and the *Beacon* for a few days. But I'll be thinking about you every hour."

She could hear the sad smile in his voice as he murmured, "Thank you, love. I'll count the minutes."

Hell, she missed him already—his touch, his warmth and humor and laughing dark eyes. But that was the cold, hard truth about being a grown-up. Sometimes, what you want takes a back seat to what needs to be done, even if you are falling in love.

Chapter Nineteen

With the new construction crew scheduled to start on Monday and Hannah busy caring for her mom, Xander found himself with time to kill.

Though trendier by far than Trappers Cove, Carroll Beach offered decent hotel prices in mid-March, so he treated himself to an overnight stay with an ocean view, hoping the change in surroundings would get him unstuck.

One way or another, his inherited building would be ready for re-opening in a month or two, and he still had to fill it with merchandise, choose a branding direction, and name the damn thing—without UFOs, aliens, or planets.

As his old Prius crested the steeply arched Astoria-Megler Bridge, the morning drizzle eased, and sunshine peaked through the clouds, lifting his mood. The picturesque port city of Astoria spread out before him, its cute Victorian houses arrayed up steep hills above the mouth of the Columbia.

"Freakin' beautiful," he exclaimed. "Note to self: bring Hannah down here for a romantic weekend."

His lips curved into a smile as he imagined a candlelit seafood dinner overlooking the port, huge freighters and sturdy fishing boats sliding past, the bridge lights twinkling like Hannah's eyes—

A hulking eighteen-wheeler nearly sideswiped him as he rounded a curve while foolishly gawking at the bridge.

Heart pounding like a conga drum, he forced his focus back to the present moment. With another hour of twisty roads to go, he couldn't afford to let his mind wander.

He switched on a playlist for the early aughts—good years before he felt the curse's weight—and belted along with The Black-Eyed Peas—because why not? No one here to complain, and like will.i.am, he had a good feeling about today.

He rolled into Carroll Beach a little before noon. After checking into his room, he unpacked his overnight bag, then stuffed a small notebook into his jacket pocket, ready to be filled with inspiration. Maybe he'd been spending too much time around Zora, but he had a hunch the answer to his branding problem would be found here. Still humming, he strolled toward Madrona Way, the town's main drag.

Now this was more like it. Unlike Trappers Cove, where Main Street was a patchwork of architectural styles from quaint to shabby, all the buildings along Madrona Way were fronted with the same redwood shake siding. Pansies nodded from planters in courtyards fronting clusters of shops.

He lingered in front of an art gallery's jewelry display. Those delicate gold earrings set with glittering red stones would look stunning against Hannah's creamy skin. And that hand-painted scarf would complement the rosy shade of her lips. He leaned in closer to check the price tags.

Yikes!

Extravagant gifts like these would have to wait until his business was in the black. Nevertheless, he snapped photos of pieces that piqued his interest, then jotted a few notes: *artistic, classy accessories for women.* He spotted a wide man's ring embossed with swirling, surf-like lines. *And for men.* Shouldn't be too hard to find local jewelry artists willing to sell their work on consignment in a dedicated corner of his new mini-mall.

While visiting a cousin in Tacoma, he'd seen something like what he had in mind—an old industrial building divided into small shops selling everything from lingerie to goth gear to handmade stationery and artisanal comics. With some cheap dividing walls, he hoped to construct something similar in Gus's building, maybe even add seating areas out front where customers could relax and enjoy Garrett's baked goodies before diving into...

He leaned against an ornate lamppost and scribbled ideas: *The Old Tar's Treasure Trove? Buccaneer's Bazaar? Captain's Booty?* Snickering, he crossed out that last one. No doubt about it, TC's quirkiness was warping his brain.

As he wandered up the street, he continued turning over possible names in his head. *Mariner's Marketplace? Ye Olde Curiosity Shoppe? Cave of Wonders?* No, he'd heard how litigious Disney was. *Mall of Magic?* Nah, that sounded like a magician's supply shop.

A couple dressed head-to-toe in designer athleisure gear cut across his path, followed by four stair-step blond children. The littlest one dawdled at a toy shop's window.

"Mo-oom, I want a kite."

"You have a kite, darling."

"Madison broke it yesterday," the kid whined.

Rigid with outrage, his sister glared. "Did not."

"Did too!"

The father rolled his eyes and herded them into the toy store.

Toys! Xander pulled his notebook out and scribbled furiously. Why hadn't he thought of that before? Trappers Cove's souvenir shops offered plenty of beach toys, but it lacked a dedicated toy shop. If he stocked those snooty educational toys from Europe, status-conscious customers would eat that shit up.

Hannah might have a nose for news, but Xander had a knack for spotting opportunities, and right now, his intuition was ringing like a Vegas jackpot bell. If he could inject a skosh more sophistication into Trappers Cove, he'd lure upscale visitors like these folks crowding Carroll Beach—an impressive crowd for a weekday before Easter. And that would benefit all the businesses in TC, even Hannah's newspaper.

Before continuing his fact-finding mission, he stopped to quell his stomach's rumbling with an overpriced "hand crafted" ice cream—lavender and honey. Pretty purple color, but it tasted like a scented candle, and he gave up after a few bites. There must be something edible nearby.

After downing an over-salted smoked salmon chowder in a sourdough bread bowl and an extremely hoppy IPA, he rubbed his overstuffed belly and waddled forth again, regretting his choice.

"Salad for dinner, my gluttonous friend," he told his reflection in an art gallery window. Hmm. Those blown-glass ocean waves were striking. He noted the artist's name. Maybe he could stock those in the artistic tchotchke corner of his new shop.

And then, reflected in the plate glass, he saw it—a bright, glimmering vision of his future. A setting so perfect, customers would want to linger all day.

Mouth agape, he spun and stared. Across the street, a driftwood arch invited visitors onto a winding, brick-paved path. Lush planters flanked a carved wooden sign: *The Galleria*. Simple. Elegant.

Tourists streamed through that arch. From somewhere down that path, the seductive notes of a saxophone beckoned, along with the rich scent of coffee.

As if in a trance, he stepped into the street and nearly got flattened by a Range Rover.

"Watch where you're going, numbnuts," the driver yelled. In the back seat, a preteen kid flipped Xander the bird.

Dodging cars, he zig-zagged through traffic until he reached shopping nirvana. *Not a bad name for my place.* Grinning like a happy drunk, he ambled up the brick walkway whose twists and turns revealed a dozen or so mini shops, each with paned windows and redwood shake facades. Some brilliant planner had taken a large lot—about the size of Souvenir Planet, in fact—and turned it into this wonderland.

"Freakin' delightful!" he crowed, drawing stares—but who cared? The answer to his entrepreneurial dream was right here!

Each tiny building bore an old-fashioned sign framed in curlicue wrought iron. There was a wee coffee shop, a Belgian waffle place, a "chocolatier" with a window display of jewel-like bonbons in satin-lined boxes, and a tiny wine bar with a chalkboard menu of mouth-watering small plates. The enticing food scents pulled visitors like bees to blossoms.

Among the non-edible offerings, one shop sold only white linen clothing—loose, comfortable, classic pieces that would wrinkle like crazy but looked so elegant on the slender mannequins.

Another sold handmade paper goods—journals and planners and fancy desk accessories, along with a huge bouquet of feathered quill pens in the window. Yet another sold "organic, earth-friendly" smelly candles and bath stuff. And the shoppers were eating! It! Up!

Vibrating with excitement, Xander snapped photos of the décor and layout, including flowery planters ringed with benches, clusters of café tables and chairs, and even a trickling fountain with a sexy stone mermaid whose smile was a dead ringer for Hannah's.

He photographed all the shops, inside and out, and chatted up shopkeepers, then dropped onto a bench and wrote it all down, his pen flying over the page until it ran out of ink. After equipping himself with a new one from the stationery shop, he ordered an overpriced coffee, sat outside the tiny café, and interrogated passersby. Few seemed to mind his manic questions, glad to show off their purchases and point out their favorite shops.

Finally, Xander closed his notebook, stretched out his legs, and sighed. Trappers Cove had nothing like this. If only he could afford to, he'd knock down Souvenir Planet's skeleton and duplicate this setup on the lot. But for now, he'd do his damnedest to create this atmosphere inside Gus's old building. It wouldn't be easy. He'd need a forest of potted plants and a textured cement floor to simulate bricks, but at last, his vision was clear.

"Who knows?" he remarked to a fat bumblebee dive-bombing his coffee cup. "In five years, I bet I'll have enough capital to knock the old wreck down and build a galleria just like this one." Anticipation buzzed in his veins, making him want to chuck his mini-vacation, zoom back to Trappers Cove, and get started immediately.

But it was Friday afternoon, and he wouldn't meet with the new foreman until Monday, so he might as well enjoy his visit, take a walk on the beach and indulge in a fancy restaurant meal—possibilities that rang flat and unappealing without Hannah. Giving her space was a challenge to his impatient nature.

He finished his organic blond caffe misto—Hannah would call it pretentious, but he enjoyed the indulgence—and doodled a potential layout for his indoor marketplace. He'd have to group the alien merchandise around that damned cosmic transmitter, but he'd keep it to a few symbolic shelves of UFO junk.

What if he turned the transmitter into a fountain? Yeah, put that at the crossroads of his fake brick paths, flanked by mini shops—maybe garden sheds with cheap siding and architectural trim from a salvage yard? As soon as he got back, he'd call that Matteo guy who upcycled furniture.

Oh! And he'd name the aisles for streets in Trappers Cove—that'd please the locals, especially Hannah. Perhaps it was the fancy coffee, but his brain was buzzing and zapping with ideas. After five weeks of feeling stuck and uninspired, this felt freakin' fantastic.

His phone buzzed in his pocket.

"Mr. Anagnos?" He didn't recognize the gruff voice.

"Yeah, what's up?"

"This is Barry Bogosian from AAA Construction. Carl Williams appointed me project manager for your reno."

"Oh. What can I do for you, Mr. Bogosian?"

"Just Barry. Listen, uh—" Papers rattled in the background. "We'll need to talk at your earliest convenience."

Worry cribbled through Xander's stomach. "I'm free now."

"It's better if we talk face to face. I can drive out there tomorrow. Say, ten?"

"Okay, sure."

"Great. See you then." The guy disconnected without further explanation.

Well, shit. This couldn't be good news. Had the old crew filled AAA in on the ghost issue? He did not relish the idea of having to bring in Zora and explain to a bunch of hard-baked worker dudes how they'd exorcised his uncle's restless spirit.

His phone rang again just as he climbed the wooden stairs to his hotel room. When he pulled it from his pocket, Hannah's smiling face lit up his screen.

God bless the person who invented video calls.

He flopped onto the bed and held the phone above his grinning face. "How are you, beauty?"

She curled her lip. "Meh. Missing you. Mom's a little better, but still groggy from the muscle relaxers. I had to send Fred and Almah out to cover stories and," she gave a wry chuckle, "let's just say they're not exactly go-getters. This week's edition is gonna be boring."

"Wish I could help somehow."

"Unless you know a nurse willing to work for free, there's not much you can do." With a sigh, she leaned back into that faded armchair beneath her window. "I hate being stuck at home. I miss your kisses, Xander."

"Yeah?" He nestled into the pillows. "Tell me more about that."

Her low, earthy laugh sent a zap of pleasure straight to his dick. "I miss smelling your cologne when I nuzzle you right here." She stroked a finger over the tender spot where her neck met her shoulder. "You smell like leather and old books."

"Mmmm. And you smell like flowers and spice. It's addictive, that scent, just like your silky skin, your soft hair..." He sighed. "Damn, Hannah. You're too far away. I need another hit."

"Is that so?" Giggling, she hooked a fingertip in the neckline of her blouse and tugged, revealing the top of one creamy breast, its soft swell contained by a lacy black bra.

"Woman, you're driving me loco."

"Oh, is that Greek too?" she teased, running her fingertip under the black lace.

"Okay, you're making me palavós." His Greek was far from fluent, but he'd heard that word flung around at family dinners, especially when discussing Gus. "Show me more."

She toyed with her buttons. "You mean, like this?" One button popped open, and her lush cleavage filled the screen.

His breath whooshed out on a moan. "Does this bra hook in the front?"

Eyes twinkling with mischief, she fingered the satin bow. The hidden clasp released, and her glorious breasts spilled out, heavy and full and begging to be sucked.

"Oh, Hannah." He slid his hand down his belly toward his aching cock.

"Yes, lover?" She circled one rosy areola with her fingernail, and the bud tightened and puckered.

"You're killing me. I need you." He fumbled with his buckle, desperate for relief. His fingers closed over his rigid shaft. Pumping slowly, he drank in the intoxicating sight of Hannah's tongue tracing the curve of her plump lower lip while her slender fingers pinched and squeezed and—

"Hannaaah," a shrill voice rang out. "Gotta pee!"

"Crap on a flaming stick," she muttered and dropped the phone. She appeared again, fully buttoned. "To be continued. Sorry!" Her sheepish smile tugged at his heart.

"It's okay. Don't worry about me." *And my poor little friend here.* Wincing, he tucked himself away. "Love you, beauty."

"Me too you." He caught a jerky glimpse of her apartment floor as she hustled to the door, and then the call disconnected.

Me too you? Does that mean she loves me?

Damn and double damn. Why couldn't Linda's bladder hold out for a few more minutes?

While he contemplated a quick shower and tug to relieve his frustration, his text alert pinged.

BTW, Col. M, the UFO guy, called again. Told him you're not interested.

How did he take it?

Like the blowhard he is.

Thx. Wish you were here with me, Han.

He decided against prodding her about what she'd meant just then. Texting was not the right venue for something so important.

Not a fan of Carroll Beach. Too snooty and expensive. TC is better.

I know, love.

He still didn't quite get Trappers Cove's shabby appeal. Carroll Beach's polished style was more to his taste, but so what? He could disagree and still love her.

See you tomorrow. New contractor wants to chat face to face.

He chuckled as he read her response: a thumbs up emoji, a kissy face, and a heart with an arrow.

She still wasn't ready to say the big L word, but she was inching closer.

Grinning, he stretched out for a nap and sweet dreams of his beautiful new love.

Chapter Twenty

After a decadent beachside breakfast of house-made smoked salmon and cream cheese on a sesame bagel, plus coffee strong enough to restart a dead man's heart, Xander drove back up the coast, his mood light and his head crackling with ideas, not to mention anticipation of reconnecting with Hannah.

That giddy optimism didn't even last until noon. When he reached Souvenir Planet, Barry Bogosian, his new contractor, was waiting for him, along with a sharp-jawed, squinty-eyed guy who reminded Xander of a buzzard.

When they shook hands, Barry squeezed Xander's a little too hard. "Good to meet you face to face, son."

Xander made a mental note to order one of those grip-strength trainer gadgets. If he was going to spend the next few months shaking hands with construction guys, he'd need it.

"Meet Oscar Babbitt, our building inspector."

Oscar tilted his chin in greeting. "S'up?"

"Building inspector?" Xander's shoulders tensed. "I've already had the building inspected."

"No offense," Barry deadpanned, "but I never start a job without a fresh report by my own guy."

Faking breezy confidence, Xander rubbed his palms together. "No problem. Shall we check it out?"

Oscar shot Barry a look Xander couldn't decipher.

Barry shrugged. "Might as well."

Xander gave them a quick walk-through, summarizing the work done so far. Right on cue, the plumbing shuddered and groaned as they passed the washroom.

Gus?

With a cluck of his tongue, Oscar pulled a stylus from his pocket and scribbled on his tablet.

So much for Zora's magic. The pipes had been quiet since Tuesday's seance, but now, only two days later, the building was grumbling again.

After a walk-through much too brief for Xander's liking, the two workmen put their heads together and muttered in the corner. There was much gesticulating, scowling, and flipping through something on the inspector's tablet.

Finally, Barry approached and heaved a sigh that raised prickles of foreboding on Xander's skin.

"We've seen enough. Is there somewhere we can sit and talk?"

"I've got some chairs in my office."

The two men exchanged a look of distaste.

"How about my buddy's bakery next door? He makes great coffee."

They adjourned to Garrett's place and claimed a table near the window. Once equipped with extra-large mugs and an assortment of pastries, Monte dropped the bomb.

"I'm sorry to be the bearer of bad news, son, but your building has catastrophic flaws. We got the previous inspector's report, and now that we've seen it up close..." He shook his head. "To bring it up to code would cost an astronomical amount."

Xander gulped. "How astronomical?"

Barry scribbled a figure on a paper napkin and slid it across the table.

Holy flaming shitballs. His stomach plummeted.

"I, uh, don't think I can raise that sum on short notice," he choked out.

"Doesn't matter." The contractor chugged his coffee. "We're not taking the job. We take pride in our work." He inclined his head toward what was left of Souvenir Planet. "And frankly, I can't take on that mess good conscience. If you want my advice..." He cocked a bushy eyebrow.

Xander nodded his aching head.

"Sell it. We've done some work for the Borna Development Group. They're hungry for coastal properties. Bet they'd make you a good offer."

Devastated, Xander squeezed his mug in a white-knuckled grip. "If I sell the property, all the profits go to my uncle's favorite charity."

"Bummer," Oscar said with a nod of sympathy. "Borna's offering big bucks, and they'd love to get their hands on a lot this big. Probably put up luxury beach condos." He turned to his colleague. "Didn't they already do something like that in Trappers Cove?"

Barry shook his head. "Nah, just a crappy apartment building."

An icy finger poked Xander's gut. "Over on Narwhal Lane?"

Oscar consulted his tablet. "Yeah, that's a Borna project."

Remembering Hannah's breakdown at the mere sight of the place, he shook his head vehemently. "No way will I do business with that company." Hannah would never forgive him.

Barry squinted at Oscar's tablet. "Nineteen ninety-nine. That was Old Man Borna's work. His sons have taken over now. Built some real nice rentals up in Pacific Shores."

"Sorry, that's still a hard no."

Barry drained his coffee cup. "Lemme know what you decide. But son, I wouldn't wait too long. This building is a ticking time bomb."

After they left, Xander stayed behind, chewing a knuckle as he stared through the bakery window at the hulking wreck beyond. Fueled by panic and Garrett's strong coffee, his mental wheels whirred. He couldn't re-open Souvenir Planet and risk injuring customers—or worse. He couldn't afford to demolish it either, and if he sold, he'd lose everything—unless he negotiated some kind of sleazy under-the-table deal. With her journalistic smarts, Hannah would find out for sure, and she'd hate him forever.

No, there had to be another way.

"Refill?" Garrett had somehow materialized, holding a coffee pot.

Xander clapped a hand over his racing heart. "Jeeezus, give a man a warning."

Chuckling, Garrett refilled his cup, then slid into the seat opposite, leaned onto his elbows, and raised one ginger eyebrow. "You look a wreck, my friend."

Xander hooked a thumb over his shoulder. "That's the wreck, and I don't know if I can salvage it."

"Bad news, eh?" The baker's icy blue eyes crinkled with sympathy.

"Abysmal." He drummed his fingers on the table. "There's gotta be a way to turn Borna's offer to my advantage."

"Borna?" Xander had only ever seen Garrett even-tempered, but now his freckled face contracted in a thunderous scowl. "That bastard tried to pressure Grandma Ella into selling this place more times than I can count. Dude, you cannot sell to him."

"No, I can't. I won't. But man, he's offering top dollar for properties like mine. If only there was a way to take that offer to the bank..."

A wide grin split his face, and he smacked the table. "That's exactly what I'll do!"

"Huh?"

"It might work, my carrot-top friend. And if it does, you and I are celebrating."

Bemused, Garret shrugged. "Good luck, then."

Xander hurried into his jacket. "I'll need it. This is probably my last chance."

Staying away from Xander until Friday evening proved damn difficult, especially after Mom's distress cry interrupted their virtual sexy times. Knowing he was back in Trappers Cove but too busy with Souvenir Planet to visit—that stung, even though she'd been the one who'd asked for a breather to handle her mother's medical care and the *Beacon*'s ticking clock.

File that away under lessons learned the hard way.

So when he knocked on her apartment door a little after seven, bearing takeout from Ali Baba Kebabs and a bottle of Prosecco, she nearly bowled him over with her overzealous embrace.

"God, I've missed you." After a torrid kiss, she released him and dashed to her tiny kitchenette for plates and silverware. "My knight in shining denim, you've saved me from another dinner of instant ramen. Are we celebrating? Or do you always drink bubbly with your kebabs?"

He removed the cork with a resounding pop. "We, my love, are celebrating something spectacular." He filled the crystal flutes she provided—souvenirs from her cousin's wedding—to the brim and raised his glass. "To The Village!" Grinning like a kid on Christmas morning, he clinked his glass to hers, then chugged it dry. "Who just got a big fat bank loan?" He pointed his thumb at his chest. "This guy. I can't wait to show you my plans."

While she blinked in bewilderment, he unpacked their dinner. "But first, let's eat. I haven't had a bite since breakfast, and that was cold Pop-Tarts."

The tiny hairs on her nape prickled. "What's the village?"

"My new shopping center."

Pretty lame name, but she'd help him find a better one. She gave her head a little shake. "Let me get this straight—you got a loan to renovate the building?"

"Sort of. Dig in, beauty." He sat and attacked his pita wrap like a starving bear.

But he wasn't fooling her with his enthusiastic chomping. He was holding something back.

She took a seat, dipped a garlicky French fry in tzatziki, and waited for him to drop the other shoe.

Xander set down his sandwich and wiped his lips, his movements jerky. "So, yesterday I met with a new contractor and building inspector."

"Right. And?"

He clasped her hand. His palm felt clammy. "Hannah, I'm sorry, but the building is structurally unsafe. It has to come down."

Her sharp inhalation lodged a chunk of falafel in her throat. "Gack!" she spluttered.

With a yelp of alarm, Xander bolted around the table and whacked her between the shoulder blades. The chewed-up bean mash tumbled onto her plate, ruining her appetite.

No, it was Xander's news that did that.

She was so flustered, she only caught half of his hurried explanation—something about structural failure and condemning the building and a cluster of mini shops.

"...so when the contractor told me Borna Development Group is offering top dollar for—"

"Borna?" she shrieked. "Are you out of your profit-addled mind?"

Xander flinched back in his seat. "Hannah, you must know I would never sell to them after what they did to you and Linda."

"Then why even mention those crooked scumbags?"

His nostrils flared, and he gripped the table's edge. "Hear me out, okay?"

"I—"

"All the way, Hannah. Please."

"Fine." She tossed down her napkin and folded her arms tight across her middle. "I'm listening." The mere mention of that evil bastard who destroyed her childhood home had her emotions locked down tight—except for anger—with a bitter dash of betrayal.

He spoke as carefully as a bomb squad boss talking a newbie through her first assignment. "Okay, you're mad. I get it. I was too when I realized the previous crew led me on instead of telling me the hard truth. Then again, they probably tried, but I was too desperate to listen to reason. And now, there's no getting around it—the building is in danger of collapse."

"But you said you couldn't afford to knock it down."

"Now I can." He leaned onto his elbows, his eyes glittering with excitement. "In a weird way, this is just the push I needed. Until the other day, I couldn't envision how to make the business my own. But look—" He tapped his phone screen and flipped through photo after photo of nearly identical shingle-fronted buildings. "When I saw this outdoor galleria in Carroll Beach, it's like the heavens opened up and the angels sang."

She wrinkled her nose. "Ugh. The bougiest beach town on the coast."

"Hey now." He scooted his chair closer and eased her fist open, cradling it gently. "I know you're not a fan of Carroll Beach, but this could work in Trappers Cove. It *will* work."

Ignoring the pleasure of his touch, she spat out, "How?"

"By giving it TC's eclectic feel. Instead of being all matchy-matchy, every shop in will look a little different, just like the shops on Main Street."

"And the bank gave you a loan for this, this...?" She waved a hand at the photos on his screen.

"Once I got a bid from Borna, just to show the market value, the loan officer got on board. In fact, she loved the idea." His gaze dropped. "Of course, I had to put the land up as collateral."

Her already frantic heartbeat ratcheted up a notch. "But if you're not successful, you'll lose everything! The bank will sell it to a developer and—"

Leaning forward, he grasped her shoulders. "I won't fail, Hannah."

But it might fail. In fact, it probably would fail if he rejected the huge mass of customers he already freakin' had, who were salivating over the merchandise he refused to sell.

And yet, she'd promised not to bring up the aliens. Damn it to infinity.

"What about your promise to Gus?"

His voice cracked under the strain. "How many times do I have to tell you? I am a man of my word. The cosmic transmitter stays. In fact, it'll be smack in the middle, surrounded by other merchandise that regular people will enjoy."

"Regular people?" she squeaked.

"Gah!" He dropped his head back as if imploring help from the angels—or the aliens. "That's not what I meant. Damn it, Hannah, why are you fighting me so hard on this? I thought you were on my side."

A surge of irritation propelled her out of her chair to pace the tiny dining room. "Okay, you're right. Mea freakin' culpa. I'm sentimental. I'm nostalgic. I wish people weren't so quick to throw away the best parts of the past like chewed-up gum."

He rose and grabbed her from behind, wrapping her in his strong arms and holding her tight against his chest. "Hannah," he murmured into her ear as he rocked her gently, "I'm in love with you. And for your sake, I'll continue to offer a small selection of alien crap, even though I hate those little green bastards with every atom in my body."

She rotated into his embrace and pressed her forehead to his, hoping to get through that thick skull of his. "Why, Xander? What's so bad about them?"

"Because Gus might still be alive if he'd pulled his head out of the stars and paid more attention to reality." Eyes ablaze, he gripped her shoulders tightly. "But hey, who needs doctors if your buddies from Planet Xormak are on their way to pick you up?" He stabbed a finger toward the street below. "Everyone in this town saw he was spiraling, but they laughed it off. 'Oh, that's just Gus.'"

The air whooshed out of her lungs. Xander was right. In truth, the sweet old guy had tipped over into full-blown delusion, and the whole town enabled his illness.

Xander gentled his voice and slumped against the kitchen counter. "I loved Gus, but in the last years of his life, the man was unhinged. And if I make my new business all about aliens, people will think I am too."

"Hey now." She gave his arm a squeeze. "Why are you so hung up on what other people think?"

Xander's eyes bugged out as if she'd asked him why he needed to breathe.

"Because my future depends on what other people think! A business needs customers. A newspaper needs readers. If we get a reputation as nut jobs, we lose our livelihood, Hannah. Don't you see that?"

Defensive anger rose hot in her throat, especially because his words held a kernel of truth, damn it. She clawed her fingers into her hair and fought for control. "Like I said before, Xander, it's your business. So, what will you sell to these so-called 'normal' people?" She couldn't resist adding snarky air quotes.

He threw his hands wide. "Normal things! Vinegar and oil. Home décor. Nice clothing, a hundred percent alien-free. Wine and small plates. Classy stuff. Upscale. Trendy."

And here they went again, round and round. "You don't understand Trappers Cove at all, if you think you're going to draw customers with that kind of bougie, pretentious crap."

He poked her hard in the sternum, right over her aching heart. "And you think plastic aliens are gonna keep time from moving forward, Hannah? 'Cause let me drop a truth bomb on you—they won't. Change is coming to Trappers Cove, and you can't stop it."

Seething, she bit back a scathing comeback. She had to make him see what a huge mistake he was making, but arguing further now could destroy their fragile bond.

She marched to the sofa and plopped down with a huff. Unable to bear this emotional turmoil for one more minute, she needed to escape into action.

She flipped open her laptop. "Okay, Xander. You'll do what you have to do. And because I care about you *and* this town, past and future, I'll do what I can to support your new project." She speared him with a final glare. "And don't try to stop me."

Chapter Twenty-One

So much for the power of longhand doodling to unlock hidden wisdom. How was it possible to fill so many pages and still come up blank?

With a frustrated grunt, Hannah chucked her completely full journal onto the coffee table and rubbed her bleary eyes.

Xander's idea about a cluster of mini shops was a good one, but not if he used those buildings to sell the same old boring, basic crap on offer up and down the coast. Trappers Cove attracted people who wanted something different, and if she couldn't make him see that, he was going to fail—and lose all the time and money he'd invested in his ill-conceived scheme.

And then he'd leave.

Or worse, he'd succeed, drawing visitors who craved a swankier beach vacation experience, and one by one, every business that made TC the quirky, funky town she loved would fall to gentrification.

"Fuckity fuck fuck fuck!" Rising, she paced to the window and back. She'd been doing a lot of that lately—pacing while she puzzled out what to do about the *Beacon*, about Mom, about Xander. Fat lot of good it'd done her—she was still as gnarled up as ever.

Zora's voice echoed in her memory. "When we indulge in rumination, we risk anxiety, overwhelm, even paralysis."

That decided it. She snatched up her jacket, shoved her feet into her boots, and headed out, stopping on the landing to poke her head into Mom's apartment.

"I'm going out for a few hours. Can I bring you anything?"

Mom's sleep-roughened voice drifted through her bedroom door. "What time is it?"

"Almost five."

"Dang it, I'm too young to be napping the day away. Bring me something from Garrett's?"

"You betcha. Love you."

"Love you too, Hannah-Boo."

"You give Linda my best, you hear?" Garrett tucked an extra apple turnover into the pink paper bag printed with a smiling cartoon cloud.

"I will. Thanks so much, Garr." She gave him a playful eyebrow waggle. "I'm going to Daphne's place next."

"Say no more." He added a mini lemon tart and a giant chocolate muffin to the bag before folding it shut.

"You should stop by after you close up."

"Might could do that." His cryptic smile revealed no inclination either way. Despite her best effort—and half of Trappers Cove's, Garrett and Daphne remained firmly in friends territory, even though they were both single, attractive, and next-door business neighbors.

Hannah chuckled to herself. *Look at me, joining the ranks of the meddling matchmakers.* Her smile faltered. *Wow, I'm getting old.*

She paused in the doorway. "Say, has Xander been in today?"

"Several times." He swabbed the glass case with a kitchen towel. "I swear, he's gonna shake that building down around his ears if he keeps on drinking this much coffee. Dude's vibrating from caffeine overload."

Should she go see him? She glanced across the empty parking lot. A light burned somewhere in the back of Souvenir Planet. Damn it, why was he rattling around in a condemned building? Worry itched like grit under her skin, but it was probably best she left him alone after last night's testy stalemate.

She found Daphne and Noah in the bookshop's reading nook, folding colorful origami paper into flowers.

"Auntie H!" Noah shot to his oversize feet, flashed an adorable, braces-filled grin, and hugged her tight.

"Hey, kiddo." She nuzzled his mop of light-brown hair, thick and wavy like his mother's. "You smell good. New shampoo?"

He shrugged. "Dunno. Mom buys it."

"Green apple and bergamot." Daphne wrapped them both in her long arms and gave her son's hair a sniff. "Deeelicious."

"I can't breathe," the skinny squirt protested and wriggled free. He eyed the paper bag in Hannah's hand. "Pastries?"

"I think Garrett may have put a little something for you in here."

Noah peered inside. "Awesome! Mom, you should totally marry him." He snatched up the chocolate muffin.

"Eew. We grew up together. That'd be like marrying my brother." She claimed her lemon tartlet. "Go put on the kettle, would you?"

"Oui oui, ma capitaine." He snapped a salute, then chomped into his treat and trotted to the back of the bookshop.

"He's got a wee crush on his French teacher." The fond smile on her friend's face made Hannah a little jealous. What would it be like to have a sweet, goofy kid like Noah? Not that she envied Daphne's single mom status—she'd seen enough of her own mother's struggles to know how hard that was.

Still smiling, Daphne shook her head. "My kiddo, the romantic artist. He's so agreeable lately, I keep waiting for the other shoe to drop."

"Let's see, he's twelve?"

Daphne nodded as she collected the paper flowers. "For our spring window display."

"Beautiful. And you've probably got another year or two before that shoe drops."

"So, what brings you here besides pastries?"

"Do I need a reason to visit my best friend?"

Daphne smiled serenely, one eyebrow raised.

"Okay, I need a new journal."

Daphne strolled to a rotating rack and gave it a slow spin. "Didn't you buy one last month? That's a lot of noodling."

"Yeah. Lots to think through."

"Hmm. Does this cogitation center around a certain handsome Greek?"

"Guilty as charged." She sank into the cushy armchair Noah had vacated. "The Greek and the little green men."

"Or women." Finished with her clean-up, Daphne sat beside her.

"Of course." She rumpled her brow. "Maybe aliens don't have a gender. They could be...what do you call it?"

"Ambisextrous?" Noah suggested, depositing two steaming mugs on the low table between them.

"I don't think that's a word, darling," his mother said, seemingly unperturbed.

"It should be. Can I go draw?"

"Sure, love."

He scampered up the back stairs.

"So." Daphne kicked off her Dansko clogs and folded her mile-long legs beneath her. "Spill."

Hannah heaved a huge sigh and let her head fall against the seatback. "I want to meddle. But I shouldn't."

"Hmmph."

Daphne would have made an excellent therapist. With a single humph, she had the power to unblock a torrent of words. Or maybe Hannah just felt safe with her bestie. In any case, it all came spilling out—Xander's plan to replace Souvenir Planet with a high-end outdoor mini mall, and her vain hopes of changing his mind.

"He's making a huge mistake. Ginormous. And when he fails, TC will lose a valuable part of our heritage."

Daphne regarded her skeptically. "You're getting awfully worked up over the loss of a tacky souvenir shop."

Indignant, Hannah glared. "It's not tacky!"

"It's gloriously tacky. That's its charm."

"Well," Hannah spluttered. "TC is gloriously tacky. Take that away and we're just another beach town. Carroll Beach has those dramatic rocks off the coast. Willow Bay has that Beer and Chowder Festival and Cannery Park. Pacific Shores has the Dunes Marathon. Westport has that cute marina and the Crab Festival."

"So what?"

"If Trappers Cove loses what makes it special, the whole town might dry up and..." she trailed off, realizing she wasn't making much sense.

Daphne reached over and gently rubbed Hannah's knee. "Hon, what's this really about? Your mom?"

Her indignation deflated like a pricked balloon.

"Yeah. And the newspaper. It feels like I'm being swept away in an avalanche of loss." She closed her eyes and massaged her aching forehead. "You're right. I'm fixating on Gus's shop and his goofy aliens because I'm afraid of losing everything that makes my life cozy and secure. Up until now, I've always felt safe in TC." Her voice squeaked. "And then the most wonderful man shows up and says he's in love with me—while he's dismantling a big chunk of the town I love."

"Oh, you silly goose." Daphne squeezed her hand. "First of all, there is so much more to this town than one shop, even if it's the most famous one. Second, I told you he was sweet on you."

"Yeah," she grumbled. "You were right. Fat lot of good it's doing me now."

Daphne's unshakable calm could really get annoying. "And Han, you *are* safe here. But if everything falls apart and you need to leave TC, you'll be fine. You're the sharpest person I know. Plus, you're compassionate, and so photogenic it's unfair. You can apply your journalism skills in a hundred different ways—public relations, writing books, travel blogging."

"Hmmph." Hannah huffed, too full of angst to acknowledge her friend's compliment. "Even if I wanted to, which I don't, I can't leave Mom when she's so sick."

"Then stay in TC and do something else. There are dozens of businesses here that'd gladly take you on as an employee if it came down to that."

She slid a sideways, tearful glance at Daphne. "Like you?"

Her gaze dropped to her lap. "Well, I don't exactly need extra help this time of year, but…"

"Don't worry, I'm not asking yet." She swiped a loose tendril off her forehead. "I'm just so damn awful at waiting for things to fall into place. I need to *do* something."

"Typical Leo, thinking you can fix any situations."

"But I know I'm right about this," she protested. "There's no way a glorified mini mall hawking basic bougie crap can compete with a legendary…" she flapped her hands, "legend like Souvenir Planet."

Daphne leveled her with a look of gentle disappointment. "It's not like you to be such a snob."

"Me? A snob?" The accusation stung—because her friend was correct.

Daphne sipped her tea, one of Zora's special blends. "There's nothing wrong with—what does he plan to sell?"

"I don't know. Probably those 'Live, Laugh, Love' signs."

Daphne winced.

"See? Totally not Trappers Cove's vibe."

"And yet, we mustn't impose our taste on others. Very bad juju."

"Gah. You're right. And I hate it."

"But you don't hate him."

"No." She sighed down to her toes. "Quite the opposite, actually."

Daphne cracked a smile. "How very Austen-esque. Well then, Miss Bennet, what are you going to do about it? What outcome do you want?"

"I want him to stay. And I want him to succeed, even if he has to tear down the—" She clapped a hand over her mouth.

"Tear down Souvenir Planet?" Daphne whispered, eyes wide.

Hannah lowered her voice too. "It's been condemned. Don't tell anyone. Though I suppose everyone will know about it as soon as the bulldozers roll down Main Street." And why was she picturing them like WWII tanks?

"Poor Xander," Daphne cooed. "He must be crushed."

And yet, he'd seemed all too thrilled about the prospect of knocking down an iconic landmark.

After swearing Daphne to secrecy, she quickly filled her in on Xander's plans.

"Okay, don't be mad." Daph waited for Hannah's nod. "That actually sounds brilliant."

"It could be, if he maintains the TC vibe."

"And the aliens?"

Hannah gave her head a sharp shake. "He hates those. Like, down to the marrow of his bones."

"Hmm. Pity." Daphne tapped her chin. "How can we convince him?"

"We?"

"You're right, of course. Souvenir Planet was iconic, and a big tourist draw, which means the whole town has an interest in Xander's success. He'll need our gentle guidance."

"Gentle is right." Hannah sipped her lukewarm tea. "If I push any harder, he'll shut me down completely."

"Oh, I think you underestimate your sway. But I see your point. Now, who can nudge your wayward boyfriend in the right direction?"

Hannah's phone shrilled, making her jump and slosh her tea.

Daphne waved her fingers in a "go ahead" gesture.

"Hannah Leone."

"Ms. Leone, it's Jim Malinowski."

For a moment, she drew a complete blank—until he gave an impatient harrumph.

"Colonel, how are you?" Eyes wide, she pointed to her phone and grinned.

Speaker, Daphne mouthed.

Why not? It was almost closing time, and no customers lingered to overhear.

"A little birdie told me some very bad news about Gus Anagnos's building."

Hannah gulped. "Little birdie?"

"My cousin works for the county planning commission. Apparently, Souvenir Planet is slated for demolition." He made more phlegmy noises of disapproval. "That's out of the question. I've left a dozen voice mails for that young man, but he hasn't returned my calls."

She chewed her lip. This could be a golden opportunity or a stinking disaster. How to maneuver the blowhard colonel and his UFO cronies into supporting Xander's new project?

A little flattery might get the ball rolling. "Mr. Anagnos has assured me that the cosmic transmitter will remain in place and accessible to the public. Maybe you could—"

"Cosmic Transmitter my pasty white ass," he said with a snort.

Daphne sprayed tea onto her lap.

"I beg your pardon?" She shot her friend a look of warning.

"Missy, you and I both know that transmitter is a bullshit DIY art project. But the cosmic vortex beneath the property, that's very real. And if that young man knocks down the building, who knows the effect it'll have on the vortex? Already, our measurements show an alarming flux in electromagnetic vibrations."

Daphne crossed her eyes and twirled a finger at her temple.

Hannah cleared her throat to stifle a rising giggle. "I'm sorry, sir, but there's nothing that can be done. The building is too dangerous to save." A lightbulb switched on in her head. "However, Mr. Anagnos is planning a cluster of small shops surrounding the transmitter. Perhaps you'd like to lease one for your—er, instruments, or an information center about UFO activity in the region."

Daphne flashed a thumbs up.

And really, it was a brilliant idea. Harnessing these alien believers' avid interest would draw hordes of new shoppers to Trappers Cove. After all, even UFO nuts go shopping. And if she offered the colonel's organization a guest column in the *Beacon*, she'd net who knows how many new subscribers. Xander might be worried about skeptics who looked down their noses at the whole UFO issue, but Hannah was too smart and too desperate to turn down a juicy opportunity like this.

Win-win!

The colonel hummed his interest into the phone. "I like how you think, little lady. We'll work up a proposal. I'll be in touch. Malinowski out."

She disconnected before she and Daphne dissolved into helpless giggles.

"Is that guy for real?"

"He's a genuine Air Force pilot. Retired, of course."

Daphne wiped her streaming eyes. "Probably medically discharged due to a knock on the head."

"Hey now, don't insult your future customer. You'd better stock up on books about UFOs."

"Roger Wilco." Daphne snapped a salute and doubled over with laughter again.

Hannah pushed to her feet. "Well, let me grab a journal and get these pastries back to Mom."

Daphne trotted to her display and selected one with a star-spangled metallic cover. "On the house, since you're bringing in new customers." She squeezed Hannah in a tight hug, jabbing Hannah's throat with her bony shoulder.

With her victory grin firmly in place and a huge weight off her shoulders, Hannah trotted back across the street to the *Beacon*.

Chapter Twenty-Two

"No, sir. Absolutely not." Jaw clenched, eyes bulging, Xander stood toe to toe with Colonel Malinowski. "You can visit the transmitter whenever you like, but the building is not for sale."

He'd already shut them down weeks ago, but for some daft reason, these two space cadets were back with a new offer—they'd buy the property and "let" him run the business inside in exchange for a "small corner" for their UFO "information center."

All this weasely language was turning his stomach. Their purpose was clear enough—they wanted to take over.

Clearly not accustomed to being thwarted, the colonel inflated like a bristly puffer fish. "You're making a grave mistake, son. Without proper stabilization, the cosmic vortex might spin out of control, and the consequences could be dire."

What a freakin' nut job. Still, the guy was a retired military officer and deserved respect for his service, so Xander confined his snark to a single raised eyebrow. "What kind of consequences?"

"Seismic activity the likes of which you've never seen," Professor Alterman asserted, her eyes crackling with outrage. "We're talkin' dangerous levels of radiation, or abductions, or—"

"Save your breath, Lois." Malinowski dropped a sausage-fingered hand onto her shoulder. "This fool isn't in the mood to listen to reason."

And what these two didn't seem to realize, thank God, was that if he failed and lost the property to the bank, their UFO fan clubs would be the beneficiaries. If they uncovered that juicy news, they'd sabotage him for sure.

Though he might end up making an unwilling donation to the UFO investigation groups, it damn sure wouldn't happen until he'd given The Village his all. And he was just getting started.

"You'll be sorry, Anagnos," the little professor snapped and jabbed a stubby finger into his chest. "You don't understand the forces you're dealing with."

The colonel gripped her arm and muttered something about Plan B.

They could sling plans from B to Z, and he still wouldn't change his mind. Obnoxious, interfering twits.

Muttering and shooting him barbed looks, the colonel and the professor stalked away, leaving Xander as wrung out as a dishcloth.

Not that he had time to feel sorry for himself, since the demolition crew would be here on Thursday. He headed back inside to finish packing up whatever fixtures could be salvaged.

Why in the literal hell would Colonel Blowhard and Professor Yappy believe he'd want to sell?

A chill slithered down his spine. Did Hannah send them? Was this a ploy to harass him into changing his mind?

He shook his head hard. No way. She'd promised to support him, not kneecap him. It had to be a coincidence.

Boop beep boop. The bakery's doorway chime sang its merry tune as Xander trudged inside seeking carbs and caffeine—his only fuel since the Colonel's ambush the day before. Great, the place was packed. Three o'clock must be peak coffee break time in Trappers Cove. As he took his place in line, he heard whispers behind him. He shook off the weird paranoid feeling. Why would his neighbors be gossiping about him? They had more interesting things to talk about than his non-progress on the derelict building.

When he reached the counter, Garrett raised one ginger eyebrow. "Again?"

Xander faked a nonchalant grin. "What, you object to repeat customers?"

"Nah, man. You're welcome anytime, but try the decaf? This is your fourth extra-large cup today."

He tugged his sleeve up over his elbow. "If I could take it intravenously, I would. Ginormous latte with three shots, please, and whatever pastry I haven't tried yet."

Shaking his head, Garrett turned to the espresso machine.

While he waited, Xander went to get a copy of the *Beacon*, but the newspaper rack was empty.

"All sold out," Garrett told him, depositing an oversize mug and a slice of carrot cake on the counter.

"Good for Hannah," he muttered on his way to the cream and sugar station. Never thought he'd be so invested in the success of a small-town newspaper, but he was rooting for the *Beacon*—and not just because it was hers. He might never love the town's crusty side, but she wasn't wrong about the we-are-family-whether-you-like-it-or-not aspect. It felt a little claustrophobic at first, when everyone seemed to be talking about the new guy, but now...

He gazed around at the familiar faces turned his way. If his plan failed, if it all went to shit, he'd miss Trappers Cove almost as much as he'd miss Hannah.

Hell, he missed her right now. Painfully so.

Three days after their last—argument? Discussion? Butting of heads? In any case, he still wasn't sure where they stood. She was definitely avoiding him, not picking up his calls, responding to his texts with mere emojis. Keeping busy helped him not to perseverate, but every time he took a break, memories of her came barreling back.

Her low, sexy voice, her sharp eyes that didn't miss a trick, her stubborn determination, her silky hair that whipped around her shoulders as she paced, the slide of her satiny skin against his... Longing smacked him right in the solar plexus, making it hard to breathe.

He'd hoped she'd share his excitement about his new plan, but having learned about her sentimental nature, he understood how disappointed she must feel. He should've been straight with her all along about how much he hated the alien theme and why. Then again, if he had, she might never have given him a chance to get to know her.

And now that he knew her easy grace and confidence, the sweet snuffling sounds she made in her sleep, the bliss of sinking into her body, he was determined to claim his place in her life. Sure, he'd give her time and space to process the loss of Souvenir Planet, but if she thought a bunch of plastic aliens would keep them apart, she had another thing coming. Another think? Whatever—he wasn't giving up.

He poured three packets of sugar into his mug, stirred, then froze, the spoon slipping from his fingers to clink on the metal counter. What had she said right before dismissing him from her apartment?

"I'll do what I can to support your new project. And don't try to stop me." The firm set of her chin was fixed in his memory.

Maybe she really had sent Malinowski and Alterman. Wracked with indecision, he started toward the door, then forced himself to sit. Charging into her newsroom in a lather was a terrible idea. He needed a moment to collect his thoughts.

It made no sense, he decided. Hannah knew that selling the building would net him zero profit and cost him everything he'd invested so far. Even if she was mad at him over the aliens, she'd never do something so dastardly. Hannah was a good person, through and through. That certainty allowed him to relax and release his blip of paranoia.

Someone had left a copy of the *Seattle Times* on his table, the perfect distraction as he sipped his coffee and munched on carrot cake. He scanned an article on the Seattle Kraken's new goalie, checked the restaurant reviews—no mention of Niko's Taverna—then yelped with surprise at the sight of Hannah's solemn face in the Regional News section.

Coastal Newspaper Fighting for Survival

A full-page story on the plight of small-town journalism featured none other than the *Trappers Cove Beacon*. What a coup for Hannah! The byline belonged to a Seattle reporter whose name he recognized, but the article included multiple quotes from Hannah and Linda, and cute photos of mother and daughter in the newsroom along with a photo of an old-timey gent, the founder of the newspaper back in 1879. With his mutton chops and round belly, he looked as solid as the brick building that housed his newspaper.

"...local journalism is crucial to an informed citizenry, which is the cornerstone of democracy." Yup, sounded like Hannah. According to the article, subscriptions for the Beacon were on the rise, but still not high enough to save the paper. The article ended with "For more Trappers Cove news, see page 16B."

He flipped the page and nearly swallowed his tongue.

Shit on burnt toast. Hannah had taken the gloves off.

"Seattle entrepreneur Xander Anagnos plans to dismantle Souvenir Planet, a beloved Trappers Cove icon, according to a local source."

Again, the byline listed a Seattle reporter, but Hannah had to be involved. Who else had connections to get *The Times* interested in such a piddly story?

The article quoted Col. Malinowski about the cosmic vortex, along with Dr. Alterman's claims of extra-terrestrial visitations to the site. In a single six-inch column, the reporter painted Gus as a kook, and Xander as a serial failure whose chances of success were lower than dirt.

Cold sweat prickled his skin. How could she betray him like this?

And he thought he'd shaken off the curse with some herbs and hot bath sex. How stupid could a man be?

Stupid enough to fall for a woman who cared more about winning than she did about him, that's for damn sure.

Garrett's gravelly voice pierced Xander's fog of shock. Pulling up a chair, he sat beside him. "Dude, have you seen this?"

A FriendBook group filled Garrett's phone screen. "Save Souvenir Planet," Xander read aloud. The group's logo was a familiar caricature of Gus grinning from a flying saucer. Beneath it, members posted photos of Souvenir Planet going back decades, along with snaps of Gus's greatest hits—alien-themed mugs, hoodies, ashtrays, pencil sharpeners, bobbleheads, lollypops, and shot after shot of tourists grinning beside that ugly cloth alien on the park bench—which now resided in a storage locker because Xander didn't have the heart to throw it away.

As he watched, the screen filled with angry-face emojis. Word of Souvenir Planet's demise was spreading like wildfire, and people were pissed.

"How long has this been going on?"

Garrett poked the About tab. "Started yesterday."

And he hadn't told anyone about his plans for the building—except Hannah.

A new post popped up: a UFO mug beside a newspaper. *"Stay informed, people. Subscribe to the TC Beacon."*

For an endless-seeming moment, anger kick-boxed with heartbreak in Xander's aching chest.

Anger won.

He pushed to his feet, resolve tightening his jaw. If Hannah cared more about little green aliens than about the life they could've shared, so be it. But he would not surrender to that damn curse. He'd lost a girlfriend over this. He would not lose the business too. Gus placed his trust in Xander, and for Gus's sake, he'd fight to the end.

Xander nearly ripped the *Beacon*'s front door off its hinges.

Hannah flinched. Damn, he must've seen the *Times* article.

Mara Choi had warned her the story might not even make the regional news section, but promised to do her best. They'd hit it off at a conference in Bellevue a few years back, so Hannah was surprised and delighted when Mara contacted her. Seems word of the *Beacon*'s potential demise had garnered sympathy among the *Times* staff, many of whom had started out at small-town newspapers.

Xander waved a crumpled *Times* over his head like a club, his blazing glare hot enough to torch the old newsroom.

He smacked the newspaper down on her desk, along with a document bearing the Pacific County seal. Arms crossed, muscles bunching, he glowered down at her. "I can't believe you'd lie to my face. Was anything between us real? Or were you just playing me the whole time?"

"Xander, I swear—"

"Now all of Seattle sees me as a loser. My family's burning up my phone, thanks to your nasty little story."

Heat flashed through her as she pushed to her feet and poked his chest. "I did *not* write that article."

His lip curled in a sneer. "Of course not. You're too smart for that. You got one of your reporter buddies to do your dirty work."

Flabbergasted, she spluttered, her tongue too thick to form words. She'd never seen this raging beast side of him, and she didn't like it one iota. "Do you really think so little of me, Xander?"

"I don't know what to think." He stabbed the paper on her desk. "This arrived this morning by overnight mail."

She bent over to read the document. "Someone filed an injunction?"

"Yeah," he smirked. "Your Colonel friend and his sidekick are trying to halt the demolition. Thanks to your interference, I have to postpone the demo and go to court tomorrow." He jabbed a stiff finger toward Main Street. "Meanwhile, that building is *dangerous*. Do you not get that, Hannah? This morning I caught a couple of kids poking around. What do you think's gonna happen if someone gets hurt?"

"I—"

"I'll be ruined, that's what. I'll lose everything before I even got the chance to try—all because you want to hang onto the little green aliens you clearly love more than me." His voice caught, but his eyes blazed with fury.

"Hannah?" Her mother's thin voice came from the stairwell.

"Mom, you're not supposed to be on your feet."

Mom's worried face poked into the newsroom. "I heard yelling."

The force of Xander's exhalation stirred Hannah's hair. "I apologize, Mrs. Leone." He leaned in close and hiss-whispered, "You broke my heart, Hannah, but you won't break my will. Souvenir Planet is coming down."

And then he whirled on his heel and stormed out.

Mom hobbled resolutely to where Hannah stood rooted at her desk. "What on earth?"

For a long moment, Hannah could only shake her head. A lone tear slid down her cheek.

"Oh, Mom, I thought I was helping." She wrapped her arms around her mother's shoulders and sobbed into her hair. "Now I've ruined everything."

Chapter Twenty-Three

"What the hell is going on across the street?" Mom asked, limping to the front window to peer outside.

Hannah hunched over her laptop, working and reworking her job posting on the headhunting website. She would not, could not bear the sight of yet another bulldozer rumbling past. Too many gut-wrenching memories. She'd watched one beloved building splinter—there was no way her battered heart could stand witnessing the end of Souvenir Planet.

Apparently, the rest of the town didn't share her misgivings, though, because people had been streaming toward Xander's place all morning, like villagers on their way to a public execution.

Better to focus on this job-posting site. Hannah was taking a hell of a chance, hiring reporters for a newspaper on the brink of collapse, but if the Xander debacle had taught her one thing, besides the foolishness of listening to her heart, it was that sometimes, the only way out is up. Either the expanded *Pacific County Beacon* would fly, or it would flop, but at least she'd know she gave it her all. And right now, a clean conscience was all the comfort she could hope for.

The racket outside wasn't helping her concentration. Neither were thoughts of Xander she couldn't shake off—his anguished expression, his certainty she was responsible for that hatchet job in the *Seattle Times* and that damn Save Souvenir Planet FriendBook group, which swelled to thousands over Easter weekend. Didn't people have better things to do with their time?

It didn't take much digging to find out an underling at NASDEV had set up the social media campaign—a fact Xander might have discovered on his own, if he hadn't been so busy blaming her.

The unfairness of his accusation burned, as did his refusal to answer her voicemails or texts. Hell, he'd probably blocked her.

Deep down, she knew she had only the thinnest sliver of a chance with Xander, but she couldn't surrender hope—not with him so near and hurting just like she was.

Almah joined Mom at the window. "Look, there's a TV news van!"

What the…? She pushed to her feet and trotted to their side in time to see picket signs bobbing past.

"Holy crapoly," Fred exclaimed, joining them. "Are they wearing alien masks?"

Some were. Others wore headbands with silver antennas. Antennae? Whatever—these people, and another group of at least ten, all dressed in alien paraphernalia, were trooping toward Xander's parking lot.

"Hannah, hon, grab my jacket." Mom said with a backward wave. "And my recorder too."

"Mom, your sciatica." Except for medical appointments, Linda hadn't left the *Beacon* building in weeks. Even hobbling down the stairs was a painful ordeal for her.

"Oh, bosh. It's just across the street. As long as my hard-headed daughter is determined to keep the *Beacon* open, I might as well contribute one last story before I hand over the reins."

"Hand over the... Mom?" Heart galloping, she snatched up the items her mother requested, along with her cane, and sprinted after the three older reporters.

The mob's chants rang out loud and clear. "Save Souvenir Planet! Save the Vortex!"

She found her mother in close conversation with a woman wearing a lime green spandex bodysuit and a UFO-shaped hat.

"Mom, are you serious? You're letting me keep the *Beacon*?"

Mom waved her off with an indulgent smile. "Doesn't look like I can stop you. We'll talk later, darling. Now, if this isn't the story of the decade, I'm not Italian. Go cover it, Editor-in-Chief."

Head spinning, Hannah urged Almah and Fred to keep a close eye on her mother, then scanned the crowded parking lot for Xander. No sign of him, but what a wild ruckus! Homemade UFOs of aluminum foil and spray-painted foam bobbed above the protester's heads. On the cab of a bulldozer, someone in a silver lamé space suit danced to EDM blasting from the old-school boom box at his feet.

Daphne bopped up wearing one of Gus's greatest hits, a headband with spring-mounted glittery alien heads. "Isn't this amazing?"

"It's terrible!" Hannah clutched her heart.

Her friend tilted her head like a confused puppy. "I thought you wanted Xander to see how much people love Gus's aliens."

"I do, but the building is unstable."

"Oh, shit, that's right." Daphne's eyes widened. "Should all these people be so close?"

"No, they definitely should not. I've gotta stop this."

It wasn't going to be easy, though, as the protest was quickly morphing into a giant open-air party. Dancers clustered around the bulldozers bounced and fist-pumped along with Mr. Silver-Butt's music, while at the other end of the parking lot, someone set huge speakers atop a muscle car and cranked up spacey techno tunes. Meanwhile, under the veranda's sagging roof, Colonel Malinowski and his equally red-faced partner in crime, Professor Alterman, took turns bellowing into megaphones, riling up the protestors.

Hannah shoved and prodded and jabbed until she reached the chief rabble rousers.

"Give me that! She yanked the Colonel's megaphone from his hand and faced the crowd, stretching up on her tiptoes.

"People! Listen up! You need to back away from the building."

At least a hundred faces turned toward her, some painted silver, some neon green.

"Save the Vortex! Save Souvenir Planet!" The chant pulsed like a wave, threatening to knock her off balance.

"Save the whales!" some smart-ass yelled.

"It's not safe here," she yelled, the megaphone garbling her voice. "Back away."

A sharp-eyed, blazer-wearing young woman slid through the crowd and thrust a fuzzy microphone into Hannah's face. "Brianna Wu, KNXT News." Her cameraman filmed Hannah batting it away.

The door behind her flew open, and Xander stormed out wearing a hard hat, followed by a half-dozen similarly helmeted guys in work clothes. His fierce glare skimmed the crowd's upturned faces before lasering in on Hannah. "What the hell, Han? What part of 'the building is falling down' don't you get?"

"It wasn't me, I swear."

His eyes narrowed, and his nostrils flared in a way that would've been sexy if not for the figurative pitchforks and torches. "You just don't know when to quit, do you?"

The Colonel puffed out his chest and stepped between them. "Now, look here, son. NASDEV is prepared to make you a substantial offer."

"GUFON too!" Dr. Alterman piped up, a yappy Frenchie to his English bulldog. "We've got the resources to save this building."

"Save Planet Gus," someone screamed nearby. The TV reporter swiveled to question them.

"Save it?" Xander grabbed the bullhorn. "This building has been condemned, people. It's coming down whether you nut jobs like it or not."

"Greedy motherfucker," a deep voice growled.

"Stop gentrification!" a shrill one added.

"Go back to Seattle, you loser," another hollered.

A loud noise sounded from inside the building—a metallic, grumbly moan.

"It's Gus!" someone shouted.

"It's the aliens!"

"It's the fuckin' pipes," Xander countered and flung the megaphone down, causing it to crackle and shriek. He stabbed a finger into Hannah's chest. "You see? This place is on its last legs. If we don't knock it down, someone's gonna get hurt, or worse."

"Where's the water shut-off valve?" One of the hard-hat guys asked.

"I'll get it." Xander stomped back into the building and slammed the door behind him.

The noise grew louder, an eerie sound like the death cry of a wounded dragon. The veranda's roof shuddered above their heads.

"Go, go, go," one of the construction guys yelled and shoved Hannah, tumbling her into the protesters. Gravel bit into her palms and scraped her knees. She righted herself just in time to see the porch roof collapse in a whoomph of broken boards and shredded tar paper.

"Earthquake!" The crowd boiled into panicked flight in all directions.

But it wasn't seismic activity. It was Souvenir Planet's dying gasp. The walls trembled and swayed as if the building were breathing. One by one, they splintered and collapsed inward with a sickening crunch.

Hannah's heart seized. "Xander," she screeched and sprinted into the wreckage, wriggling free from the strong hands that clutched her arms and ripped her jacket.

Inside, shafts of sunlight pierced the shattered roof. Fallen beams lay like pick-up sticks. From somewhere in the back, a geyser of icy water sprayed skyward.

"Xander, where are you?" Using her phone's flashlight, she scanned the rubble. Its beam glinted off something metallic—the cosmic transmitter. A faint groan emerged from that direction.

"Don't move! I'm coming." Scrambling like a crab, she picked her way over and under debris until she spotted him curled in a fetal position around the transmitter's base, pale and dusty but alive. Falling beams had knocked his hardhat off, and blood trickled from his ear and lips.

"Oh God Oh God Oh God." Splintered wood and jagged metal bit into her hands as she wrenched away the fallen beams separating them. With a sharp curse, she swiped at the tears blurring her vision. She couldn't lose him now. Fate couldn't be that cruel.

Sirens wailed outside, growing nearer.

"In here!" she screeched and reached for him, then jerked her hands back, afraid to injure him further. A tsunami of emotion pushed her babbling into warp drive.

"Oh, Xander. I'm so sorry. You could have died. What were you thinking? I love you so much. Don't you *ever* scare me like that."

Shivers quaked through her. What if this was his last moment? What if he died believing she'd orchestrated this catastrophe?

Gingerly, she took his hand and lifted it to her lips, kissing his scraped skin over and over. "I should have supported you. I should have listened, love. Please, don't leave me."

His dusty lashes fluttered. "Gus?"

She thrust her face closer. "No, it's me, Hannah."

"Hannah left me." His ragged cough turned into a sob. "She hates me."

"No, I don't. I love you, do you hear me? I'm not giving up on us."

Maybe he did hear, because his lips twitched before he shuddered and went deathly still.

Chapter Twenty-Four

The inside of Xander's eyelids felt like sandpaper. His mouth tasted like fishy chalk. His ears vibrated with an odd ringing sound. And *everything* hurt.

"Well, good morning, handsome." A plump, dark face floated into view, though his vision was too blurry to make out the details. The woman tutted. "Let me get you some ice chips."

"Who... Where..." he croaked. His tongue felt too thick and slightly numb, and his throat stung like crazy.

A cool, soft palm stroked the hair back from his forehead, and then something cold—a spoon?—slid between his parched lips and deposited the most delicious ice he'd ever tasted. "You're in the hospital, hon," his guardian angel cooed. "You had quite a bump on the head. Doctor Bakshi will be in to see you soon. I'm Tamara, your nurse." She fiddled with an IV bag beside his bed. A thin plastic tube ran from the bag to the inside of his alarmingly purple arm.

"Got some nasty bruises, didn't you? Don't worry, they'll heal up in a few weeks."

"How did I… " He wiggled his fingers—all operational, ditto his toes—then blew out a sigh of relief that made his ribs ache.

She checked the adhesive pads stuck to his chest. "Building fell down around your ears. Don't you remember?"

Shards of memory flashed behind his closed lids: horrible sounds like crunching bones, a high-pitched hiss, followed by pain and darkness. He remembered thinking, "This is it. This is how I die." Then an angel appeared, pale and beautiful, floating above him, calling his name. Gus was there, too, his jowly face haloed in a silvery glow. His uncle had smiled. "Not your time yet, son. You've got work to do." After that, sirens and warm raindrops kissing his skin.

"Oh good, he's awake," a second voice chirped. "His girlfriend's been camped out in the waiting room for hours. Refuses to leave."

"Hannah's here?" he ground the words out with difficulty. At the mention of her name, a wave of sadness washed through him, an ache every bit as painful as his multiple injuries.

"Rode with you in the ambulance. You wouldn't let go of her hand, so they packed her along." Nurse Tamara slipped a gadget onto his fingertip.

"Is she okay?" He tried to sit up, but arrows of pain shot through his body.

The nurse gently pushed him back onto his pillow. "Mostly scratches and contusions. Needed stitches on her hands." She chuckled. "According to the EMT, she was determined to tear that building apart board by board until she got you out." She fiddled with a dial on a metal box beside his bed. "You, on the other hand, have some serious healing to do."

"What's wrong with me?"

"Fractured fibula, three cracked ribs, and a probable concussion."

When he reached for his aching forehead, the IV needle in his arm pinched painfully.

Nurse Tamara leaned in for a closer look. She smelled of rubbing alcohol and coffee. "Twelve stitches. Afraid that's going to scar. Honey, if you hadn't been wearing a hardhat, your skull would've cracked like an egg."

A shiver wracked his body. That damn building had nearly claimed his life. And it could've taken Hannah's as well. Even though pain meds blurred his senses and muddled his thoughts, one thing was clear—no argument was worth losing the woman who braved a collapsing building to save him.

"I need to see her." He clutched the nurse's busy hand.

"Who, hon?"

"Hannah."

Another woman bustled into the room wearing a white coat. "No visitors until we're finished testing. Tamara, let's get this patient to Imaging for a CT scan."

"Off we go." The bed began to roll, triggering a wave of nausea and panic.

"Hannah," he bellowed.

A soft hand patted his shoulder. "Relax, hon. She's not going anywhere. She made that clear with some choice words to the intake nurse. Now, hush, before the doc orders sedation." Lights flashed by overhead, fading to darkness again. Surrendering to sleep felt so damn good.

Dozing in the world's most uncomfortable plastic chair, Hannah woke to a gentle poke and the sound of her name. A fifty-something nurse with wide hips and a sweet smile beckoned. "Your friend is awake and asking for you. Come on back."

Heart slamming her ribs, she sprang up and followed through swinging doors, down a corridor lined with medical equipment and gurneys, to Room 14. Dimly, she registered surprise that Trappers Cove's little hospital even had that many rooms.

The nurse knocked softly. "Xander, someone to see you."

A muffled, masculine grunt came from inside.

"I'm glad you're here, hon," the nurse told her. "His family's up in Seattle, and he didn't want us to call them." She swept the door open with one hand and sailed into the room.

Timidly, Hannah followed and braced herself. After the terrible accident she'd indirectly caused with her meddling, she was astonished he'd even deign to speak to her, much less let her see him in this vulnerable state.

The nurse fiddled with his IV line, then stepped aside, revealing a sight so horrible Hannah had to jam a fist in her mouth to stifle a gasp.

Dark bruises mottled his face, arms and hands—and probably the rest of him hidden beneath his hospital gown and thin blanket. His left eye was swollen shut in a wicked shiner, and a swath of hair had been shaved above his left temple for the row of stitches there. His left leg wore an inflated air cast and rested on a pillow.

"Hi," he rasped and waggled the fingers resting on his chest.

"Oh, Xander." She lurched toward him, but the nurse gripped her elbow.

"No hugs. He's got three cracked ribs." She squinted into Hannah's face. "You're white as a sheet, hon. Here, you better sit."

Good thing the nurse had such sharp eyes, because Hannah broke out in a queasy cold sweat at the sight of him lying pale and battered on that narrow hospital bed. Pretty hard to beg forgiveness when you're passed out on the floor. She let the nurse ease her into a chair beside Xander's bed.

He scanned her face with his good eye and croaked, "You...rescued me?"

She wiped her tear-streaked cheeks. "No, the firefighters and EMTs did that. I just showed them where you were."

"Hannah." He reached out his hand, a gesture that broke her heart afresh because she didn't deserve tenderness after nearly getting him killed. "You should've waited outside. You could've died in there."

"Seems we've got a standoff," the nurse remarked with a chuckle. "The doc will be in shortly."

With a grunt, Xander pushed up onto his elbow. "Was anyone else hurt?"

"Nothing major. A few sprains and such from the stampede." The nurse gave a wry smile. "I saw the footage on FriendBook. To say you were lucky is the understatement of the year. Someone must be watching out for you two. Now then—" She set down her tablet, her expression all business. "Xander will need to stay at least forty-eight hours for observation. Afterward, he'll be groggy from pain meds. He'll need someone to look after him."

He rumpled his brow in a sheepish gesture, then winced. Damn, those stitches had to hurt.

Hannah straightened her shoulders. "I'll stay with him." When Xander started to protest, she added, "This is my fault, and I'll do what I can to fix it."

The nurse tilted her head. "Your fault? How?"

"It's complicated. Let's focus on what Xander needs."

The doctor, a petite woman with a brusque manner, bustled in holding a tablet. She peppered Xander with questions, then turned to Hannah. "You're going to be his caretaker?"

She nodded grimly. "Tell me what to do."

"Don't worry, we'll supply you with detailed care instructions when he's discharged." With a conspiratorial grin, the doc hooked a thumb toward Xander and whispered, "Will he cooperate? Or is he stubborn?"

"Not as stubborn as me."

That earned her a laugh from the medical crew.

"Just make sure he gets plenty of rest." The doc pointed her pen at Xander, her expression stern. "And Mr. Anagnos, it's vital that you get plenty of rest and take your pain meds. Deep breaths will be uncomfortable for the next few weeks, but it's crucial you use your spirometer. Shallow breathing can lead to pneumonia."

He groaned. "I need to work. So does Hannah."

The doc wasn't having any of his excuses. "Mr. Anagnos, you are lucky to be alive. If you don't give your body the rest it needs, your healing could easily drag on for several months, not to mention the effects a close brush with death can have on your mental health." She swiveled to Hannah. "That goes for you too, Ms. Leone. Do not underestimate the impact of this trauma."

Hannah gingerly took Xander's hand and squeezed, though the motion tugged her stitches painfully. His one-eyed gaze lasered onto hers, and a silent understanding passed between them. Whatever their differences, they'd narrowly escaped disaster yesterday. This kind of second chance is not something you squander.

She rubbed her thumb over the back of his bruised hand, memorizing the fine bones, the delicate lines of blue veins beneath his skin. The realization of what she'd almost lost suffused her body with aching remorse and giddy gratitude. "We'll both rest up, doctor." She lifted his hand to her lips. "Even if I have to tie him to the bed."

The doctor and nurse exchanged amused looks. "Sorry, but that kind of fun is off the menu for at least two weeks. We'll re-evaluate at your follow-up appointment. Until then, no exertion, Mr. Anagnos. No alcohol, no stress, and absolutely no heavy lifting." She patted his uninjured leg and hurried out, pausing in the doorway. "Oh, and happy birthday."

His eyes closed on a groan.

"Helluva birthday present," Hannah muttered under her breath. What had poor Xander ever done to deserve this?

"How old are you today?" Nurse Tamara sing-songed as she fetched Xander's belongings from a locked cabinet.

"The big four-oh." With Hannah's help, he rose to a sitting position. "I used to wonder how I'd celebrate this day." He gave a dry chuckle. "No disrespect to Zora, but her curse cure is crap."

"By the way." The nurse opened a cabinet and shook out Xander's torn, blood-stained clothes. "You might want to fetch him something to wear home. These won't do, and hospital gowns are kinda drafty." Grinning, she left them alone.

Hannah clutched his shredded shirt to her chest. "Oh, Xander, I'm so sorry. I thought if I nudged Malinowski and Alterman, they'd support your mini mall by renting out one of the shops. I had no idea they'd try to take over." She dabbed her streaming eyes with the dusty rag. "I should've seen that coming. I swear, I'll never interfere with your plans again."

He studied her for several seconds of agonizing silence before rasping out, "If you hadn't meddled, the demo would have taken place on time and without a crowd. It's a miracle we were the only two hurt."

She hung her head under the weight of his well-deserved condemnation.

A soft touch under her chin raised her gaze back to his. "But you ran into the wreckage to find me. Hell of a brave thing to do, Hannah. So, thank you."

His watery smile rekindled her hope. It wouldn't be easy, and it would take time, but maybe they could recapture the love that had started to bloom before it all came tumbling down.

Chapter Twenty-Five

Two weeks cooped up in an RV? Not fun.

Hannah's quiet presence kept him from coming completely unglued, but she refused the deep conversation he craved, insisting he rest up and heal.

Being confined with a cranky, restless patient couldn't have been much fun for her either, yet despite her responsibilities as new editor-in-chief of the *Pacific County Beacon*, she stayed stubbornly put in their little sick bay for two.

By day, she worked from the tiny dinette at one end of the RV while he made phone calls and pored over insurance documents from his bed at the other end, his injured leg elevated on a pile of pillows. Eagle-eyed and fierce as any mama bear, she thwarted his every effort to get out of bed except to limp to the toilet.

By night, his mental wheels spinning, he listened to her faint snores and mumbled sleep-talk. Knowing her sleepy-soft body was only thirty feet away was sheer torture. And hearing her morning shower in the tiny RV conjured memories of her slippery wet skin beneath his hands, warm water trickling between her breasts, dripping from the curls between her thighs...

"Arrgh." He tossed aside yet another packet of insurance claim forms.

Footsteps hurried toward him. Hannah's worried face popped around the accordion door. "What's wrong?"

He stretched as far as his injured ribs would permit and stacked his palms behind his head. "You."

"Me?" Her nose wrinkled adorably as she tried to puzzle what the hell he was talking about.

He patted the mattress, but she just folded her arms and leaned against the narrow doorframe. "None of that. Doctor's orders. Besides, you and I have unfinished business to tackle before we re-open that can of worms."

"I miss you, Han," he protested. "And you're right there, twenty-four seven. It's unbearable."

"You'll see Doctor Bakshi on Wednesday." He caught her gaze skimming down his supine body. She missed their connection as much as he did, yet she kept their physical contact to a minimum.

She was annoyingly smart that way. Probably still chewing on her guilt too.

Jumping back into bed together wouldn't solve the clashing goals that led to their current mess. Not that he was in any shape to jump. Thirteen days after the collapse, his ribs screamed whenever he coughed, and his broken leg throbbed if he accidentally touched it to the ground. At least he was off the damn painkillers that made him thick-tongued and fuzzy-brained.

Clearer thoughts were also a mixed blessing. On the one hand, he was able to sort through the insurance labyrinth that would ultimately yield a payout big enough to cover half the rebuilding costs. *If* he stuck with his plans. Should he?

Pretty hard not to see a building collapsing on your head as a sign from the gods or the universe or whatever to retreat from the whole business.

Gus's ghost was no help—his uncle had well and truly flown the coop. He almost missed those rattling pipes.

And there was no comfort to be found in stilted phone calls with his parents and siblings, who regularly threatened to drag him back "home." That was a showdown he'd like to see, after Hannah handed Dad his ass during Gus's memorial.

Whatever Hannah's thoughts about his next steps, she resolutely stuck to her promise not to interfere.

"C'mon, Han," he whined from his sickbed. "I'm facing some tough choices. I need someone to talk this through with."

She shook her head, her ponytail whipping behind her. "Nope. We both know what happened the last time I got involved. Your business, your decisions."

A rap sounded on the door, and Garrett's gravelly voice called, "Okay to come in?"

"Yes!" Xander shouted before Hannah could object. "Please, thank you, and hallelujah."

Garrett climbed aboard, pecked Hannah's cheek, and handed her an extra-large to-go cup, then slid past her, holding a bulging paper bag.

By the time his cast came off, Xander would need bigger pants. Ever since Hannah gave Trappers Cove her okay, edible offerings had been showing up on their doorstep: Linda Leone's excellent banana bread, the Delaney sisters' hippie lentil casserole—surprisingly good despite looking like mud, plus kebabs from Ali Baba's, chowder from the Salty

Dog, dumplings from the Sea Dragon, even a crab and spinach lasagna from Casa Francesca, the swanky Italian restaurant up on the South bluff.

"Can you stay a while, Garrett?" Hannah glanced toward the door, no doubt just as claustrophobic as he was.

"Sure. Mondays are slow, and Tessa's at the till."

"Thanks." She gave him a sweet grin and Xander a sharp look. "Promise me you'll stay put."

He spread his hands wide. "Where am I gonna go, beauty?"

She huffed a hank of hair from her forehead, then made her escape.

Garrett perched on the edge of the mattress and opened the bag to reveal an assortment of goodies, including Xander's favorite apple turnovers. Crumbs be damned, these were too good to resist.

"So..." Garrett scrubbed bony fingers into his close-cropped ginger hair. "You and Hannah—everything okay?"

"Man, I have no idea. She's so—" He waved a crumb-dusted hand— "stubborn, I guess. She won't talk much, except to say how sorry she is."

"And have you forgiven her?"

Xander opened his mouth, then snapped it shut. He had, mostly, but did she know that?

"It's complicated."

With an annoying grin, Garrett kicked off his leather high-tops and sat cross-legged on the bed. "Explain."

Just as obstinate as his pretty roommate, Xander jutted his jaw. "Why?"

"Because I drove all this way with pastries, numbnuts. And you clearly need an ear that isn't hers."

"You won't tell her?"

Garrett mimed zipping his lips.

Xander heaved a dramatic sigh. "You know how sometimes you get a song stuck in your head?"

"Yeah, sure."

He hummed that famous riff from The Kinks' "Should I Stay or Should I Go."

"Ah." He nodded slowly, a wise ginger guru. "One of life's toughest questions, especially when there's a lady involved."

"Yup. I can't help feeling like the universe keeps smacking me down, you know? And whenever things start to hum between us, it's like a switch flips, and *bam,* we're butting heads again. Maybe we're not meant to be—Hannah and me, Trappers Cove and me."

"Huh. That's one way to look at it."

Xander arched an eyebrow. "You got another?"

"Well." Garrett stretched and scratched his belly. "You believe in signs, right?"

"Sorta, I guess." Should he tell his new friend about the curse, the ghost, and the whole eerie mess? Nah—better to have Garrett think him sane.

Garret regarded him, his spooky pale gaze inscrutable. "So, what survived the destruction?"

"Well, uh—" He tapped his chest.

"And...?"

"The cosmic transmitter thingy."

"The one thing Gus wanted you to hang onto. Interesting." He shifted on the mattress. "What'll happen to it if you sell the property?"

Xander shrugged. "I guess I could plant it in the town cemetery." Unless the UFO people decided to keep it as a shrine to their departed friend.

Garrett guffawed. "Good luck getting Father Ochinang to agree to that."

Irritation tightened Xander's brow. "You got a suggestion, smart-ass?"

He scrunched his lips to the side in a comically pensive expression. "You know, that FriendBook group's still active."

"Yeah, I saw." A few days ago, he checked the site in a moment of boredom. New posts had slowed to a trickle, but there were tons of video clips of the melee—the sickening crunch as the walls collapsed, billowing clouds of dust, water pumping skyward like blood from a severed artery. It turned his stomach to think of how many people could've been hurt and how narrowly he'd averted a life-destroying lawsuit.

Huh. Perhaps Gus was looking out for him after all.

"And the TV news piece," Garrett prodded, "you saw that?"

"Yeah, of course." That cute reporter had Xander's misfortune to thank for her story going viral. Should've been Hannah who got the credit, but she was too busy trying to pull his ass from the rubble.

"So, are you gonna use that momentum or just slink back to Seattle with your tail between your legs?" Garrett picked crumbs from the blanket. "'Cause if I had a lady like Hannah rooting for me, I know what I'd do."

A tingle of warning prickled Xander's nape. "Garrett, look at me."

Ice-blue eyes met his.

"Are you sweet on Hannah?"

Ice-blue eyes rolled heavenward. "Nah. She's not my type. Besides, she's stuck on you. But she's a quality person, you know? Loyal, smart, easy on the eyes. I wouldn't be so quick to give that up."

Xander sank back onto his pillows. "To tell the truth, Hannah's the main argument for staying."

"Wow. Trappers Cove sucks that much?" Garrett looked genuinely taken aback.

"No, I—" He was making a hash of this. He actually hated the idea of leaving this cute little coastal town for Seattle's crazy traffic and yet another round of job hunting. "I kinda like it here."

Garrett's big hand smacked the mattress. "Then stay. Show us what you're made of."

Another knock on the door.

"Got it." Garrett bounced to his feet—a movement Xander deeply envied.

He returned a moment later and tossed a large padded envelope onto the bed. "For you."

Xander ripped it open and extracted a pair of flannel pajama pants printed all over with cartoon aliens. On the greeting card, Spielberg's ET flashed a peace sign. He read the inscription aloud. "Get well soon, junior space man." It was signed "a fan," with an Oregon address.

"Huh. Cute." A few weeks ago, in the thick of his anti-alien tirade, he'd have tossed this gift in the trash. No, make that the shredder. But there was no way to interpret this offering as hostile—unless it was impregnated with itching powder.

He ran a hand inside the legs. No itch, just soft cloth. He gave the garment a sniff. It had that sharp new-clothing smell.

"Seems a legit gift. I thought those UFO people all hated my guts."

"I wouldn't say that." Garrett tilted his chin at Xander's phone, lying face-up on the bed. "Check the FriendBook group."

Xander pulled up the app. At the top of the feed, there was a new post by someone called TC Native. Their avatar: a silver-skinned alien from some 1950s sci-fi movie.

Stop the hate, friends.

I grew up in Trappers Cove. I love this town—its people, its funky vibe, its history. I knew Gus Anagnos well, and I loved him too. Visits to Souvenir Planet were the highlights of my childhood.

But friends, Gus was a flawed human being, just like the rest of us. Since losing his wife, a truly great lady, he spiraled into grief and obsession, and he neglected the building that housed his business.

He left that business to his nephew, someone he loved and trusted to take Souvenir Planet to new heights, not to freeze it in the past.

Gus is gone, folks, and hating on the new owner won't bring him back.

Delaying the demolition of Souvenir Planet almost cost Gus's nephew his life.

Think about that.

If you loved Gus, support his legacy, whatever form that takes.

I know I will.

As Xander read, the likes and hearts ticked upward into the high triple digits.

"Check out the comments," Garrett urged him.

Some posters disagreed, a few vociferously, but most seconded TC Native's comments.

One reply in particular, from someone called BeanMeUpScotty, drew almost as many likes as the original post:

If you're worried about the cosmic vortex in Trappers Cove, do y'all really think a race intelligent enough for interstellar travel is gonna be deterred because a cruddy old building fell down? Use your brains, people!

He raised wide eyes to his new friend. "Did Hannah post this?"

Garrett rubbed his freckled nose. "I can neither confirm nor deny the identity of TC Native, but she—er, *they* speak for a lot of us." He gathered up the paper wrappers littering Xander's bedspread. "Anyway, I've known Hannah for a long time, and I can tell you, she's not the type to give up easily. The question is, my wounded Greek friend, are you?"

With that, he unfolded his long limbs, pushed to his feet, and stretched. "Cute place you've got here, but in your shoes, I'd be looking for something bigger. Cheryl Rossi's a good place to start—if you plan to stick around."

Chapter Twenty-Six

An hour later, raised female voices outside jerked Xander's attention from the ridiculousness he and Garrett were constructing.

"Shit, she's back. Get my crutches."

With his friend's help, he hobbled to the door and held up a finger. Clear and loud as a church bell, Hannah bellowed, "What part of No don't you understand?"

"Our viewers have a right to know—"

Garret peered through the café curtains. "News crew," he whispered.

Hannah's outline appeared in the door's frosted window. Perched on the top step, she hollered, "Until he's healed, your viewers can shove it up their collective—"

Xander flung open the door and smiled wide for the camera trained on his furious, marvelous girlfriend—because he'd be damned if he'd let go of a woman this sexy and loyal and fierce.

"Hey, Han, I didn't know we were expecting company."

She whirled so fast her ponytail whipped his cheek. "Xander! You're supposed to be in bed."

Holding the door frame for balance, he snugged her against his side and whispered, "The minute the doc gives her okay, beauty, you and I are gonna break every spring in that bed."

Lids lowered, she hummed deep in her throat, too softly for anyone else to hear, and ran her hand over his chest. That private moment lasted only a second or two, but it was enough to give him hope. Hannah might be traumatized and eaten up with remorse, but she was still his.

Her caress turned into a bug-eyed stare when she registered his goofy outfit: the alien-print pajamas, slit to the knee on one side to accommodate his cast, plus a vintage Souvenir Planet hoodie, UFO-shaped sunglasses, and a ball cap topped with a light-up flying saucer, all salvaged from Gus's inventory as Christmas presents for his nieces and nephews. He pressed a button on the band, and the plastic craft spun and made pew-pew noises.

"Just getting in the Trappers Cove spirit," he told her.

Behind him, Garrett giggled.

"Hi there," Xander greeted the gaping reporter and her crew. "I remember you from the day of the—" he scratched his chin. "What should we call it—the collapse? The disaster? The big kaboom?"

"I, uh," the young reporter spluttered.

"Shit, man, you look like hell," the cameraman blurted.

The reporter shot him a death glare.

"Sorry, no offense," the guy said.

"None taken." Hell, two weeks after the accident, Xander jolted at his reflection if he didn't brace himself. Most of his bruises had faded from purple to green and yellow, but he still resembled a tie-dye project gone horribly wrong. At least this UFO cap covered his bald patch and ugly stitches.

Recovering her composure, the reporter thrust a mic in his face—well, she tried, but Hannah knocked it away with a Jackie Chan chop. "Sorry," she whispered. "I've been deflecting their calls for two weeks."

"It's okay, beauty." He released the doorframe, wrapped his free arm around her waist, and kissed her cheek. "You've been the most devoted bodyguard ever to guard a body, but it's time for me to—er, pull up my big boy pants and handle my business." He flapped the fabric of his comically large pajama pants.

The cameraman chortled.

"Now then, Ms.—"

She tugged the hem of her blazer. "Brianna Wu, KNXT News."

Might as well have a little fun with the intruder. "Ah yes. We saw your clip online—over and over and over." He waggled his eyebrows. "You're welcome."

Flustered, she inquired about his recovery.

"Coming along as well as can be expected. Anything else?" He squeezed Hannah's waist. "Pacific County's best journalist and I have a lot to discuss."

Hannah made a cute little squeak and flushed rose pink.

"Mr. Aganos,"

"Anagnos," Hannah corrected her.

"Sorry. Mr. Anagnos, the Pacific Northwest community of UFO investigators is up in arms over the loss of the cosmic vortex. What would you like to say to them?"

"Pfft." He shot Hannah a 'can you believe this idiot?' look. "The correct term is UAPs, unidentified anomalous phenomena."

Stuck in bed and half-mad with boredom, he'd researched the topic that obsessed his uncle. Despite his skepticism, he had to admit the stories were intriguing. Not that he was packing for his trip to Alpha

Centauri anytime soon, but Hannah was right—it couldn't hurt to keep an open mind.

"Besides," he continued, "the vortex is centered deep underground, so it won't matter what we build above." He'd made that part up, because if he had to pander to the space-cadet crowd, why not join in the fun?

He straightened his shoulders and gazed directly into the camera. "To all those involved in the search for extraterrestrial intelligence, I invite you to visit the cosmic transmitter's new home in our shopping center located on the site, opening Memorial Day weekend." He'd have to race like hell to meet that deadline, but Hannah and Garrett were right—a smart businessman would take advantage of the hype.

He showed the camera his cheesiest grin. "You won't find a finer place to spend the holiday weekend than Trappers Cove."

The reporter gulped, and so did Hannah. "You're staying?" she whispered.

He pressed a kiss to her temple and murmured, "When the woman I love is here, wild aliens couldn't pry me away."

Heedless of the camera, she threw her arms around him and kissed him breathless, a move she was damn good at.

"One last question, Mr. Anogos."

"Anagnos," they both chorused.

"What are going to call your new shopping center?"

"Yeah." Hannah goosed his butt. "What are you going to call it?"

He goosed her back. "That's a surprise." Turning to the news crew, he waved a cheerful goodbye and shut the door in their faces.

Back inside the RV, Hannah squealed and squeezed him painfully tight, then jumped backward at his yelp of pain.

"Oh God." She clapped her hands over her mouth. "I'm sorry, Xander."

From his seat at the dinette, Garrett gave them a slow clap. "Outstanding." He pushed to his feet. "Welp, I'll leave you to sort out the particulars."

"Wait," Hannah blocked his exit. "Were you in on this?"

"Nah." The big beanpole grinned. "All the good parts were Xander's idea. I was just stage crew." He tipped an imaginary hat. "Evening, you two."

The door closed behind him with a bang.

"C'mere, beauty." Leaning on his crutch, Xander hobbled to the dinette, sat down, and patted the bench. "Gimme those gorgeous legs."

She scooted in beside him and gingerly placed her legs over his lap. "This doesn't hurt?"

"Not one bit. Now, we've put this off long enough." He stroked and kneaded her calves, gratified by her purr of contentment. "You've been apologizing for the past two weeks, so please, I need you to understand something." He threaded his fingers into her hair. "I forgive you, Hannah. You were trying to help me."

Unshed tears glittered in her beautiful chestnut eyes. "My help could've gotten you killed."

"Not if Colonel Space Fart had listened to you. You had no way of knowing he'd file an injunction and summon a mob." He traced her cheekbone with his thumb. "Did you, TC Native?"

Laughing, she leaned into his caress. "Busted."

"Beautifully so." He skated his fingertips over the curve of her breast. "And thanks for calling off the rabble."

"It's so unfair of them to blame you. I mean, they saw the building fall down with their own eyes. They watched the ambulance carry us away."

He raised her hand to his lips and kissed her palm. "You endangered your own life to save mine."

A tear trickled down her cheek. "I didn't think. I just ran." Seizing his hand, she kissed his palm. "Because I love you, Xander."

Joy filled him like sunshine, making him so buoyant, he'd have floated away if not for Hannah's legs anchoring him. "Really?"

Gingerly, she eased onto his lap and pressed her lips to his, whispering into her kiss, "Really, truly, deeply, madly, a thousand million percent yes."

Just as carefully, he shifted his hips, pressing his arousal into her soft ass. "I'm the happiest man who ever breathed."

Hannah chuckled, a deep, seductive sound. "You'll be even happier as soon as the doctor says it's okay."

Chapter Twenty-Seven

Five weeks later, with the new shopping center nearing completion, Xander was still keeping its name under wraps—literally. A canvas tarp wrapped in chains and secured with a padlock obscured the wooden archway Matteo had installed at the entrance this morning. Beside it, two large lumps, each around five feet tall, stood likewise shrouded. Even the signs on the mini shops were covered.

It was enough to drive a curious reporter up a wall.

Staring out the window of the *Beacon*, Hannah huffed loose hair out of her eyes. She hated, hated, hated being kept in suspense. But part of patching up things between her and Xander was proving she respected his judgment. Boundaries and all that. Besides, her efforts to help had done enough damage.

So she'd kept her mouth shut as she watched Gus's cosmic transmitter craned into place. She'd hushed as the bricklayers constructed a circular plaza around it with brick-paved paths wending to the four corners of the lot. She'd zipped her lips as Matteo dumped load after load of architectural trim in the parking lot, and his crew of tight-lipped locals hammered into the night, giving each mini shop a unique front—some vaguely Victorian, some Tudor-ish, some shingled, each with its own color scheme.

In just six weeks, Xander had transformed a muddy lot and some mismatched prefab garden sheds into a funky little village where everything sparkled and nothing matched. Totally TC.

He finally got it.

From her vantage point at the editor's desk, Hannah watched out-of-towners and locals enter the temporary construction office, equipped with a ramp for Xander's knee scooter. This past week, with the doctor's blessing and a lightweight walking boot, he trotted around the site with only the slightest hitch in his step.

His ribs were better too, as long as she didn't squeeze him too tight. Now that Mom was feeling better, she and Xander spent most nights in his little RV under the pines, where they could love as loud as they pleased. Well, almost. With Memorial Day weekend approaching, the RV court was filling up with visitors, and the last thing they needed was a visit from the police on reports of a woman's screams.

The memory of their steamy nights brought a blush to her cheeks and a grin to her lips. He might be over forty and recovering from a close brush with death, but her Xander was *fierce* between the sheets. And in the shower. And on the dinette table. And one night she'd never forget, on the RV's little deck, beneath a pile of blankets while the wind whipped through the pines, and the stars shone as brilliant as her love for him.

Infatuated with their long-term renter, the Delaney sisters had outfitted his wooden deck with strings of Edison lights, and as spring crept toward summer, they spent many a starlit night snuggling there and talking for hours about everything *except* his new shopping center.

"Just trust me, Hannah. You're going to love it."

Whenever she slipped and started prodding him for details, he'd distract her with deep, drugging kisses and whispered praise as his hands deftly removed her clothing. And before she knew it, she'd be riding him again—carefully, so as not to aggravate his injuries—so drunk with pleasure she couldn't hold a thought except for how much she loved him.

Even if his sneaky-poo secrecy was driving her nuts.

Around five o'clock, her mother came humming down the staircase. Since her official retirement six weeks ago, the color had returned to her face and the sparkle to her smile. She'd put away her cane, too, thanks to thrice-weekly physical therapy with a very cute PT.

Mom clucked her tongue. "Hannah girl, aren't you ready yet?"

The *Beacon*'s old-school landline jangled a summons.

"I'll get that." Mom flapped her hand at Hannah. "Go get dressed."

"Dressed for what?"

"Xander's party, of course. Now scoot." She lifted the receiver. "*Pacific County Beacon*...Good evening to you, dear heart...Yes, I'll have her ready in a jiffy."

Hannah racked her brain but drew a blank on any mention of a party. Clearly, Mom and Xander were in cahoots. What could they be celebrating the Monday before Memorial Day weekend? Not Xander's birthday—they'd commemorated his fortieth with a belated birthday dinner at Casa Francesca weeks ago. Despite downing a bottle of excellent Chianti between them, their post-dinner sexy times had been spectacular. "A good omen," Xander murmured afterward, his fingertips tracing lazy spirals over her skin.

So, what the hell was he up to tonight? Secrets upon secrets. Shaking her head, she climbed the stairs to her apartment.

"Wear something pretty," Mom called after her.

"Something pretty," she grumbled, flipping through her over-stuffed closet. What she'd give for a proper walk-in with room to spread out. She dug deep into her jumbled wardrobe and extracted a floaty chiffon blouse in sunset hues, Xander's favorite. What else?

She went to the window and stuck her head outside. Balmy, with just a slight breeze, but it would cool off soon. She fished out a midi-length flared skirt and a knit throw she'd picked up at last summer's art fair. She finished the look with soft suede boots, spritzed on rose and spice cologne, fastened dangly gold earrings, and fluffed her hair to curl loosely around her shoulders.

"Not bad for a woman of almost forty-one." She grinned at her reflection. "Let's see what my boyfriend is up to."

Boyfriend. Sounded funny at her age—but saying it aloud made her giggle with delight. After four years of stubborn loneliness, she had a most excellent boyfriend, one who adored her and supported her and challenged her to think bigger than she'd ever dared.

When she descended the stairs, she found Xander talking to Mom and Luz Oloroso, the *Beacon*'s newest reporter. Fresh out of WSU's journalism school, she'd been thrilled to land a job in Trappers Cove where she could keep an eye on her grandmother, who lived behind Saint Sebastian's Church.

Hannah could forgive Luz for gawking starry-eyed at Xander. He truly was a gorgeous man. Day or night, dusty from the worksite or shined up for a dinner out, or even naked—especially naked—he took Hannah's breath away. But tonight, he'd gone all out: a crisp white dress shirt with the sleeves rolled up and the top button open. Muscled forearms and just a hint of chest hair—yum! Dark slacks hugged his thighs, and his leather shoes gleamed. His unruly curls were neatly combed—an effort that would last only until the next breeze because they were as determined as he was.

She hadn't seen him this polished since Casa Francesca, and she was going to have so much fun rumpling him as soon as she could get him alone. Her mouth watered at the thought.

"There's my beauty." Xander beamed. "Are you ready?" He crooked his arm in an old-fashioned, courtly gesture.

"Ready for what?" She slid her arm through his. "And if you tell me it's a secret, I'll smack you."

Xander tutted in mock consternation. "Violence in front of your mother?"

"Go on, you two," Mom said with a laugh. "Xander's kept us waiting long enough."

"Right as always, Linda." He gave her his other elbow, and together, the three of them promenaded across the street.

Once again, the parking lot held a crowd—a smaller one, this time, and Hannah recognized all the expectant faces turned their way.

"Is the whole town here?" she asked.

"Pretty much."

His smug grin was so unbearably cute, she had to give his butt a quick squeeze, onlookers be damned.

Xander put two fingers to his lips and let fly a piercing whistle. Conversations dwindled and stilled.

"Friends, thanks for coming out tonight. We'll all be busy over Memorial Day weekend, so I wanted to take this chance to introduce Trappers Cove's newest attraction to the people who made all this possible. Truly, I couldn't have done it without you." He grasped Hannah's hand and gave her a wink. "But first, let's have some bubbly."

The sound of popping corks carried in the expectant stillness, and soon, bartender Quinn and her Salty Dog crew were circulating through the gathering with trays of plastic champagne flutes. Even

Ryan Lee, the brew pub's owner, and Lilo, his girlfriend and head brewer, helped serve.

Xander claimed two glasses and offered one to Hannah, then raised his high. "A toast to the lady who helped me understand Trappers Cove." Twinkling with affection, his eyes locked on hers. "I didn't make it easy for her. But she never gave up on this stubborn Greek, and I think—I *hope* I've got it right. Everyone ready?"

Gripping her hand, he walked her to the shrouded archway, now minus its chains, she noted. He nodded to Matteo Verducci, who nodded in turn to his two helpers, young guys she recognized from the Sons of Italy dinner-dances.

Hal Horvat, their silver-haired mayor, stepped forward, holding a giant pair of scissors.

"Xander?!" Hannah squealed, bouncing on her toes. "You said you'd be working right up to the weekend."

"We still have some interior work to finish, but I wanted to give our friends and neighbors a sneak peek." He squeezed her tight in a side hug. "You've been so very patient," he teased before releasing her. "Ready, Luz?"

The new reporter stepped forward and lifted her camera.

"Drumroll, please."

Tongues trilled and hands patted thighs as, laughing, everyone awaited the great unveiling.

"Now!"

The tarps tumbled to the ground, revealing a driftwood archway spangled with glittery stars. Dangling from chains at its crest, a carved wooden sign read *Souvenir Galaxy.*

Cheers and applause rang out in the golden evening air.

Hannah clapped her free hand over her gaping mouth. Unable to speak, she gawked up at Xander, her whole face a question.

He gave a sheepish shrug. "So, I may have been unfairly prejudiced against the UFO schtick." He touched his glass to hers. "Do you like it, beauty?"

Like it? She didn't have words to express how much she loved the idea, loved him for finding room in his dream for those goofy aliens and room in his heart for Trappers Cove—and for her.

She gripped the back of his neck and crushed her mouth to his.

Hoots of approval rose from the onlookers.

Hannah thrust her glass in the air and hollered, "To Xander!"

"To Xander!" the cry echoed in the evening breeze. Someone struck up a chorus of "For He's a Jolly Good Fellow," and everyone joined in.

When they'd drained their glasses, Xander guided her through the happy mob, stopping along the way for hugs and back slaps, until they reached Quinn's temporary bar table. Glasses refilled with nose-tickling bubbly, they made their way to the wide red ribbon across the archway. Together with the mayor, Xander cut it and welcomed his guests inside. "The shops aren't open yet, folks. We're still stocking and finalizing the interiors, but you're welcome to stroll around. You'll find refreshments as you go."

He hugged Hannah close. "Ready for your tour, love?"

"Can't wait." She grinned up at him and patted one of the human-sized fiberglass aliens flanking the entrance, wide, welcoming grins across their neon green faces.

"Are these from Gus's roof?"

"Yup. They were pitted and peeling, but Matteo gave them a makeover."

She kissed him again. "You've thought of everything, you brilliant man."

"Oh, we're just getting started." He pecked her nose. "But feel free to kiss me whenever you see something you like."

She giggled and slid her hand into his back pocket. "Prepare for the worst case of chapped lips ever."

While jazzy beats played from hidden speakers, Xander squired her from shop to shop. First stop: Galactic Goodies. Outside, a college-age guy refilled platters of canapes, already well picked over by the strolling guests. "Evening, boss. Saved you some of the salmon pate and goat cheese."

"Much obliged, Cody." Xander handed her a paper plate.

"Wow, delicious." She crunched through her snack, realizing how long it had been since lunch.

"Right?" He brushed crumbs from his shirt front. "Here we'll sell that saltwater taffy Gus loved so much, along with Garrett's cookies, cheesecake from Cassie's Café, Washington smoked salmon and huckleberry jam, cheese and cured meats from Ben York's farm, herb blends from Jesse's, and tea from Zora's shop. I even talked Francesca into stocking jars of her marinara sauce."

"It's your gourmet market," Hannah exclaimed.

He patted the shingled wall and smiled proudly. "Yeah, I'm allowing myself a do-over. I cast my net too wide in my first gourmet shop. I figure I'll have better luck focusing on locally produced goods."

"Smart man." She gave him another smooch.

Speaking of do-overs, next door, he introduced her to the Stardust Wine Bar, a tiny chalet decorated with starry garlands and fronted by mismatched café tables and star-spangled umbrellas. "This will feature a small selection of Washington and Oregon wines and a daily menu of small plates." He gave a sheepish shrug. "Experience has proved I don't know squat about wine, so I arranged for winery interns to run this one."

An oddly familiar sixty-something woman emerged with a tray of flatbreads speckled with roast peppers and olives. She gave Xander a crisp nod.

"Hannah, meet Cassie's sister, Margaret Cartolucci."

The chef gave Hannah a once-over and a fraction of a smile. "Been wanting to move out here for years. When my baby sis told me about this job, I jumped." She tilted her chin toward the young woman pouring red and white wine. "What's your poison, boss?"

"I'll try the Columbia Valley Malbec. Hannah?"

"Something white and dry, please."

They sat at a cute table painted with planets and stars while she enjoyed a tart Walla Walla Pinot Gris and a slice of flatbread.

Annie from the antiques shop tugged her billionaire boyfriend to their table and clapped her hands together, jiggling with enthusiasm. "It's all so pretty, Xander. And these lights!" She gestured to the strings of star-shaped twinkle lights crisscrossing overhead. "It's cute, but classy. You captured Gus's spirit and dressed it up for a new generation. Well done, you!"

Michael Garwood, a newcomer to TC, gave Xander a thumbs up. "Great idea, great execution."

"Wow!" Hannah whispered once they'd passed. "High praise from a tech tycoon."

Xander shrugged. "Met him at Garrett's bakery. He's cool—just another guy who fell in love with a woman from Trappers Cove. Shall we?"

He showed her Andromeda's Boudoir, a tiny emporium of bath goodies, including fancy soaps from the Sea Queen Spa, and "magical" herbal bath salts and oils from Zora's shop. "See, this way, people can sample stuff made by TC merchants."

"Mutual promotion. What a brilliant idea." She laced her arms around his neck and laid another smooch on him.

His cheeks darkened in an adorable blush. "Well, a certain lady likes to get frisky in the bath, so I wanted to make sure she's always well-supplied."

"Like I said, brilliant."

"This next one might not fly, but I had to give it a try." He pointed to a blue and white striped mini cottage with plaster columns holding up a portico. Its sign showed an astronaut planting a Greek flag on the moon.

"The Cosmic Greek. I love it! What will you sell here?"

"Greek fisherman's hats, sweaters, olive oil, 'Kiss me, I'm Greek' mugs. The full range of corny tchotchkes. See, I'm leaning into Trappers Cove's aesthetic."

"Here's to kitsch." Feeling a little tipsy from the wine, she kissed him again.

"Easy now, don't fall into the water."

Turning, she beheld the weirdest public fountain she'd ever seen.

"The cosmic transmitter!"

"Right on its original spot, just like I promised Gus."

"It's, er, really something." The transmitter stood on a cement dais, ringed with bug-eyed alien heads that spit water into a surrounding basin. Nestled inside the rebar structure, a plexiglass box held Gus's artistic urn. A bronze plaque listed his name, date of birth and death, and *Ad Astra per Aspera*.

Xander sighed. "Kinda creepy, I know, but Gus is resting where he wanted to."

"Through hardship to the stars." She wound her arms around him from behind and rested her chin on his shoulder. "Pretty much describes our start together, eh?"

They lingered there, linked together beneath the brilliant stars. Xander raised her hand to his lips, pressed a soft kiss to her knuckles, and turned into her embrace. "Beauty, I'm dying to get you alone, but I've got one more thing to show you."

"Lead on, Space Captain." She linked her arm through his. "You know, you'd look damn fine in one of those shiny astronaut jumpsuits.

He threw his head back on a belly-shaking laugh. "I'll wear one if you will."

On the other side of the fountain, two larger sheds stood side by side, both painted deep blue with silver stars. The sign above one entrance read, *Souvenir Planet Museum*. The other, *Souvenir Starship*.

Hannah clapped her hands to her mouth and squeaked, "Xander?!" After all their strife and struggle, he'd made peace with the aliens? This was more than she could've hoped for.

He wrapped his arms around her from behind and pressed his cheek to her temple. "I hope you like it, love. Come inside and give me your verdict."

On indigo walls painted with stars, galaxies, and nebulae, Xander had arranged photos of Souvenir Planet, including several she recognized from back issues of the *Beacon*. "Your mom helped me with this part," he admitted. A few relics from the old shop held pride of place, including a cabinet of vintage souvenirs and the mummified mermaid. "I talked the historical society into returning this ugly critter," he said, patting the glass case.

Hannah's chest swelled with love and gratitude. "Oh, Xander." She hugged him tightly. "This will mean so much to everyone who remembers Gus's shop."

He nuzzled her hair. "I don't care about the others. Just you, beauty."

"Whatever happened to that life-size alien on the bench?"

"Afraid that one disintegrated when we tried to move it. But—" He gestured to the connecting doorway, framed in silver and winking lights to look like a spaceship's portal.

There he sat, between shelves of kitschy alien-themed souvenirs, the same lumpy cloth alien, gazing stoically into the distance, waiting for visitors to snap selfies and sit on his squishy lap.

"You fixed him?"

"The original was beyond repair. This is a replica made by the Trappers Cove Quilters Guild."

"He's absolutely identical!" Hannah bit her lip. "Xander, would you...?" She pulled her phone from her pocket.

"My pleasure."

She plopped onto the bench and threw her arm over the spaceman's shoulders, mashing her cheek against his.

Xander held the phone up, then scowled. "This shot needs something."

He sat beside her, tugged her legs across his lap, then snapped a group selfie.

"Lemme see." Giggling, she examined the photo of their star-struck, goofy grins. "It's perfect. This whole place is perfect—the ultimate expression of the Trappers Cove vibe, and yet, a hundred percent you."

"Well, I've had a good teacher." He brushed his lips across hers. "The best, I'd say."

"I love you, Xander Anagnos." She peppered his face with kisses. How had she ever found those three little words difficult to say? Tonight, she wanted to shout them from the rooftops and sky-write them across the spring twilight.

"And I love you, Hannah Leone." Pulling her onto his lap, he fused his mouth to hers in a hot, drugging kiss. With a lust-drunk moan, she matched him stroke for stroke.

When she finally came up for air, she drawled, "Oh my" in her best Sulu impression.

Catching her cheesy sci-fi joke with nary a wince, he cocked an eyebrow. "Shall we take this to my private quarters?"

She wiggled on his lap, relishing his hard length against her thigh. "Mine are closer."

"Think again." He pulled her to her feet and led her outside to another shed tucked behind the museum. Plainer than the others, this one was marked, "Employees Only."

"Your office?"

"Yup." He switched on a soft light. "Furnished for comfort."

The cozy space was paneled in pale wood. A desk sat in the corner, flanked by old-fashioned filing cabinets that held a collection of seashells, a miniature Seattle Space Needle, a triathlon trophy, and framed photos.

She lifted one of a skinny, curly-haired boy grinning beside a young, dark-haired Gus. "Is this you?"

"Yup. I must've been around ten. I wanted a reminder of my uncle at his best. I like to think he'd love this place."

She grasped his waist and snugged him close. "He absolutely would." Over his shoulder, she spotted her own face smiling from a silver frame. "It's us!"

During his birthday dinner at Casa Francesca, Trappers Cove's elegant, old-school Italian restaurant, someone had captured her and Xander gazing at each other starry-eyed over their wineglasses, looking as blissed-out as she felt right now.

"This is my favorite photo of us." He traced the frame with his fingertip. "Fair warning, Han, I plan to do whatever it takes to keep you looking at me just like you did that night."

If he kept this up, she'd end the night in a puddle of happy tears.

After another tender kiss, he switched on a little Bluetooth speaker and tapped his phone. The small space filled with the sexy saxophone jazz she'd confessed to loving one wine-soaked night in his RV.

Gripping her hips, he danced her backward to the sofa that took up the office's back wall. "I want to talk to you about something, Han."

"Yeah?" She swayed to the slow beat. "Can we discuss it sitting down?"

"Or lying down." He wound her hair around his fist, tugged her head back, and trailed kisses down her neck. "I do my best thinking lying beside you, beauty."

"Is that so?" She pulled him onto the cushions, then rolled to straddle him, raking her fingers into his soft curls, and kissed him hungrily.

"So." He arched his throat, inviting more kisses. "I've been talking to Cheryl Rossi."

"The rental agent?" She nibbled her way down to his collar bone, unfastening his shirt buttons to bare more delicious skin.

"She handles some sales too. She's got a client looking to unload her beach cottages."

Hannah bolted upright. "Xander?"

His smile glimmered with happiness and hope. "What do you say, Han? Both our places are awfully small. Would you consider sharing a bigger home with me?"

"In Trappers Cove?"

"Where else? As long as you're here, there's no place I'd rather be. If I sell my Seattle condo, we could—"

She mashed her lips to his. To hell with the boring details. She'd heard all she needed to hear.

"Is that a yes?"

Laughing into their kiss, she crowed, "That's definitely a yes."

He rolled her beneath him and cradled her face in both hands. "I truly am the happiest alien-peddler on the planet." And then he kissed her so deep and hot and sweet she saw stars.

And when she opened her eyes, they were still there, floating above their entwined bodies.

"Xander?" She tapped his shoulder.

"Mmm?"

"I see stars."

Desire glimmered in his dark eyes. "Me too, love."

"On the ceiling."

"Oh, right." Chuckling, he rolled off her and gazed up as he finished undoing buttons on his shirt. "When I was a kid, Gus gave me glow-in-the-dark star decals for my bedroom ceiling. I found a distributor and ordered some for the gift shop. You like 'em?" He attacked her blouse buttons with nimble fingers.

"I do. Let's put some over our bed."

His movements stilled, and the most beautiful smile dawned across his face. "Our bed. I love the sound of that."

"We'll need a big one." Wrapping her arms around his neck, she drew him down again. "With sturdy bedposts in case I want to tie you up."

He inhaled on a hiss. "Please want to, Han."

Her laughter turned to whimpers as he skillfully peeled off her bra and closed his mouth over one aching nipple while thrumming the other with his thumb.

How lucky was she to have found this sweet, stubborn, funny, generous, sexy man? Then and there, she vowed to never take one minute of their time together for granted.

The scruff on his chin scraped deliciously as he nibbled down her trembling belly. He tugged at the waistband of her skirt, but it didn't budge.

"Hooks in the back," she gasped, impatient for more.

But he continued his downward path, gathering the cloth and lifting it to expose her black lace panties.

"You sexy minx," he growled as he spread her thighs wide.

Thank God she'd been warned to dress pretty.

Xander's hot breath set her core tingling, and when he worked one finger beneath the elastic to glide between her slick folds, the intense pleasure drew a hiss.

"That's right, love." He pulled the lace aside and stroked his thumb lightly over her seam, then pushed deeper, opening her to his ravenous gaze. "Show me what I've been craving. Do you know how hard I've been all night, watching this skirt swish around your legs, knowing what you're hiding beneath?"

His words fired her blood just as surely as his touch, and she spread herself wider, silently begging for what she needed.

Xander sealed his mouth to her core and laved her with broad strokes of his tongue. Shocks of pleasure jolted her body with each pass, and when he slid two fingers into her channel and twisted in some magical way, she nearly levitated.

"Xan," she pleaded, clutching his soft hair, "I want you inside me."

"Soon, love. Give me this first. Let yourself go." With a wicked grin, he dove in again and unleashed a flurry of rapid tongue-flicks that rocketed her over the edge. Biting into her own arm, she stifled a scream of bright, electric bliss.

"God, you're beautiful." Kneeling between her splayed knees, he drank her in with a gaze so heated she felt its trail sizzling over her skin. With brusque, impatient movements, he shoved his pants down, rose between her thighs, and notched himself at her entrance, and filled her in one hot surge.

Still quaking with aftershocks, she cried out, jolted by pleasure almost too intense to bear.

"That's it, angel. Squeeze me tight."

She did as he commanded, winding her arms and legs around him as her inner muscles clutched his cock. Too far gone for slow sweetness, he pummeled her. A second climax coiled at the base of her spine, each thrust driving her higher until he froze, buried to the hilt while his cock pulsed deep inside her and she tumbled with him into a vortex of blinding pleasure.

Sweat-slicked and panting, sprawled halfway off the couch, she was the first to giggle. Xander collapsed atop her, shaking with laughter. "Holy flaming comets, that was amazing."

He lifted his head, his gaze alight with joy. "Have I told you how completely, helplessly in love with you I am?"

She brushed his hair from his sweaty forehead. "A few times, yeah. But feel free to tell me as often as you like." Curling forward, she peppered his face with kisses. "I love you to the stars and beyond."

He propped his chin on her chest. "Maybe there's something to this cosmic vortex business."

Happiness sparkled inside her, as bright as any star. "Nah. That's just us, love."

Chapter Twenty-Eight

"Whew!" Fanning his flushed face, Xander opened the kitchen windows to air out the heady scent of garlic and lamb wafting through their cottage. "No vampires will bother us tonight."

Hannah looked up from the cutting board where she was slicing crusty bread. "Your moussaka smells amazing. Can't believe you made me wait this long to taste it."

"Well, we've both been a little busy, eh? And Yiayia's recipe takes all day." In fact, his grandmother would be scandalized by the shortcuts he'd taken. He could just hear her scratchy grumble, "Bechamel in the microwave? Bah!"

But that's the thing about family traditions—you've gotta find a way to make them your own.

Nuzzling Hannah's neck, he grasped her knife hand and snatched a slice of bread.

"Thief!" Grinning, she bumped him with her hip. "That's for our guests. Think we have enough?"

He eyed the three brimming bread baskets before smooching her cheek. "Yeah, plenty."

Although they'd moved into this three-bedroom cottage back in June, the summer tourist season had kept them both so busy they hadn't had a chance to celebrate properly until now, the weekend after Labor Day. Not that either was complaining. Souvenir Galaxy had raked in even more profits than Xander had hoped for, and he was well on his way to repaying his loan early. The expanded *Beacon* was flourishing too, thanks to Hannah's expert management and nose for news.

And yeah, turned out she'd been right about the UFO nuts. Hundreds had come to pay homage to Gus's legacy, and most of them left with full shopping bags. Though Colonel Malinowski and Professor Alterman hadn't bugged him again, he was in talks with a third group, WASETI—Washington Searchers for Extra-terrestrial Intelligence—about leasing one of the mini shops for a UFO information center. Gus would've liked that, and Xander definitely owed him one.

Hannah poked her head outside and declared, "Gorgeous! We couldn't ask for more perfect weather."

He joined her in the doorway, the tight space giving him the perfect excuse to squeeze her close—not that he needed an excuse. His favorite after-work pastime was finding new places in the house to get frisky with his lady love. In fact, they hadn't tried the garden shed yet...

But for now, they had less than half an hour before their guests arrived. The morning's patchy cloud cover had given way to clear skies and balmy temperatures, allowing their celebration to spill out into the front and back yards—plenty of room for the friends and family they'd invited to a combination housewarming party and launch party for the children's book they'd co-written over the summer: *Gus and the Aliens.*

Wiping her hands on her "Kiss me, I'm Greek" apron, which she adored despite her thoroughly Italian roots, Hannah hugged his waist and gave him a look of concern. "So, your brother's not coming, after all?"

He smooched her forehead. "His kids have a soccer tournament. To tell you the truth, I'm kinda glad they can't make it."

He hadn't heard a peep about the curse since the business's grand opening. Two of his sisters, Irida and Sofia, had visited over the summer and no doubt reported back to his parents, who'd sent congratulations via a sterile greeting card. There was a time when that paltry gesture would have stung, but honestly? He was over it. Starting over in Trappers Cove had snapped the thread that tied his self-image to his family's opinions. With Hannah's help, he'd discovered the joy of not giving a crap. And poof! The curse was broken.

"Hey, before the party starts—" He dashed to the coat closet, where he'd hidden a package under his raincoat. "A little something from me and Gus to you."

Hannah opened the gift bag, dug through the glittery tissue paper, and extracted a flying saucer wind chime, complete with a star-shaped crystal prism that transformed sunlight into flashes of rainbow.

Hannah's giggle of delight warmed him, body and soul.

"Zora recommended hanging a wind chime by the front door to repel negative energy."

"But an alien, Xan?" she teased. "Out where everyone can see?"

Okay, he'd earned some ribbing on that subject, after all his grumbling about Gus's little green aliens.

"Call it a tribute to TC's funky vibe." He tapped the tiny spacecraft. "These little guys showed me how to embrace my inner weirdness." He gathered her into his arms. "Most importantly, they led me to you."

She nuzzled the crook of his neck. "And they taught me to accept change." Her hands tunneled beneath his shirt to stroke his back. "Actually, no. You get the credit for that. You showed me I can let go of the past without losing myself. So thank you, my sexy spaceman."

"Anytime, beauty." He pecked her nose. "Now, let's hang this guy up before the horde arrives."

Good thing he'd already installed a hook while she was at work, because a procession was heading their way, headed by Zora, dressed for the occasion in a purple caftan and matching turban.

"What the—?"

Hannah grinned. "That's my surprise to you. Zora's leading a house blessing."

Xander threw his head back and laughed. "Of course she is." He waved. "Welcome, friends."

The crowd filled their sandy front yard, unavoidable when you lived this close to the beach, and overflowed onto the sidewalk. Standing beside her aunt, Gemma Moore held a large thermos and a stack of paper cups. Jesse del Toro, her boyfriend, carried a backpack that jingled when he shifted it to one shoulder.

Xander instantly understood Jesse's sympathetic grin and half-shrug. Life in Trappers Cove came with a brimming side dish of woo-woo, and that was fine by him.

Zora spread her arms wide in greeting. "A long-delayed congratulations to the happy couple. Xander, we are so glad to welcome you into our family."

"Hear, hear," Garrett called from the sidewalk. Hannah's friend Daphne elbowed him.

Under Zora's direction, Jesse passed out a collection of bells to their guests: little brass bells he recognized from Zora's shop, Christmas jingle bells, and a few old-timey school bells with wooden handles. Gemma filled paper cups and handed them around.

"Consecrated salt water," she explained, "to clean away any residual bad vibes. Works as well as smudging, and it won't set off your smoke alarms."

Hannah gave Xander a sheepish smile. "You don't mind, do you? This house has been rented out to God knows who, so I figured a spiritual cleaning was in order."

"Mind?" He squeezed her in a side hug. "I love the idea. What do we do, Zora?"

'A joyful noise' was the perfect description of what happened next. The old hippie mama led a merry procession through the house, bells clanging and jingling, salty water sprinkling into every corner and cranny, until she pronounced their new home cleansed.

Afterward, everyone filed through the kitchen to load up their plates with Xander's moussaka, Hannah's Greek salad, and dozens of other dishes their guests had brought to share. Garrett served up a giant sheet cake decorated with—of course—little green aliens.

"Who knew these little buggers were so tasty?" Xander joked, wiping green frosting from his chin.

"You're tasty," Hannah whispered, nuzzling his neck.

"Hey, now." He gave her butt a squeeze. "Don't start something you can't finish."

"Oh, we'll both finish. I promise you that." She smooched his cheek. "Mega happy ending." And off she trotted to giggle with Daphne as they set up the next event: his first and probably only book signing.

Who'da thunk it? Xander Ioannis Anagnos, a published author. He and Hannah had dreamed up the idea for a children's book one starlight night over post-sex wine and snacks. Giggling, they'd sketched out a story about a boy named Gus who made friends with visiting aliens and went for a ride in their spaceship. No one believed the kid, but he learned not to care what others thought. Daphne helped them find an illustrator and a local printer, and voilà! Their picture book was born.

"Book time," Daphne sang out and plunked down a carton of slim volumes. "Get your copy signed by the authors."

He took his seat beside Hannah and uncapped a green Sharpie. "Did you ever imagine yourself doing this?"

"Nope." She scribbled her signature on the title page, then passed the book to him. "Is there a *New York Times* bestseller list for picture books?"

He laughed as he scrawled his signature below hers. "That's my Hannah, always shooting for the stars."

When the line died down, Daphne plopped onto the bench between them. "Thanks, you two. You've given my bottom line a nice boost."

"Thank *you*," Hannah insisted.

"Don't mention it." She pecked her friend's cheek. "I love supporting local authors. Speaking of..." She pulled a sour face. "I sent your interview request to Finn Abrams, but he turned us down. You'd think an author whose fictional town looks so much like Trappers Cove could spare the *Beacon* a few minutes, but noooo. He's such a snot." She wrapped a long arm around each of them and squeezed. "Not like my two favorite kid lit authors. You're the cutest couple in TC, and I'm so glad you got together. Hey, I'm gonna get more cake. You want some?"

"None for me, thanks." Xander patted his overstuffed belly.

Hannah shook her head, so Daphne left them for a moment of sweet peace.

"Finn Abrams. Isn't he that mystery author?"

Hannah nodded. "Has a reputation as a reclusive grump. Sets all his stories on the Washington Coast. Every year, Daphne invites him to do a signing, and every year, he turns her down."

"Hmm. Our next picture book: Daphne and the Grumpy Author?"

"Nah, I'm thinking something about a ghost."

"Han and Xan and the Ghosties?"

"You goofball." She laid her head on his shoulder and sighed. "I'm so happy, Xan."

"Me too, Han." He pulled her onto his lap, not an easy move on the wobbly picnic bench. "Happier than I ever thought I could be. We've got a beautiful home in the best beach town."

"Damn straight," she murmured into the crook of his neck, her soft lips delicious against his skin.

Something about Hannah's warm presence brought out the poet in him. "We've got the sea next door, the stars above, and—"

She stiffened in his arms and pointed skyward, her eyes wide and round. "Look!"

Hovering high above their heads, an eerie greenish light pulsed. Too big to be star or satellite, too quiet to be a helicopter, it hung perfectly still in the deep blue twilight.

A hush fell over the party as, one by one, people noticed him and Hannah gawking upward and then spotted the mysterious light. For several seconds, the craft glowed brighter, pulsed faster, then it streaked seaward at incredible speed and disappeared.

All the little hairs on Xander's skin stood on end. Speechless, he clung to Hannah, whose mouth opened and closed like a goldfish. "Did you see that?" she finally croaked.

His lips stretched in an incredulous grin. "Holy flying spaceballs, beauty. Gus's friends came to the party!"

Thanks for reading Xander and Hannah's story! If you enjoyed Love, Legacy, and Little Green Aliens, pretty please consider leaving a review on **Goodreads, Bookbub**, or your **favorite online bookstore**.

Up next, Daphne and Finn's story, coming autumn of 2024. For exclusive previews, special deals, and giveaways, please visit me at **sadirastone.com** and sign up for my reader newsletter. As my thank-you for subscribing, you'll get a free steamy silver-fox novella from my ***Bangers Tavern*** series.

And don't miss the rest of the ***Trappers Cove Romance*** series!

Passion in the Cards: An Opposites-Attract Metaphysical Beach Town Romance (novella)

Headstrong, homebody farmer clashes with freedom-loving hippie chick, but their blazing chemistry is unstoppable. Though Jesse knows the bewitching fortuneteller Gemma will never settle down in their quirky beach town, he can't resist playing with fire. When a harmless secret backfires, Gemma discovers just how deeply she's wounded Jesse, and how desperately she wants to keep him.

Passionate Brew: An Enemies-to-Lovers Beach Town Brewery Romance (novella)

When a control-freak brewery owner is forced to partner with a prickly master brewer, their business and their hearts will never be the same. Working side by side ignites sizzling desire. But when a high-stakes craft beer competition arouses their fierce rivalry, can new love survive this battle of wills? Come to Trappers Cove for a sizzling enemies-to-lovers small town workplace romance.

The Billionaire's Christmas Castle: A Silver Fox Holiday Beach Town Romance (novel)

His billions can't buy what he craves most—her love. Can a spoiled tycoon and a fiercely independent entrepreneur cross an ocean of differences to forge a love that lasts past the holidays? Come to Trappers Cove for an Over-40 Christmas beach town billionaire romance that'll steam up your windows and warm your heart!

Acknowledgements

It is a truth universally acknowledged, that an author in possession of sharp eyes, a sound mind, and proofreading software will still miss an embarrassing number of errors and plot holes.

Huge thanks to my talented beta readers Laurie Ryan, Lyann Blanton, Jodi Turchin, and Roxanne Blackhall, marvelous authors all. If you're as homesick for the Washington State coast as I am, check out Laurie Ryan's **Willow Bay** romance series. Delightful!

And thanks to my wonderful, sharp-eyed editors Jessica and Saya from Red Quill Editing. Without your eagle eyes, I'd look very silly indeed.

About the author

And more books by Sadira Stone

Award-winning contemporary romance author Sadira Stone spins steamy, smoochy tales set in small businesses—a quirky bookstore, a neighborhood bar, a vintage boutique. Set in the U.S. Pacific Northwest, her stories highlight found family, friendship, and the sizzling chemistry that pulls unlikely partners together. When she emerges from her writing cave in Las Vegas, Nevada (which she seldom does), she can be found in dance class, strumming her guitar, exploring the Western U.S. with her charming husband, cooking up a storm, and gobbling all the romance books. For a guaranteed HEA (and no cliffhangers!) visit Sadira at sadirastone.com.

Visit Sadira on All the Socials!
https://linktr.ee/SadiraStone

Also by Sadira Stone

The Bangers Tavern Romance Series
The Bangers Tavern Romance series, set in a neighborhood bar in Tacoma, Washington, offers super-steamy, laugh out loud love sto-

ries, chosen family, diverse characters, fabulous bar food and creative cocktails, a home away from home you'll want to return to again and again...and the best tater tots in Tacoma!

Christmas Rekindled

When two Scrooges unite to save a bar in trouble, a kiss under the mistletoe sparks the steamiest Christmas miracle ever. Bartender River hates Christmas and the sexy, snarky server who once squashed his ego. When she sashays back into Bangers Tavern, his holiday goes from blah to dismal. Come to Bangers Tavern for enemies-to-lovers, fake dating, chosen family, snowed-in shenanigans, holiday cocktails, and grumpy, snarky love.

Opposites Ignite

Aspiring tattoo artist Rosie is too smart to fall for her adorably straight-laced coworker at Bangers Tavern, until they share too much New Year's Eve bubbly, and Rosie wakes up in Eddie's bed! For Eddie, their New Year's surprise is a dream come true—until his grandma walks in on them! Eddie begs Rosie for a few fake dates to appease his old-fashioned family. But their lies spin out of control, and the longer he pretends, the deeper he falls.

Delicious Heat

Bangers Tavern chef Diego meets a woman who makes his heart sing. Trouble is, she's pregnant with another man's child. With one belligerent ex and two overprotective families intent on breaking them up, Anna and Diego need more than red-hot passion to pull them through. His career and her baby's future are on the line. Come back to Bangers Tavern for a spicy tale of forbidden love that will warm your heart...and other parts...and make you hungry for empanadas!

Sweet Slow Sizzle

Bangers Tavern's hunky bouncer Jojo has been crushing on server Lana for years, but her sole focus is keeping her orphaned teen brothers together in the only home they've ever known. When their teen shenanigans land them in trouble, Jojo may be the only person who can save them. This slow burn, sizzling hot friends-to-lovers workplace romance celebrates the glorious chaos of 21st century family—the ones we're born into, and the ones we gather to our hearts.

Cupid's Silver Spark: A Bangers Tavern Novella

At Bangers Tavern's Anti-Valentine's Bash, Carla collides with a swoonworthy silver fox. Could a no-strings fling be the remedy for her tattered heart? He seems perfect for the job: suave, attentive, and oh so tempting. Trouble is, his real estate firm has the hots for her building. To keep her business, Carla must dare to trust the enemy. Will her silver fox prove a predator, or will Cupid's arrow strike true?